Looking into My Sister's Eyes: an Exploration in Women's History

Looking into My Sister's Eyes: an Exploration in Women's History

Edited by Jean Burnet

1986
The Multicultural History Society of Ontario
Toronto

This book is dedicated to
the memory of
MARTA DANYLEWYCZ

We wish to thank the Multiculturalism Directorate, Office of the Secretary of State for its generous assistance in the preparation of this volume.

Canadian Cataloguing in Publication Data

Main entry under title:
Women in ethnicity

Papers presented at a conference Immigration and ethnicity in Ontario: an exploration in women's history, held at the University of Toronto in May 1985.
Includes bibliographical references.
ISBN 0-919045-27-8

1. Women immigrants — Ontario — History — Congresses.
2. Women immigrants — Canada — History — Congresses.
I. Burnet, Jean R., 1920- II. Multicultural History Society of Ontario.

JV7282.W7W7 1986 305.4'88'009713 C86-093262-1

ISBN: 0-919045-27-8

Cover photo: By David Levine

Published 1986.
Printed in Canada.

The Multicultural History Society of Ontario
43 Queen's Park Crescent East
Toronto, Ontario M5S 2C3

Contents

Preface

The Multicultural History Society of Ontario and the Ethnic and Immigration Studies Program have over the last decade sponsored conferences on the history of a number of Ontario's ethnocultural groups. At each of those conferences, the intersection of the history of migration, ethnicity, women and labour has stood out as an intriguing and clearly critical matrix—a natural point of departure for studying networks, identity and strategies for maintaining or improving the quality of family, ethnocultural and economic life. Studying women in migration as well as their place in the life of the *ethnie*, the historian encounters questions about the work place and attitudes about work, about the home and values held about family roles, and about the *ethnie* in terms of ethnic women's sense of fellow-feeling and of the need for institutions—churches, associations, unions—to nurture such fellow-feeling.

As mothers, mothers-in-law, daughters, daughters-in-law, sisters and sisters-in-law, women provided the networks of obligation and caring which made most *ethnies* more than the lonely cultureless sojourning stops of migrant male labour. As everything from sodality workers, trade unionists, nuns, members and officers of ethnonational associations, or their women's auxiliaries, they worked and were often worked by men to sustain that intensity of activity and concern at the crucial levels of cadre, which makes ethnic organizational life more than a paper reality or the braggadocio of male immigrant intellectuals. History of ethnic groups, informed by a male view of events by both the immigrant actors and their chroniclers, most often conjure up a picture of a row of smiling and servile ladies "from the auxiliary" being paraded to the front of an ethnic hall for applause after cooking and serving an old-country-style meal. The role of women and food as representing the folkways of the *ethnie* should not be seen as trivial, but it is hardly representative of women's place in immigration and ethnicity.

Women's history, as exemplified in this volume, should remind the reader of the demotic revolution of sensibilities of the 1960s which led to a new concern in history writing for all the people. The skilled interweaving of family, sioco-economic and cultural history shows that immigrant and ethnic women clearly possessed tactics to try to impose their values in the work place, at home, or in outside employment. They cared about the quality of life and found in both ethnic and cross-cultural forms of associations, from neighbourhood friendships to formal organizations, opportunities for sisterhood and for asserting rights and dignity. The volume's title derives from a poem, *Tree of August*, by Mary di Michele.

Professor Jean Burnet and all those who participated in Immigration and Ethnicity in Ontario: An Exploration in Women's History and contributed to this volume were compelled by a special sense of the need to demonstrate how valuable a frame for scholarship women's studies can be. For as the conference was in preparation, they were faced with the tragic and untimely death of one of Canada's most promising historians who had contributed much to the field and had been a good friend to many of the participants. Marta Danylewycz of York University's History Department died in the prime of her life and scholarship at the age of thirty-six.

This volume is dedicated to her memory in the hope that it achieves the high standards of her work.

Robert F. Harney
Professor of History
University of Toronto

Introduction

Jean Burnet

The recent celebration of the bicentenary of the Province of Ontario has awakened curiosity about and pride in its history. It is appropriate that the curiosity and the pride include the history of women, who, by the 1981 census, make up more than half of the population, and of people with at least some ancestry that is not British, French, or Native, who are well over a third of the population. This volume, a collection of papers given at a conference held at the University of Toronto in May 1985, is a contribution to women's studies and to immigration and ethnic studies in Ontario.

The subtitle, *an exploration in women's history*, underlines the fact that most of the papers are pioneering enterprises. Conventional Ontario history, like Canadian history generally, has been a history of men and of the public life in which women's participation has been restricted. The few women who have won a place have done so by manly exploits: the legendary Laura Secord, for example, carried messages through enemy lines in time of war, and Agnes Macphail won a seat in the hitherto entirely male House of Commons.

Conventional Ontario history, like Canadian history generally, has also been a history of people of British origin, with some attention to the French and a few footnotes about the Amerindians. Those of other ethnic origins who have earned mention have usually prior to this shed all or most of the stigmata of difference: little seems to have been Polish about Sir Casimir Gzowski except his name, and Sir Adam Beck probably was not very German.

Ontario history has not only been a history of men of British origin but it has been told by such men. Academics, including historians, have until recently been male and British. That the Department of History at the University of Toronto was even slower than many other departments to admit women to its faculty is a matter of record. It also failed to show daring in admitting to its ranks those of other than British origin, even if sanified by Anglomania or by their choice of specialty. Women and members of other ethnic groups were forced to satisfy any urge to do history as record-keepers for families and associations and as local historians. Their work, though useful to academic historians, especially biographers, was treated scornfully.

But it has been said (by sociologist Everett Hughes) that the great American game is to break in where one is not wanted. Women and members of other ethnic groups—and in considerable numbers those who belong to both categories—have recently been breaking into Ontario history. At first they took pains to prove they belonged by the orthodoxy of their work, but today they are trying to develop new perspectives and to pay attention to people and to areas of life previously ignored. They have been encouraged to do so in women's studies by the women's movement and in immigration and ethnic studies by the governmental policies of multiculturalism. It is not necessary, however, to be a feminist or a militant "ethnic" to want to tease out from Ontario history the part played by immigrant and "ethnic" women. All that is required is a determination to give a new and richer nap to the fabric.

Immigration and ethnicity are almost invariably linked, and for good reason: it is through the meeting of peoples that ethnic consciousness develops. Yet two of the papers in this collection are reminders that a major part of the Ontario population has been made up of people who considered themselves to be neither immigrants nor "ethnics"—the equivalent for their times was "foreigners"—and the descendants of such people. The English and Anglo-Irish women of the nineteenth century of whom Hopkins writes and the British domestics of the early decades of the twentieth century of whom Barber writes did not think of themselves as anything other than Britishers moving to another part of the British realm. They did have to adapt to the Canadian climate and Canadian ways, but they had an initial advantage in their serene Britishness.

Hopkins's women had additional advantages. They were gentlewomen—members of the upper-middle class; they were educated, as few women were in their time and place, and not simply, in Virginia Woolf's bitter phrase, daughters of educated men; they had leisure time; Moodie and Traill even had marketable skills, having begun in England careers as writers and editors that they could pursue in their new homes. The women who by their writings shaped our view of immigrant life in the nineteenth century in the backwoods and the towns of what is now southern Ontario were thus exceptional and privileged.

Their situation provides a backdrop against which to view the situation of both British and "foreigners" who came to Ontario between the turn of the century and the outbreak of World War Two. During that period the number of people of British origin in the province increased by almost a million, the number of people of other origins than British, French or Native by well over a third of a million. Most of those of other origins were Europeans, of peasant or working-class background; most were men, who came first as sojourners and then, when they were able to bring out their wives or fiancées, as settlers.

Single women did come, among them both Britishers and northern Europeans, to fill the insatiable demand for domestic servants. Barber describes the British domestics, Lindström-Best the Finnish. It is remarkable that neither seem to have been as oppressed and exploited as some, at least, of their modern counterparts. The British girls (who undoubtedly did not mind that appellation) profited from sharing the ethnicity of the dominant groups in the population. The Finns were secure in the support of their ethnic community and in their high reputation among employers. Both moved in and out of domestic service in accordance with its advantages and disadvantages for them.

The majority of women immigrants, however, came as members of families. As Sturino points out, with regard to southern Italians, women played an important role even before their arrival, as unmarried sisters requiring dowries that could only be earned by sojourners, or as fiancées or wives who encouraged men to migrate and influenced the timing of the move and its destination. During settlement their work was essential, whether paid or unpaid.

The paid work was often of the sort reformers decried as sweated labour: work in the home for the garment industry and the food processing industry. However, several authors suggest that even as before migration the peasant or working-class woman had played a more spirited part than is sometimes assumed, so after settlement did she do so in the ethnic community. Like keeping a boardinghouse or working in a family grocery or restaurant, home work was not a matter of oppression but a source of pride. It was a contribution to a family enterprise, in which, although the man was the designated bread-winner, the woman's part was indispensable and not that of a mere dependant.

The death or desertion of a husband sometimes thrust new responsibilities on a woman. If she had no relatives in Canada and decided to stay and raise her children here, she had to take a more assertive part in the labour force than her sisters. Nipp tells of the widowed mother of eight children, head of the only Chinese family in North Bay, who operated first a laundry and then a small restaurant, while suffering repeated personal tragedies.

Since their prime roles were as wives and mothers, women's participation in the extra-familial life of the ethnic community was limited. Women's associations were usually formed later than men's associations and as adjuncts to them: the term that was applied to a few of them, ladies' auxiliaries, was apt for most. Except among socialists, with their ideological commitment to equality, the formation of women's associations seems to have been related to the emergence of a middle class and to acculturation. The tasks assumed by or allotted to them, even among the socialists, were supportive rather than decisive; they had to do with charity, education and fund-raising. Those tasks could be considered to be extensions of women's familial roles, yet in regard to them as in regard to other matters in the community, men set policy. Petroff's reference to the fact that Macedonian women helped to decide upon tenants of the church hall only underlines how limited their powers were.

Yet she and other authors make clear that women contributed vitally and creatively to the adaptation of ethnic groups to North American life, to the coherence of the groups and to group persistence. One means of doing all three was by being devoted subalterns, both as teachers and as fund-raisers, in the classes formed to transmit mother tongues to new generations. As Polyzoi describes for the Greek community in Toronto and Kaprielian for the Armenian communities in Hamilton, St. Catharines and Brantford, teaching brought women into the work-force; support of the schools helped to preserve some measure of unity among factions in the ethnic community; and, however, resentful young scholars may have been of their hours in supplementary school, some knowledge of homeland traditions and tongue was passed on in an assimilative, if not hostile, Ontario environment.

Draper and Kojder, writing about Jewish and Polish women's associations, pay tribute to their contributions: Draper calls them the backbone of communal life and Kojder describes them as crucial to survival. But both also describe them as peripheral to the ethnic community. Perhaps the key to the contradiction lies in the fact that ethnicity in Canada during the period before World War Two, indeed before 1960, was itself peripheral and not central, or, in terms of another pair of awkward antonyms, was private rather than public. It therefore was relegated in good part to the women's sphere.

Swyripa uses the word peripheral in another context, as a reminder that before World War Two it was not to Ontario but to Western Canada that many eastern and central European immigrants gravitated. Southern Ontario was considered to be a British stronghold. Ethnic groups of other origins looked to the United States, to Montreal or to Western Canada for definitions of themselves as North Americans. For the Ukrainians the heartland was the prairie provinces, a very different environment from the industrial towns and cities of Ontario.

In the postwar period, as immigrants flocked to Canada, the situation changed. For many old ethnic groups and for most new ones Ontario became the cynosure: it received more than half of all immigrants. And it became a very different place. Iacovetta describes the southern Italian immigrant working women in Toronto in the early postwar years, 1947-62, and the similarities between her findings and Sturino's for the first decades of the century are striking. But the dimensions of the postwar immigration; its variety, which increased with changes in immigration regulations in the 1960s and the new Immigration Act in the 1970s; the changing ideology and public policy concerning human rights, women and ethnocultural diversity; the expansion and new directions of the economy—all contributed to create a dynamic and cosmopolitan environment. Historians, with their distrust of the contemporary, have only begun to explore women's place in immigration and ethnic communities since 1960. Epp and Epp offer an indication of the direction of change in their finding that some Mennonite women have moved from the periphery towards the centre both in Mennonite organizations and in the world of work.

One function of exploration is to indicate how much remains to be learned. The thirteen papers in this volume have dealt with the role of women in only a few of the scores of ethnocultural groups that make up the population of Ontario; Nipp's is the only paper to have looked at women in one of the several different "visible minorities," whose numbers have increased spectacularly in the 1970s and 1980s and whose Canadian experience has included and still includes racism. The papers have covered a number of topics, but exhausted none: for example, although women's role as educators has been outlined, virtually nothing has been said about the kind of education given to girls within various ethnic groups. The impact upon them of the biases within the formally egalitarian public schools; the attitude of family and community to education for them as compared to their brothers; their access to and treatment within classes for immigrants and ethnic full-time and supplementary schools—such matters, best explored through autobiography and oral history, have not yet been probed. Some intriguing topics—for example, women and the churches—have been referred to by several authors but never more than incidentally. Finally, with a few exceptions the papers concentrate upon Toronto, yet in the first four decades of the century ethnocultural diversity was more characteristic of northern than of southern Ontario, and in the postwar era, while Toronto has been the braggart immigrant boom town, most of the province has shared in ethnocultural enrichment. The lot of women in immigrant and ethnic communities in Thunder Bay or Welland cannot be extrapolated from what is known about Toronto.

Thus, the authors represented in this volume have opened out the history of women in a number of ethnic groups. They have indicated the richness of the field of research. A beginning has been made; much remains to be done.

A Prison-House for Prosperity: the Immigrant Experience of the Nineteenth Century Upper-Class British Woman

Elizabeth Hopkins

This article centres on the stories of five British gentlewomen who immigrated from Britain to Ontario in the first half of the nineteenth century. Mary Gapper O'Brien, Frances Stewart, Susanna Moodie, Catharine Parr Traill and Anne Langton all left behind written accounts of their experiences in the New World. As might be expected, these accounts have many common characteristics, but they differ from each other in ways that make the task of generalizing about the gentlewoman's adaptation to pioneering a very risky business indeed. In part this is because each of the five women clearly exposed her personal reactions to her new life and one finds oneself trying to brush aside interesting personalities—some optimistic, some pessimistic, some stoic, some enthusiastic—in order to arrive at a picture of a specific class in a specific place at a specific time in our history. So, in general, I propose to proceed on a case-by-case basis, trying to avoid my literary concerns and activate my historical and sociological reasoning as best I can to make some general observations about upper-middle-class immigration in the early nineteenth century. In the end, though, I must leave you, as Susanna Moodie says at the end of *Roughing It in the Bush*, "to draw your own conclusions"![1]

The existence of personal, written accounts of what it was like to settle in Canada in the early 1800s is in itself a revealing matter. It means that the women who wrote these letters, diaries, journals and manuscripts were educated. They recognized the uniqueness of their own adventures and shared them in generous detail with their readers, whether distant relatives or the book-buying public.

Furthermore, especially in the case of their letters and private journals, they must have raised families and written to friends who appreciated the interest and rarity of such accounts enough to preserve them through the years. The fact that the five women all had time to write, daily and lengthily, about their experiences while they lived them also shows that they were, at least to some extent, leisured—some had servants in Canada, four eventually had large families who in time were able to help run the home and thus free their mothers to write. Finally, the fragile yellow manuscripts that we can read today in the Public Archives and other collections remind us that, at the time they were written, the very materials needed to engage in writing were scarce and expensive in the backwoods. Pens, ink, paper, postage and even the artificial light from candles or lamps were luxuries not to be used frivolously in most households. Even our five gentlewomen used them carefully— writing on both sides of the page, sometimes across their horizontal lines of script, writing by firelight, complaining of frozen ink and profusely thanking relatives and friends for parcels from home containing pens and paper. Thus, the very fact that we have these women's stories in their own words is a sign of their privileged backgrounds, their relative comfort in the New World and the kind of values they passed on to their children.

The education of these women deserves a little more comment than its quick mention above. In the early 1800s, with few exceptions, only the children of the well-to-do middle and upper classes received anything resembling a formal education. In the case of the sons of such families, education begun at home under a tutor would be continued at a "public" school when the boy reached the age of eleven or twelve and finished at university if he was destined for one of the professions. For the daughters of such families, education was acquired only at home under the guidance of parents and governesses or tutors. Furthermore, the curriculum in most households was a very different matter for boys and girls. The latter were seldom exposed to mathematics or the sciences (beyond a polite smattering of nature study) and spent hours studying decorum, music, dancing, fine needlework, drawing and painting. By the 1820s the picture was beginning to change as the *nouveau riche* British middle class set up their own "public" schools for sons and daughters. The five women in this study, however, were educated at home. The unusual feature of their schooling was the emphasis their parents and guardians placed on a well-rounded curriculum for both sons and daughters. This curriculum was one of the most valuable assets they carried to Canada as young adults. It meant that they could do more than write about their experiences; they were not helpless, unskilled or ignorant. Indeed, it clearly enabled them to survive and succeed where so many others struggled and failed.

In the Public Archives of Canada there is an unpublished memoir of her girlhood in Suffolk written by Catharine Parr Traill, sister of Susanna Moodie.[2] In it she gives a detailed account of the education their father, Thomas Strickland, devised for his six daughters and two sons. They were all taught the same subjects—reading, writing, Latin and a little Greek, history, geography, philosophy, mathematics, physics and botany. They were encouraged to read in their father's extensive library—though fiction was definitely discouraged. There were frequent walking excursions into the countryside surrounding Stowe House and Reydon Hall, their early Suffolk homes (which were also large working farms). Their father made these trips the occasion for more lessons on the care of farmland, the habits of wildlife, the art of fishing and the patterns of plant life. The only segregated part of their education came when their mother took the girls for training in small animal husbandry, the dairy, the vegetable garden and other domestic realms while their father coached the boys in farm operation. There were daily religious observances in the Strickland home, and the children were encouraged to make their own toys and games in what little leisure time they had. Needless to say, while good behaviour and polite manners were insisted upon, very little time was given to the decorative arts, though Susanna later took lessons in drawing and painting and Catharine became an accomplished embroiderer. One can hardly imagine a better education for the lives that three of the young Stricklands would one day lead.

Mr. Strickland died rather suddenly in 1818, leaving his large family in fairly restricted financial circumstances. A few years later young Samuel Strickland set out for Canada. His brother Tom joined the merchant navy, and the girls began careers as professional writers and editors while they helped their mother operate the Reydon Hall farm. After further training as a surveyor for the Canada Land Company, Samuel settled near present-day Lakefield, Ontario, and eventually prospered. Realizing that the gentleman settler's main problem was the absence of practical backwoods and farming knowledge, Samuel later established a school at Lakefield for the sons of gentlemen wishing to settle in Canada.

This digression on the education of upper-middle-class settlers helps to explain why so many of the women seemed to adapt to the practicalities of the life of a Canadian farmer's wife with relative ease. It was only when necessity forced them to help in the fields or when the isolation of the bush farm became depressing that they began to complain. In fact, most of the immigrant gentlewomen from the English and Irish countryside were much better prepared for their life in Canada than one would think. Milking cows, working in the dairy, curing and preserving meat, tending large vegetable gardens, chickens and children were tasks they approached with much more confidence than their more narrowly trained descendants could do today.

If their education made them better prepared for the life of an immigrant, however, social class and habits from the old country often threatened their new existence. Used to polite company, the sophistication of London, readily available literature, doctors, religious ministers, elegant furniture and inexpensive servants, these upper-middle-class settlers had in many ways more to learn about the New World than their less privileged fellow immigrants. Susanna Moodie's conclusion to *Roughing It in the Bush* summarizes the problem:

> I have given you a faithful picture of a life in the backwoods of Canada, and I leave you to draw your own conclusions. To the poor, industrious working man it presents many advantages; to the poor gentleman, *none*! The former works hard, puts up with coarse, scanty fare, and submits, with a good grace, to hardships that would kill a domestic animal at home. Thus he becomes independent, inasmuch as the land that he has cleared finds him the common necessaries of life; but it seldom, if ever, in remote situations, accomplishes more than this. The gentleman can neither work so hard, live so coarsely, nor endure so many privations as his poorer but more fortunate neighbour. Unaccustomed to manual labour, his services in the field are not of a nature to secure for him a profitable return. The task is new to him, he knows not how to perform it well; and, conscious of his deficiency, he expends his little means in hiring labour, which his bush farm can never repay. Difficulties increase, debts grow upon him, he struggles in vain to extricate himself, and finally sees his family sink into hopeless ruin.
>
> If these sketches should prove the means of deterring one family from sinking their property, and shipwrecking all their hopes, by going to reside in the backwoods of Canada, I shall consider myself amply repaid for revealing the secrets of the prisonhouse, and feel that I have not toiled and suffered in the wilderness in vain.[3]

Susanna's "prisonhouse" was the bush near present-day Lakefield where she and her husband struggled to establish a farm for the seven heart-breaking years described in her book. She wrote these words in 1850 in the relative comfort of her stone cottage at the corner of Sinclair and Bridge streets in Belleville, Ontario. In 1839 her husband, like many British gentlemen immigrants, had been offered a government post as sheriff of Hastings County. Life in growing, bustling Belleville meant modest prosperity for the Moodies: a stone house instead of a log cabin, schools for their children, a piano from Montreal and a few servants. Although the position of sheriff carried no salary (a sheriff was expected to support himself on the proceeds of successfully prosecuted cases, and John Wedderburn Dunbar Moodie was a scrupulously honest sheriff), the Moodies managed to invest in mortgages and purchase small parcels of land as savings for their retirement. Their two daughters married "well"—the eldest became Mrs. John Vickers, wife of the owner of the Vickers Express Company in Toronto, while her sister's second husband was Brown Chamberlin, Queen's Printer in Ottawa. Two of the three surviving Moodie sons sought their fortunes in the United States, while the youngest, Robert, built a career in the service of the Grand Trunk Railway and later in the Vickers Express Company. Although she worried constantly about money during her widowhood, when she died in Toronto one hundred years ago, Susanna left an estate of $4,700. But if her material prosperity was modest, the opportunity for social contact and literary achievement that her arrival in Belleville afforded her provided a claim to posterity.

In England Susanna Strickland had been a minor literary figure, publishing children's books, verses and sketches in Christmas gift books and such journals as *La Belle Assemblée*, and a single volume of poetry on the eve of her departure for Canada with her new husband and baby daughter. In Canada as a writer she became "a big fish in a little pond" as the principal contributor to John Lovell's *Literary Garland*, the co-editor with her husband of the short-lived *Victoria Magazine*, and the author of *Roughing It in the Bush*, *Life in the Clearings*, *Flora Lyndsey* and half a dozen other novels. She was a figure of some notoriety in the new province, as she reports in *Life in the Clearings*, becoming known as "that woman what writes," a person who "tells lies and gets paid for it."[4]

In Belleville the Moodies were members of the establishment—prominent families of the town were among their social circle and, as educated British gentlefolk, the Moodies were looked to as arbiters of social and moral standards in the community. Even the many political difficulties of Sheriff Moodie's profession did not detract from their social standing, their position as pillars of the community. When J.W.D. Moodie resigned under troubled circumstances in 1863, a local paper reprinted testimonials to his exemplary character.

For Susanna Moodie, then, the general pattern of her life in Canada was typical of immigration experiences: early years of hardship and emotional rebellion were gradually replaced by years of adaptation, acceptance and comfort, the prison-house bush gave way to the relative prosperity of Belleville.

I have started with this very brief sketch of Susanna Moodie's story because she provided the title for this paper and because *Roughing It in the Bush* is probably the account of pioneering most familiar to Canadians today. Its themes, the reasons for immigration, the high expectations for the new land, the painful separation from the old, the struggles with a hostile environment, constantly threatening poverty and emotional despair, and the final acceptance of a much-modified version of comfort and success are common to gentlefolk and poorer immigrants alike. What Susanna's background and social position did offer her was the possibility of escape from hardship and a position of influence as a writer and arbiter of social values in the new land. The stories of her sister Catharine Parr Traill, along with those of their friend Frances Stewart and the experiences of Mary O'Brien and Anne Langton, share more of these themes, but also reveal these women's differing responses to them.

Catharine Parr Traill arrived in Canada in the same year, 1832, as Susanna and for the same reason. She had married an officer of the British army, retired on half-pay after the Napoleonic Wars and suffering the ignominy of genteel poverty as the second son of Scottish landed gentry. With few respectable prospects for improving his fortunes in Britain, Thomas Traill, like hundreds of his fellow officers at the time, opted for the chance to build his own estate on the 400 acres of land granted to retired officers as inducement to settle and increase British influence in Upper Canada. In 1836 Catharine published her first account of their transatlantic voyage and early struggles in the dense cedar bush north of Peterborough. This book, *The Backwoods of Canada*,[5] takes the form of letters written home to Suffolk in which she describes her new life with enthusiasm and wonder:

> Yet I must say, for all its roughness, I love Canada, and am as happy in my humble log-house as if it were a courtly hall or bower; habit reconciles us to many things that at first were distasteful. It has ever been my way to extract the sweet rather than the bitter in the cup of life, and surely it is best and wisest so to do. In a country where constant

> exertion is called for from all ages and degrees of settlers, it would be foolish to a degree to damp our energies by complaints, and cast a gloom over our homes by sitting dejectedly down to lament for all that was so dear to us in the old country. Since we are here, let us make the best of it, and bear with cheerfulness the lot we have chosen.[6]

At least in public Catharine hid her suffering, for her true story was even more heart-breaking than her sister's. Her actual, rather than her fictional, letters reveal her horror and sense of isolation in the bush, though she does her best to maintain a brave face.[7] Thomas Traill shared her shock and horror in the woods, but unlike his wife, he succumbed to long periods of serious depression in the face of back-breaking labour and constant financial worries. The growing family (they eventually had nine children) gave up the bush for a series of partially cleared farms on the Rice Lake Plains where contact with neighbours and friends was a little easier. However, they suffered endless illnesses and twice lost their homes and possessions in serious fires. Thomas never recovered from the last of these in 1856 and died a broken man in 1859. Catharine, however, with characteristic fortitude and her strong Christian faith, lived on until 1899, supporting herself with her writing and her increasingly absorbing botanical studies. Her brother Samuel Strickland built a cottage for her in Lakefield and in her long widowhood she finally achieved modest comfort and a permanent escape from the terrifying isolation of the woods. She corresponded with botanists all over the world and was eventually granted a small pension and an island as a reward for her literary and botanical efforts.

One of Catharine's closest friends was Frances Stewart, another early Peterborough region settler. The Stewarts came to Canada from Ireland in 1822—yet another case of immigration to better the sagging fortunes of the genteel but poor. Frances had grown up in the family seat of her relatives, the Beauforts. Her education was similar to the young Stricklands' and she, too, relieved the isolation of her early years in the Canadian bush by sharing the thoughts she could not speak with distant relations and friends in long letters. She was a cultured settler, an accomplished musician and water-colourist, and she and her husband brought a large library with them to Canada. This library was kept current with frequent parcels from home and was often used by Susanna Moodie and Catharine Parr Traill as a way of keeping up to date with the world of books in Britain.

In 1889 Stewart's daughter, Ellen Dunlop, edited and published her mother's letters in *Our Forest Home*.[8] The Stewarts' difficult first ten years in the bush were just beginning to be succeeded by greater comfort when the Moodies and Traills arrived in Canada, thus Frances was able to give very real emotional support and encouragement to the new settlers. She too had suffered the hardships, depressions and isolation they were just embarking upon. The Stewarts eventually achieved considerable prosperity and prominence in their new community. Thomas Stewart served as a Justice of the Peace for many years, and Frances came to be regarded as a kind of Canadian "squire's lady." She was noted for her efforts to maintain certain graces in her home—her silver tea service was brought all the way from Wilmont Hall in Ireland to the dense cedar bush that was to become their home, named "Auburn" after one of the Stewart family's Irish properties.

Mary Gapper came to Canada in 1828, accompanying her mother who wanted to visit Mary's brothers, both of whom had settled on farms, north of the City of York, in what is now Thornhill. The visit stretched into a permanent immigration for young Mary who met and married an Irish gentleman settler, Edward O'Brien, in 1830. For almost ten years from the moment her ship set sail from Bristol, Mary Gapper O'Brien kept a daily journal of her life in Canada which she sent at frequent intervals to a sister who had remained in England. In 1968 Audrey Saunders Miller edited these journals for publication as *The Journals of Mary O'Brien.*[9]

The Gapper family were west country folk. They lived in yet another fine country house and were well-educated, primarily under the tutelage of their father, an Anglican clergyman. His unexpected death prompted two of his sons to immigrate to Canada. They, too, were pensioned officers—veterans of the Napoleonic Wars—and thus entitled to free grants of land. By the time Mary and their mother joined them in Thornhill, they were well-established, prominent leaders in the young community, on friendly terms with Sir John Colborne, the governor, whom they frequently visited on day trips down Yonge Street to York. Sheltered in the prosperous surroundings of her brothers' farms, introduced to their many friends and anxious to learn all about the new colony, Mary Gapper suffered none of the hardship or depression of the Moodies, Traills and Stewarts. She enthusiastically recorded her adventures and seems scarcely to have had a moment of homesickness, even when she made her decision to remain in Canada as Mrs. O'Brien.

As a new bride she settled on a farm farther back from Yonge Street and more recently cleared than her brothers' properties. She joked in her journals about her first rude home, which rapidly expanded and began to fill up with fine furniture and servants.

But her husband's dreams lay farther afield. He had claimed a beautiful point on Shanty Bay, Lake Simcoe, and dreamed of recreating an Irish estate out of the unbroken bush there. By May 1, 1832 the young couple, their year-old baby, servants and possessions found themselves camping in a shanty while Edward O'Brien's log mansion took shape on the rise above the bay. O'Brien himself drew up the plans for "The Woods," as the house was called, and oversaw its construction with the help of escaped slaves who had found their way to the shores of Lake Simcoe.

Friends and acquaintances came to visit, and the O'Briens took trips down to Thornhill and York. They had congenial neighbours, help with the farm clearing and labour, and they were involved in establishing local roads, a church, the militia, a ferry service across the lake, a lending library and numerous other public endeavours. Mary, like many female settlers of her class, was particularly concerned with education for the young, teaching reading and writing to numerous girls and boys who in exchange helped her with the O'Brien babies and chores. By 1838 when Mary O'Brien's journals end, she and her husband had a large and growing family of young children and they were beginning to worry about the education of their two eldest sons. In 1845 they moved to Toronto, living at Shanty Bay only in the summer, so that the boys could attend Upper Canada College.

The O'Briens lived in Toronto and Shanty Bay until their deaths in the mid-1870s. Two of their sons became lawyers, a third, a civil engineer. Their experience seems to have had no "prisonhouse" element, alleviated as it was by social contacts and considerably more wealth than the Lakefield settlers had brought with them. The O'Briens moved through the stage of physical discomforts quickly, and Edward saw his dream of a Canadian estate come true. Samuel Thompson in his *Reminiscences of a Canadian Pioneer* described "The Woods" as "a perfect gem of civilization set in the wildest of natural surroundings."[10] Mary O'Brien took to the life of a Canadian settler with enthusiasm, humour and grace:

> June 11—Edward took me round his fields and then I went to my household work while he went to superintend the making of the road past our lot. I went afterwards to see what they were doing and found them placing logs across a swamp to make a corduroy.
>
> I also stirred a bowl of cream into butter, in which I succeeded much to my heart's content, sitting under the verandah and reading Milton all the time. Only I found to

> my sorrow when my work was finished that I had ground off one of my nails.[11]

The last of the gentlewomen, whose account of a settler's life offers an interesting and cultivated analysis of her experience, is Anne Langton, the sister of John Langton who had settled on Sturgeon Lake, near the site of Fenelon Falls, in 1833. The Langtons were from yet another upper-middle-class English family who found their fortunes reduced. John came to Canada first, settling at Sturgeon Lake because it offered neighbours of his own class who shared his interests. He quickly built a log house and seemed content to enjoy a leisurely, if modest, bachelorhood looking after his needs and pursuing his reading and writing. In 1837 he was joined by his parents and sister who soon made themselves indispensable in helping with the daily tasks. Indeed, Anne, who had been deaf from an early age, never married and took it upon herself to become her brother's housekeeper until his marriage in 1845, after which she was a much-loved "Aunt Anne" to his children, a permanent member of his household in Sturgeon Lake and later Toronto, except for long visits to England, until her death in 1893. Anne's journals from 1837-46 were edited for publication by a Langton descendant in 1950, under the title *A Gentlewoman in Upper Canada*.[12]

In addition to the usual enthusiastic responses to scenery, surprise at homestead chores and Canadian customs, Anne's journal/letters show an analytical bent that is rare in such accounts. For example, she comments on the role of gentlewomen in the New World as follows:

> I have caught myself wishing an old long-forgotten wish that I had been born of the rougher sex. Women are very dependent here, and give a great deal of trouble; we feel our weakness more than anywhere else. This, I cannot but think, has a slight tendency to sink us, it may be, into a more natural and proper sphere than the one we occupy in over-civilised life, as the thing I mean and feel, though I do not express it well, operates, I believe, as a safeguard to our feminine virtues, such virtues, I mean, as the Apostles recommended to us for I think here a woman must be respectable to meet with consideration and respect. The greatest danger, I think, we all run from our peculiar mode of life is that of becoming selfish and narrow-minded. We live so much to ourselves and mix so exclusively with one community. It is not only that the individuals are few, but the degrees and classes we come in contact with are still more limited.[13]

Anne's contemplative nature made her an excellent backwoods schoolmistress, aware of her own and her pupils' limitations under the circumstances:

> I am quite sensible that the instruction I give goes a very small way indeed towards complete education, and I have felt a misgiving lest, in some cases, the fact of a child being sent to me for two or three hours twice a week affords an excuse for neglecting it at home. I endeavour to impress it upon their friends that I by no means charge myself with the whole education, but am willing to give a little assistance such as may be in my power.[14]

Like the O'Briens, the Langtons were rather more prosperous to begin with, and certainly became more successful as their lives in Canada progressed, than the Moodies or Traills. Their motive for emigrating had not been *absolute* necessity, and Anne was able to return to England on visits from time to time. She had friends of her own class and enjoyed enough leisure to exercise her considerable talent as an artist. More importantly, the initial expectations of Mary O'Brien and Anne Langton were realistic compared with those at Lakefield. Thus the former were able to respond cheerfully when conditions improved. Neither Mary nor Anne was reduced to manual labour or suffered the threat of starvation, hence their views of their new lives are much more encouraging than those of Moodie, Traill or even Frances Stewart. What common elements might, then, be drawn from these five stories of upper-middle-class immigration?

First of all, while it was never an easy life for a woman of that period, it was a great deal more comfortable for an upper-class woman of the colonizing nation than for her poorer sister. The former crossed the Atlantic in a private cabin, not in the horrors of steerage accommodation. She was often tended by a maidservant on board ship and at least in her early years of settlement, thus allowing her some freedom to respond to her new land in aesthetic rather than purely practical ways. Despite the hardships and deprivations of bush life, the upper-class immigrant was confident in her knowledge of who she was and what her role as social and moral leader should be. Her education sometimes provided a means of earning extra income and always offered her philosophic and artistic relief from depression. While she shared homesickness and isolation with poorer female immigrants, she could write, read and eventually travel—sometimes to larger centres in Canada, sometimes even back to Britain. The lack of companionship of her own class was gradually circumvented by settlement in areas like Lakefield, Thornhill and Sturgeon Lake where other upper-middle-class settlers had preceded her. Government appointments in the militia, as a Justice of the Peace, or a county sheriff were much more likely to bless her family than that of a lower-class immigrant. In short, difficult and different though her lot in the New World was, she enjoyed class advantages that were not unlike those she might expect in the old country.

At the same time, she established a pattern of order, hard work and community service that would not have been necessary in her homeland. She was, in effect, an early version of the North American woman who, as far as she is able, does what has to be done whether or not it is woman's work. This was often a difficult lesson to learn, and was not, of course, the preserve of upper-class female immigrants alone; but for such women, with their education and expectations, it often resulted in quite remarkable achievements.

Finally, I think it is true to say that, though the reality of their lives may not have matched their hopes when they left Britain, they all did improve their family's security and material prosperity, however modest the latter. And for those who ended with modest estates there was literary and national renown.

Notes

1. Susanna Moodie, *Roughing It in the Bush* (Toronto: Coles, 1980).
2. Traill Family Collection, MG29 D81, Public Archives of Canada (PAC), Ottawa.
3. Moodie, *Roughing It in the Bush*, pp. 562-63.
4. Moodie, *Life in the Clearings*, ed. Robert McDougall (Toronto: Macmillan, 1959).
5. Catharine Parr Traill, *The Backwoods of Canada* (Toronto: Coles, 1980).
6. Ibid., p. 310.
7. The majority of Mrs. Traill's extant letters are in the Traill Family Collection, MG29 D81, PAC, Ottawa.
8. Frances Stewart, *Our Forest Home*, ed. E. S. Dunlop (Toronto: Presbyterian Printing and Publishing Co., 1889).
9. *The Journals of Mary O'Brien, 1828-1838*, ed. Audrey Saunders Miller (Toronto: Macmillan, 1968).
10. Ibid., p. 118.

11. Ibid.
12. Anne Langton, *A Gentlewoman in Upper Canada*, ed. H. H. Langton (Toronto: Clarke, Irwin, 1950).
13. Ibid., p. 73.
14. Ibid., p. 134.

The Role of Women in Italian Immigration to the New World

Franc Sturino

My statements will very much be an exploration of the role of women in the migratory process as it was played out between Italy and Canada, and by no means definitive. The article is chiefly derived from oral testimony collected in on-going research into emigration from southern Italy to Canada. It is part of a case study documenting the migratory process as it emanated from Cosenza province in the southern region of Calabria in the early part of this century. The study examined emigration from eight neighbouring communes in Cosenza; I will use the term *paesani* to refer to this population, a term the immigrants themselves used to refer to those from the same local area. The study was particularly concerned with the process of kin-linked chain migration of *paesani* who had been former peasants, and as much as possible an effort was made to understand this process from the point of view of the historical actors themselves.[1] Though our interpretation is based upon a specific case study, I believe that by virtue of being southerners, by virtue of being former peasants and by virtue of making their way to Canada via kinship chains, the general contours of the Cosenza immigrants' experience may be indicative of the experience of many other Italian immigrants prior to the Second World War.

What can one say about women in Italian immigration? First of all, on the basis of the experience of the Cosenza immigrants, I believe it is of little use to talk about women as such within the context of southern Italian culture and immigration. That is to say, empirically the category "women" (or men) as a unit of study does not get us very far in understanding southern Italian immigration. To talk of women (or men) as a unit of study implies that females participated in emigration by virtue of belonging to the category "women"; it connotes that females acted primarily as women rather than in some other capacity. We know, however, that this was not the case.[2]

First and foremost, women (as well as men) migrated by virtue of their role in the family. In a basically traditional society that had yet to witness effective intervention and encapsulation by the modern state, and subsequent individualization, people first of all acted as members of corporate families, the basic building blocks of the community. Within the family unit women had rights as well as obligations, as men did, and it was with respect to this unit that they defined themselves. The decision to emigrate, the manner of migration and the nature of subsequent settlement patterns were determined not by women or men as individuals, but by families. Though one may focus on the role of women—which implies the role of men and a sense of position within community social structures—this is quite different from focusing on women as a singular category that empirically needs specialized attention when examining Italian migration. Furthermore, while families provide us with the basic unit of study when attempting to comprehend Italian migration, the actual process of migration, the link in the chain, was provided primarily by kinship, that is, blood ties up to the degree of fourth cousin and, to a lesser extent, by *paese* (or commune) ties.

It is only by considering family and kinship adequately that one can come to a phenomenological understanding of the migratory process; that is to say, an understanding that takes into account the experience of the migrants themselves. In our study of Italian and similar migrations, we must beware not to use automatically categories borrowed from our own industrial, bourgeois, mass society, which often reflect more of what is salient to us as individuals today than what was important to past women and men who were often part of very different societies.

In the migration process, the role of women within the home setting of Cosenza roughly corresponded to their position in the life cycle. First, as young, single women open to courtship, it can be said that they changed the nature and upgraded the quality of the local marriage market. They did this by adding "emigration" to the list of attributes defining a desirable husband. Women knew that *americani*, upon their return from the New World, found that their credit rating had gone up, that their accessibility to social betters had improved, and that they were rendered increased respect by *paesani*. Hence, it is not surprising that their desirability as potential husbands also improved.

Indeed, within the "culture of emigration" that emerged in Cosenza, one provincial mayor reported in 1910 that it had become a matter of shame or dishonour if a young man did not attempt to better his socio-economic status by immigrating to the New World.[3] It was reported that sometimes a father would refuse to consent to his daughter's marriage if the young man had not been, or was unwilling to go, to America. Conversely, young suitors could often marry peasant women above their station and be given handsome dowries on the promise of emigrating. In such an arrangement, part of the dowry was often used to finance the voyage and the marriage itself was usually just a civil ceremony and unconsummated until the spouse returned.[4]

In any case, there is little doubt that as emigration became an increasingly accepted strategy for the attainment of social and economic goals—ultimately leading to the purchase of a home and, if one were fortunate, land—women increasingly valued young returned, or prospective, *americani* over more sedentary men. In this way women actively had an input into the social capital associated with emigration and, hence, they acted as an additional stimulus to the overseas exodus.

In addition to their influence as potential spouses, women as sisters stimulated emigration in the common case where male siblings, as part of their familial obligations, travelled overseas to put together the dowry required of young brides. To give but one example of the importance played by the provision of dowries as a spur to emigration, one Cosenza immigrant related concerning his father:

> He went [to America] for his mother and father. He wanted to give them a nice home. People worked for their family then. My father had three sisters and he married them all off himself because his father didn't have any money. Back home you had to have all the dowry. My father did it all for all three sisters. It was mostly my father that set them up.[5]

The person spoken of worked as a navvy on various railroad lines throughout North America in order to place his sisters in a respectable position within the local marriage market. The provision of dowries was a common, immediate motivation behind emigration, primary to the male emigrant investing in his own family formation.

But even more directly than through the workings of the marriage market, women played an important part in decisions regarding emigration once they had married and become wives. It was especially the young wife, newly married, who was likely to see the emigration of her spouse as a potential threat to marital stability. A considerable amount has been written of "jealous Italian men," but the powerful emotion of jealousy was not restricted to males. And, indeed, local norms which winked at the moral transgressions of men gave women precious little consolation in their worries. One young woman, for example, was against her husband immigrating to the United States in the late nineteenth century for she believed that slavery still existed and he might be tempted to take as personal chattel a black woman. Another young woman discouraged her husband from immigrating to Buenos Aires, where one of his aunts had settled, for it was popularly believed that Argentinian women were even more of a threat to fidelity than American women.[6] In fact, in the Italian *boca* colony of Buenos Aires there was a well-known red light district that catered to the many Italian sailors and transients who passed through the harbour area. On the other hand, few wives worried about the potential temptations posed by Ontario.

Most wives encouraged immigration, however, for they believed that only through the migration of their husbands could they acquire a better future. Encouragement was especially forthcoming when women became mothers, and the burden of a growing family started to be felt. As a mother, the woman's first duty was now to her children, and any reservations about her husband were put aside. Also, it is quite likely that since the husband was now a father, women felt more assured that added familial ties would lessen the possibility of moral infringements and hence decrease the chance of marriages being damaged.

Sometimes, however, the encouragement of wives was to no avail. Some husbands who considered themselves quite well off refused to emigrate, and often their wives never forgave them for this. While necessities were provided, such women resented that there was never enough cash to improve the home or dress their children nicely; and they resented the fact that socially inferior families whose bread-winners had emigrated were able to improve their condition while their own remained stagnant.[7]

It can be concluded that women were far from passive in the migratory process. They added input into the social capital that was associated with emigration in their local society, and they were active participants in the culture of emigration that permeated Cosenza in the early part of the century. Also, their role in the migratory process was very much related to the process of family formation. They influenced emigration primarily as potential wives, as wives and as mothers, rather than as women *per se*.

During the sojourn phase of migration, which predominated up to World War One, a married woman could expect that her husband would be absent for several years. During this separation the support wives and children could expect from kin mitigated the hardships involved. Close relatives, especially those on the male side, would help maintain wives and children during the sojourner's absence. Female relatives would provide wives with both domestic help and emotional support. Families were assured that should the sojourner be injured, or even lose his life overseas, close kin would help support the wife and children. Such assurances made sojourning easier to accept for both women and men. The increased economic role that women played working in the fields and their central socializing role raising children during the absence of men were also important.

In addition to such considerations, however, the predominance of sojourning, which saw men make the transatlantic journey several times in a lifetime, and the prevalence of astonishingly long separations were rendered acceptable to *paesani* by certain social values. For men, the centrality of their role as the family's provider, which was linked to a peasant ideology of hard work and sacrifice, made deprivation in North American work camps tolerable since it was expected that their *sacrificio* would later be redeemed in the village by the attainment of a home, land and increased respect. But what was perhaps even more fundamental in facilitating sojourning was the value of female honour.[8]

Among the respectable peasantry, while a husband provided for his wife and children through hard work and self-deprivation, a wife reciprocated by remaining sexually faithful. Just as a man's social capital rested upon his ability as a provider—and emigration was a strategy to attain this—a woman's social capital rested upon her capacity to protect her sexual honour. Any slight on her honour affected the reputation and status not only of the woman, but of the whole family (just as would be true if the male proved to be an inadequate provider). With *paesani* remaining away from wives and daughters for years at a time, the strict peasant restrictions on female sexuality, which it was the responsibility of close kin to help maintain, reassured migrants that their absence from home would not lead to dishonour. It assured migrants that their families would remain intact, for indeed the sojourn itself would have little meaning without the safe assumption that there would be an honourable family to return to afterwards. In short, it was the knowledge that the honour of their wives and daughters would be protected and the family's social capital remain untouched that made sojourning psychologically possible for the males.

As Germaine Greer recently pointed out after observing Calabrian and similar peasant women, they did not experience the pervasive emphasis on female honour as something forced upon them by men,[9] any more than men experienced their role as providers as forced. Female honour was part of the fabric of society, which women internalized as young children and, indeed, a mother-in-law or aunt could be just as strict a protector of this social value as any man. The origin of this value must be sought beyond personalities in the material base of peasant society. The system of small landed property in a state of scarcity made the middling peasantry exceedingly jealous of protecting its patrimonial plots and exceedingly zealous that such land be inherited by progeny who were in fact one's own.[10] Only confidence that one had legitimate heirs could validate the "sacrifice" of labour expended by small peasants in acquiring a patrimony, which ultimately, it was hoped, would ensure the family's corporate unity through generations. The social value of female honour, then, was grounded in the system of small holdings of family property, which families strove to acquire and maintain, and initially they sought the capital for such proprietorship through the strategy of male sojourning.

When aspirations of gaining stable peasant proprietorship in Cosenza ended in disillusionment, as they usually did, sojourning gave way to immigration to the New World. Wives and children joined the male bread-winners who had preceded them, and with family reunification women came to play an important role in settlement.

The initial years of settlement invariably involved a period of boarding with kin or *paesani*. During this phase the first priority of the family was to attain ownership of its own home, an aim which reflected the former peasants' drive for landed status. Ownership of a home provided a concrete focus for the family's social unity. Further, it marked an attempt to stabilize and add economic reality to the family as a corporate group—the members of which were to hold property in common.

Home ownership was virtually the definition of a "good" parent. Insofar as *paesani* thought in terms of "mobility" currents, it is clear that the focus of their aspirations for improvement was not occupation, education, or even income as such, but ownership of a home.[11] Home ownership was intimately connected with a prime purpose of the corporate family, which was to make possible the *sistemazione* of offspring—setting up children at marriage with the proper economic and social wealth necessary to establish respectable new families.

For the immigrant family, then, work, home ownership, family cohesion, and *sistemazione* were all interwoven. Women contributed actively to this constellation, but most concretely to the world of work, which materially underlay the other aspects. It is now well established, primarily through the research of Virginia Yans-McLaughlin, that the work of Italian immigrant women, even when it involved the factory, did not place undue stress on the immigrant family as many prior scholars had assumed. McLaughlin has shown that, for the most part, Italian women sought out occupational niches which placed minimal strain on family relations and allowed them to earn income while still maintaining traditional roles.[12] This was certainly the case with *paesani.*

In Toronto, for example, for the minority of women who worked outside the home, jobs in the city's clothing industry were by far the most common. This preference often reflected Old-World experience in textile and clothing production, and such work was seen as an acceptable female activity. Moreover, since women went to work in village groups and sometimes even the foreman was a *paesano*, it was generally regarded that sexual honour would be preserved.

Nonetheless, factory work was often seen as a compromise which took away from the man's primary definition as provider. When possible, it was often preferred that women work at home. This was particularly true of immigrants who had come from the better-off, landed, peasant strata. Home work for women, of course, could take many forms: the running of boardinghouses where families had excess rooms to let, work in family businesses such as grocery stores or shoe stores, work alongside men who were moonlighting as furniture makers or petty salesmen and, for the most fortunate of women, running their own home businesses as seamstresses.

More common, however, was taking in home work from the city's garment manufacturers. *Paesani* women took in simple jobs and often also involved their children in these. A common task was the scissor cutting of appliqués from large machine-made sheets, which would later be sewn at the factory to blouses, dresses, hats and the like. Another form of home work involved the city's food processing plants. For example, the Laing Company would distribute bushels of onions to be peeled and washed by *paesani* women at home, after which they would be further processed and put in jars at the factory. In any case, women were paid on the basis of piece-work, and they often laboured in small groups of kin in order to break the monotony and boredom.[13]

Aside from such work for which they were paid, women, of course, contributed to the family economy through performing numerous domestic tasks. This involved fairly standard responsibilities common to most housewives such as shopping, cooking, laundering, knitting and sewing clothing, caring for the children and, commonly, managing the family purse.[14] Other tasks contributing to the family economy, however, were a direct transplantation of "pre-industrial" work done in the home society. First and foremost, this involved the production of food. Women tended home gardens, they gathered their own vegetables for preserves from farms (often Italian-owned) on the city's outskirts, and they were not above gleaning edible greens such as chicory and dandelion from Toronto's parks and railroad rights-of-way. They made tomato purée, pickled vegetables and, along with the men, worked at the annual production of preserved meats and wine. Through their domestic labour, especially the growing, collection and preparation of food, *paesani* women were able to cut the family's household expenses to a minimum.

It has been noted in several studies that Italian women showed a greater preference for paid home work than any other ethnic group.[15] Several factors contributed to this: such work recalled their Old-World past, it allowed children to help, and it allowed the fulfilment of traditional roles regarding child-rearing and domestic responsibilities. Lastly, because paid home work was seasonal and low paying, the woman's wages did not approach those of her husband. Hence, the male's role as provider was not threatened and family cohesion was maintained.

While these factors have been commonly cited, there was an additional element that was primary in accounting for the prevalence of home work; that is, the pervasive concern over female honour, which underlay a woman's proper performance of responsibilities as mother and wife. But in speaking of the importance of female honour, it is not sufficient to simply refer to the "Mediterranean attitude" of the immigrants. The southern Italians' concept of female honour was more complex and more concretely linked to everyday reality than much of the literature suggests. We have already mentioned the connection between the honour complex and small peasant property which families strove to acquire and bequeath to their children. Moreover, a family's good standing among *paesani* was determined not only by its economic wealth, but also by its social capital. Corporate wealth without corporate honour, particularly as manifested through the female, was empty.

A family's striving for social and economic status in the New World, especially through home ownership, made little sense if this was to be spoiled by dishonour. Home work, while allowing for the woman's input into the family economy, provided an avenue by which the family's prestige could be preserved. Though home work—because of its poor remuneration compared to factory work—compromised maximization of the family's potential income, this compromise was consciously made to ensure the family's social capital, so that what wealth *was* accumulated would remain honourable.[16]

Home ownership was arguably the most important single aspiration of southern Italians during the early settlement phase of migration. Women, through patterns of work consonant with traditional social values, contributed significantly to the setting up of immigrant homes. Moreover, their balancing of economy and social values enabled women to contribute to the cohesiveness of the corporate family and the honourable *sistemazione* of children. By playing an instrumental role in the settlement of their families, women, in their own way, helped lay the foundation for Italian community and ethnicity in the new land.

In discussing the role of women in Italian immigration, I have presented a view stressing their facilitation of the migration process as it unfolded from Old-World village to New-World settlement. Obviously, I believe that the emphasis placed on women as part of wider family strategies and as contributors to successful transplantation corresponds with historical reality. But while I have maintained that relations between men and women were essentially corporate in nature, this corporateness should not be taken to mean that conflict between the sexes was absent. Though the primary roles of man as provider and woman as the repository of family honour placed limits on the freedom of action of both sexes, there is little doubt where power within the family lay.

Because a woman's behaviour was always under surveillance and because the limits on her freedom involved, much more than the man's, the private sphere of life, women felt the constraints of their community—both within the Old World and the New—more acutely than men. While *paesani* women from early childhood had sufficiently internalized the precepts of female honour to deter transgression, the constant checks on the part of fathers, husbands, brothers and uncles was not taken by some without resentment and sometimes hostility.[17] With respect to the work sphere, some women related how, had their husbands approved, they would have chosen to contribute to the family economy through factory work rather than home work—especially in the interval before the birth of their children or after their infancy—because it was better paid, more readily available, and was seen as less monotonous. As daughters, some women complained that their fathers' concern for their honour, in conjunction with the emphasis on their future roles as wives and mothers, prevented them from completing the education they desired, thus restricting their potential entrée into non-factory jobs.[18]

In short, life within the immigrant family was not an idyll. The family functioned as a corporate group, but conflict too existed. Cooperation did not mean egalitarianism. Power was skewed along sexual lines in the man's favour, at times leading to dissatisfaction on the part of women. Nonetheless, though strife existed, one must not lose sight of the immigrant family's total reality. Despite the dissatisfaction occasionally expressed by women, the stability of the family unit prevailed. In order to contribute to the family's economy and coherence, men had to pay the price of exploitation on the job. For their contribution towards the same end, women also had to pay a price by adhering to the pervasive demands of the honour complex. For both, however, their *sacrificio* was made for the benefit of the greater whole of the corporate family by which they were primarily defined. Since migration came to be viewed as a prime strategy for familial advancement, women as well as men were inexorably linked to the contours of its development, past as well as future.

Notes

1. The account presented here is derived from interviews with both men and women gathered during field work with Cosenza immigrants in Toronto in the 1970s. For a discussion of the original research upon which much of this article is based, see Franc Sturino, "Inside the Chain: A Case Study in Southern Italian Migration to North America, 1880-1930" (Ph.D. diss., University of Toronto, 1981), introduction.
2. An incisive discussion regarding women in the migration process is provided by Anthony Leeds, "Women in the Migratory Process: A Reductionist Outlook," *Anthropological Quarterly*, vol. 49, no. 1 (January 1976), pp. 69-76. This issue as a whole is of relevance since it is devoted to the theme of women and migration.
3. Francesco Nitti, *Scritti sulla questione meridionale*. vol. 4, pt. 1: *Inchiesta sulle condizioni dei contadini in Basilicata e in Calabria (1910)* (Bari, 1968), p. 160.

4. See Adolfo Rossi, "Vantaggi e danni dell'emigrazione nel mezzogiorno d'Italia (Note di un viaggio fatto in Basilicata e in Calabria)" *Bollettino dell'emigrazione*, anno 1908, no. 13 (Roma: Ministero degli Affari Esteri, Commissariato dell'Emigrazione, 1908), pp. 33-34.
5. Interview with Eugenio S., 17 April 1976.
6. Interviews.
7. Ibid.
8. A readable, though somewhat haughty, account of some of the social values and patterns discussed here is given by A. L. Maraspini, *The Study of an Italian Village* (Paris, 1968), especially the middle chapters dealing with familial aspects. Also see Alain Morel, "Power and Ideology in the Village Community of Picardy: Past and Present," in *Rural Society in France: Selections from the Annales; Economies, Sociétés, Civilisations*, ed. Robert Forster and Orest Ranum (Baltimore, 1977), p. 113, and Alessandro Mastro-Valerio, "Remarks upon the Italian Colony in Chicago," in *Hull-House Maps and Papers: A Presentation of Nationalities and Wages in a Congested District of Chicago, Together with Comments and Essays on Problems Growing Out of the Social Conditions* (Boston, 1895; facsim. rpt., New York, 1970), p. 132.
9. Germaine Greer, *Sex and Destiny: the Politics of Human Fertility* (London, 1984), pp. 95-97.
10. For the genesis of the relationship between female fidelity and small property see F(riedrich) Engels, *The Origin of the Family, Private Property and the State* (Moscow, 1948; English ed.), p. 58 *passim.*
11. According to the 1971 Census, Italian immigrants had the second highest proportion of home ownership (77 per cent) of any group in Canada, after the Poles (79 per cent), and the highest proportion for Toronto with over 83 per cent of Italians owning their own homes. Anthony H. Richmond and Warren K. Kalbach, *Factors in the Adjustment of Immigrants and their Descendants* (Ottawa: Statistics Canada, 1980), pp. 404-07.
12. Virginia Yans-McLaughlin, *Family and Community: Italian Immigrants in Buffalo, 1880-1930* (Ithaca, New York, 1977), chapt. 7.
13. Aside from McLaughlin's work, a number of other studies have appeared in recent years dealing to a lesser or greater extent with the work world of Italian immigrant women. Among these are Colomba M. Furio, "The Cultural Background of the Italian Immigrant Woman and Its Impact on Her Unionization in the New York City Garment Industry, 1880-1919," in *Pane e Lavoro: The Italian American Working Class*, ed. George E. Pozzetta (Toronto, 1980), pp. 81-98; and the articles by Judith E. Smith, "Italian Mothers, American Daughters: Changes in Work and Family Roles," and Sharon Hartman Strom, "Italian-American Women and Their Daughters in Rhode Island: the Adolescence of Two Generations, 1900-1950," both of which appeared in *The Italian Immigrant Women in North America*, ed. Betty Boyd Caroli et al. (Toronto, 1978). This volume was published by the Multicultural History Society of Ontario and contains the proceedings of a 1977 conference on the Italian

immigrant woman, which is probably the best collection to date treating the subject.

14. For a provocative analysis of the labour value of the housewife's work, see Wally Secombe, "The Housewife and Her Labour under Capitalism," *New Left Review*, 83 (1974), pp. 3-24.
15. For example, a 1916 American government study of home finishers in the garment industry found that 46 per cent of such workers were Italian (the next largest group were the Jews with just over 17 per cent). U.S. Department of Labor, Bureau of Labor Statistics, *Summary of the Report on the Condition of Woman and Child Wage Earners in the U.S.*, Bulletin No. 175 (Washington, 1916), p. 294. See Furio, "Cultural Background of the Italian Immigrant Woman," pp. 88-89, for similar studies.
16. A recent study of Italian immigration to Canada, which considers the twin issues of social values and home ownership, is provided by Jeremy Boissevain, *The Italians of Montreal: Social Adjustment in a Plural Society* (Ottawa, 1970), pp. 9-18.
17. See Leonard Covello, *The Social Background of the Italo-American School Child: a Study of the School Situation in Italy and America* (Leiden, Nether., 1967), p. 196 *passim.*
18. Interviews.

"I Won't Be a Slave!"—Finnish Domestics in Canada, 1911-30

Varpu Lindström-Best

> It is with deep sorrow and longing that I inform you of the death of my beloved daughter Siiri Mary who became the victim of a terrible death in her place of employment in Nanaimo, B. C. on the first of May at 04:00 in the morning. As she was lighting the fire in the kitchen stove with kerosene it exploded and the fire ignited her clothes and she burnt so badly that on the fifth of May she died in the Nanaimo hospital at 11:30 in the evening. She was born on January 1, 1906 and died on May 5, 1922 at the age of 16 years 4 months and 4 days. Father remembers you with bitter sadness and longing.[1]

This touching funeral notice reveals some of the dark realities about domestic service in Canada. Why was the sixteen-year-old girl having to start her work day at 4:00 A.M.? What knowledge did she have of kerosene? And what protection in case of an accident? Who could she turn to for advice, or what avenues for complaint did she have? While the domestic servant looked after all the members and guests of the household, who looked after her? These questions were hotly debated in the various organizations established for Finnish maids in North America. Despite the many negative aspects of domestic work, it was the most common occupation for Finnish immigrant women.

The domestics themselves are quick to point out the many positive features about their life as a *haussi-meiti* (housemaid). From the discussions emerge important differences in the society's view of domestic service as a low-status occupation and the maid's own view of her work. This article will probe into both the positive and negative aspects of life as a domestic, taking the examination beyond the work place and into the community. In the process the study will discuss the organizations and communication networks which were established to assist the Finnish domestic servants.

Supply and Demand

The University of Toronto probe into the conditions of female labour in Ontario in 1889 noted that the demand for domestic servants exceeded the supply and that it was necessary to import domestic servants from the British Isles.[2] Barber's thorough examination of the recruitment and settlement of the British domestic servants as the most welcome women shows to what great extent the government and employers would go to recruit domestics.[3] Young girls, often orphans from England, were brought to Canada through various benevolent agencies and ended up as domestic servants.[4] Still, as poignantly illustrated by Makeda Silvera's book *Silenced*, the chronic shortage of domestic servants has continued until the present day.[5] There have, of course, been periodic fluctuations in the demand, and some communities felt the shortage of domestic workers more severely than others, but generally the supply of maids did not meet the demand.

After the turn of the century, Finnish domestics were enticed to come to Canada. The federal government bent immigration regulations, created special categories and made easier travel arrangements for women who promised to work as domestic servants.[6] In fact, it was the only category, in addition to farm worker, in which a single woman from Finland during the twenties was allowed to enter the country.[7] Like the British, they too were welcome. The following riddle in a Finnish paper illustrates the point:

> I am not beautiful,
> Yet, I am the most wanted woman.
> I am not rich,
> Yet I am worth my weight in gold.
> I might be dull, stupid,
> Dirty and mean,
> Yet, all the doors are open for me.
> I am a welcome guest
> All of the elite compete for me.
> I am a maid.[8]

Finnish women entered the industry during its "transitional period," when the proportional importance of domestic service as a major occupation for women was declining. In 1921 domestics represented only 18 per cent of all employed women in Canada. New opportunities were enticing Canadian women away from domestic service and the resulting gap was partially filled by newly arrived immigrants.[9] The largest proportion of foreign domestic workers still came from the British Isles—75 per cent before World War One and 60 per cent during the 1920s.[10] Among the other ethnic groups, the Scandinavians and Finns showed an exceptionally high propensity for domestic work. While the British women, who were able to speak English, also had other opportunities for employment, the Finnish women were almost exclusively concentrated in the service industry. In Finnish jargon "going to work in America" became synonymous with "going to be a domestic servant in America."[11] During the twenties, the Finnish domestic servants made up 7-8 per cent of all female immigrants classified as "female domestics." In the fiscal year ending March 31, 1929, for example, 1,288 Finnish women arrived in Canada under this category out of a total of 1,618 adult female immigrants from Finland.[12] This does not necessarily mean that all women actually settled into their declared occupations in Canada. In fact, the Finnish Immigrant Home Records indicate that there was considerable diversity of skills among these "excellent domestic servants." Letters of recommendation from Finland often included revealing additions such as "she is also an experienced seamstress," or "this woman is a skilful masseuse."[13] The domestic service category was simply the most convenient for immigration purposes.

Nevertheless, the vast majority of working women in Finnish communities were maids. Calculations based on the two largest urban centres indicate that of all the Finnish immigrant women employed outside the home during the twenties at least 66 per cent were maids in Toronto and Montreal.[14] Except for a handful of women who worked in restaurants, "all Finnish women in Winnipeg were maids."[15] This single, overpowering concentration of Finnish women in domestic work had a great impact on the community which had to adapt to the life patterns of the maids. Just as mining, lumbering and construction work coloured the life of the Finnish men, influenced their economic status, settlement location and political thinking, domestic work shaped the world-views of the Finnish women.

The nature of domestic service was also changing from the predominance of live-in maids around the turn of the century to "day workers" by the depression. For example, the percentage of laundresses in the service occupations doubled between 1901-11.[16] It was becoming increasingly difficult to find women willing to live in and, consequently, more of this work was left to the newly arrived immigrants—the greenhorns—whose occupational choices were limited. The Finnish women knew upon arrival that there would be no problem in finding a job. "I could have worked thirty hours a day, eight days a week," commented one tired woman;[17] and a man shamefully recollected:

> There was no work for me, nothing, but my wife was always able to get work as a live-in cook. What to do? I had to take women's work. Oh, I didn't like it. I was to look after the liquor, but in the morning I had to do some dusting too. I hated women's work and the pay was not good either, but we had a place to live and food to eat. As soon as I could get man's work, I left.[18]

The consequent role reversal, which heightened during periods of economic slow-down, was a bitter pill for many men to swallow. "My mother worked," remembered a dynamic leader of the Finnish community, "she could always find work in the houses, and my father stayed home with the children." Then she laughed, "He never liked it, but he did a good job!"[19] By 1928 when the Great Depression had hit the lumbering industry—one of the biggest employers of Finnish men—the frustrated "house-husband" syndrome spread beyond the urban centres. Letters to Finland explained how "women are the only ones who find work and men stay home to look after the children."[20] Women gained in status as "they were the only ones with money to spend."[21] Even during the depression in 1937 when all doors to immigration were shut, the government launched a special scheme to bring in "Scandinavian and Finnish Domestics." Most of the women who came under this plan were Finnish and in their late twenties and early thirties.[22]

Thus, the Finnish women who came to Canada from 1900-30 when the supply of domestics was dwindling and the demand for live-in maids still strong were in a good economic position. They came mainly as single, mature women who were used to hard work, and many had been domestics prior to emigrating. This combination, the availability of work and the ability to do it, was the main reason why Finnish women, both in the United States and Canada, were found in such large numbers in domestic service. In addition, there were other positive features about domestic work which attracted the newcomers.

The Bright Side of Domestic Work

The most pressing concerns of newly arrived immigrants included where to live and where to work. As a live-in maid both worries were taken care of at once. While the Finnish men spent much of their first years in Canada in rooming-houses or bunk-houses, or roaming around in search of work, the live-in maids at least had a solid roof over their heads. Their homes might only be damp cellar quarters, or, more commonly, cold upstairs rooms, but they could also be sunny rooms in luxurious mansions, with beautiful gardens and comfortable feather beds. Lice-covered blankets, hair frozen to the bunk-house wall, or the unpalatable smell of dozens of sweaty socks were not part of the maid's experience. Instead, the domestics usually lived in middle- and upper-class homes in safe and relatively clean neighbourhoods. No time was spent looking for housing and no initial investment needed to buy furniture or basic kitchen utensils.

The maid's limited free time was carefully monitored by the employers. "The family" was sure to report any unexpected absences or late arrivals of the maids. In case of serious trouble or illness at least someone would notice and beware. The stories of unidentified Finnish men found dead by the railroad tracks, lost in the bush, or dying alone from an illness did not have their female counterparts. Someone, whether from reasons of moral concern or meanness, was keeping tabs on the maid's whereabouts and routines. For many younger women, the employers became the surrogate family, disciplining and restricting their social activities. This, of course, was a double-edged sword. One summer evening when a Finnish maid in Toronto failed to come home from the local dance at the agreed-upon time of eleven, the employers swiftly called the police. In her case the alarm was too late as her beaten-up body was found on the outskirts of Toronto in 1916, but her friend was saved from a similar fate.[23] While appreciating any genuine concern, many women resented the strict scheduling of their free time. A Port Arthur maid remembers her first evening off in 1910:

> I have been rebellious ever since I was a child. On my only evening off, I was supposed to be back at 10:00 P.M. Well, I went to the hall to see a play and to dance afterwards and didn't get back until one in the morning. I found the door bolted from inside and my blood rushed to my head. They treated me just as if I was a small child incapable of looking after my own affairs. I banged on that door so hard that

> they finally opened it, and I shouted in my broken English: 'I not dog! I Sanni! I sleep inside!'[24]

In addition to a safe "home" the domestics received regular meals. Many farm girls who were used to hearty dinners, however, complained of the small portions served. They had to sneak extra food from the kitchen. Others went to a local Finnish restaurant on their afternoon off "and stuffed themselves with pancakes" so that for at least a day they would not go hungry.[25] One woman noted an ideological difference about eating and explained in a letter to her mother: "Canadians don't give enough food to anybody. They are afraid that if you eat too much you get sick and the Finns are afraid that if you don't eat enough you get sick."[26] Others complained of the miserly manner in which the mistress checked all food supplies. In one millionaire's home in Montreal, the maids were not allowed to have cream in their coffee. "When the lady asked for the hundreth time if there was cream in the coffee," explained one frustrated maid, "my friend took the entire cream pitcher and threw it against the wall." With a thoughtful sigh she added, "We Finns, you know, we have such temper—that *sisu*—has caused many a maid to lose her job."[27] On the other hand, many women were fed good balanced diets, were introduced to white bread, various vegetables and fruits unknown in their own country. Not only did they receive regular meals, they learned to "eat the Canadian way."

Living with a Canadian family they also learned to speak some English, usually enough to manage in the kitchen. Jokingly they described their language as *kitsi-Engelska*. Many were taught by their employers who found communication through a dictionary too cumbersome, others took language classes provided by the Finnish community during the "maid's day." The maids themselves realized the importance of learning the language:

> ...I am so thankful that right away I was placed in a job where there are only English-speaking people so that I just have to learn when I don't even hear anything else and here that is the main thing to learn to speak English first even when looking for work they don't ask if you know how to work but if you know the language of the country....[28]

Along with language skills, the maids were also given an immersion course on Canadian home appliances, customs and behaviour. On-the-job training included the introduction to vacuum cleaners, washing machines and the operation of gas ovens. The maids attentively observed the "ladies" and were soon acquiring new role models. In amazement Finnish men complained of the profusion of make-up used by the maids who had started to *playata laidia* (play the lady).[29] Women's clothing reflected the new image—hats, gloves and silk stockings being among the first items of purchase. Having obtained these symbols of Canadianization, the maids rushed to the photography studios and sent home pictures of themselves lounging on two-seater velvet sofas, sniffing at a rose and revealing strategically placed silk-stockinged legs. Other pictures showed women with huge hats, the likes of which could only be worn by the nobility or the minister's wife in Finland.[30] We can imagine what effect these photographs had on the relatives back home, or on the girlfriends still wearing tight scarves and wool stockings. Only one month in Canada, and the photographs showed a total transformation of a poor country woman into a sophisticated "lady" sipping tea from a silver pot, some needle-point resting on her knee.

The reality, of course, was much different from the illusion created by the props in the photographers' studios. Undeniably, there were many advantages to being a live-in maid—an instant "home," on-the-job training and immersion in the country's language and customs. On the other hand, there were also serious complaints.

The Proud Maid

A recent study of domestic service in Canada blames the long working hours, hard work, lack of privacy and low status of domestic work for the unpopularity of the job.[31] The Finnish immigrant women certainly agreed with many of these complaints, but because of their cultural background, their position in the community and their special immigrant conditions, their view of domestic work was somewhat different.

Historians have suggested that for the young Irish girls in Boston domestic work actually represented upward mobility, since they had been unable to obtain any kind of work in Ireland. A study of Swedes in Chicago indicates that domestic work was reputable and accepted as the norm for the first-generation Swedish women who were almost exclusively working as maids.[32] This trend is evident among the Finnish domestics in Canada. When the community was so overwhelmingly composed of domestic servants, comparisons with other occupations became irrelevant. Instead the domestics created their own internal hierarchy. Their status came from a job well done and they took pride in their honesty, initiative and ability to work hard "to do what previously had taken two women."[33] Together they worked to create a sound collective image and to improve their working opportunities. Any deviance from this norm, any Finnish woman perceived as "lazy" or dishonest, was severely chastised in the Finnish-Canadian press for ruining the reputation of Finns as "most desirable and highly paid domestic servants."[34]

On an individual level, pride in their work—in their profession—is reflected in the comments of the domestics interviewed for this project. "My floors were the cleanest on the street," or "my laundry was out the earliest every morning" are typical of the self-congratulatory mood. Comparisons with other women were used to illustrate these points:

> Nobody had scrubbed that dirt off, did they look at me when I took off my only pair of shoes, got on my knees and scrubbed that muck till you could have eaten from the floor. Women weren't supposed to show their naked ankles, but heck, I wasn't about to ruin my shoes. Another Finlander, they thought![35]

They worked hard to gain the trust of their employers, and then they boasted, "If I said the sky was green, then the sky was green."[36] Finnish women, often showed a strange mixture of an inferiority and superiority complex. While they might have respected the position of the "Missis," they often felt great disdain for "her inability to do anything right." Helmi, who worked for a wealthy family in Sault Ste. Marie during the early twenties is a prime example of the confidence and control that shines through from many of the stories told by domestics:

> When that Mrs. noticed that I could take care of all the cleaning, all the dishes and all the cooking, in fact, I ran the entire household, she became so lazy that she started to demand her breakfast in bed. Healthy woman! Just lying there and I had to carry the food to bed. Oh boy, that hurt the Finlander's *sisu* that a woman makes herself so shamefully helpless. What to do, what to come up with, when there was no point to *kikkia* [kick back]. So I started making the most delicious old-country pancakes, plenty of them and thick, and I added lots of butter and whipped cream. Every morning I carried to the Mrs. a huge plateful, and the Mrs. ate until she was as round as my pancakes. The Mr. ordered her to go on a diet, and Helmi no longer had to take breakfast to bed![37]

When Nellie McClung chose to make a Finnish domestic the heroine of her novel *Painted Fires*, she agreed with the image that

Finnish domestics had of themselves. Having had a Finnish maid, she was surprisingly familiar with their manners, pride, temper and customs. The Finns, on the other hand, greeted the book with exalted praise as it showed the Finnish maids "exactly as we like to think we are."[38] The novel was promptly translated into Finnish and sold thousands of copies. The heroine, whose name was also Helmi, was honest to a fault, loyal, extremely clean and hard working. She was also strong, stubborn and defiant. For example, in one scene Helmi slams the dishtray on the head of another domestic who had not pre-rinsed the greasy plates. In the ensuing chaos the employer asks, "Isn't that kind of behaviour so typical of the Finns, Maggie? They are clean, swift, but so hot-headed."[39]

McClung's stereotype of a spirited Finnish domestic finds many counterparts in the literary tradition of Finland and of Finns in North America. Because of the Finnish women's love of theatre, of acting and performing, they were often in the position to choose and even write plays for the stage. Invariably the maid was portrayed as "intelligent and honest," constantly involved in her self-improvement while the masters were corrupt, lazy and often stupid. In the Finnish-Canadian socialist literature, the class struggle is depicted through scenes of superior servants suffering under less capable masters. The beloved poems of Aku Päiviö, the best known Finnish-Canadian socialist writer, reinforced the superiority of the victim. One woman confided: "Every time I read the poem 'Woman's Day,' I just cried. It was so true that I could feel it in my bones. The book, you know, was censored by the government, so I removed a tile from the kitchen floor and hid it. When I was in the kitchen by myself, early in the morning, I would read the poem over and over again. It was my private source of strength."[40]

Another woman, Sanni, describes the Finnish domestics by taking examples from the writings of Minna Canth and Juhani Tervapää. The latter's play *Juurakon Hulda* (Hulda from the Stump District) gave Sanni her inspiration and role model. Hulda was a poor farm girl who took employment as a domestic servant, but through hard work and persistent studying in the middle of the night, she eventually outshone her employers in wit, intelligence and honesty.[41] "You might be a servant," said Sanni, "but it doesn't mean you are dumb":

> When you can read, a whole new world opens up for you. It doesn't matter where you live, how far from the civilization, or in what poverty. Once I got started, I read everything I could get my hands on...Finnish women are like that Juurakon Hulda, they come from such poor circumstances with nothing

> in their name, but through hard work and self-education they try to get ahead, find dignity, learn to see beyond their own neighbourhood.[42]

Of course, not all Finnish domestics fit this collective image. Many a woman quietly cried herself to sleep, "too tired to get up to get a handkerchief."[43] The image, however, did create a role model of a domestic that Finnish women ought to emulate, and if they reached this goal, if they convinced their friends and the community that they had earned the respect of their employers, they also gained the support and respect of the community. A maid who was not afraid to take the household reins into her hands had high status in her community. Many bizarre stories emerge when women explain that really they were the ones in control in such families as the Molsons, Otises and Masseys. Perhaps the most outrageous comes from a woman who served the widow of a Governor General in Quebec. She discovered that her living quarters on the first floor of the house were infested with rats. Having spent one entire night catching them, she laid the seven fat specimens on the breakfast table.[44]

Within the social hierarchy of the domestics, those who specialized and worked for the "millionaires" had the highest status within the community. The salaries reflected the experience and the nature of the work, ranging from $15 a month before the First World War and during the twenties to as high as $50 a month. The cooks were at the top of the hierarchy and so too were nursemaids and companions. Chamber-maids, kitchen helpers and "generals" following in that order.[45] For women with a Finnish cultural background, domestic service was not necessarily a "low status occupation." Furthermore, the maid's own view of her work and the community's response to it might indeed see it as reputable, well paid and even independent work.

"When You Are a Domestic You Are Nothing but a Slave"

While the generally perceived low status of domestic work was not a serious deterrent to the Finnish immigrant women, the demand for submissiveness was almost impossible for Finns to meet. The most serious and persistent complaints came from those domestics who bemoaned their lack of privacy, their loss of individuality, their sense of being totally controlled by a strange family. Domestics who stayed with the same family for a long period of time lost their chance to have a family of their own. Children and husbands were seldom tolerated by the employers. Those lucky couples who were able to hire themselves out as butler-maid teams were rare exceptions.[46] Not many husbands were satisfied to have a part-time wife who was available only every other Sunday and one afternoon a week, although such "hidden" marriages did exist. More often, the maid became an extension of somebody else's family and an integral part of the daily routines, but not necessarily any part of the emotional life. As years went by and the maid aged, the chance of ever having a family of her own became an impossible dream. The exceptionally high age of the women giving birth in Montreal to illegitimate children—37.6 in 1936-39—suggests that some women made a deliberate decision to have a child of their own while it was still physically possible.[47]

A Finnish pastor of the Montreal congregation during the late seventies regretted the fate of some of his parishioners, most of whom were women who had worked as live-in domestics in Montreal during the twenties and thirties, and now were totally alone.[48] The families did not provide pensions, nor take much interest in the whereabouts of a retired maid. To make matters worse, the maid had no family, no home, no life of her own. "All my life, I just worked and worked, I seldom went anywhere or met anybody," remembers one resident of a Vancouver old-age home, "and now I know nobody, I am just wondering why God keeps me alive?"[49] The tremendous personal sacrifices demanded from a reliable domestic, the willingness to become a shadow, a quiet figure in the corner tending to the household tasks, was described by one maid as "equal to being buried alive."[50]

This sad fate fell on some Finnish domestics, but many others vigorously fought against it. The free time, the precious Wednesday or Thursday afternoon off, when the maid was allowed to exercise her own will, to be a decision-making person and to meet people of her choice, was carefully planned in advance. Here the Finnish community was of special help and support.

Community Support

The Finnish communities quickly adjusted to the maid's unusual time schedules in order to have some social activity. Finnish organizations, which until the thirties were largely socialist locals of the Finnish Organization of Canada (FOC), scheduled their social occasions, gymnastics practices, theatre rehearsals and dances during "the maid's day." The halls kept their doors open so that the maids could relax after their weekly pilgrimage to Eaton's. They could go and have coffee, meet each other, discuss the work situation, find out about new job opportunities and for a few brief hours escape from their employers. The FOC locals were not the only groups vying for the maid's attention. Finnish congregations, especially in Toronto and Montreal, also catered to them, scheduling their services for Wednesday and Sunday evenings and providing social coffees and reading-rooms for the maids.

When the Finnish consul of Canada, Akseli Rauanheimo, tried to convince Canadian industries, railroads and the government to contribute to the building of a Finnish immigrant home in Montreal, one of his chief concerns was the welfare of the maids. "Many of them have nothing to do on their afternoons off except sit alone on park benches." The home was not only to be used for entertainment, it could also function as a refuge for those women who were mistreated by their employers and who had no other "home" to go to then.[51] Similarly, such temporary shelters for maids in other major communities were usually provided by those women who ran the maids' employment services.[52] Thus, the Finnish domestics could have a sense of belonging to a community, they could share their work experiences with other domestics, and they knew that if their conditions became intolerable other options were open—they could quit and leave and know that they didn't have to spend the night on the street.

This added to the bargaining power of the Finnish domestics who knew that their services were in demand and who had the means to contact new employers. Most Finnish maids did take advantage of their ability "to slam the door so that the chandeliers were shaking," or alternately to "sneak out of the backdoor so that nobody would notice." During their first year as domestics in Canada, the women changed jobs frequently. For example, the Finnish Immigrant Home in Montreal accommodated women who were changing their jobs for the sixth time within a year.[53] Similarly the biographies and interviews concur that at first women took almost any work and then shopped around until a suitable family came along.

The Finnish employment agencies were the key to the domestic's flexibility. They were quick to advise the women not to accept intolerable conditions. Many enterprising women kept rooms for just such a purpose, and there is every indication that they kept close watch on the "greenhorns" who were most vulnerable to exploitation. Still, even with a helpful Finnish woman, the hiring was a harrowing experience. Elli remembered it vividly:

> The first lady who came picked me because I was obviously the cheapest and strongest one, she wanted a greenhorn who would work like a dog...I cried and washed her floors and I was always hungry, but I stayed there for four months until I went back to Mrs. Engman.... She got me a new job right away, but this time I quit after one crazy day, sneaked out secretly.... In my third place I stayed for seven and a half months and was able to demand $35.00 a month, but I quit that place too... because I had to be home at eleven o'clock and it broke my heart to leave the dances during the intermission and see my good-looking boyfriend stay behind.[54]

As the maids gained confidence in their own ability to work, they became more defiant in the work place and often refused to be treated like slaves. Hilja explained:

> In one place where I worked the lady started to shout at me because I hadn't got up early enough to do the washing at 6:00 A.M. I told her that nobody shouts at me and I quit. I decided to take that day off and went to stay at Ilomaki's [home for maids], but as soon as I got there the phone rang for me. It was the employment office calling, they figured that I had quit because my lady had called for a new maid. They phoned me to let me know that a new job was already waiting for me. Next day I was working again.[55]

In addition to the private agencies which received payment for every maid they placed, the Finnish Immigrant Home and many churches arranged for employment for the maids. The system was the same kind of "cattle auction." Ida remembers that "the women just stood in a line and the ladies came to pick which one they wanted."[56] While most Finnish-Canadian sources claim that the Finnish maids were sought-after workers, there are also examples to the contrary: "There were places that would take only Finns, but there were also places that wouldn't take a Finn for any money. Once I was told bluntly that 'We won't hire Finns, because they are all red and stubborn.'"[57]

One woman remembers being told to quit singing the "International" while washing the kitchen floor. "I'll sing what I want," she replied and with that lost her job.[58] Nellie McClung also referred to the reputation of Finnish maids as socialists and trouble-makers.[59] But on the whole the employers were not interested in the private lives of their maids, not to speak of their political opinions, as long as the floors were scrubbed, the laundry washed and the family fed. Edna Ferber vividly describes the family's ignorance of the maid's private world in her short story of a Finnish maid in the United States.[60]

The Class-Conscious Maid

To some Finnish domestics, the availability of work and the supportive networks within the community were not enough. Instead they sought a more elusive goal—a strong collective spirit.

Class consciousness, unlike such characteristics as temper or shyness, is acquired through experience, cultivated by self-study and cemented by daily injustices. Finland was swept by a socialist fervour during the first two decades of the nineteenth century and the question of maids was hotly debated in both the legislature and media. Special homes for maids were established where women could acquire domestic skills. A newspaper, *Palvelijatar* (Maid), discussed at length "maid's rights" and suggested protective measures. The paper's editor, Miina Sillanpää, a Social Democratic member of Parliament since 1907, raised the grievances in the Finnish legislature.[61] Thus it is highly possible that many maids who arrived in North America had already learnt to accept the socialist world-view in Finland.

Because domestic service was the major occupation for Finnish women, it received much attention from the Finnish socialists in North America. The socialist leaders were worried that the live-in domestics would adopt the "capitalist outlook of their employers when they are clearly an indistinguishable part of the working class."[62] They were baffled as to how to organize the domestics who were serving thousands of different "bosses" all over Canada. In the end, the main impetus was placed on raising the individual consciousness, making each maid fight for her own rights within her particular place of employment, while the community would provide her with the best possible support: knowledge, training, cooperative housing and minimum guide-lines for wages and working hours. Unsuccessful efforts at unionizing the maids were also made in major urban areas.

The key to bringing the maids into the socialist fold was to give them hope of improved working conditions by frankly discussing the problems and solutions through the Finnish North American press. In this the socialist women's newpaper, *Toveritar*, which had over 3,000 subscribers in Canada in 1929, played a vital role.[63] In a special issue for the maids, on May 9, 1916, the editor, Selma Jokela-McClone, analysed the situation:

1. While the factory worker is seldom in direct contact with her employer, the maid has personally to face her boss on a daily basis and negotiate her undefined work.
2. A maid is a highly skilled worker, yet she has no possibility to learn her trade before she starts working.
3. Maids do not necessarily work for the big capitalists, many serve the middle class and even the more prosperous working class, which can confuse the issue of class struggle.

To deal with these problems Jokela-McClone suggested that:

1. Because the maid meets her employer as a human being she must have the self-confidence and the sense of self-worth to demand decent human treatment.
2. Maids must become professionals by improving their skills to the utmost of their ability. The key to successful bargaining is the ability to perform well.
3. They must organize maids' clubs, cooperative homes, employment exchanges and raise the class-consciousness of the maids before they can put forth strong demands.[64]

These guide-lines were adopted by Finnish socialist women's groups in Canada, but not without a debate. Many questioned "the need for special skills," or the argument that a maid was a professional, or a highly trained worker. There were those who saw the maid as "an appendix to the parasite class" and not a trustworthy member of the working class. Maids themselves asked what good would training centres or clubs do when the maids didn't have the free time to attend them. Despite the scepticism, attempts were made to implement the plan.[65]

In New York and San Francisco well-organized and highly effective maids' cooperative homes were established. These were seen as a model for other communities to emulate. In Canada the cooperative maids' home movement among the Finns had sporadic support at best. The need for such homes in Canada was partially met by private establishments which provided temporary housing when necessary. The employment exchange for Finnish maids was also in the hands of Finnish women who were generally trusted and reliable, unlike the situation in Manhattan, for example, where several large American agencies "competed for the Finnish maids." [66] Besides, in 1916, both the United States and Canada were experiencing shortages of domestic servants, "giving the maids great opportunities to be selective." In 1922 an article in *Vapaus* concluded that obtaining work was the least of the maids' problems, but rather the inhumanly long working days.[67]

By the mid-1920s, when socialist activity among the Finns had taken a more radical turn toward communism, the question of maids' unions and organizations rose again. This time, the response was at least lukewarm. The first Palvelijatar Yhdistys (Maids' Organization) was founded in Toronto on December 6, 1925.[68] Prior to this the Finnish Organization of Canada's Toronto local had given their Don Hall free of charge for the maids to use on their afternoons off. In 1926 the organization placed a permanent advertisement in the *Telegram* and set up a job exchange at the hall. Later the advertisement was only placed in the paper if someone was in need of work. At times the organization had over twenty paying members and then it seemed to "go to sleep." The last time it was "woken up" was on January 6, 1929, under the name of "Finnish Domestic Club."[69] A year earlier the Chinese community of Toronto had established a union of domestic workers at 87 Elizabeth Street complete with an employment exchange. Among the Finns a cooperative home for the maids was discussed, but it never materialized.

In 1927 Vancouver women also decided to establish a cooperative home and employment exchange for the maids. They set up a fund for this purpose, but by the end of 1928 gave up the idea. Instead, they decided to investigate the possibility of joining the existing Domestic Servant's Union, mainly made up of Chinese domestics. Nothing came of this joint venture.[70]

The largest Finnish maids' organization was established in Montreal, where the need for protection was the greatest since the city was the immediate recipient of all the newly arrived maids coming off the transatlantic steamers. Here a cooperative home was not only discussed but also established in 1930, only to be dissolved within two years by the depression. This home and job exchange was in competition with the Finnish Immigrant Home established by the Consul of Finland and the Seamen's Mission in 1927. From the beginning the housing co-op had over thirty members.[71] In 1928 an article in *Vapaus* pointed out that the city had about 500 Finnish women of whom less than 2 per cent were housewives; the rest were all working as maids or in the service industries. A newly arrived maid might only receive a wage of $20 a month, and the only weapon used by Finnish women to improve their working conditions was to change jobs constantly in search of a better employer.[72] The maids' organization was founded in September 1928 and was quite active. The success of actually getting a cooperative home off the ground was not unbiased because: "so many of the women who joined up were former members of workers' organizations and unions in Finland and thus, right from the beginning we were able to have experienced, capable women to carry on the cause."[73]

Similar maids' groups were established in Sudbury in 1928, in Sault Ste. Marie in 1929 and more sporadically in Port Arthur and Timmins during 1928-30. Common to all these maids' organizations was the desire to achieve minimum wage levels. The women in Sault Ste. Marie all swore that they would not "scab" for lower wages.[74] In Sudbury the maids were keen to establish insurance schemes for the sick and unemployed.[75] In all locations great emphasis was placed on self-education, not in domestic skills, but in class-consciousness and in understanding the role of women in a communist society.

In total, a rough estimate would suggest that about 200 Finnish domestics belonged to the organizations designed for the specific purpose of promoting maids' interests. The small numbers suggest that domestic servants did not have the time or will to give their only afternoon off for meetings, especially since other Finnish women's groups could carry on the task. In northern Ontario the Timmins domestics suggested total integration of women's organizations instead of splintering women into small interest groups.[76] Finnish men "did not take the organizations seriously," and the groups were not strong enough to have any concrete impact on wages. "Despite this," concludes a published assessment of the maids' organizations, "they had great impact in making the maids realize that they too were part of the working class and most welcome in socialist circles."[77]

> No matter how good the family you work in, when you are a maid, you are nothing but a slave. I won't be a slave![78]

Domestic service, the greatest employer of Finnish women, clearly had many problems such as long hours, hard work and lack of privacy. Still, it continued to attract Finnish women, at least initially, because of the perceived advantages of room and board and learning the language and customs of the employers. It was also work that Finnish women were able and accustomed to doing, and the pay was sufficient to meet their immediate demands. Women could see considerable upward mobility within the hierarchy of domestic service and could conceivably double their wages within a year. The stigma of low status work was not very relevant in the Finnish community where most women were, or had been, domestics. Furthermore, the number of Finnish maids in the urban centres was great enough to force the community to set up their activities around the maids' schedules, thus lessening the pain of isolation.

While the Finnish communities could claim that many of their maids were class-conscious workers, they did not succeed in establishing long-term unions or cooperative homes. Still, by collectively keeping up their good image, Finnish domestics were some of the highest paid in the country. The more informal arrangements of maids' meeting-rooms, employment exchanges and private "homes" increased the flexibility of the Finnish domestics and gave them greater bargaining power with the employers. Yet domestic service demanded great personal sacrifices which most women were unwilling to make. As soon as other opportunities presented themselves, Finnish maids left their live-in situations and tried to find more independent work.

Notes

1. *Vapaus*, 30 May 1922, signed by Adolf Leaf.
2. Ramsey Cook and Wendy Mitchinson (eds.), *The Proper Sphere: Woman's Place in Canadian Society* (Toronto, 1976), pp. 172-74.
3. Marilyn J. Barber, "Below Stairs: The Domestic Servant," *Material History Bulletin*, No. 19 (Ottawa, 1984); Marilyn Barber, "The Women Ontario Welcomed: Immigrant Domestics for Ontario Homes, 1870-1930," *Ontario History*, vol. LXXII, no. 3 (September 1980).
4. Joy Parr, *Labouring Children* (London, 1980); Kenneth Bagnell, *Little Immigrants* (Toronto, 1980); Gail H. Corbett, *Barnado Children in Canada* (Woodview, Ont., 1981).
5. Makeda Silvera, *Silenced* (Toronto, 1983).
6. Ibid., pp. 11-40; Genevieve Leslie, "Domestic Service in Canada, 1880-1920," in Janice Acton, Penny Goldsmith and Bonnie Shepard, eds., *Women at Work* (Canadian Women's Educational Press, 1974), pp. 71-125; in 1985 live-in domestic servants are allowed to enter Canada without immigrant status as temporary foreign workers.
7. "Emigration from Finland 1893-1944," New Canadian Immigration Regulations concerning emigration from Scandinavia and Finland, RG 76 vol. 651 C 4682, Public Archives of Canada.
8. *Toveritar*, 10 Feb. 1925, poem by Arvo Lindewall.
9. Leslie, "Domestic Service in Canada," Table A, p. 72.
10. Barber, "Below Stairs," p. 38.
11. The term in Finnish is *piikomaan Amerikkaan*.
12. Dominion of Canada, Report of the Department of Immigration and Colonization for the Fiscal Year ended March 31, 1929.

13. "Finnish Immigrant Home Records," MG 28 V128 Vol. 1 File 1.
14. For Montreal figures see Varpu Lindström-Best, "Finnish Immigrants and the Depression: A Case Study of Montreal," Ph.D. II paper (York University, 1981) and for information on Toronto see her "Tailor-Maid: the Finnish Immigrant Community of Toronto before the First World War," in Robert F. Harney, ed., *Gathering Place: Peoples and Neighbourhoods of Toronto, 1834-1945* (MHSO, 1985).
15. Interviews with Martta Norlen and Mary Syrjälä, Winnipeg, 1983.
16. Census of Canada, 1911, Volume VI, Table I, "Occupations of the people compared for all of Canada."
17. Interview with Tyyne Pihlajamäki, Timmins, 1982.
18. Interview with Rolph Koskinen, Parry Sound, 1983.
19. Interview with Helen Tarvainen, Toronto, 1978; see also Joan Sangster, "Finnish Women in Ontario, 1890-1930," *Polyphony*, vol. 3, no. 2 (Fall 1981).
20. American Letter Collection, LOIM:IV Letter from Aino Kuparinen, a maid who came to Toronto in 1924.
21. Interview with Lahja Söderberg, Vancouver, 1983.
22. "Scandinavian and Finnish Domestics," RG 76 Vol. 436 File 654504.
23. Interview with Martta Kujanpää, Toronto, 1978.
24. Interview with Sanni Salmijärvi, Thunder Bay, 1984.
25. Interview with Martta Norlen, Winnipeg, 1983.
26. American Letter Collection, EURA:XXI Letter from Aino Norkooli who immigrated to Fort William, Ontario in 1923.
27. Taped recording of Ida Toivonen's reminiscences in Thunder Bay, 1983 and her handwritten notes, both in the author's possession.
28. American Letter Collection, KAR:CXXVI, letter from Sylvia Hakola in Schreiber, Ontario dated 26.09.1926.
29. Carl Ross, "Finnish American Women in Transition, 1910-1920," in Michael G. Karni, ed., *Finnish Diaspora II: United States* (MHSO, 1981).
30. For example see Varpu Lindström-Best and Charles M. Sutyla, *Terveisiä Ruusa-tädiltä: Kanadan suomalaisten ensimmäinen sukupolvi* (Helsinki, 1984), especially the chapter on "Valokuvaajalla" (At the Photographers), pp. 143-56.
31. Leslie, "Domestic Work in Canada," p. 85; *Toveritar*, 20 June 1916, an article explaining why women do not like to be domestic servants.
32. Ulf Beijbom, *Swedes in Chicago*, Studia Historica Upsaliensia XXXVIII, especially pp. 197-98.
33. "Consulate of Finland Correspondence," MG8 G62 Vol. 2, File 59.
34. Interview with Hilja Sihvola, Parry Sound, 1983.
35. Ida Toivonen Recordings, Thunder Bay, 1983.
36. Interview with Lahja Söderberg, Vancouver, 1983.
37. Interview with Helmi Vanhatalo, Sault Ste. Marie, 1981.
38. Nellie L. McClung, *Painted Fires*, was translated into Finnish by Väinö Nyman, *Suomalaistyttö Amerikassa* (Helsinki, 1926).
39. Copies of related correspondence courtesy of J. Donald Wilson.
40. Aku Päiviö poem "Naisten Päivä."

41. Juhani Tervapää, (Hella Wuolajoki) *Juurakon Hulda* (Helsinki, 1937).
42. Interview with Sanni Salmijärvi, Thunder Bay, 1984.
43. Interview with Saimi Ranta, Niagara Falls, 1974.
44. Ida Toivonen Recordings, Thunder Bay, 1983.
45. Interview with Rolph Koskinen, Parry Sound, 1983.
46. Butler-maid, cook-chauffeur, etc., combinations were especially popular during the depression when men could not obtain any other kind of work.
47. "St. Michael's Finnish Ev. Lutheran Church," Province of Quebec Registration of a Live Birth, MG 8 G62 Vol. 7, Files 23-25.
48. Discussion with Rev. Markku Suokonautio, Montreal, 1979.
49. Interview with Impi Lehto, Toronto, 1974.
50. Interview with Martta Huhtala, Waubamik, Ontario, 1983.
51. "Consulate of Finland Correspondence," MG8 G62 Vol. 2 File 59.
52. In Toronto alone, there were at least twelve women who took in maids and found them jobs on a more or less permanent basis.
53. Immigrant Home Registers for Women list a total of 3,044 women between 1927 and 1931, MG 28 V128 Vol. 6 Files 1-3.
54. Interview with Elli Mäki, Parry Sound, 1984.
55. Interview with Hilja Sihvola, Parry Sound, 1983.
56. Ida Toivonen Recordings.
57. Ibid.
58. Interview with Sanni Salmijärvi, Thunder Bay, 1984.
59. McClung, *Painted Fires*; the heroine is often confused in the novel with a socialist Finnish woman who has the same last name but a reputation as a trouble-maker.
60. Edna Ferber, *Every Other Thursday*, a short story about the life of a Finnish Domestic in New York City.
61. Oma Mäkikossa, *Yhteiskunnalle omistettu elämä: Miina Sillanpään elämän ja työn vaiheita* (Helsinki, 1947).
62. *Toveritar*, 18 Jan. 1916.
63. *Toveritar*, 9 May 1916; see also Varpu Lindström-Best and Allen Seager, "*Toveritar* and the Finnish Canadian Women's Movement 1900-1930," a paper presented in Frankfurt, West Germany, February 12-15, 1985.
64. *Toveritar*, 9 May 1916.
65. *Toveritar*, 6 June 1916.
66. Ross, "Finnish American Women," pp. 239-55.
67. *Vapaus* article, "Nais palvelijain asema Kanadassa" (The position of female domestics in Canada) was also printed in *Toveritar*, 30 May 1922.
68. *Vapaus*, 6 Dec. 1925.
69. *Vapaus*; 18 Jan. 1926; 26 Jan. 1926; 28 Dec. 1926; 18 Jan. 1927; 29 Jan. 1929.
70. *Vapaus*, 19 June 1926; 07 June 1927; 05 June 1928; 12 Feb. 1929; the organization stopped earlier on 13 Dec. 1928.
71. "Finnish Organization of Canada Correspondence with Montreal," MG 28 V46 Vol. II File 7.

72. *Vapaus*, 15 Aug. 1928.
73. *Vapaus*, 24 Sept. 1928.
74. *Vapaus*, 01 Oct. 1929.
75. *Vapaus*, 29 Jan. 1929.
76. *Vapaus*, 18 Mar. 1930.
77. *Vapaus*, 20 Dec. 1929.
78. Interview with Sanni Salmijärvi, Thunder Bay, 1984.

Sunny Ontario for British Girls, 1900-30*

Marilyn Barber

Jean Burns, who worked in a Dundee carpet factory, had no experience as a domestic when she came to eastern Ontario in 1913. Attracted by notices about Canada, "the land flowing with milk and honey," she eagerly applied when Mackie Bros., the steamship agent, placed an ad in the local Scottish newspaper seeking domestic servants for Canada. Since Jean was only eighteen, she had to obtain her mother's consent to emigrate. She recalls: "I thought, 'Well I won't be going.' But anyway, I went home and talked it over with mother and she said 'If you think you're going to better yourself by going out to Canada I'll no keep you back.' "

The agent selected a suitable position for Jean on an Ontario farm where there was other household help and where she would look after a baby. Agreeing to repay the fare which her Ontario employer advanced, Jean travelled to Canada with three other girls from Dundee bound for the same eastern Ontario town near Ottawa. Since they were not in a conducted party, they found comfort in numbers. On the train from Montreal, a cattle buyer who knew the employer of one of the girls offered his assistance, stating, "It's going to be dark. I'll look after you when you get to town." The Dundee agent had warned Jean to be very careful in talking with strange men, but this man seemed honest and respectable. He took them to a hotel for the night. In the morning men with buggies arrived and drove the girls to their country homes, each in a different direction.[1]

Jean Burns was one of over 170,000 British women who came to Canada between 1900 and 1930 declaring their intended occupation to be domestic service—90,000 in the decade before the Great War and another 80,000 in the 1920s. Like Jean, many found employment in Ontario, but the exact proportion that came to the province cannot be determined. The term "British," as used in Canada in the early twentieth century, included immigrants from England, Scotland, Northern Ireland and Wales. The majority of British domestics, like the majority of British immigrants in the period 1900-30, came from England. In the decade before the Great War, 60 per cent of the British domestics came from England, 29 per cent from Scotland, 10 per cent from Ireland and 1 per cent from Wales. The domestics thought of themselves as English, Scotch, Irish, or Welsh, and their Ontario employers often asked specifically for an English or a Scotch girl rather than just a British maid.[2] Similarly, religious affiliation divided the domestics from the British Isles, with the separation between Protestants and Catholics being the most pronounced. The proportion of Protestant and Catholic domestics remains unknown because, as the superintendent of immigration explained to one MP, it had never been considered advisable to tabulate religious denomination.[3] The significance of both ethnic and religious divisions requires much further examination. Nevertheless, domestics from various parts of the British Isles came to Canada through similar immigration arrangements and, in Canada, became identified as British in distinction from both Canadian-born and foreign domestics. Therefore, for the purposes of this paper, the British domestics will be considered as one immigrant group.

The demand for domestic servants in Ontario consistently exceeded the supply. Housework became less strenuous in the twentieth century with technological improvements and the lower birth rate, but women who wanted to meet higher standards and expanding social responsibilities continued to need domestic help.[4] Because Canadian-born women preferred employment in factories or in the increasing number of offices and shops to domestic work, Ontario housewives increasingly turned to immigration to solve the servant problem. In the early twentieth century, approximately 40 per cent of Ontario domestics were born outside Canada. Most immigrant domestics in Ontario came from the British Isles, although the proportion from continental Europe did increase during the 1920s.[5]

Most British women who came to Canada as domestics hoped to better themselves by taking advantage of higher wages and wider opportunities in the new country, although a variety of personal and family considerations also influenced each individual decision. While the combined push and pull of perceived economic differences between Britain and Canada explained much of the interest in emigration, the British connection helped unaccompanied young women to take part in the mass movement of people across the Atlantic. The settlement of Canada by British immigrants in the nineteenth century established a network of family, friends and acquaintances who might provide information on Canadian conditions and assist in overcoming the difficulties inherent in emigration. In addition to the personal ties, institutional links often enabled women to make the final decision to travel three thousand miles from home. Governments, women's societies and religious organizations on both sides of the Atlantic supplemented the work of transportation companies in promoting the migration of women from Britain to Canada. Canada needed domestic servants and gave preference to British immigrants over other nationalities. As a result, British women interested in emigration received encouragement and support from a range of agencies which joined recruitment in the British Isles with placement in Canada. Like Jean, these female emigrants could obtain passage loans and guaranteed employment even if they knew no one in Canada. Of course, in order to receive the assistance and the guarantees, they had to agree to work as domestic servants.

Immigration literature reinforced the image of Canada as a British country, not a foreign land but an integral part of the British Empire. Ontario, in particular, stressed the British heritage of the province. In *Sunny Ontario for British Girls*—a recruiting pamphlet published in the early 1920s—the Ontario government promised British women seeking household work that in Ontario, "one of the nearest-to-England Provinces of Canada," they would find not only wide opportunities but also a familiar British country where "the same old flag flies." *Sunny Ontario for British Girls* even ascribed an English appearance to the Ontario landscape with its green fields and woods, hills and dales, and many familiar wild flowers, trees and plants. More important was the message that Ontario society retained British traditions:

> The people of Ontario are largely of British descent and nowhere in the Empire to-day are British sentiment and British traditions stronger than in Ontario. Anyone going from this country will certainly feel quite at home with the people of Ontario; indeed in such cities as Toronto there are so many Old Country people that you sometimes wonder if you are in Canada at all.[6]

In spite of government assurances, the "same old flag" did not guarantee British domestics a smooth transition in familiar surroundings. Institutional networks operated more effectively in bringing British domestics to Ontario than in assisting them to accommodate to Ontario society. Employment in household work dispersed some British immigrants to rural areas or small towns and placed even those working in Toronto or Ottawa in isolated situations in private homes with little time to make social contacts. In their efforts to adjust to new conditions, the British domestics relied on family and friends when possible, on institutions to which they had access and on their own initiative and determination.

The ensuing stories of four British domestics show how individual personality and circumstance combined with general economic and social structures to influence both emigration and adaptation in Canada. They have been selected to illustrate a range of background, of family or institutional support and of placement in Canada. In addition to Jean Burns, who was a factory worker, Ann Fisher, a trained cook, also came from Scotland to eastern Ontario before the First World War. Mary Craig, a Northern Ireland factory employee with domestic science education and Kate Brown, who had both factory and domestic experience in England, came to Toronto in the 1920s, as did an increasing number of British domestics.

Before the Great War, many British women, like Jean Burns, made their emigration arrangements through the network of government immigration agents and steamship booking agents that linked Britain with Canada. The agents, who served as intermediaries between British women interested in emigration and Ontario employers, not only provided guaranteed situations but also the passage loans so essential for many female immigrants. Women earned less than men, yet daughters frequently contributed more regularly to the support of their families than did sons.[7] As a result, fewer women than men could afford the cost of emigration. Federal government agents, stationed in London and other key British centres, recruited domestics for situations obtained from a similar group of government agents in Canadian cities and provided the domestics with advanced fares from their Canadian employers. Commercial booking agents operated in a similar manner and some increased their domestic servant business by using their own money to advance fares. One of these, George Macfarlane of Glasgow—described as "an enthusiastic little fellow"—established contact with W. D. Scott in the Ottawa Immigration Branch and through him forwarded domestics to Ottawa employers.[8]

A British woman's destination and choice of employer often depended on the contacts established by a local booking agent. Of course, once a number had gone to a particular community, others wished to follow in order to be near relatives or friends. In addition, earlier immigrants sometimes wrote back to agents, requesting that someone with whom they could be friends also be sent to another situation in their neighbourhood. Although engaged for a particular situation, the immigrant who received information only from a booking agent knew little about her prospective employer or the conditions of work which awaited her. Like Jean Burns, she also might have to find her own way to her place of employment once she arrived in Ontario. Scott instructed Macfarlane to tell one Scottish domestic employed by a family in Ottawa South to "get on a Bank Street car and go to the south end of the city as far as the car goes. It will be very near to her situation, and any person in that vicinity will be able to direct her."[9] Another Ottawa employer, who did not receive notice of her domestic's arrival, observed that "the girl had good courage to find the place all by herself."[10]

Even British domestics able to pay their own way to Canada often turned to agencies to obtain a situation for them before departure. Ann Fisher, the daughter of a Scottish coal miner, had exceptionally good domestic training when she came to the same Ontario community as Jean Burns in 1914 at age twenty-five. Growing up in a family of nine, she had to help so she chose cooking. In her words, "You have to have something at your finger ends." Cooking appealed to her because the cook was the head servant and received the highest wages. After some local experience, she attended an Edinburgh cooking school and worked for wealthy families, becoming assistant cook on a large estate. She too heard stories about higher wages and better opportunities in Canada, being told "when you go to Canada you'll be picking up money in your apron." When wages dropped in Scotland at the beginning of the war, Ann, with the encouragement of her father, decided the time had come to follow others who were leaving for Canada. Although Canada too experienced a recession in 1914, which curtailed general immigration activities, the demand for trained domestics did not diminish. With her experience, Ann was offered a choice of situations by the Glasgow agency to which she applied. Because she had worked in one of the higher-paid domestic positions, she could pay for her own passage. Ann's possessions indicated her relative prosperity. She lugged her sewing machine to Canada but sold her beaver hat and, to her later regret, her bicycle. Like Jean, Ann relied on friends and acquaintances for companionship and assistance during the journey. She met five girls on the boat with whom she later kept in contact for some time. Arriving in Montreal at night, Ann stayed with a friend from Aberdeen whose address she had; at her final destination she was met by her new employer, the manager of the Bank of Montreal.[11]

By travelling to Canada with a conducted party, a British woman could avoid many of the problems with which the individual immigrant had to cope without formal assistance: the mysteries of the new currency, the different operation of the transportation and baggage system and arrival in a strange community, possibly late at night, without much money. Beginning in the late nineteenth century, several British religious and women's societies as well as individuals sponsored conducted parties to Canada for a variety of philanthropic, imperial and business motives. Voluntary societies of the Church of England, such as the Girls' Friendly Society, which had direct links with Canada, helped to initiate the system. In the 1880s, Mrs. Ellen Joyce, widow of an Anglican cleryman at Winchester, expanded from her emigration work with the Girls' Friendly Society to help form the British Women's Emigration Association (BWEA). With Scottish and Irish branches and workers in almost every provincial town, the BWEA built on its reputation for careful selection and good care to become the major British association sponsoring female immigration to Canada.[12] Because the BWEA insisted that its protected parties must go only to centres with hostels, the Toronto Local Council of Women, led by its president, Mary Agnes FitzGibbon, established the Womens Welcome Hostel in 1905. Supported by the Toronto élite and by provincial and federal grants, the Toronto Hostel served as the chief Ontario receiving centre for British domestics.[13]

In spite of its prominence, the British Women's Emigration Association by no means held a monopoly on conducted party travel for female immigrants. The Salvation Army, which sought and received government support for its extensive immigration activities, placed its Ontario parties of domestics through the Salvation Army Toronto Hostel on Jarvis Street. In addition, a few enterprising women in Canada established Domestic Guild businesses and worked in conjunction with a steamship line and British agents to bring over groups of domestics whom they placed through the guild homes and offices. Probably the best known of these women, Mrs. E. K. Frances, the daughter of a Montreal lawyer, established the Women's Domestic Guild of Canada with headquarters in Montreal and placed many domestics in Ontario.[14]

In Toronto Mrs. Sarah McArthur, a former Belfast steamship agent, established the Canadian Domestic Guild for Irish domestics in 1912.[15] During their period of operation before the war, the guilds benefited from a government bonus paid on British domestics as well as from fees collected from both immigrants and employers.

In the 1920s imperial ties continued to provide connections which facilitated the movement of British domestics to Canada, but more direct government control replaced the system of subsidizing private agencies and voluntary societies. The new women's division of the Department of Immigration sent staff officers to Britain authorized to give final approval in the selection of British domestics. In Canada it established a chain of Women's Hostels to receive the domestics who travelled in conducted parties and were placed in situations by the new government employment service. The Canadian Women's Hostel in Toronto continued the work of the Womens Welcome Hostel, reinforcing the dominance of Toronto as a centre for British domestics. In smaller Ontario cities such as Ottawa and London, the YWCA received those British domestics who could be persuaded that life existed outside Toronto. In addition, governments provided funding to those domestics who needed passage assistance. After the British government passed the Empire Settlement Act to promote migration within the empire, both the Ontario and the federal governments cooperated with the British government in giving loans and, after 1926, very low fares to qualified domestics. Thus, in the 1920s, women in all parts of the United Kingdom who sought to emigrate encountered more centralization and standardization in direction and procedures.

Among the first party of Empire Settlement Act women to arrive in 1923 was Mary Craig, age twenty-four, of County Armagh, Northern Ireland. She recalls with pride that they were met at Quebec by Miss Burnham, head of the women's branch of the Immigration Department, who told them, "You're very precious. You're the first to come under the Empire Settlement Act." The act enabled Mary to fulfill her dream of immigrating to Canada. Mary's father, a mill worker, died when she was quite young, so from age thirteen Mary had worked in the linen mill to assist her mother. She received her domestic training at home from her mother, who was an immaculate housekeeper, and at night school where she studied home economics.

Even as a young girl, Mary wanted to go to Canada because her grandfather constantly talked about the country where he had worked several summers as a farm labourer. On her grandparents' farm, Mary observed the gold letters on the green farm machinery which read "Massey Harris, Toronto, Ontario, Canada." She read everything she could find about Canada, learning, among other facts, that 94 per cent of people in Canada had bank accounts. Her work at the linen factory had been cut back to three days a week, so she also had an economic incentive to emigrate. When large signs appeared on billboards advertising the Empire Settlement Act, "Come to Canada: A Welcome Awaits You," Mary already had prepared her belongings. After an interview at the Canadian government office in Belfast, she travelled in a group to the Toronto Hostel. Unlike the prewar emigrants who had an employer selected for them in Britain, Mary obtained her situation after arrival in Ontario. Thus she was able to make a better informed choice. Through Miss Duff at the Ontario employment bureau, she selected a position in a Toronto Rosedale home.[16]

Even British women with family connections in Ontario made partial use of the provisions of the Empire Settlement Act to arrange for emigration. In 1927 Kate Brown, age twenty-two, came from Manchester to Toronto as a domestic, although her primary reason for emigration was to join her family. Kate's father, who had been in the army in India, died when she was two, and during the war her mother moved to Canada, so Kate lived with an older brother in England. When laid off by the factory where she worked, she obtained a position in a private home. When a possible marriage did not develop, Kate agreed to join her mother and another brother and sister in Canada. At the Canadian shipping office where she applied, she was told that she could save her mother the cost of the fare if she worked as a domestic for one year. Kate agreed to repay the fare loaned to her and travelled to Toronto with a large group of other women from England and Ireland. Because she had family in Toronto, she did not go to the Women's Hostel nor did she receive employment through the government. Her brother, who worked at Eaton's, met her in Toronto and introduced her to her new employer, a manager of Eaton's drapery department.[17]

British women who chose to immigrate to Canada as domestics expected to better themselves in the new country, whether they decided to settle permanently or only to work for a few years to earn money before returning to Britain. Often the conditions which they found made realization of their aim much more difficult than anticipated. Jean Burns had been placed in what seemed to be a light position where supposedly there was other hired help in the home. But on arrival at the Ontario farm, Jean discovered that the other help was a young girl from the Quarrier Home at Brockville, so her work actually involved much more than caring for the baby. In her words, "I had no idea I had to get up at 5 A.M. and, besides looking after the baby, was expected to work, work from morning till night." Jean had expected to be taken into the family when she agreed to work on an Ontario farm, but, as she said, she soon had her eyes opened. She had no time off and never left the farm except to go to the little church across the road on Sunday. She could not please her employer and after paying back her passage fare in three months, she determined to leave because, in her words, "I'm not going to be in jail for the rest of my life." She had become friends with a neighbour who helped to manage the farm, so she told him her intention to give notice. Appearing the next morning with his horse and buggy, he took her for a drive, but the ride did not change her mind.

Jean turned to friends from Scotland for aid in solving her employment problem. She contacted one of the Scottish girls with whom she had come to Canada who arranged for her transportation to town where she could get another job. At a restaurant in town, much to her surprise, Jean met three carpet weavers from her old Dundee factory who told her she could get employment at the local carpet factory. She was hired immediately at four dollars a week and found a boardinghouse also at four dollars a week. Jean's inability to live on her standard factory wage showed the advantage of domestic work for those who could not board at home. As the only Scottish girl in the factory, Jean attracted attention. Her boss, who wondered how she would manage, raised her pay two dollars a week by giving her the title of forewoman and also informed her of a cheaper room. When the factory closed during the war, Jean returned to domestic work. As she was in a better position to choose, she obtained a situation in town where she was well treated. In her free time, she sang in the Presbyterian church choir, gave readings and went out with the farmer who had earlier given her the buggy ride. After three years in Canada, Jean married him and settled on the farm where she raised a family of four.[18]

Canada widely advertised its British character and British connections, yet even experienced British domestics found that British skills did not entirely prepare them for Canadian homes. Indeed the same immigration literature which promoted Canada as a British country stressed that British women must learn "Canadian ways." A 1921 pamphlet advised the domestic worker:

> Even to the one who has had experience in domestic work in this country or who may have taken a course in household service, there will be much in a Canadian house that will

> be strange, and she must be ready to give up many of her old ideas and methods and adopt those of her new environment.... When she goes to her first position, the terms of her agreement with her employer will be based upon her unfamiliarity with Canadian household methods and on the understanding that she will have to be taught.[19]

Considerable investigation still needs to be done in the realm of material history to explain how Canadian ways differed from British ways, although Hilary Russell has published a helpful article in the *Material History Bulletin*, focusing primarily on differences in cooking.[20] Communication among immigration workers and complaints from employers emphasized food preparation as the greatest problem area. The Canadian cook stove, generally gas or electric in urban homes, bore little resemblance to its British counterpart. Kate Brown from England failed in her efforts to bake good cakes in the gas stove, but had much better success with the wood-burning stove at her employer's summer cottage. Many items of diet also differed, and in baking the British domestic had to use unfamiliar types of flour, yeast and measuring tools. The Toronto Hostel began offering classes in domestic science because "the Overseas girls all claim that Canadian cooking is so different to that in the Old Country."[21] Differences in climate and technology required adaptation in other aspects of housework as well. In Ontario the British domestic had to remember to keep food cool in summer, to shut screens to keep out flies and to stoke the furnace regularly even though it was out of sight in the basement.

While warning British women of the need for adaptation, immigration literature stressed the advantages of Canadian ways. The pamphlets consistently conveyed the message that housework was easier in Canada, especially in city homes. The design of Canadian houses saved steps and reduced cleaning. Houses generally had only two storeys, or three storeys at the most, with the kitchen conveniently located on the ground floor adjacent to the dining-room rather than in the basement. There were no stone sculleries, area ways or stone doorsteps to be scrubbed, and front doors were not adorned with brass plate which had to be polished every morning. Central heating eliminated much of the labour of tending numerous fireplaces and reduced dirt. The domestic also benefited from the Canadian concern with efficiency which even simplified meals and increased the use of labour-saving equipment including the telephone and electrical appliances. *Sunny Ontario for British Girls* featured illustrations of the electric iron and vacuum cleaner, and Jessie Duff, head of the women's division of the Ontario Employment Bureau, on a recruiting mission in Britain further explained the advantages of working in Ontario homes: "The basement cellar, that *bête noir* of English households, is almost unknown here; 'carrying coals' up long flights of stairs and through endless halls has become obsolete since the introduction of furnaces and, then, that British institution, early morning tea, has very few advocates in Canada."[22]

Some British domestics agreed that Canadian technology and custom made housework easier. Satisfied domestics who responded to the invitation to send their views for possible publication in *Sunny Ontario for British Girls* generally expressed pleasure with lighter work in Canada.[23] As two in Toronto wrote: "We have had several years experience of domestic work in England, so we feel able to give our opinion of work over here. The work is much lighter, the hours shorter, and we get much more freedom.... We came from country life in England to find city life in Toronto with all its modern conveniences most interesting."[24] Similarly, Mary Craig from Northern Ireland, who had always cleaned carpets by spreading tea leaves and using a whisk broom, was delighted to find vacuum cleaners in Toronto. In her words, "I thought it was great when I came to Canada and there was vacuums. I thought I'd died and gone to heaven."[25]

In spite of the vaunted superiority of Canadian ways, not all British women who became domestics in Ontario felt that they had improved their conditions of work. Complaints about hard work and long hours offset the praise for easier work and shorter hours. Like Jean Burns, many found that they had little or no free time. Rural homes did not share equally in the technological improvements, and as recent American studies of household technology have shown, urban housewives often used new technology to improve standards rather than to reduce work.[26] In addition, with the purchase of labour-saving appliances, employers sometimes decreased the number of servants hired or expected the maid to undertake work, such as the laundry, which previously had been done outside the home. Hence, British domestics joined Canadian-born domestics in objecting to the continued long hours and lack of free time which characterized household work. Some who previously had enjoyed more regulated hours in factories, shops, or hotels found the lack of spare time particularly irksome. One Toronto domestic whose letter was not published in *Sunny Ontario for British Girls* wrote: "There are no advantages here for girls. I myself have always been in Hotels as a waitress but I can't find a suitable place here as that, so had to take to private service. Here you are up at 7 in the morning and work until 8 at night—hardly time to wash and change in the afternoon."[27]

Even domestics who had been in service in Britain complained that they had not improved their position. One English maid discovered that she had more work in Canada because she was the only servant for a family of five, with all the washing, whereas in England she had been employed in a two-servant household for a family of two, with no washing required. She wrote to the Toronto *Star* in 1914: "The agents tell the women over in the old country... that there is much more liberty here. I have not seen it yet. Those two or three hours in the evening are better done without. In the old country a maid gets a whole day off every month, that is some good, besides her afternoon and evening a week and Sundays."[28] Kate Brown from England had experience in domestic work and immigrated to such urban employment in Canada in the 1920s, but she considered the work harder than in England. She remarked that in England she never worked after supper and she cleaned one room a day, not all through the house as was often expected in Canada. Her first Toronto employer gave many dinner parties which kept her busy, but did pay her five dollars extra to take charge of the furnace.[29]

A British immigrant's experience of Ontario household employment cannot be judged solely by her first situation. British domestics, like Canadian-born domestics, moved to better themselves and gain higher wages, prompting employers to complain that domestics left almost as soon as they obtained some training. Domestics never found the illusory pot of gold in Ontario; whether they managed to benefit in a modest way from crossing the Atlantic is more difficult to determine. Wages offered by Ontario employers varied considerably, since even the low standards set by the minimum wage legislation of the 1920s did not include workers in private homes. The average monthly wage seemed higher than in Britain but so did the cost of living. Even with room and board provided, domestics still had expenses. One English maid complained: "Clothes are much more expensive here as everyone knows, and everyone dresses to their last cent. My uniform never cost me anything at home, as that all came to me in birthday and Christmas presents."[30] In Ontario a domestic had to pay her medical expenses whereas in Britain after 1912 they were covered by insurance.[31] An irate Toronto domestic found the service as well as the cost annoying:

> If you are ill, as I have been for 10 days, and call in a doctor he looks your tongue, does not even sound you. You pay for your own drugs then he has a cheek to send in a bill for $6.00. What for—for looking at your tongue. In England

> you have the insurance, doctor free, also drugs and you get sickness benefit, but there is nothing like that here."[32]

In addition, the cost of passage to Canada to be repaid more than offset any increase in wages for a number of months.

Whether or not a British woman improved her standard of living as a domestic in Ontario, the work did possess certain economic advantages over other types of semi-skilled work available to the female immigrant. As Jean Burns discovered, for young women unable to live at home, domestic employment generally provided higher net earnings than factory work. Domestic employment also meant steady work without seasonal lay-offs. Although some urban employers did not retain their servants during summer holidays and some rural employers did not keep help during the slack winter period, the scarcity of servants enabled the laid-off domestics to obtain another situation immediately.

In contrast to the economic advantage of having room and board provided, domestic employment often made successful social adaptation difficult. As the majority of domestics worked alone or with one other person, being in service isolated the immigrant. The British domestic met few people through her work, and she had little free time to see or make friends elsewhere. Employment in an Ontario home thus introduced the British immigrant to Canadian ways but not to Canadian society. The low social status accorded domestic service reinforced the physical isolation. In most cases, often even on farms, the domestic was not treated as a member of the family. The social inferiority implied by her subordinate position in a personal service relationship within the household hampered her acceptance by the community. As one domestic said, "If we go into a private place everyone looks down upon us, the world as well as our employer."[33] Other young people often avoided friendship with domestics because they feared such association would be regarded as demeaning. A Scottish domestic working in a country district before the war described her experience in a letter to the *Globe*:

> I am Scotch, and was in a shop in the old country.... I was only making as much as fed and clothed me, so decided to try Canada... My mistress is exceedingly good and kind to me, and at first introduced me to some of the shopgirls, but I was not long in seeing how much I was looked down on. They were always quite polite and nice to me, but they were always very careful not to invite me to their homes when anyone else was expected. It is amusing to think how one is shunned by one's own class. Some of those girls are not

> brought up as well as myself. But I am a domestic servant, and they are young ladies in a shop.[34]

In smaller communities, there were few organizations to provide familiar links with the old country and assist British domestics in adapting to the new society. The only institution with which many domestics had any contact was the church. Domestics always had time off on Sunday to attend church. For some the church offered both social and religious support, but for others Sunday church attendance did not alleviate loneliness. When possible, British domestics in smaller centres relied on nearby friends or relatives from the old country for assistance in overcoming problems, but these rural domestics were also less insulated from Canadian society than those in cities with a larger British immigrant community.

Ann Fisher, the experienced cook from Scotland, encountered fewer problems than Jean Burns, partly because her background enabled her to start work in a better situation. After a year in the bank manager's employ, she wanted to go to Ottawa—following the pattern of moving to obtain more money and improved conditions. In Ottawa she worked as a cook for wealthy families who employed a large staff, including J. R. Booth, the lumber baron. She took pride in her position as head servant, acquiring status from the social standing of her employers. As she explained, it was a genteel life because she worked only for genteel families. Even though the prediction that she would pick up money in her apron did not come true, she earned a good wage and put that money in the bank. She never found life lonely because she had an interest in everything. In the first town she chummed with two Scottish girls who worked across the street, and she made other friends through the Baptist church. In Ottawa she went to the homes of friends whom she met though McPhail Baptist Church. In the city she also was able to attend night school, studying millinery and cooking. Like Jean, she retained ties made through her first situation and returned to visit Baptist friends in the area. Aften ten years in Canada, she married a farmer whom she met through these friends. On the farm she had to learn many new skills as she raised her four children.[35]

Far more institutions existed to give support to British domestics in Toronto—the main centre for British immigrants. Even the churches in Toronto were better organized to serve their needs. In the 1920s the Church of England and the Presbyterian church both employed women church workers who visited domestics. The Girls' Friendly Society (GFS) operated a lodge on Charles

Street which was a centre for GFS activity. The YWCA in Toronto, as part of an international organization, was well known among British immigrants. For example, the Toronto *Star* published the story of a lonely English domestic in Cape Breton who had the address of the Toronto Y from England. She established a correspondence with British domestics at the Toronto Y and when she had enough money joined her new friends in Toronto.[36] Most important was the Toronto institution specifically designed for British domestics, the Women's Hostel.

The Women's Hostel, well advertised in Ontario and federal immigration literature, helped to draw British domestics to Toronto. The hostel served as a home for British domestics, and associations formed at the hostel helped to take the place of absent family for the women. Before the establishment of the government employment bureau, hostel supervisors found employers for the immigrants. Throughout the period, domestics returned to the hostel for accommodation between situations and sought assistance from the hostel at times of illness or other crises. British domestics celebrated special festivities, like Christmas, at the hostel, and a number chose to be married there. The hostel also provided emotional support on a more regular basis for British domestics who used it as a social centre on their days off. As Mary Craig from Northern Ireland recollected: "It was home. The hostel was home and you always met your friends there. It was great."[37] The hostel organized social evenings, summer picnics and Sunday afternoon teas for the domestics, since "Sunday seems to be the day when they miss the Homeland more than any other time."[38] Before the war, the Agnes FitzGibbon Chapter of the Imperial Order of the Daughters of the Empire also met at the hostel on Wednesday evenings and sewed for the children of the Tuberculosis Preventorium Hospital.[39]

The Women's Hostel helped to reinforce and sustain the British domestics' sense of ethnic identity. With the exception of the occasional immigrant from western Europe, only domestics from the United Kingdom came to the hostel. In the 1920s the group was narrowed to Protestant domestics from the British Isles as the government sent Catholic immigrants to the Catholic Women's Hostel in Toronto. The hostel supervisors consciously fostered the British atmosphere. As one member of the hostel committee explained in 1921, "Our aim is to make the girls feel that this is merely another room of the British Empire."[40] The Women's Hostel eased the period of adjustment to the new country; those domestics who successfully adapted began to depend less on its services as they established other contacts. Jessie Duff, as hostel superintendent in the latter 1920s, noted the need to loosen the bonds with the hostel: "There is always the girl, and their number is fairly large, to whom the Hostel seems to be the only Haven. They have joined no other group except their own group at Church on Sunday, and have made no other friends. As a rule these are among our problem cases."[41]

One of the Toronto domestics who enjoyed the hostel was Mary Craig. She changed employers in Toronto for a higher wage, as she wanted to send money to her mother in Ireland, but she continued to meet her friends at the hostel. Miss Anderson, the hostel superintendent, told her she was working too hard and offered her a job at the hostel. Mary liked the activity at the hostel but objected to some of the ethnic rivalries. She noted that some Scottish girls seemed to think nothing was right unless it was Scottish, and some English girls tried to put down the Irish.

While the hostel aided Mary's adaptation to Canada, it did not perform such a central role for all British domestics in Toronto. As Kate Brown was met an arrival by her brother in Toronto, she never saw the hostel. Since Kate had her own family in Ontario she did not need its support. Her brother arranged her first situation and during the depression advised her to remain in domestic work because it provided a sure income.

Both Mary Craig and Kate Brown changed jobs in Toronto in order to better themselves. The range of employment opportunity, as well as the educational and social activities available, helped to make the city attractive. After Miss Anderson died, Mary obtained a job baking at a Toronto restaurant, and she lived in a rooming-house. Like many domestics who left private homes for work in restaurants, hotels or other institutions, she liked the greater freedom. Through the cashier at the restaurant, she met her husband who worked at a paper mill. With marriage, she gave up her job, but after raising a family returned to daily work when her husband fell ill.[42] Kate Brown worked for four Toronto employers, including Sir Joseph Flavelle, before the Second World War. She joined a club at the YWCA and met other girls at church. Studying kept her from being lonely, so she enrolled at Danforth Technical night school in cooking, first aid and nursing courses. Kate did not marry, but after working in a war factory she became a licensed practical nurse as she had always enjoyed nursing.[43]

British women joined the mass migration movement of the early twentieth century and came to Canada as domestics for economic and personal reasons. Jean Burns, Ann Fisher and Mary Craig sought higher wages and better opportunities while family ties drew Kate Brown to Ontario. The network of institutions and agencies which linked Britain and Canada made possible the emigration of women like Jean Burns and Mary Craig who could not afford to pay the full passage fare and assisted others like Ann Fisher who obtained a situation before leaving Scotland and Kate Brown who did not have to rely upon her mother for help. While the constant demand for domestics in Ontario enabled British women without family connections to emigrate, the structure of domestic service hampered social adaptation. Working long hours in isolated situations in private homes, British domestics had little opportunity to make friends or to participate in organized activities. Nevertheless, a major attraction of Toronto was the existence in the city of institutions such as the Women's Hostel and the YWCA where British domestics could meet and seek aid if necessary. Mary Craig enjoyed the use of the hostel while Jean Burns, Ann Fisher and Kate Brown turned to friends or family for advice and assistance. In making the transition to permanent settlement in Canada, all relied on their own initiative and determination to succeed.

Notes

* I wish to thank the Social Sciences and Humanities Research Council of Canada for financial assistance provided through the research grants programme.

1. Interview, Ontario, 2 July 1981. The names of the women interviewed have been changed to protect their anonymity.
2. Calculated from Canada, *Sessional Papers, Annual Report of the Department of the Interior*, 1904-14, and Report by Miss MacFarlane to Mr. Jolliff on the establishment and work of the women's division, 3 August 1944, PAC, RG 76, File 22787. "Scotch" not "Scottish" was the term commonly used in the early twentieth century to designate those born in Scotland.
3. Scott to Herbert Ames, 17 March 1915, PAC, RG 76, Files 22787-6.
4. See Ruth Schwartz Cowan, *More Work for Mother* (New York, 1983) and Susan Strasser, *Never Done* (New York, 1982) for an analysis of the impact of technology on the American home.
5. Calculated from *Census of Canada*, 1911, 1921, 1931. By 1931 one-quarter of immigrant domestics in Ontario were from continental Europe.
6. *Sunny Ontario for British Girls* (Ontario Government, n.d.), p. 4.
7. See Louise Tilly and Joan Scott, *Women, Work, & Family*, for an analysis of the position of women in the family economy in England.

8. Booking Agent—Glasgow, Murphy to Burnham, 29 May 1923, PAC, RG 76, 652806.
9. Ibid., Scott to Macfarlane, 15 October 1909, File 652806-2.
10. Ibid., Mrs. Kenny to Macfarlane, 11 May 1910.
11. Interview, Ontario, 2 July 1979.
12. James Hammerton, *Emigrant Gentlewomen* (London, 1979), Chap. 8.
13. See Marilyn Barber, "The Women Ontario Welcomed: Immigrant Domestics for Ontario Homes, 1870-1930," *Ontario History*, LXXII, 3 September 1980, pp. 155-56.
14. Women's Domestic Guild, PAC, RG 76, File 266957.
15. Ibid., Mrs. Sarah McArthur, Booking Agent, File 806038.
16. Interview, Victoria, 25 October 1979 and 30 April 1984.
17. Interview, Winnipeg, 16 June 1984.
18. Interview, Ontario, 2 July 1981.
19. Mabel Durham, *Canada's Call to Women*, CNR Pamphlet, 1921, p. 31.
20. Hilary Russell, "'Canadian Ways': An Introduction to Comparative Studies of Housework, Stoves and Diet in Great Britain and Canada," *Material History Bulletin* (Spring 1984), pp. 1-12.
21. Canadian Women's Hostel, Report February 1922, PAC, RG 76, File 356358-4.
22. *Globe*, Toronto, 26 July 1923, p. 14.
23. H. Macdonell, Director of Colonization, Dept. of Agriculture, Colonization and Immigration Branch, to Burnham, Toronto, 8 May 1922—seven out of the ten letters published mentioned easier work—PAC, RG 76, File 990380-1.
24. *Sunny Ontario for British Girls*, n.d., pp. 13-14.
25. Interview, Victoria, 25 October 1979.
26. See Ruth Schwartz Cowan, *More Work For Mother*, and Susan Strasser, *Never Done*.
27. R. O'Hara, 8 Beaumont Road, Rosedale, to H. Macdonell, Director, of Colonization, 4 April 1922, PAC, RG 76, File 990380-1.
28. *Toronto Daily Star*, 29 July 1914, p. 6.
29. Interview, Winnipeg, 16 June 1984.
30. *Toronto Daily Star*, 29 July 1914, p. 6.
31. Pamela Horn, *The Rise and Fall of the Victorian Servant* (Dublin and New York, 1975), pp. 161-63.
32. R. O'Hara to H. Macdonell, Rosedale, 4 April 1922, PAC, RG 76, File 990380-1.
33. Ibid., Canadian Women's Hostel, Toronto, Report, 2 April 1921, File 356358-3.
34. *Globe*, Toronto, 24 June 1908, p. 6.
35. Interview, Ontario, 2 July 1979.
36. *Toronto Daily Star*, 10 Sept. 1912, p. 10.
37. Interview, Victoria, 25 October 1979.
38. Annual Report of Canadian Women's Hostel, Toronto, 31 October 1923, PAC, RG 76, File 356358-5.
39. Ibid, Annual Report of Womens Welcome Hostel, Toronto, 1912, File 356358-2.

40. Ibid., *Mail and Empire*, Toronto, 29 December 1921, File 356358-3.
41. Ibid., Canadian Women's Hostel, Toronto, Report May-June 1927, File 356358-7.
42. Interview, Victoria, 25 October 1979 and 30 April 1984.
43. Interview, Winnipeg, 16 June 1984.

Abraham's Daughters: Women, Charity and Power in the Canadian Jewish Community

Paula J. Draper and
Janice B. Karlinsky

> For I have singled [Abraham] out, that he may instruct his children and his posterity to keep the way of the Lord by doing what is just and right.
>
> (Gen. 18:19)

However important the role of women and their associations has been in Jewish life, being female has translated into powerlessness in the political structure. Jewish women—energetic, skilled and committed as many have been and continue to be—operated on the periphery of the community. Without women, synagogues, schools, hospitals, homes for the aged, fund-raising organizations and representative federations would have been hard pressed to function effectively. Through fund-raising, women provide the bulk of the finances that enable the community to undertake social welfare programs. Yet within these community associations women have generally been barred from the decision-making process.[1]

While an examination of the status of women in Judaism is outside the confines of this study,[2] the relationship between religion and the position of Jewish women within their community structure should be recognized. Traditionally the role played by Jewish women has not differed significantly from the general role of women in Western society. Domesticity controlled women, kept them subservient and restricted their opportunities. Exclusion from education solidified their secondary status. Yet within the European Jewish family structure, women were the undisputed rulers of the household. Although their absence from synagogue-centred ritual activity and their secondary legal status kept them outside the sphere of real power in the community, many Jewish women were the economic as well as spiritual mainstays of their families. Women were delegated responsibility for the moral development of their children and often their economic support while their spouses withdrew to study and pray. But the weight given to the cultural significance of the role of women in the family was deceptive. Religious celebrations were presided over by fathers; male children studied long hours under exclusively male tutelage. The Jewish woman in eastern and central Europe often worked outside the home, her materialistic role always being secondary to but supportive of the male pursuit of spirituality.

In a world which excluded Jews from property ownership, participation in certain trades, political activity and even citizenship, the sphere of Jewish women was necessarily limited. Only with the emancipation of Jews in the eighteenth and nineteenth centuries did Jewish women in western Europe taste liberation. Daughters of the well-to-do benefited from a combination of the Enlightenment and traditional Jewish values which prized education.[3] Indeed Jewish women often surpassed their Gentile sisters in a society which valued intellectual astuteness as a social grace. Many Jewish women quickly overtook their husbands in the race for acculturation, which often led to the conclusion that only conversion to Chritianity would enable them to obtain complete acceptance. For however well-educated and freed from household duties upper-class Jews became, strong social and religious barriers remained.

Meanwhile, the growth of the Reform movement in Germany freed Jewish women from many traditional religious restraints. The movement's ideology opposed many of the barriers which limited female participation in religious ceremonies, and efforts to eliminate them began to be implemented.[4] Yet political power in the community eluded women. They were still regarded as enablers who worked for the benefit of husbands and sons; their role remained family centred. Satisfying their own personal psychological need was regarded as selfish, often by men and women alike. It was with this modernized yet still ethnocentric baggage that the first permanent Jewish women settlers arrived in Canada.

As an identifiable ethnic group, Jewish immigrants had a head start in the formation of self-perpetuating community institutions. Unlike most other ethnic groups, they were coming from countries wherein they had always experienced minority status. They arrived with a pre-established minority mentality and frameworks for cultural and religious institutions. The British and German Jews who came to Canadian cities like Toronto in the nineteenth century found a New World in which conversion was not the only means to integration.[5]

Mostly middle class themselves, Jewish women adopted the new perception of religion as a feminine field. Absorbing male-imposed stereotypes, women accepted the notion that their nurturing qualities made them uniquely qualified to relieve suffering. Jewish women had a new vocation, a logical extension of their family role—charity. One of the cardinal precepts of Judaism, the concept of *tzedekah*, or charity, obliged every Jew to give to the less fortunate. Indeed the Hebrew translates as either "righteousness" or "justice," and it has been central to Jewish life from biblical times. Social assistance was institutionalized in European Jewish communities through charity boxes, soup kitchens, the giving of clothing and burial societies. Boxes were circulated in homes, in the synagogue, in the cemetery—wherever Jews assembled. Taxes for relief of the poor were often levied on communities in order to care for orphans, the sick, handicapped and aged, to school the poor and provide low-interest or interest-free loans. This central theme of Jewish life, previously dominated by men, now tied Jewish women into the widening female sphere. The relative wealth and high degree of acculturation of Jews from western Europe allowed for rapid adjustment to New-World feminine ambitions, just as it reinforced their fear of any threat to their integration into Canadian life.

Women of the Jewish establishment were fuelled by a desire to Canadianize the new immigrants from eastern Europe. Yet they failed in their attempts to make these new Canadian Jews over in their own image. Indeed, by 1920 the character of Canadian Jewry had been completely transformed. Anti-Semitism intensified and the position of Jews in Canada suffered irreparable damage. Jews strove to succeed in Canada but found with each advance that growing anti-Semitic sentiment curtailed their prospects and hindered their assimilation.

The community turned inward, and women became essential participants in blossoming communal organizations. Jewish women enthusiastically took over the philanthropic demands of Jewish life. They created Ladies Hebrew Benevolent Societies. Charity as an extension of home duties became a way of life for a whole generation. But since the devotion of Jewish women to social welfare work could not overcome the traditional male dominance of benevolent and communal associations, they soon moved to create their own. In so doing, the militant social reformers of the turn of the century became "professional volunteers."

The unique nature of each major women's organization resulted from its ability to fulfill the particular social needs, language, religious and political orientation of its members. The first such Canadian women's organization, the National Council of Jewish Women (NCJW), was formed in 1897 in Toronto, just four years after its establishment in the United States.[6] At the American organizing conference, the religious justification for this new sphere of women's work was clarified. "All Israel suffers in the degradation of its poor," stated an organizer. "Woman is the Messiah come to deliver them from their second bondage of ignorance and misery. She is the educator, the reformer, and the reward of her labor will be the evolution of a nobler race of worthy citizens and respected members of society."

The National Council of Jewish Women was devoted to religious, philanthropic and educational activities considered to be female pursuits. NCJW volunteers served the larger community through the provision of schooling, scholarships, orphanages, recreation and summer camps for children and working girls, childrens' libraries, scientific research and clubs for the aged. During the Second World War services were provided for both Jewish and non-Jewish servicemen, mobile blood donor clinics were established, and bundles sent to Britain. Postwar activities saw this volunteer sector extend its programs from social welfare and immigrant and refugee absorption to contemporary Jewish affairs, social legislation and even international affairs. Throughout its history, however, the NCJW has remained an association of women, not particularly feminist-oriented, with as its basis the principle of charity as women's work.

For first-generation western European Jewish immigrant women, social reform was a revolutionary and fulfilling role. For their daughters in the 1920s—the professional volunteers—self-esteem and a sense of career were equally rewarding. But the 1930s saw a narrowing of their activities as paid professionals, most of them male, took over the social action aspects of their work and left them with the grass-roots tasks of organizing and fund-raising. Middle-class Jewish women, who neither needed nor sought employment, discovered themselves relegated to organizations which began to operate as female social clubs. Postwar options with the Jewish communal structure were increasingly limited, while higher education for women and the decline of anti-Semitism opened new doors in secular Canadian society.

While Jewish immigrants from western Europe and their daughters followed a pattern of community work best exemplified by the activities of the National Council of Jewish Women, their eastern European sisters organized their own groups. Indeed the creation of social service work as a field for women resulted from an urgent societal need.

The Toronto chapter of the Zionist Hadassah organization was established in 1917 by women who had settled in Canada in the 1880s and 1890s. These women and their daughters had risen into the ranks of the middle class yet saw themselves as worlds apart from the acculturated, North-American educated and leisured National Council women. Hadassah was founded by the daughter of a Baltimore rabbi, Henrietta Szold. After visiting Palestine in 1909 she became a determined advocate of the provision of modern health care for the peoples of Palestine. Her intelligence and indomitable spirit inspired thousands of Jewish women to focus on the concerns of building a Jewish state as an outlet for their talents. Within the Zionist Movement, however, the women of Hadassah were often referred to as "diaper Zionists." They had to struggle to maintain a separate voice, a voice which they expressed through control and allocation of the funds they raised.

While the NCJW concentrated its work for the benefit of Canadian Jewry, Hadassah focused on the creation of a Jewish homeland in Palestine. Hadassah had no particular ideological bent; its concerns were directed at the provision of social services, particularly health care, to Jews in the Holy Land. Hadassah's stated principle was that: "Women understand the art of healing, and nation building is only an abstraction."[7] Motivated solely by benevolence, Hadassah members gave no formal recognition to the important political and social role of Jewish women in the rebuilding of the Jewish homeland.

This was not the case for a third segment of Canadian Jewish women. Immigrant working-class women—Yiddish-speaking, politicized and religiously unaffiliated—joined the Pioneer Women's Organization (PWO),[8] a left-wing Zionist group affiliated with the Labour Zionist (Poale Zion) movement.[9] These women came from backgrounds that rendered them socially and philosophically unsuited for membership in organizations composed of the wives of their husbands' bosses. In eastern Europe their mothers laboured with their fathers in small family businesses. Modern liberal thought spurred many youths to trade traditional Judaism for equally fervent beliefs in socialism and political Zionism. They turned their backs on Judaism but not on Jewishness. Many secular Jews observed Jewish holidays and kept kosher as a means of maintaining their commitment to Jewish culture and peoplehood. Education acted as a catalyst. One Pioneer Woman explained: "Books lit my mind on fire. Herzl and Marx made me think about my life and the life of the Jews. They made me so mad that we had waited so long and suffered so much. I got many ideas and became free of religion."[10]

Many future Pioneer Women were involved with formal Zionist and socialist organizations in Europe. Socialism showed them the dignity of labour; Zionism pointed to labour as the means for cultural, social and economic redemption of the Jews as a nation. They became infused with new expectations of participating in the task of nation-building. They carried these expectations to Canada.

Arrival in Canada often meant the end of formal schooling for immigrant women. Many worked in factories or cared for their children, finding little time and energy to attend English classes. Yiddish remained their primary language and for this reason many shied away from joining English-speaking groups, like Hadassah. Likewise, they would not consider joining secular organizations for they maintained strong ties to Jewish culture if not religious observance. Canadian experience, especially with trade unionism, further distanced these women from pre-existing Jewish organizations. So they joined the Labour Zionist Movement, which had been formed in 1904. This male-dominated organization raised money for Palestine, supported the activities of organized labour in Toronto and sponsored social and educational activities for its membership. By 1925 women in the movement had become disillusioned by their exclusion from its political process. Encouraged by the success of other women's organizations, the women created the Pioneer Women's Organization (PWO). Its purpose was to educate children in the Labour Zionist tradition and promote women's participation in building the Jewish state. The PWO became the most ideologically based Jewish women's organization in North America. Its founding members felt part of an historic event in women's history. This feeling is reflected in the preamble to its constitution:

> The Jewish woman who occupies so distinguished a place in the life of our people has a great mission to fulfill in this period of our national rebirth and the reconstruction of Palestine... as part of the Jewish people, which suffers most, she has the high duty to place herself in the front ranks of a great movement for the rehabilitation of our national, cultural and political life.[11]

The formation of the PWO was in direct response to the exclusion of women from power in the Labour Zionist Movement rather than the urge to fulfill a feminine role. "We felt like second-class citizens," one member recalled.[12] "Major decisions were made by men, women weren't consulted.... They didn't think women capable of making political decisions."[13] Once the split was effected, however, Pioneer Women pursued a truly feminist goal: becoming the first Jewish women's group, outside Palestine,[14] to focus on the role of women. Funds raised by the PWO were to go to help women and children in Palestine and to raise the cultural level of women in Canada so they could make more valuable contributions to Jewish life. Through the PWO, women would finally have the opportunity to enter the front ranks of the Zionist movement. For the next twenty-five years, the PWO grew in membership, including English-speaking second-generation women, and it played a vital part in the creation of the Jewish state.

Two generations of women joined the PWO in Toronto. The initial members were inspired by the early women's movement and political enfranchisement. They were also searching for personal fulfillment. "Homemaking is very important and dignified work," wrote an early American member, "but homemaking alone for these women who had a revolutionary background with its keen interest in humanity, that was not enough for them.... In our organization, these women found their place and a opportunity for self-expression."[15] The women who joined the PWO in its formative years wanted both to benefit others and derive recognition from the community. The PWO offered them a role which neither synagogues, male-dominated organizations, the NCJW, nor Hadassah could. One woman explained that: "I once attended a Hadassah meeting. But, coming here, being a greenie, I felt out of place. Hadassah didn't suit me socially. Maybe they were too big for me, I mean rich."[16] In the PWO Yiddish language and cultural values were shared, and meetings were held in evenings or on weekends, so working women and those with small children could attend.[17]

The Second World War and the virtual end to eastern European immigration to Canada limited traditional sources of PWO membership just as the needs to raise funds for Jews in Palestine intensified. The organization looked to their daughters. Most of these women had participated in youth groups run by the Poale Zion and were familiar with the ideology and organizational life of Labour Zionism. They became a new and dynamic element in the PWO, for they had lived with the ideology since birth.

In 1939 a new chapter was formed comprising fourteen women who had grown up together within the Labour Zionist Movement. Most had married men from the same backgrounds. "Everything we did revolved around the Labour Zionist movement," explained one early member. "We were so tightly knit that if we came to a dance with someone who was not in the movement, we were boycotted by the other Young Poale Zion members.... We used to tell each other who to date."[18] The movement shaped their politics as well. "We were very idealistic, and very dedicated to the Labour Zionist principles."[19] These principles also shaped their view of secular Jewish life. "We never felt the need to join synagogues or temples. Belonging to the movement gave us our fulfillment."[20] In short, they joined the Pioneer Women because to do otherwise would have been an unnatural break with family and friends. Membership allowed them to continue their way of life, to work as a team and perhaps an extended family—with their parents, husbands and friends—for Labour Zionism and its ideals. It represented the vehicle through which they could become formally involved in a social and political group that represented their interests in the public sphere.

By the late 1940s the PWO had once again reached a plateau in its growth. Fortunately, its desire to attract still more members coincided with an increased interest on the part of Jewish women in joining Zionist organizations in light of the formation of the State of Israel. Although new members were often the same age as existing members, one woman explained: "I never had anything to do with Labour Zionism till I joined the PWO. I never knew anything like that existed."[21] Some of the new members had been in Hadassah in other cities; some were from orthodox religious families, and others were the daughters of Jews from England who had little or no Yiddish cultural background. They were all there because they wanted to work for Israel. "After the Holocaust, how could we not work for Israel? Working for Israel became very important."[22] Yet these women were not Labour Zionists. Their social activities took place outside the Labour Zionist milieu. They were affiliated with synagogues and did not socialize with other PWO members outside of meetings. One old-timer complained that "after they joined, it just wasn't the same; I think everybody felt that."[23]

The Holocaust and the creation of Israel caused a major shift in ideology and attitude for all North American Jewry. Old-World ties were destroyed and a new identity, focused on political nationhood, began to take shape. For those women not willing to re-establish themselves in Israel, Zionist organizations offered an avenue for expression of new concerns. Few new members carried on a family tradition of Zionist or political activity. The PWO offered a chance for socializing with friends while fulfilling the traditional charitable function, nothing more. Despite the fact that the cohesion of the PWO suffered, the new members were vital to the organization. Without them, it could not have raised as much money for Israel.

What the PWO did not lose sight of were its feminist goals. From its inception, it laid emphasis on the need to increase women's political and social awareness in Palestine and North America. Articles it published, such as "The Progress of Working Women in the Depression," "International Women's Movement" and the "Housewife and the Histadruth," were intended to generate women's interest in "raising the economic, social and cultural level of Jewish women."[24] Although the Pioneer Women in Toronto did not consciously design their program with these goals in mind (this was the rhetoric of the leaders, not the rank and file), the women understood, as one member protested, that "men didn't know everything and shouldn't do everything in Palestine."[25] They understood that women had an important part to play in the building of the Jewish state and that the PWO was working to equip women to do their share, whether in North America or in Palestine.

Through its practical program, the PWO encouraged women to think about things beyond their homes and families. While many members "were not consciously thinking about raising the level of women,"[26] they believed that they succeeded in doing so. One woman explained: "The PWO succeeded in raising the Jewish woman up a little more. When you're a Pioneer Woman, and you go and think about your people, that makes you more than just a plain woman that sits at home."[27] The Toronto Pioneer Women also participated in the annual celebration of International Women's Day. While they did not take seriously the requests by national leaders to "identify with the women's movement throughout the world,"[28] they did feel a strong bond with women in Palestine. One member vividly recalled that, "Years ago we didn't talk so much about women's rights and equality. At that time we had one aim—to help build Israel and help the women there to live and work."[29]

One activity managed to bridge the gap between ideology and practical programing—fund-raising. Money collected would shape the experience of women in Palestine and assist in national self-realization. The first generation of Pioneer Women took their financial responsibility to Palestine very seriously and raised money in every way they could. In the beginning, no matter what the weather was like, they canvassed door to door to collect coins to fill their assigned quotas. Although the average contribution was fifty cents, they persisted year after year and sometimes they were especially fortunate. As one woman recalled: "We went to one man; he asked us if we had a cheque book. I said we have receipts for 25¢, 50¢ and $1.00. He said I need a cheque, so my partner ran to get him one. The man donated thirty dollars! We nearly went crazy. We started to dance in the streets."[30]

The Pioneer Women were aggressive fund-raisers. One woman had a particularly effective scheme: "I used to go to one chicken dealer and show him the receipt from the other. He'd have to match the donation to save his face."[31] Sometimes the women's enthusiasm got them into awkward situations:

> I once went collecting with a friend. One woman I went to, she knew I had bad feet and it was hard for me to climb the stairs to her place. Well, I got there and she said 'I'm not giving you any money.' So my friend gave her hell and she called the police. Later the PWO told us we shouldn't insult people.[32]

Working class and often poor themselves, Pioneer Women actually displayed great compassion and understanding while canvassing:

> Once I went collecting and the woman at home was old and sick. I said to her, we're out for house collection for women and children in Palestine. She gave me two pennies. My heart was aching. She was so poor, I thought to give her money instead, but I didn't want to hurt her feelings.[33]

Other schemes included selling light bulbs and oranges and donating a day's wages or selling baked goods.

Fund-raising was also done collectively. The PWO's largest undertaking was its annual bazaar, preparations for which were elaborate and time consuming. They baked hundreds of pieces of gefilte fish and other delicacies for the food stand and collected saleable goods from generous businessmen. One bazaar was barely over before preparations began for the next. Other annual projects included teas, Hannukah parties and Passover celebrations. Women would prepare food and plays to entertain their guests who in turn were expected to make donations. When representatives of the Moetzet Hapoalot (a Palestinian women's organization) came to Toronto, the PWO charged admission to their lectures. In 1929 the most famous member of Moetzet Hapoalot, Golda Meir, brought in six hundred dollars for the Toronto branch.[34]

The PWO gave its members many things in return for their devotion, including confidence in group dynamics. Besides fund-raising techniques, women learned organizational skills. One member recalled how "women came in raw, took positions and learned how to be organizers." Commenting on the members' increasing ease as public speakers, she further explained that "I learned how to get up at a meeting and talk."[35] The PWO also gave its members "something to believe in, something to live for"[36] outside of their families and homes. Involvement in the organization gave them purpose and meaning. In return they received recognition from the community and praise from their families. "My children are so proud," said one member, "that I don't sit around and play cards all day."[37] Through meetings and special programs many women, denied secular education in their youth, were now able to learn. The educational activities of the PWO made information from the English-language newspapers accessible to women who could not read English, kept women informed about important issues and expanded women's knowledge of Palestine and the world. Women who were recent immigrants relied heavily on the PWO to satisfy their thirst for knowledge:

> The greenies needed the PWO very much. Speakers, seminars was their way to understand what was going on. They couldn't read a newpaper and they didn't go much to the movies and things like that. They couldn't afford it. There wasn't much things for them to do except for the Pioneer Women.[38]

At local and national conventions women heard a variety of prominent speakers and exchanged ideas with women from across North America. Conventions also prepared women for leadership roles through exposure to organizational structure and procedure.

For first- and second-generation immigrant members in particular, the PWO was a formative and progressive experience. "To me," explained one woman, "the Pioneer Women's Organization was very important. I lived out my life there, socially and politically. All my activities were there. I knew no other life."[39] Yet changes in membership, the PWO's consistent relegation to a female and, therefore, secondary role in the Zionist movement in Canada and the new political reality which followed the creation of the Jewish state moved the organization away from its roots and gradually destroyed its appeal.

Ironically, the establishment of Israel brought a crisis of ideology which has never been overcome. Some Pioneer Women did take up the challenge and emigrate. This was, of course, the logical conclusion to a program which focused on supporting women in state-building by establishing day-care facilities and training women for agriculture and industry. The ideals which differentiated Pioneer Women from other voluntary associations, however, were disappearing. Israel replaced the Yiddish secular culture (which was destroyed by the Holocaust) as a source of Jewish identification. Zionism, originally a political and nationalist ideology for creating a state, became a philosophy for support, largely financial, of Israel. The PWO no longer enjoyed a monopoly on Zionist passion. Meanwhile the membership had slowly moved into the middle class, and they had lost interest in the problems of working women. Its feminist dimension was quickly dissipating. Concerns shifted to children, their welfare and education in Israel. Yet the most devastating shift in ideology was the loss of socialist commitment. Although their pro-labour sympathies were unaltered, Pioneer Women were often no longer working and their children were becoming professionals. The creation of a Jewish state in which Labour Zionist principles played a major role, the increasing preponderance of Jews in the middle class and the increase in government sanctioned welfare legislation and unionism dissipated socialist fervour. With the winding down of the socialist component, the transformation of Zionism into a synonym for Jewishness and the devaluation of its feminist dimension, the PWO was in danger of losing its identity and its appeal.

The PWO was truly pioneer. It was the first Zionist women's group to separate from a male-dominated organization. It actively supported political causes long before other Jewish womens' groups did. Rather than depending on the established Jewish community or the NCJW, the PWO taught immigrant women that they had organizational skills and talents, encouraged a distinctly feminist outlook and fostered public speaking and political awareness among them.

Today the PWO appears to be an association which has lost its ideology and, therefore, its prestige. It has become a social club, a female ghetto whose previous functions have been taken over by the Jewish state. Yet its problems seem to be tied to the basic issue of women's powerlessness in the Jewish community.

Women took over the voluntary aspects of Jewish life and made significant contributions to its qualities, yet they were taken for granted. Women, and therefore volunteerism, have not been held in high esteem. Women have remained subservient in every sphere of Jewish life while providing the enthusiasm and funding to maintain its structural base. Meanwhile presidents of women's associations run multi-million dollar budgets and organize huge networks of regional groups.[40] Yet they are seldom given access to the ladder leading to communal decision-making. Historically, that power has been kept in the hands of perhaps 16-20 men in large urban centres—successful and wealthy businessmen and professionals in their sixties and seventies.[41] With only a few exceptions, the Jewish establishment in cities like Toronto has always been completely male. Likewise, in community organizations composed of men and women, virtually all important decision-making positions are monopolized by wealthy men.[42]

In 1975—the UN International Women's Year—a female member of the National Executive of the Canadian Jewish Congress (CJC) noted that only sixteen of the 116 members of Canadian Jewry's governing body were women and that that imbalance was perpetuated nation-wide at every level of the community. She advised that immediate steps be taken to rectify this injustice.[43]

In 1983 at the Congress Plenary Session, a women's workshop was forced on the organizers and, despite omission from the program, on the last day of the Plenary, 300 people packed the room to listen to speakers attack discrimination against women by the Jewish religious and political establishment. A survey vividly demonstrated under-representation in positions of power by women in both the volunteer and paid sectors.[44] On May 5, 1985 a women's workshop, "Involving Women in the Political Process," was presented at the Canadian Jewish Congress's Ontario regional conference. Women were urged to utilize their experience as organizers to achieve positions of power. The obstacles to overcome—to remove wealth as a prerequisite for power and to convince men to step aside—were no small tasks.

Jewish women, their perceptions altered by the feminist movement and increasingly professional, no longer see voluntary work in feminine ghettos as viable expressions of their Jewish commitment. If Canadian Jewry is to survive, the community must redefine the role of women. Neither can their traditional roles be minimized or overlooked.[45] As a former president of the Toronto chapter of the NCJW wrote in her book *Three Cheers for Volunteers*:

> Women are responsible for a great wave of compassionate action. The weak, the fallen, the aged, the young, the sick, and the lonely are all benefiting from the deeds of women. Without women, much that is planned would never be realized, and much that is dreamed would never come into being.[46]

Notes

1. For an examination of the role of Jewish women in the United States see June Sochen, "Some Observations on the Role of American Jewish Women as Communal Volunteers," in *American Jewish History* 70, no. 1 (September 1980), pp. 23-34.

2. For recent evaluations of the role of women in Judaism see: Charlotte Baum, Paula Hyman, and Sonya Michel, *The Jewish Woman in America* (New York: Plume Books, 1977); Susannah Heschel, ed., *On Being A Jewish Feminist* (New York: Schocken Books, 1983); Elizabeth Koltun, ed., *The Jewish Woman. New Perspectives* (New York: Schocken Books, 1976) and Sally Priesand, *Judaism and the New Woman* (New York: Behrman House, 1975).
3. For in-depth studies of the effects of emancipation and the Enlightenment on European Jewry see Jacob Katz, *Out of the Ghetto* (Cambridge: Harvard University Press, 1973) and Michael Meyer, *The Origins of the Modern Jew* (Detroit: Wayne State University Press, 1967).
4. For the effects of the Reform movement on Jewish women see Ellen Umansky, "Women in Judaism: From the Reform Movement to Contemporary Jewish Religious Feminism" in Rosemary Ruether and Eleanor McLaughlin, eds., *Women of Spirit. Female Leadership in the Jewish and Christian Traditions* (New York: Simon and Shuster, 1979).
5. Early Jewish life in Toronto is examined in Stephen A. Speisman, *The Jews of Toronto* (Toronto: McClelland and Stewart, 1979).
6. See Ethel Vineberg, *The History of the National Council of Jewish Women* (Montreal: National Council of Jewish Women, 1967).
7. Hadassah Organization of Canada, *Hadassah Jubilee Book* (Canada: 1927), p. 131.
8. This examination of the Pioneer Women's Organization is based on Janice B. Karlinsky, "The Pioneer Women's Organization: A Case Study of Jewish Women in Toronto" (M. A. thesis, University of Toronto, 1979).
9. By the end of World War One many different brands of political Zionism had evolved. Labour Zionists (also known as the Poale Zion or Socialist-Zionists) shared the conviction that Jewish national redemption could not be separated from the movements aiming at the liberation of oppressed classes in all nations. They adapted Marxist determination to the General Zionist slogan: "If you will it, it is no dream" by explaining the establishment of a Jewish state as the inevitable result of the Jewish proletariat's search for a base from which to conduct the class struggle. The new Jewish state would give rise to a cooperative socialist society built by Jewish labour.
10. Karlinsky, "The Pioneer Women's Organization," p. 19.
11. *Pioneer Woman* (New York), March 1927.
12. Karlinsky, "The Pioneer Women's Organization," p. 49.
13. Women in the Poale Zion in the United States faced the same problem: "We were...active *chaveras* [members], but as usual, it was our male comrades who did all the planning... We merely helped." Recollections of a founding member in *Pioneer Woman* (New York), October 1945.

14. The Moetzet Hapoalot was the women's branch of the Histadrut in Palestine, also a Labour Zionist group. This became the PWO's sister organization and funds raised in North America supported their projects.
15. *Pioneer Woman* (New York), November 1945.
16. Karlinsky, The Pioneer Women's Organization," p. 104.
17. The daytime scheduling of events and meetings by Jewish women's organizations has once again become a significant factor, causing membership to remain dominated by middle-aged, leisured women as increasing numbers of young women remain in the work-force after marriage and children.
18. Karlinsky, "The Pioneer Women's Organization," p. 119.
19. Ibid.
20. Ibid.
21. Ibid., p. 124.
22. Ibid., p. 125.
23. Ibid., p. 127.
24. *Pioneer Woman* (New York), February 1934, December 1935, December 1936, March 1927.
25. Karlinsky, "The Pioneer Women's Organization," p. 111.
26. Ibid., p. 112.
27. Ibid.
28. Ibid.
29. Ibid.
30. Ibid., p. 113.
31. Ibid.
32. Ibid.
33. Ibid., p. 114.
34. Ibid., p. 115.
35. Ibid.
36. Ibid.
37. Ibid., p. 116.
38. Ibid., p. 117.
39. Ibid., p. 118.
40. See Sochen, "Some Observations on the Role of American Jewish Women."
41. See Waller, "Power in the Jewish Community."
42. For a discussion of the situation of Jewish women in a North American perspective see Amy Stone, "The Jewish Establishment is not an Equal Opportunity Employer," in *Lilith* 1, no. 4 (Fall/Winter 1977-78).
43. Dorothy Reitman, "What are the Roles CJC Women are Playing?" in *Congress Bulliten*, September 1975.
44. Telephone conversation with Judy Feld Carr, 25 April 1985; *Canadian Jewish News*, 5 May 1983, p. 5.
45. For further discussion of the historical background of Canadian Jewish women see Paula J. Draper, "The Role of Canadian Jewish

Women in Historical Perspective,'' in E. Lipsitz, ed., *Canadian Jewish Women of Today. Who's Who of Canadian Jewish Women, 1983* (Toronto: J.E.S.L. Educational Products, 1983), pp. 3-10.

46. Ruth Hartman Frankel, *Three Cheers for Volunteers* (Toronto: Clarke and Irwin, 1965), p. 15.

Women and the Polish Alliance of Canada

Apolonja Kojder

Efforts to involve women in the Polish community in secular organizational life were first evident just prior to World War One when the Polish socialists established a branch in Toronto. Soon other groups, such as the Sons of Poland, a mutual benefit society, composed exclusively of men, came to recognize the need for Polish women to organize. However, these early endeavours, often unsatisfactory and short-lived, revealed underlying problems. Within the small Polish community found in Toronto in the early 1900s, there existed a broad spectrum of views on the role of Polish immigrant women in the New World. The early precursors of the Alliance, which were to merge eventually and form the largest Polish lay organization in Ontario, represented these divergent elements within the community, ranging from the traditional to the progressive. The history of women in relation to the Polish Alliance of Canada is largely the struggle to come to terms with what role women should play.

Contradictions become apparent almost immediately in examining the women's position within the Alliance. As previously alluded to, the origins of these contradictions can be traced back to the way in which the Alliance was formed. As well, the ambiguity of women's position within the organization can be accounted for by the changes in their roles as women upon immigration. Briefly, women were crucial to the survival of the organization and yet at the same time always at the periphery of the organizational structure. On the one hand, the women kept within tradition by assuming supportive roles and, on the other hand, they attempted to be part of the mainstream, as they saw it, in North America by forming their own women's organization. A look at women's involvement in the Alliance reveals the underlying conflicts in the lives of these immigrant women—attempting to come to terms with the old and the new, the traditional Polish heritage and the North American ways.

Some in the Polish community perceived women as being equal but different, and thus saw separate women's organizations as the most suitable vehicles for women to fulfill their supposedly special functions. Others accepted equality for women without reservation, although probably not appreciating the difficulties to be faced in maintaining such a stand in a traditionally patriarchal society. Yet others simply chose to ignore the women, either through lack of awareness or through refusal to cope with the issue.

Early Women's Groups

Reference was first made in 1915 to the need for a Polish women's group by the Sons of Poland (formed in 1907). But it was not until 1917 that a committee was finally established to discuss the formation of a women's organization—the Ladies' Circle (Koł Pań):

> . . . a debate was carried on as to the improvement of the condition of Polish men and women in Toronto, and namely, it was considered crucial that a committee be established to organize a Ladies' Association which would have as its goals taking care of emigration matters pertaining to the female sex, watching the moral behaviour of women, visiting sick sisters and brothers as well as collecting funds for the poor and impoverished Polish families not belonging to any organization.[1]

By 1918 the Ladies' Circle, known also as the Ladies' Association (Towarzystwo Pań), had transformed itself into the Polish Women's Committee (Komitet Polek). It worked closely with the Citizen's Committee (Komitet Obywatelski), organized in 1917 in Toronto to collect money for the Polish army in France and to recruit volunteers. The Polish Women's Committee was responsible to the National Department (Wydział Narodowy) of the Central Relief Committee in Chicago.[2] However, the women's involvement with the group was short-lived, when in 1919 it transferred its allegiance to the less conservative rival, the Polish Democratic Council (Demokratyczna Rada Polska) in Toronto.

In 1921, in a move to gain strength, the two mutual benefit societies—the Association of the Sons of Poland (Towarzystwo 'Synowie Polski') and the Association of St. Stanislaus (Towarzystwo św. Stanisława)—united to form the Polish Alliance of Canada (Związek Polaków w Kanadzie). In 1923 when the former socialist turned self-improvement group—the Polish National Progressive Society (Spójnia Narodowa 'Postępowa' Polska)—joined the Polish Alliance, women in the Polish community of Toronto no longer had any organizational affiliation, as the Polish Alliance was seen as exclusively male. In reaction to this, a group of women formed the Polish Women's Alliance of Canada (Związek Polek w Kanadzie).

Initially the Polish Women's Alliance was conceived of as a mutual benefit society, but several months later this idea was rejected in favour of a progressive-educational society. The constitution was to be modelled on the men's Polish Alliance of Canada. It had an ambitious program and set of aims as evidenced in the constitution (see Appendix). Although initial membership was restricted, a broad base was soon secured when the constitution was changed to extend membership not only to Polish women, but to "every woman of an upright character, regardless of her religious beliefs and political view,"[3] despite some opposition that the society would no longer be purely Polish. The wording of the constitution reveals a great optimism that women would be a regenerative force in the world. Although perceiving themselves as quite progressive, these women still also saw themselves in the traditional supportive roles, looking to the needs of society and the family as nurturers.

The women's relationship with the early men's Polish Alliance was ambiguous. Although there was cooperation between the two, for example, in drawing up the women's constitution and in sponsoring social functions, there was also an undercurrent of animosity. Most illustrative of this was the decision of the women not to call upon the men to speak at rallies because "the men from the Polish Alliance of Canada had replied once already 'that whoever undertakes to organize some kind of work should also know how to manage it.'"[4] During the two years that the women's organization existed, the men's Alliance was not faring very well, despite the union of the various Polish men's groups. Some members had returned to a newly independent Poland and many of the remaining men were unemployed. By the winter of 1924, the Polish Alliance had reached a crisis, and it was the women who came to the rescue at the critical moment, providing the essential financial aid and lending their organizational skills to the floundering men's group.

At the end of 1924, the decision was finally made to allow women membership in the Polish Alliance of Canada. No doubt at this time it became evident to the men that it would be expedient for their Alliance to draw upon the resources of the Polish women. Also, according to K. J. Mazurkiewicz, former president of the Progressives and president of the Alliance in 1923, the women were accustomed to organizational life, and if they had remained separate much longer they would never have joined the Alliance.[5] For the women, however, there were doubts concerning their future in spite of their apparent success. For example, the establishment of a Drama Circle by the men was regarded as sufficient reason for them to consider seriously joining the men's Alliance.

Women in Early Polish Secular Organizations

By 1911 the Alliance of Polish Socialists had established a branch in Toronto called 'The Power,' to which Polish women could belong (Związek Socialistów Polskich—Oddział 'Potęga'). Although a small group, the socialists were very active and vocal within the Polish community. However, their organization's existence was short-lived when the police disbanded the group during the First World War. Women played mainly a supportive role within this group. The central figures—whether as speakers, organizers or correspondents—were male.

In 1918 several former members of the now disbanded Polish Socialists in Toronto regrouped to form the Polish National Progressive Union (Spójnia Narodowa 'Postępowa' Polska). Women were also allowed membership in this self-improvement group. They were involved in the education committee, in organizing social functions, in the choir and drama. Their activities ended though when the male members joined the Polish Alliance in 1923.

In 1919 the former Polish Ladies' Circle merged with the newly formed Polish Democratic Council (Demokratyczna Rada Polska). The council was established as a reaction to the existing National Department in Chicago, which it regarded as representing the upper-class, conservative, clerical elements within the Polish community, rather than the working class. As an umbrella organization, it concerned itself with the affairs of the newly independent Poland

and with the Poles in Canada. Its first vice-president and correspondent to the English press was a woman, and women were quite active in projects involving aid to Poland. As the situation in Poland became somewhat stabilized, however, the Democratic Council started to lose its initial impact and women no longer took an active part in it.

In 1920 the Polish Bond Committee (Komitet Polskiej Pożyczki Państwowej) was established in Toronto. During its brief but relatively successful existence women took an active part in it.

Polish Women and Organizational Life

Prior to 1924 Polish women in Toronto were active in various organizations. However, they were usually on the periphery of those organizations that allowed for female membership. Their small numbers, their other commitments, economic conditions and the prevailing attitudes no doubt inhibited greater participation in the male-dominated associations. Only in the women's organizations were conditions favourable for the women to develop their organizational skills. Even women's groups exhibited a lack of confidence in having frequent recourse to the men's organizations for aid or advice. Nevertheless, these were the first ventures, transitory though they were, by Polish women into organizational matters. The women showed that they had both the desire and ability to organize. A key leadership figure that emerged during this early period was Karolina Ejsmond. She was prominent in the Ladies' Circle, the Polish Women's Committee, the Polish Women's Alliance, the Polish Democratic Council and the Polish Bond Committee.

Once women were admitted to the Polish Alliance of Canada in 1924, they became involved primarily in the theatre, youth groups and education. The amateur theatre circle 'Joy' (Uciecha), established in 1924, assumed tremendous importance in the interwar period, being responsible for the artistic-cultural activities of the Alliance. It had a broad range of activities, from arranging balls and picnics, readings and discussion groups to forming a dance group, a choir and a women's sports department. In the years 1927-30 the drama circle became better known and more popular than the Alliance. As a result, it soon had more members and operating funds than the Alliance. Women were an integral part of this very successful group, being involved in every aspect, ranging from administration, directing and committee work to acting.

Besides their involvement in theatre, women and girls in the Polish community became involved in the Alliance's youth groups. In the 1930s numerous youth groups were organized and young girls and women became involved in both the activities and the governing of these groups. Members participated in such activities as Polish national celebrations, theatre, sports, choirs, musical and dance groups, gymnastics and outings.

Once the focus of education shifted from adults to children with the maturing of the Polish population, women very gradually became involved in education. Although most of the volunteer teachers in the evening or Saturday Alliance Polish language schools for children were the better-educated men from the Polish community during the mid-1920s and the 1930s, by the 1940s and 1950s professionally trained female teachers were starting to make an appearance. The gradual changes in the role of Polish women during the depression when they were forced to work outside of the home facilitated acceptance of women as teachers in the schools. Although there was a great influx of well-educated Polish women and teachers after the Second World War, these women were often forced to look elsewhere for full-time jobs with better pay. It was only by the 1960s that professional women teachers came to dominate the Polish part-time schools.[6] Several professional women teachers emerged in those formative years, helping to shape the educational policies of the Alliance, such as Stefania Romankiewicz in the 1930s, Barbara Głogowska in the 1940s and Michalina Wolnik in the 1950s. They had to cope with numerous difficulties, such as lack of qualified teachers and textbooks, inadequate curriculum and facilities. Despite the problems, these women distinguished themselves through their dedication and involvement in the various aspects of education, whether class-room teaching, administration, innovation, or curriculum development.

One area that women were notably absent from in the Alliance was the governing body. At the yearly general assemblies there was usually either no female representative or else a conspicuous lone woman present. Over the years their numbers fluctuated but, nevertheless, remained very small. Women holding executive positions within the Polish Alliance at the local level and in the main body were uncommon. The teacher, Stefania Romankiewicz, showed considerable promise in organizational work in the 1930s. So did a woman from Hamilton, Anastazia Kozłowska, who kept reappearing as a representative to the general assemblies and the local group, as well as acquiring prominence in the highest offices of the Alliance—a remarkable lifelong commitment to the Alliance from the 1930s to the present. Perhaps it was because of her strong leadership qualities that the Hamilton branch usually had a woman on its governing body and at the general conventions.

By the mid-1930s the Alliance was definitely feeling the effects of the depression:

> Group 2 of the P.A.C. apparently like other Polish organizations faced the prospect of bankruptcy because of ever dwindling financial returns. Under such circumstances the idea arose to create a women's organization as a separate division of the Group. Mrs. Anastazja Kozłowska assumed that the new organization would financially strengthen the Group through its undertakings. And so it happened.[7]

Under such conditions, the Women's Club, later called Ladies' Circle, was formed in 1935 in Hamilton. By 1937 Mrs. Kozłowska was named general organizer of the Polish Alliance Ladies' Circles (Kół Polek Związku Polaków) and as such established circles in other Alliance groups throughout the Province of Ontario. Somewhat reminiscent of an earlier period, Polish women were again organizing.

Part of the rationale for the organizing of the Polish women was simply recognition of their contributions. From the beginning, women had been involved unofficially in committee work.[8] However, often men would interfere.[9] Once confronted with the notion of women organizing, the men of the Alliance apparently viewed it as being to their advantage: "We thought organized women would put in even more effort to the extent they would by-pass men."[10] No doubt both the men and women viewed the move as a step towards greater efficiency. But for the women, organizing must have meant more than just that:

> The women worked like slaves and had nothing for it. The Ladies' Circle would give them something to hold on to. It would show themselves and others, that they'd accomplished something . . . organizing the Ladies' Circle was a reasonable answer to the Polish women's desire to show what they had put into the main body.[11]

No doubt the women had felt that often their work was thankless. As one woman put it, "A lot of unrecognized hours were put into the Alliance by women."[12]

As already mentioned (or suggested), economics played a decisive factor in the formation of the Ladies' Circle. According to Mrs. Kozłowska, the key figure in this move to organize Polish women:

> It was sheer need—the women's group. It was the depression. There was a lot of work to be done. There was the problem of acquiring money to keep the programs going and to pay for the local hall, and the library (reading-room). I didn't plan it at all. At a meeting, it just came to me to organize the women. . . . The men were quite sceptical.[13]

Although the women had not responded particularly well to appeals from the men for involvement in Alliance activities, they did respond to a call for a women's organization. The Ladies' Circle raised funds through bingos, bazaars, bake sales, balls, teas, picnics, banquets and activities centred around various festivities. In a time of uncertainties, the women stepped in and brought a new vigour to the floundering organization. They were unabashedly acknowledged as the saviours of the organization during the depression.

The Ladies' Circle also served the particular needs of immigrant women. Many were isolated in their own homes, looking after children. Added to this was the language barrier, which increased their sense of isolation, their feelings of being different. Prejudice, child care and loneliness for their families and for Poland were other common problems they had to face. There was a desire to belong, a need to share and talk to other Polish women about their problems, common experiences and aspirations. Thus, the Ladies' Circles came to serve both a social and a therapeutic function: "Polish women! Married women! Single women and widows! All of our troubles and yours, as well as consolation, we must share together and only we know how to find comfort in each other, no one else."[14] There they found the support and company of other Polish women. There they could talk about work, children, husbands and health. For many, the Ladies' Circle brought much happiness to an otherwise very difficult life. The Ladies' Circles allowed the Polish immigrant women to help themselves. Once a week they had their evening out.

Although often acknowledged as vital to the well-being of the organization, many of the women were self-conscious and self-effacing about their contributions to the organizational life of the Polish community: "During this yearly period of time we did a little—not much—maybe too little, let others form their own opinion about us. We won't praise ourselves, what we could do, we did. The rest is ahead of us to do . . . ."[15] In response to this modesty, the editor of the Alliance newspaper commented that "they do not work for praise but rather for the common good and they themselves even want their work to remain anonymous . . . work so commendable."[16] Perhaps the character of the Ladies' Circle encouraged such an attitude of self-effacement. As an auxiliary of the branch of the Polish Alliance of Canada, in many respects the Ladies' Circle took on a supportive role, a role the women were all too familiar with in the traditional and patriarchal Polish society. The women were reluctant to assert themselves in the Alliance. Only in a strictly women's organization would the majority of women find the confidence to participate and articulate their ideas.

Formation of Polish women's groups was an attempt to modernize community activity. Women's associations of all kinds were seen everywhere, why not in Ontario. In organizing themselves, the women felt that they were following the example of Polish women in the United States and other countries where Poles had settled. And, of course, there were the Canadian women's organizations to emulate. Yet, even years later, the Polish women still did not feel confident in relation to these other groups. For example, when two delegates, who supposedly understood English well, were sent to a local Council of Women meeting, they reported the following:

> . . . When they [the Polish delegates] went there to register, they were taken aback because a very high class of ladies belongs there and they [the Polish delegates] sensed that it would be too uncomfortable for us to belong to them because we do not have such ladies who can express themselves in English.[17]

The Ladies' Circle espoused the view that women were equal but different. Because of their supposedly special qualities, they were to be custodians of Polish cultural traditions. Their special roles were well defined within the family context. Their primary concern was to be the maintenance of Polishness (*polskość*) among the youth. The Ladies' Circles became involved in such humanitarian endeavours as helping the unfortunate in Poland and Canada—the sick, the invalids, the elderly, the victims of natural disasters and war. Besides bringing up children, they were creating an environment for their children they regarded as conducive to cultural maintenance through the upkeep of the Polish schools, libraries, youth groups and the organization of various community events in the Polish halls which they helped to maintain.

The Ladies' Circle was not without its problems. With the passage of time, misunderstandings between the old and new Polish immigrants appeared. Society itself was changing and where once activities such as picnics, banquets and theatre were successful, with the advent of radio, television, cars and general family affluence, they no longer drew the crowds as in the past. And, of course, there was always the problem of women not being either able or willing to participate because of their commitments at home.

Women and the Polish Alliance Press

A discussion of the role of women in the Alliance would not be complete without looking at the newspaper, *Alliancer* (Związkowiec)—the official organ of the Polish Alliance of Canada. Soon after its founding in 1933, the newspaper began to include a regular women's column. The material for this column was most likely extracted from Polish newspapers in the United States and Poland. Apart from this women's column, other sources of information concerning women were letters to the editor, editorials, news clippings, feature articles and poetry.

Although newspaper accounts cannot be taken as a total reflection of reality, it is most vital to look to the *Alliancer* for articles referring to women because generally women were the least vocal and visible members of the Polish community and organization; they did not even appear as writers of letters to the editor. Besides reflecting current issues, the articles also attempted to shape Polish immigrant life, and, as such, had to deal with women—their roles, problems and concerns. As well, the paper offers some insight into contemporary views about women and the interests of Polish women both in North America and abroad.

The first editor of the *Alliancer* was A. J. Staniewski, who was to shape the policies of the newspaper from 1934 to the time of his death in 1941. Under his editorship the newspaper was very strongly pro-labour, socialist and anti-clerical, and the articles concerning women very much reflected this man's beliefs. In many ways, Staniewski represented many of the best elements of the old wave of Polish immigrants—the self-made man with a sense of mission. But by the 1940s the paper started to lose its earlier tone with the influx of professional Polish journalists and the new wave of Polish immigrants. A conservatism set in, reflected in the articles on women. Gone was the challenge to readers for marked social change. Instead, the position became simply one of adapting and promoting liberal attitudes.

Despite the changes that occurred in the *Alliancer* over time, the articles concerning women that appeared in the early years certainly were some of the most interesting to be found in the newspaper. Its editor was a man socially aware, having been involved in the workers' struggle in Europe and Canada and no doubt exposed to the women's rights movement of the early 1900s. The numerous sensitive and insightful articles in the *Alliancer* of the 1930s, concerning women, were without a doubt thought-provoking and controversial to many of its readers. Topics covered a broad spectrum—wife-battering, alcohol abuse, unemployment, the women's movement, conditions of women throughout the world, politics as it affected women and the changing roles of women, as well as child care, health and personal appearance.

During the thirties the *Alliancer* frequently had articles on women's particular vulnerability to exploitation and hardship during the depression—as young girls, married women, mothers and workers. One result of the economic crisis was role reversal, with the wife out working and the man at home. Although a few articles described what was being done to help unemployed women world-wide in the existing political and social structures, others called for a new social order. In lending his support to the newly formed Ladies' Circle within the Alliance, the editor addressed the Canadian Polish women as follows:

> . . . You are the sisters, the wives and mothers of Poles, belonging to the large working class. Where shoulder to shoulder, in solidarity of membership, you must struggle for a better economic survival and an advantageous position for Polish women, in this Anglo-Saxon society, along with your husband, father and brother.[18]

The recurrent theme here and elsewhere was the condemnation of the capitalist system and the pursuit of social justice for the oppressed working class. There was also an anti-clerical approach in these editorials where religion was condemned for encouraging women to accept their lot unquestioningly.

The ideological stance of a majority of the articles pertaining to women in the *Alliancer* of the 1930s was anti-capitalist, anti-fascist and pro-women's rights. The editor condemned the fascist dictators, Mussolini and Hitler, for relegating women to the role of "baby machines," with no control over their own bodies. Nor was Stalin spared these attacks. Even the Quebec legislature was branded fascist for refusing women the vote.

Basically the *Alliancer* supported women's rights. The women's movement was seen as a positive force. The emancipated, modern woman was portrayed in glowing terms. A new and better world was envisioned with the participation of these liberated women. There were repeated pleas in the *Alliancer* for women to expand their horizons beyond the home. The articles on women showed that change was possible, despite seemingly insurmountable barriers, and implied that many options were open to women and that much of women's status was determined by custom and tradition.

The *Alliancer* was not oblivious to the great changes occurring in women's roles. It was there to help the Polish people of Canada to come to terms with these changes. Although Polish society was basically traditional, changes began taking place in the Polish family, structure and relationships. The process of migration contributed to these changes. The economic crisis of the depression dramatically altered the patriarchal structures of the Polish family, as reflected in role reversal. Also, the absence of a support system to reinforce the traditional patriarchal ideal of family relations played a major part in the changes occurring in the status of women. The early *Alliancer*'s basic policy was to aid readers in making adjustments, in changing old habits and forming new attitudes.

An illustration of the *Alliancer*'s concern with the changing roles of Polish immigrant women in Canada was a feature article in 1936 entitled "Women's Problems" (Babskie Kłopoty). This witty and perceptive article described in detail the often bleak and hopeless position of wives in the old country, their hardships in Canada and the eventual breakdown of marriages. The article began as follows:

> One still finds people with old ways of thinking who hold and strongly believe in the view that so long as the woman [*baba*] was in the old country and didn't know Canada, she was an 'all right' woman. From the moment of arrival in Canada, something happens to the woman, as if she's not the same. If I may say so, it's as if something had bitten her, or the devil itself had possessed her.[19]

In closing, the author concluded that the breakup of Polish immigrant marriages occurred: ". . . through the inability to adapt to new conditions and foreign circumstances. Through overcrowded homes, where several families live, several boarders. Through the cruel behaviour of the man and his relationship to women, etc."[20]

The implications are that immigration was a great advancement for women—it freed them from strict social controls. Also, the urban industrial society allowed women to become economically independent through wage labour. With the higher standard of living, women could aspire to a better life for themselves. Supposedly this would eventually lead to a redefinition of relationships between men and women to one of more equality. The author described the process of change without condemnation because in the new order he saw more emancipated conditions. This unusual article was a strong statement against the oppression of women.

The challenge offered by the above article brought several interesting and contradictory responses from readers of the *Alliancer*. One man's advice to married men follows:

> 1. Don't keep single boarders in your home, especially those who are unemployed.
> 2. Don't allow your wife to go out to the cinema, the park or a picnic with your boarders or other boarders.
> 3. Live usually by yourselves, let there be one room less and let it cost a few dollars a month more, but for this you will have peace of mind and certainty in your home, that no one will seduce your wife.
> 4. Don't hang around the pool-rooms, nor hotels night and day.[21]

A single man objected, stating that unemployed young boarders were too busy looking for bread to seduce women.[22] One woman's response to the male correspondents was to condemn their double standards and the feudal mentality of Polish men in Canada:

> . . . it all just amounts to this, that they are—men, just because they're husbands, as if simply that label, gave them the right to ownership of women, as if they were—objects. The concept, on the other hand, of the individuality of women's spirit, as an independent human being, has not worked itself out yet in the average man's brain and this is simply an example of his own ignorance, which lowers him in the eyes of women.[23]

In 1939 there appeared a series of letters to the editor apparently from a Polish woman in Toronto, touching upon various issues of concern to the Polish community. The numerous letters covered a broad spectrum of topics, such as sexual harassment in the work place, boardinghouses as a cause of marital conflict, poor living conditions in boardinghouses and role reversal with its concomitant double burdens. Also the inappropriate behaviour of the young, with their superficial adaptation to Canadian life and denial of their roots, was discussed. Poor upbringing in Polish families and the public school system in Canada were described as reasons for the rapid Canadianization of the youth.

Of course, in response to her letters of censure, other readers offered their own objections or understanding of these issues.[24] Here again as an open forum, the *Alliancer* was playing a role in the cultural and social adjustment of the Polish immigrant readers.

Notes

1. Sons of Poland Minute Book, 17 Mar. 1917, Polish Alliance Friendly Society, vol. 1, Public Archives of Canada (PAC), MG 28 V 55.
2. See Edward R. Kantowicz, *Polish-American Politics in Chicago, 1888-1940* (Chicago: University of Chicago Press, 1975), pp. 110-11.
3. Polish Women's Alliance Minute Book, 27 June 1923, Polish Alliance Friendly Society, vol. 48, PAC, MG 28 V 55.
4. Ibid., 13 May 1923.
5. Frank Kmietowicz interview, July 20, 1981, Toronto.
6. Michalina Wolnik interview, May 2, 1985, Toronto.
7. "Praca Społeczna Daje Zadowolenie," *Związkowiec* [Toronto], 11 May 1960, p. 5.
8. Stanisław Konopka interview, July 20, 1981, Toronto.
9. Kmietowicz interview.
10. Konopka interview.
11. Ibid.
12. Mary Kiczma interview, Multicultural History Society of Ontario—Oral History Collection.
13. Anastazja Kozłowska interview, June 30, 1981, Toronto.
14. "Wyjątki z Protokołu Zjazdowego 'Kół Polek' Związek Polaków w Kanadzie," *Związkowiec* [Toronto], 12 June 1938, p. 5.
15. H. Staniewska, "Nadchodzi Czas!" *Związkowiec* [Toronto], 11 December 1938, p. 5.
16. "Koło Polek Gr. 1-szej i ich Praca," *Związkowiec* [Toronto], 13 March 1938, p. 6.
17. Letter from F. Przedrowek to A. Kozłowska, 20 March 1957, Windsor, in Anastazja Kozłowska Collection, Multicultural History Society of Ontario.
18. "Witajcie Polki," *Związkowiec* [Toronto], 29 May 1938, p. 4.
19. "Babskie Kłopoty," *Związkowiec* [Toronto], 31 May 1936, p. 4.
20. Ibid., p. 7.
21. M. Z. A., "Moje Uwagi," *Związkowiec* [Toronto], 21 June 1936, p. 6.
22. S. Sorek, "Kłopoty Małżeńskie," *Związkowiec* [Toronto], 5 July 1936, p. 6.

23. Marja D., "W Obronie Czci Kobiety," *Związkowiec* [Toronto], 19 July 1936, p. 6.
24. A series of twenty letters to the editor were written by Florcia Drygalska, entitled "Miss Florcia has a Voice" (Panna Florcia ma Głos), to the *Alliancer* in the period 30 July 1939-14 January 1940. Responses to her letters were found in the *Alliancer*, 17 September 1939 and 5 November 1939.

Appendix

Constitution of the Polish Women's Alliance of Canada, 1923-24

Aims

The goal of the Polish Women's Alliance is to be the unification of all of women's conscious strengths, with the aim of acquiring all-round moral development so that people's universal aspirations are realized in deeds, through uplifting the moral life of the family, society and community.

Methods of Achieving Goals

1. With the goal of unification, conducting rallies, lectures, family social evenings and amateur plays.
2. Educating ourselves through conducting self-educating circles, reading books and newspapers of a progressive nature.
3. Establishing exclusively Polish language schools for the illiterate and for the children, and English for the adults.
4. School for needlework, lacemaking, crocheting, etc.
   School of home economics.
   Lectures on hygiene.
   Athletic school for youth, as well as moral upbringing in the Polish spirit.
   Promote and assist morally and materially the members of the Polish Women's Alliance as well as other progressive organizations.

Greek Immigrant Women from Asia Minor in Prewar Toronto: the Formative Years

Eleoussa Polyzoi

Following the tragic defeat of the Greek forces in 1922 by the Turkish army in Asia Minor and the resulting exodus of more than one and a half million Greek refugees to mainland Greece, a sizeable number of refugees managed to enter Canada. Although the émigrés from Asia Minor constituted the first major wave of Greek immigration, they have rarely, if at all, been systematically studied. Since they embrace the founding period of the Greek community in Toronto, it is important to examine this distinctive ethnic subgroup.

The objectives of this paper are: a) to address the historical and political circumstances surrounding early Greek immigration to Toronto from Asia Minor, 1900-39; b) to discuss the appeal to the Canadian government to accept Greek refugees from Asia Minor; c) to examine the social adjustment of this early immigrant group and its unique ethnocultural position in the early Greek community; and d) to explore women's participation in early Greek institutional life, focusing on their contribution to the establishment of the first Greek Ladies' Philanthropic Society and the founding of the first Greek language school in Toronto. Primary sources upon which the present study is based include associational papers, parish records, the Greek press and the oral histories of individuals who grew up in the Greek neighbourhoods of prewar Toronto. Federal archival records, the Canadian census, city records and the English-language press are also utilized. Secondary sources include translations of Greek government publications regarding prewar Greek emigration, analyses of United Nations documents on the Greek refugee problem and related articles addressing Greek immigration in general. The primary sources cited in this paper are all part of the collection of the Multicultural History Society of Ontario.

Circumstances Surrounding Early Greek Immigration to Toronto from Asia Minor, 1900-39

As early as January 1915 the Allies tried to tempt Greece into entering the First World War with the promise of territorial gains in Anatolia. Freeing "unredeemed" Greek territory under Turkish rule since 1453 was a national ideal that occupied the hearts and minds of the Greek people for years.[1] From the onset of World War One, however, it was clear that the prime minister of Greece, Eleftherios Venizelos, and King Constantine differed regarding the country's participation in the war. Their differences were to last beyond their lifetimes and divide Greeks politically, for generations, into royalists and republicans. This division was repeated on a smaller scale in Greek communities all across North America. Toronto was no exception.[2]

Eleftherios Venizelos, encouraged by the prospect of expanding Greek territory, sided with the Allies. His political platform rested essentially on the premise that, by joining in the fight, Greece would be permitted to "liberate" Smyrna region, with its large Greek population, from Turkish rule.[3] King Constantine, however, wanted no part in the war. He assured the German Emperor William II (whose sister, Sophia, he had married) that, although officially neutral, he was, in fact, in sympathy with Germany's position. King Constantine's persistent neutrality eventually led to Venizelos's resignation. In September 1915 Venizelos established his own revolutionary government in Crete, and in November he declared war on the Central Powers and Bulgaria. He then worked with the Allies and waited for an opportune moment to regain power in Athens.[4]

Following a number of increasingly strong Anglo-French ultimatums, King Constantine was forced to leave the country, and in June 1917, Venizelos returned to Athens as prime minister of Greece. With renewed vigour, Venizelos exacted fulfillment of the Entente promise, and the Allied Supreme Council in Paris authorized the landing of Greek troops in Smyrna in May 1919. This was the beginning of disaster for both Venizelos and Greece.

Four months later, Venizelos was defeated at the polls and Constantine was restored to his throne on the crest of a wave of public emotion. The following year, the occupation of Smyrna developed into a catastrophic war with Turkey led by Mustafa Kemal Atatürk. The Greeks, either ill-advised or improperly restrained by the Allies, launched a general offensive in Anatolia. By September 1920 they were in full retreat.[5]

Greece appealed to the British to intervene while France entered into accord with Turkish leader Mustafa Kemal. Britain, itself unclear on policy in the Near East, was unable to rally its allies to a common policy. By 1922 Greece's position became desperate. In August of that year, the Turks launched a final offensive which drove the Greeks out of Anatolia amid brandishing swords, burning cities and crowds in panic, fleeing to the sea for evacuation and safety. This sad scenario marked one of the most tragic periods in modern Greek history.[6]

On Friday, September 8, 1922, the lead headline of the *Toronto Star* read, "Evacuation of Smyrna Begun by the Greeks."[7] The Near-East crises captured the attention of the Canadian public for several weeks in mid-September of that year. Other stories vying for second place included: "Prime Minister William Lyon Mackenzie King Opens Unemployment Conference in Ottawa"; "Record Year in Finances Reached by the Canadian National Exhibition"; and "Credit for the Complete Discovery of Insulin Given to Dr. F. B. Banting." Adjacent news reports proclaimed the Turkish leader Kemal's intent to pursue the Greek army into Thrace, the British government's determination to prevent his crossing the Dardanelles, and the British Labour leaders' warnings that the British public would not tolerate another war.

On October 20, 1922 Ernest Hemingway, at the time a reporter for the *Toronto Star*, described the tragic events that were beginning to unfold in Eastern Thrace:

> In a never-ending, staggering march, the Christian population of Eastern Thrace is jamming the roads to Macedonia. The main column crossing the Maritza river at Adrianople is twenty miles long, twenty miles of carts drawn by cows, bullocks and muddy flanked water buffalo, with exhausted, staggering men, women and children, blankets over their heads, walking blindly along in the rain beside their worldly goods.[8]

On September 18, 1922 Great Britain had invited Canada to be represented by contingents in the British force taking part in the defense of the neutral zone in the Near East. This announcement followed the semi-official statement by the British government that the effective and permanent freedom of the Dardanelles was of vital necessity.[9] At first, Canada was uncertain whether her support of the mother country was to be "actual and military or only moral."[10] However, following Prime Minister Churchill's request, the Canadian Department of Militia and Defense was flooded with offers of service from all parts of the Dominion. Battalions were ready to be dispatched from St. Catharines, Edmonton, Port Arthur, London and Vancouver.[11] Later, reports in the *Globe* indicated that the crisis in the Near East was exaggerated, and Canadian contingents were not necessary. Thus, Canada's response to Britain's request for assistance never actually materialized.

After the evacuation of Asia Minor, Greece accepted 1,221,848 refugees,[12] including approximately 100,000 Armenians.[13] This represented an increase equal to one-quarter of its prewar population.[14] The majority of the refugees who fled Turkish territory came from Asia Minor, Eastern Thrace and Pontos, although sizeable numbers also came from Bulgaria, the Caucasus, Constantinople, Russia, Serbia, Albania, Dodecanesos, Romania, Cyprus and Egypt.[15]

The Greek government, totally unprepared for dealing with the problem created by this sudden influx of refugees, solicited the aid of the League of Nations. In 1923 at the close of the Fourth Assembly and upon the suggestion of Dr. Nansen, the League's High Commissioner, a Committee for the Resettlement of Refugees was created containing provisions for facilitating an international loan to provide funds for the settlement of the refugees in Greece.[16]

Distribution centres were promptly established at all major ports of entry in Greece. Government officials were dispatched to settlement posts to oversee the processing of incoming refugees. Through a massive national effort, a major distribution program was established through which refugees were systematically resettled throughout Greece. The great majority were placed in areas that were left vacant by Moslem families who left Greece in the compulsory exchange of Moslem and Orthodox populations between Greece and Turkey, in accordance with the Treaty of Lausanne, 1923.[17] Approximately 60 per cent of the Greek refugees from Asia Minor eventually settled in Macedonia and Thrace. The remainder were dispersed throughout areas of Central Greece, the Aegean Islands, Crete and Epirus.[18]

Faced with the immediate problem of offering relief and shelter, Greece provided whatever dwellings were available. These ranged from houses specifically built by the state to "... requisitioned buildings ... warehouses ... barracks, schools, churches, inns, hospitals, railway carriages and tents...."[19] Many refugees suffered from cold and exposure[20] as well as infectious diseases such as malaria[21] and tuberculosis.[22] Others were suddenly confronted with the uncomfortable social stigma of their new "refugee" status.[23]

The Appeal to the Canadian Government

In October 1922 Greece inquired whether Canada would be willing to accept any refugees from Asia Minor.[24] The Canadian government's position was made very clear in a letter signed by J. C. Smith, superintendent of Emigration for Canada:

> The general conditions under which Canada can receive and care for emigrants require that such persons desiring admission to our Dominion should be of a class and have sufficient ability to assimilate with citizens of Canada and it has been held, time and again, that persons of the type and nationality above mentioned [Greek, Armenian, Russian] do not succeed in Canada and are not considered desireable immigrants. By this it is not exclusively meant that the people themselves are udesireables, but that their conditions of life, their training, their ability preclude their finding employment of a satisfactory character in Canada and ... indeed, all approaching Canada from these countries must necessarily submit to the stringent regulations that are in existence.[25]

At the turn of the century, Canada was in the midst of a massive international promotion campaign to attract farmers to settle and develop its western frontier.[26] Based on the notion of "nordic superiority," Canadian immigration laws reflected a preference for settlers from northern Europe, Scandinavia and Britain while southern and eastern Europeans were considered less able to assimilate and thus less desirable.[27]

Between 1900-20 three million immigrants—including large numbers of British labourers, American farmers and eastern Europeans—had entered Canada. Between 1901-22 Canada's population had increased by 43 per cent, and the proportion of immigrants in the country as a whole reached 22 per cent. In 1911 people of non-British and non-French origin formed 34 per cent of the population of Manitoba, 40 per cent of the population of Saskatchewan and 33 per cent of the population of Alberta.[28]

Many Canadian authors, writing on immigration in the early 1910s and 1920s, perceived immigrants as "service- or welfare-consumptive."[29] Indeed, it was not uncommon for these authors to be active in those institutions most involved with social change—that is, government, social welfare agencies or church organizations. As a result, at this time concerns about immigrants, including the Greeks from Asia Minor, were frequently examined within the context of program development and usually promoted the assimilationist program of the specific institution involved.[30] Although virtually all Canadian immigration authors espoused the need for cultural assimilation,[31] many authors refused to accept the assimilability of certain ethnic groups and joined those advocating more rigid regulations governing their entry into Canada.[32]

Despite the strict regulations of the Canadian Immigration Office regarding entrance of refugees from Asia Minor, a great majority of Greek immigrants did manage to enter Canada as "farmers," but then quickly moved to more lucrative employment in the country's urban centres.[33] Unfamiliar with the farming techniques and produce of a "flatter" and colder Canada, unwilling to accept the isolation of its rural areas, and lacking capital, these early Greek immigrants preferred to live in the cities. An urban environment offered the anxious new arrivals an opportunity for immediate employment. In expanding centres like Toronto, business and industry were often ready to use the services of unskilled labour. Those independent in spirit and venturesome of character soon struck out into small commercial enterprises of their own—a fruit or flower stand, an ice-cream parlour, a shoeshine shop, a confectionery store, a café, or perhaps even a small restaurant.

According to the Canadian census, by 1900 more than 250 Greek immigrants from mainland Greece had entered the country. By the outbreak of the First World War their numbers had risen to nearly 4,000, and by 1931 over 9,000 Greeks had immigrated to Canada.[34] Most came by way of Ellis Island, New York, on American-bound steamship lines. Those who entered Canada directly came through Halifax or Montreal and then continued by rail to Toronto, Vancouver and other smaller cities.

One must approach the early Canadian census figures, however, with some caution due to the confusing "nationality issue." Those Greeks who migrated from "unredeemed" Greece, that is, Greek territory still under Turkish rule—Greek Macedonia and Epirus before 1912, Thrace before 1920 and Asia Minor before 1922—of necessity entered Canada with Turkish passports. Those refugees who emigrated in subsequent years entered the country with Greek passports. By simply examining Canadian census figures, then, it is impossible to distinguish between Greek immigrants who came from Asia Minor, those who came from mainland Greece and Turks who came from Turkish territory.[35]

It must be noted, too, that a small influx of migrants from Asia Minor originated prior to the "Great Catastrophe." Prompted by a number of political and religious grievances against the Turks, the insecurity of life and property under Turkish rule and the requirement of rendering military service in the Turkish army (an outcome of the Young Turks Revolution of 1908), Greeks from "unredeemed" Greece began to emigrate in small numbers as early as 1900.[36]

In Toronto, for example, there were approximately fifty Greek immigrants from Asia Minor who had emigrated in the early 1910s. By 1918 there were over 100 residing in the city.[37] This group not only constituted the first major wave of Greek immigration to Canada but also represented the founding period during which the first Greek community in Toronto was established. By 1926 the number of Greek immigrants in Toronto from Asia Minor increased to approximately 200. This represented about one-fifth of the total Greek immigrant population (approximately 1,000) that had settled in Toronto up to that time. Indeed, many immigrants who entered Canada after 1922 through chain migration came to join families who had preceded them before the great exodus.[38]

The Social Adjustment of the Early Greek Immigrants from Asia Minor

The social adjustment of the early Greek immigrants from Asia Minor who settled in Canada was unusual due to their refugee status. For those who emigrated before 1922, once the outbreak of war began in Asia Minor and the mass evacuation of people was initiated all hopes for a return to their homeland were destroyed. If they had considered their stay in Toronto as temporary, they soon became resolved to permanent residence. Thus, for those prewar sojourners, immigration replaced migration. For those who entered Canada after 1922, the hope of returning to Asia Minor was shattered at the point of original departure. Having suddenly lost their property and possessions in the war, and being faced now with poor economic conditions in Greece, many left their refugee homes in search of a more secure financial and social position. Both groups, regardless of their year of arrival in Canada, were faced with the problem of coming to terms with the New World and adapting to a primarily Anglo-conformist institutional and cultural life.

With time, subtle changes in their identity began to take place. Their search for conformity in the face of the larger Anglo society contributed to the eventual disappearance of the sub-identity that originally marked their distinctiveness. The upheaval in Asia Minor, the loss of family, home and property, and the years of living under Turkish rule all contributed to the formation of an identity different from that of the mainland Greek immigrants. When the great exodus began and these Greeks were forced to flee to Greece, they had to contend with the additional social stigma of being perceived and treated as "refugees." Upon arrival in Canada, however, this distinction began slowly to fall away. Their new surroundings, similar needs and common shared experiences of life as immigrants in Toronto helped shape a unique Canadian ethnic identity different from that experienced in mainland Greece and different still from that experienced in Asia Minor.

Although no "interior" history of this Canadian immigrant group exists or research examining their frame of mind, their levels of expectations upon arrival, or their sense of permanence in the New World, an examination of the adjustment patterns of the Greek immigrants from Asia Minor offers us a unique understanding of the changing sentiments, intentions and ethnic identities of those who were forced to leave their homeland.

Women's Participation in Early Greek Institutional Life

Shortly after the First World War, political disharmony split Toronto's Greek community along the lines of the national disruption taking place in Greece. Defamation and slander were readily tossed about, social and religious relationships became strained and intra-group boycotts injured many business establishments.[39] As one informant observed, "The community was divided; the church was divided; even coffee houses were divided."[40] By 1923 friction became so intolerable that the small Greek Orthodox church on Jarvis Street, established in 1909, had to be shut down temporarily.[41] By 1930 political squabbles in Greece, repeated here in miniature, began to subside as the community once again found common interests.

Throughout the era of political infighting, the Greek population in Toronto continued to grow. By 1930 the Greek business sector, concentrated along Yonge and Dundas streets, was visibly expanding.[42] With a permanent Greek population of approximately 850 in 1921,[43] a small yet noticeable Greek residential area was developing around the St. George Greek Orthodox Church on Jarvis and Shuter streets.[44] As the community grew, so did the number of social institutions designed to ease the transition of the immigrants from Greece to Canada. Of particular interest to the Greek immigrant women of the community was the Greek Ladies' Philanthropic Society. This society, or Philoptoho as it was called, was founded in 1925 by Mrs. Maria Haraka, an immigrant from Smyrna, Asia Minor.[45] The Philoptoho served not only to encourage community solidarity in the midst of a strange and often threatening Anglo-conformist environment, but also helped mitigate the harshness of entry into Canadian city life for Greek migrants.

Philoptoho literally means "friends to the poor." The Greek Ladies' Philoptoho Society was also known as the Charitable Greek Church Fraternity or Sorority of Ladies. Such benevolent organizations were commonly formed wherever a Greek church was established. Although the first Greek Orthodox church in Toronto was founded in 1909, one can only speculate why its counterpart Philoptoho was not formed until sixteen years later. In 1909 there were approximately 200 Greeks in Toronto—most of them transient labourers. Although the early Greek immigrant influx was characterized by a strong male bias, by 1920 more women and children began entering Canada.[46] Perhaps the early Greek community's small numbers and scarcity of women precluded the formation of a Philoptoho Society. Perhaps the early Greek immigrants, closely knit as they were, were able to meet their own needs within the community without the aid of a formal society. Regardless of the reason for its late development, the Philoptoho Society once formed played a vital role in preserving community cohesiveness.

The pioneer ladies of the Philoptoho were considered the right hand of the church and as such always worked very closely with the priest of the Greek community. The members of the Philoptoho were exclusively women (the charter group numbered only a handful), its weekly meetings were held on the premises of the Greek Orthodox church and its objectives were purely philanthropic. As with most charitable organizations, not only were women considered more adaptable to the "caretaking" role but, so too, the appeal of conducting charitable work tended to attract only the more affluent members of the community. In Toronto the early members of the Greek Ladies' Philoptoho Society were the wives of the most prominent Greek businessmen of the community. Many women from Asia Minor were particularly active and helped develop the Philoptoho through its formative years. These women had greater freedom of movement and were familiar with participating in activities outside the home from the Old World.

Through church, collections, bake sales, community dances and the annual celebration of the Vassilopita (the cutting of the New Year's Bread), the Greek Ladies' Philoptoho Society of Toronto helped raise funds for a number of charitable objectives. For example, in the early twenties they helped purchase desks and other class-room furniture for the first after-four Greek school in Toronto. During the depression they provided clothing and food for the poor. They visited the sick in hospitals and homes, and they offered assistance in the burial expenses of the destitute. The society's influence, however, went beyond the confines of Toronto. After the great exodus from Asia Minor in 1922, the Philoptoho provided aid to the Greek refugees in mainland Greece. In 1945 it helped support the Greek War Relief Fund, an effort in which all Greek settlements across Canada and the United States joined together. The Philoptoho also helped furnish a room in the newly established New York City orphanage and initiated support for the Greek-American School of Theology in Pomfret, Connecticut.[47]

It must be noted that the home and family constituted the main sphere of influence of the Greek immigrant women in Toronto, and their purely voluntary participation in the Philoptoho did not conflict with their family values. The women were able to integrate their work in the Philoptoho with their domestic responsibilities. Their participation in the society was thus perceived as a mere extension of their "caretaking" role.

Another involvement which tended to attract particularly the Greek women of the community was the after-four language school. Women who participated in this institution by definition also entered the work place as wage-earners. However, their economic role in this arena similarly did not conflict with their domestic roles. Their participation in the Greek language schools not only helped fill a need within the community to formalize the communal desire for cultural continuity, but also was perceived as an amplification of their role as educators of the immigrant and Canadian-born children.

The pressing need to form a Greek language school to accommodate the community's youth became an increasing priority by the early 1920s as the number of Canadian-born second-generation children began to increase. Putting aside their political differences and aided by the women of the community, the Greek immigrants of Toronto in 1921 pooled their resources to establish the first Greek language parochial school. That same year, a Greek school was opened under the auspices of the St. George Greek Orthodox Church on Jarvis Street.[48] As in many Greek settlements across North America, the church served as the backbone of both the Greek community and the Greek school.[49] Indeed, the first responsibility traditionally relegated to the church was the establishment of a school and, in the early years, classes were often initiated under the guidance and tutelage of the priest himself.

Approximately fifty Greek children in Toronto, immigrant and Canadian-born, enrolled in the one-room school on the second floor of the church. Elementary classes began in both Greek and English. The church cantor taught Greek and an English-speaking teacher—approved by the Toronto Board of Education—taught English.[50] Although fees were nominal and texts were free, the all-day parochial school was soon converted to an after-four school where the language of instruction was confined to Greek only.

Since the reasons for such a conversion are difficult to ascertain, only speculation can be offered. Perhaps operating costs were prohibitive. Perhaps the Greek communal program ran counter to the official Toronto Board of Education standards. Or alternatively, perhaps the Greek parents' priority to teach their children English lay in the Canadian school system. Regardless of the reasons for the Greek school's conversion to an after-four program only, community support for the school remained strong.

By the mid-1920s an increasing number of refugees from Asia Minor began entering Canada and settling in Toronto. Many were well educated, of middle-class backgrounds and from an urban environment.[51] In 1925 Mrs. Smaro Pavlakis, a certified teacher educated in Constantinople, Asia Minor, and dissatisfied with the poor reception of the refugees in Greece, immigrated to Canada as a "picture bride."[52] She first established a household in Prince Rupert, British Columbia. Within a year, she and her husband moved to Toronto where she was hired by the Greek community to initiate and organize a new Greek afternoon school. She was joined in 1930 by Miss Sophie Samara (later Maniates), also a refugee from Kasaba, Asia Minor, and by a recent graduate of the Teacher's Academy in Mitilini.[53]

Although a number of other Greek immigrants from Asia Minor were able to find employment in the Greek afternoon school, sometimes temporarily (for example, Kleoniki Zerva, 1930-31, and Despina Mouhtari, 1933-37), it was Mrs. Pavlakis and Mrs. Maniates who succeeded in shaping the Greek elementary school system and in influencing the lives of the children of the early Greek immigrants in Toronto. Mrs. Pavlakis's teaching career lasted twenty-one years and Mrs. Maniates's lasted twelve years.[54]

The school conducted classes on the second floor of the church on Jarvis Street for over ten years, albeit with a minimum of furniture and curricular material and, as one student remembered, "primitive heating facilities that did not always work in the cold winters."[55] It moved in 1937 to a new location. In that year the present Greek Orthodox church at 115 Bond Street was purchased through the efforts of the president of the Greek community, who travelled thoughout the Province of Ontario to raise funds for the project.[56]

Dedicated to teaching and paid very little in the inaugural years of the school's operation, the Greek school teachers believed in and worked towards instilling the Canadian-born Greek children with an appreciation of their heritage. The Greek texts—principally published in New York, with some imported from Greece—tended to reflect a strong ethnocentric bias. Subjects taught included reading, writing, grammar, Greek geography, history, religious studies and mythology. Injunctions for cultural and linguistic maintenance among the increasing number of Canadian-born youth in the Greek community were echoed and re-echoed by the Greek Archdiocese in New York,[57] the Greek press, the church and the local community leadership in general.

However, instilling an appreciation for Greek language and culture did not always proceed smoothly. Although belatedly appreciative of the rudimentary knowledge of modern Greek, student informants readily recall the resentment they felt at having to attend a second school from 5:00–7:00 P.M. daily while their non-Greek schoolmates were free to play or engage in extra-curricular activities. The subject matter of the Greek school generally bore little relationship to their everyday life in Toronto and often seemed out of step with the world outside the school. As a result, and much to the exasperation of the teachers, students were often listless, tired and difficult to motivate.[58]

That parents, in contrast, showed dutiful and almost fervent support of the Greek school can be seen from the high enrolment. Financed by the payment of one or two dollars in fees per month per family, by supplementary weekly collections in the church and by the generous patronage of the Greek business sector of Toronto,[59] the Greek communal school grew slowly at first. By 1930 it had 150 students and by 1945 the enrolment rose to 230.[60]

With a Greek population in the city of approximately 1,200 at the beginning of World War Two, it appears that the majority of the approximately 250 Greek families then residing in Toronto must have helped to support the school.

Yet if numbers underscore the degree of community support for the school, they fail to explain the reasons for that support. It would be facile to argue that the teachers saw the school as a solid buttress against the assimilation of the Greek immigrant youth. While this element was present, the women from Asia Minor, who had already given up the expectation if not the dream of returning to their homeland, were themselves caught up in an endless series of adjustments necessary to "making it" in their new environment. The school, too, could not escape the uneasy tension between the two worlds. In its effort to capture the essence of the Greek culture, the school was forced to deny an urban North American Greek experience which provided both its *raison d'être* and its student body. The child who grew up in Toronto did not see the world through the eyes of his Greek-born, Old-World-educated teachers and, accordingly, questioned the curricular relevance of the Greek communal school. Nevertheless, while it is perhaps impossible to calibrate, the Greek after-four school, for all its problems, did help create a degree of Greek self-identity in immigrant and Canadian-born children, which in turn shaped their lives. And it is the work of a small group of women from Asia Minor that made it possible.

Although the exact number of immigrants from Asia Minor who gained entrance into Canada in the 1920s and 1930s is difficult to ascertain by simply examining Canadian census figures, the impact of this unique immigrant group on the formative years of institutional life in the Greek community of Toronto is evident. Through the Philoptoho Society and the Greek communal school, the Greek immigrant women of Asia Minor were able to help maintain community cohesiveness in the face of a new world, while at the same time themselves adjusting to the forces of a new and strange environment. The Greek Women's Philanthropic Association was founded by these women in response to the need to provide assistance for the Greek community's increasing immigrant population. The Greek school was established and developed in its early years by this same group of women in response to the community's need to maintain a sense of cultural continuity between the Old and New World cultures. The effort to promote the language of the homeland and to keep the Canadian-born second generation aware of their national heritage was the driving force behind the Greek school. And it was to the Greek women from Asia Minor that the role of cultural mediator between the Greek-born immigrant parents and their Canadian-born children was relegated.

Notes

1. The campaign for the annexation of lost territory with mainland Greece was often referred to as "The Great Idea." See T. Saloutos, "Greek-Americans and the Great Idea," in *The Greeks in the United States* (Cambridge, Mass.: Harvard University Press, 1964), pp. 169-84.
2. E. Polyzoi, "The Greek Communal School and Cultural Survival in Pre-War Toronto," *Urban History Review* (Special Issue: Immigrants in the City) 1, no. 2 (1978), pp. 74-79.
3. G. F. Abbott, *Greece and the Allies: 1914-1922* (London: Metheun, 1922), p. 32.
4. M. Housepian, *The Smyrna Affair* (N.Y.: Harcourt Brace Jovanich Inc., 1971), pp. 37-39.
5. M. L. Smith, "Catastrophe," in *Ionian Vision: Greece in Asia Minor, 1919-1922* (London: Allen Lane, 1973), pp. 284-311.
6. G. Horton, *The Blight of Asia* (Indianapolis: Bobbs-Merrill Co., 1926), pp. 112-67.
7. The *Toronto Star*, "Evacuation of Smyrna Begun by the Greeks," 8 September 1922, Sec. 1, p. 1.
8. The *Toronto Star*, "Exodus of Greeks in Eastern Thrace," 20 October 1922, Sec. 1, p. 1.
9. The *Globe* (Toronto), "Premier Summons Cabinet in Extraordinary Session to Consider Britain's Call," 18 September 1922, Sec. 1, p. 1.
10. The *Globe* (Toronto), 18 September 1922, Sec. 1, p. 1.
11. The *Globe* (Toronto), 18 September 1922, sec. 1, p. 1-2.
12. I. N. Angelis, *I Apokatastasis Ton Prosfigon Tou 1922* (The Resettlement of the Refugees of 1922) (Athens: Ministry of Social Services, 1973), p. 7.
13. Housepian, *The Smyrna Affair*, p. 208.
14. Angelis, *I Apokatastasis*, p. 11.
15. E. Sandis, "The Settlement of the Asia Minor Refugees in Greece," in *Refugees and Economic Migrants in Greater Athens* (Athens: National Centre of Social Research, 1973), p. 157.
16. *League of Nations*, "International Loan for Greek refugees and Other Works of the Financial Committee," Report of the Second Committee to the Fifth Assembly, Geneva, 27 September 1924.

17. For more detail on the exchange of populations, see A. A. Pallis, *Greece's Anatolian Venture and After* (London: Metheun and Co. Ltd., 1937), pp. 166-76.
18. Angelis, *I Apokatastasis*, p. 12.
19. *League of Nations*, Sixteenth Quarterly Report to the Refugee Settlement Commission, Geneva, 21 November 1922, p. 8.
20. *League of Nations*, Report to the 4th Assembly of the League of Nations on the Work of the Council, Geneva, 28 June 1923, p. 91.
21. *League of Nations*, Refugee Settlement Commission, 13th Quaterly Report, Geneva, 25 February 1927, p. 6.
22. *League of Nations*, Refugee Settlement Commission, 13th Quarterly Report, Geneva, 25 February 1927, p. 6.
23. See, for example, taped interviews with Smaro Pavlakis, 24 August 1977, and Angela Dallas, 18 November 1980. Such discriminatory attitudes lasted for over fifty years. As a result of the refugee legislative measures established in 1922, which served to protect all refugees and provide "special" treatment to Greeks from Asia Minor, an inadvertent government discriminatory practice was created. Feelings of resentment were evident among mainland Greeks towards this group of people who were receiving favoured government support. This lasted until December 1971, at which time the Greek government removed the word "refugee" from all protective legislation (see I. N. Angelis, p. 10).
24. Immigration Branch, RG 76, vol. 645, File 998358, Part 1, "Greek Immigration; 1908-1951," Public Archives of Canada.
25. Immigration Branch, RG 76, vol. 645, File 998358, Part 1, Public Archives of Canada.
26. H. Troper, *Only Farmers Need Apply* (Toronto: Griffin Press Ltd., 1972).
27. Ibid.
28. H. Palmer, "Mosaic versus Melting Pot: Reality or Illusion?" unpublished paper, Ontario Institute for Studies in Education, Toronto, 1976.
29. H. Palmer and H. Troper, "Canadian Ethnic Studies: Historical Perspectives and Contemporary Implications," *Interchange* 4, no. 4 (1973), p. 14.
30. Classic works reflecting this assimilationist attitude include: J. S. Woodsworth, *Strangers Within Our Gates* (Winnipeg: Methodist Church, 1909; reprinted, Toronto: University of Toronto Press, 1972); J. T. M. Anderson, *The Education of the New Canadian, a Treatise on Canada's Greatest Educational Problem* (Toronto: Dent, 1918); and R. England, *The Central European Immigrant in Canada* (Toronto: MacMillan, 1929).
31. See the representative articles by W. B. Hurd, "A Case for a Quota," *Queen's Quarterly* 36 (1928), pp. 145-59; W. A. Carrothers, "The Immigration Problem in Canada," *Queen's Quarterly* 36 (1929), pp. 517-31; A. Lower, "The Case Against Immigration," *Queen's Quarterly* 37 (1930), pp. 592-602; and L. Hamilton, "Foreigners in the Canadian West," *Dalhousie Review* 7 (1938), pp. 448-59.

32. H. Palmer and H. Troper, "Canadian Ethnic Studies," 1973.
33. Immigration RG 76, Vol. 645, File 998358, Part I, Public Archives of Canada.
34. *Census of Canada*, 1901, 1911, 1921, 1931.
35. It was not unusual, too, for the very early immigrants to have resided several years in the United States before settling in Canada, a phenomenon which further complicated Canadian Census immigration figures. See E. N. Papamanoli, *Perliptiki Historia Tou Kanada Ke Hellino-Kanados Odigos* (A Canadian-Greek Publishing Co., 1921-22).
36. Housepian, *The Smyrna Affair*, pp. 18-19; J. P. Xenides, *The Greeks in America* (N.Y.: George H. Doran Co., 1922), pp. 39-40.
37. Due to the confusion in immigration statistics for Canada (as addressed earlier) and because of the absence of any statistics for Toronto, these estimates were provided by a number of early immigrants from Asia Minor: see taped interviews with Smaro Pavlakis, 20 December 1983; Bill Dimopoulos, 27 June 1978; and Emily Andoniades, 14 December 1983. Despite their small numbers, by 1918 the immigrants from Asia Minor established a parochial club, "Karteria." Its membership consisted exclusively of immigrant men from various parts of Asia Minor, and its main concern was the welfare of the people whose region it served. Examples of families who emigrated before 1922 are: Maria, Angelos, Philitsa and Nick Killismanis; John, Mike, Sophoclese and Nick Haralambidis; Steele Basel; Andreas, Vassilios, Emanuel and Sophia Andoniades; Peter and Maria Marmaroglou; Gus and Stelios Barbarikis; Phillipas Basilaras; Alex Gremakos; Alex Christophorides; Eleftherios and Apostolos Dallas; Nick Solomos; George and Joseph Dimopolos.
38. Taped interview with Smaro Pavlakis, 24 August 1977.
39. Taped interview with Politemi Janetakis, 6 April 1977.
40. Taped interview with Peter Palmer, 13 October 1977. In Toronto the Greek coffee-houses became politically aligned according to either royalist or republican loyalties. The dominance of political discussions in the coffee-houses and their catering to clientele of similar political and regional loyalties was not uncommon. However tensions quickly broke out on a more emotional front. Because of the disagreement over the church chanting of the *polichronion* (hymn for the king), the Benezelist faction withdrew and soon took steps to initiate a new church. Although a second church was not actually established, separate services were held for some time afterwards. See L. Douramakou-Petroleka, "The Elusive Community: Greek Settlement in Toronto 1900-1940," in *Gathering Place: Peoples and Neighbourhoods of Toronto, 1934-1945*, ed. R. Harney (Toronto: The Multicultural History Society of Ontario, 1985), p. 268.
41. It must be noted that, in addition to the partisan conflict that existed within the community, the official policy of neutrality in the state of Greece created additional difficulties for the Greek immigrants in Toronto. Canadian officials who resented and were fearful of the

pro-German sentiments of the Greek government insisted on some form of official action for dealing with the presence of the "potential enemies among us." (See Public Archives of Canada, Immigration Branch, RG 76, vol. 645, File 998358, Part I, "Greek Immigration; 1905-1951.") On August 7, 1914, the *Globe* proposed the following plan to control the growing hostility of native Canadians: "Every member of a race hostile to us should be forced immediately to register and a passport should be issued to him without which he dare not leave his residence. Our foes should not be permitted to travel without authority and they should report immediately on arrival at their destination; must be indoors at dusk...." (The *Globe* (Toronto), "Is Canada at War? A Plea and some Advice to the Canadian People," 7 August 1914, Sec. 1, p. 6). Soon after, immigrant men in Toronto whose nationalities were associated with the enemy nations were required to report to the office of the Registrar for Alien Enemies on Adelaide Street. See also L. Petroff, "Macedonians: From Village to City," *Canadian Ethnic Studies*, IX, no. 1 (1977), pp. 29-41.

42. Papamanoli, *Perliptiki Historia*, pp. 341-74.
43. *Census of Canada*, 1921.
44. This was the general observation of a number of oral sources contacted. See taped interviews with: Maria Letros, 20 November 1976; Politemi Janetakis, 20 November 1977; Peter Palmer, 30 October 1977; Sophie Maniates, 15 August 1977; and Smaro Pavlakis, 24 August 1977.
45. G. Vlassis, *Greeks in Canada* (Ottawa: Le Clerc Printers, 1942), p. 44. Subsequently elected presidents include K. K. Kilismani (1930-31). Kleoniki Zerva (1931-32) and Despina Mouhtari (1933-37). All were immigrants from various parts of Asia Minor (Interview with Smaro Pavlakis, 11 May 1985).
46. Substantiated by *Census of Canada*, 1911, 1921, 1931. In 1911, for example, of the 3,594 Greeks listed in Canada, 3,064 were men and 530 were women. Of the 9,444 Greeks in 1931, 6,055 were men and 3,389 were women. By 1941 the number of males was still greater than females although the proportion was declining: 7,210 men to 4,482 women. Because the great majority of early arrivals were either boys or older males devoid of normal family relations, their adjustment was more difficult. This same male bias characterized the flow of Greek immigration to the United States as well. See G. Abbott, "A Study of the Greeks in Chicago," *American Journal of Sociology* 15 (1909), pp. 379-93; H. Balk, "Economic Contributions of the Greeks to the United States," *Economic Geography* 30 (1943), pp. 270-75; T. Saloutos, *The Greeks in the United States* (Cambridge: Harvard University Press, 1964), p. 45.
47. Mrs. Smaro Pavlakis and Mrs. Politemi Janetakis have donated a number of valuable documents to the Multicultural History Society of Ontario, which deal with the early history of the Greek Ladies' Philoptoho Society in Toronto. Among them is a copy of the original constitution of the first Greek Ladies' Philoptoho Society, Enosis,

a number of photographs of its early members and several pictures of their fund-raising activities. The official stamp adopted by the Greek Ladies' Philoptoho Society of Toronto was that of Mother Mary and Child—thus their title Enosis, or Union.

48. Papamanoli, *Perliptiki Historia*, p. 342.
49. The importance of the church in Greek settlements across North America has been documented by a number of Greek-American historians. See, for example, T. Saloutos, "The Greek Orthodox Church and Assimilation," *International Migration Review* 7 (1973).
50. Papamanoli, *Perliptiki Historia*, p. 342.
51. T. Saloutos, "The Greeks in the Unites States," *South Atlantic Quarterly* 44 (1945), p. 70.
52. This was not an uncommon practice among early Greek immigrants to Canada.
53. Taped interview with Sophie Maniates, 15 August 1977.
54. Taped interviews with Smaro Pavlakis, 24 August 1977 and Sophie Maniates, 15 August 1977. Note that both Mrs. Pavlakis and Mrs. Maniates also participated actively in the Philoptoho Society throughout its early years.
55. Taped interview with Mary Manetas (née Fallis), 4 December 1977.
56. Vlassis, *Greeks in Canada*, p. 43.
57. Although the Greek communal schools were formally under the jurisdication of the Greek Archdiocese of New York, they, nevertheless, enjoyed substantial freedom and independence.
58. This is what a number of former students expressed, taped interviews with Reta Harris, 26 July 1977; George Letros, 20 November 1976; Helen Janetakis, 27 November 1977; Mary Manetas, 10 December 1977.
59. Taped interviews with Sophie Maniates, 15 August 1977 and Smaro Pavlakis, 24 August 1977.
60. Taped interveiws with Sophie Maniates, 15 August 1977 and Smaro Pavlakis, 24 August 1977.

Contributors to Ethnic Cohesion: Macedonian Women in Toronto to 1940

Lillian Petroff

The majority of Macedonian males who first came to Toronto before World War One did not intend to stay. They were "target migrants," seasoned sojourners who came to earn good industrial wages. They lived frugally in the East and West Ends of the city taking advantage of cheap housing in the neighbourhoods (the Junction, Cabbagetown and the Niagara Street district) around and about their work sites. They were committed to using their hard earned salaries for the daily needs and rising expectations of their families and small holdings in the Old World.

The Macedonians' commitment to a temporary stay in Toronto was altered by the end of the Balkan War in 1913. The Ottoman Empire's long-standing and oppressive domination of Macedonia now gave way to the rigours of a Greek hegemony and repressive regime. Hopes for a freer Macedonia faded quickly when Bulgarian language schools and churches in Macedonia were ordered closed by the ruling Greeks. Villages were forced to billet Greek soldiers who conducted comprehensive searches for the hidden rifles and ammunition of rebellious peasants. This unhappy situation in the old country convinced the men abroad that their future and that of their families lay in the New World. As sojourners, the suitors, husbands and fathers worried about the survival and well-being of their womenfolk and children left behind. As settlers, they continued to do so; their concern inspired their decision to bring their families to Toronto.

The purpose of this article is to examine the role of women within the context of Macedonian migration history, settler work and enterprise, group religion and politics in Toronto before 1940; to study perceptions—how women in transition saw themselves and others.

Marriage and new households, but more especially family reconstruction in the form of young wives coming to Canada, was the central fact of the ethnic group in the 1920s. It created a community of families, but involved a peculiar cultural gap. Brides who, more often than not, had been left behind—since the preparation time needed by women to come over (e.g., the acquisition of passports, etc.) proved incompatible with their husbands' need to maximize earnings versus costs in seasonal migration or sojourning—arrived in numbers, but not until their odyssey had been further delayed by World War One. Typically, a tailor from Gabresh, who had married in 1914, remembered that he could only bring out his wife in 1920 after the "roads opened up."[1] In fact, the Toronto settlement received not just more womenfolk, but women who had lived through a further decade of Macedonian history, who lacked their husbands' sense of the New World and needed the linguistic and cultural reassurances of an ethnic community.

The majority of bachelor settlers chose to write their families, asking them to select and dispatch acceptable girls as prospective brides. Characteristics and attributes that were demanded for Old-World unions now became the stuff of New-World marriages. These prospective brides were expected to be chaste and to come from families of good repute. For as residents of Zhelevo argued, "even when you choose a dog it must be from a good stock." They also had to demonstrate a flair and capacity for hard work. Gina Petroff's hard work at the riverside (e.g., fetching water, washing clothes) and in the fields, during the planting and harvesting seasons, made her one family's choice as a bride for their son, a barber thousands of miles away in Toronto's Junction area. Similarly, Tina Vassil found herself sent as bride-to-be to an East-End restaurateur. In her case, her diligence and good nature so impressed the restaurateur's landowning family that it was willing to overlook the sins of her father, who had been stripped of his share of the family holdings because of his marriage to a Greek.[2]

Few, if any, girls came out on their own initiative to seek their fortunes or find a husband. A Macedonian village woman went from being a man's daughter to being a man's wife. Fathers and husbands-to-be wanted their women to stay within these perimeters, and older females abetted this system of a male-centred society. Female conduct was monitored; men made their thoughts and expectations known. Preparing to leave for Toronto, Gina Petroff was cautioned by her father who said: "[You] find some trouble, the boy don't want, I can take you home when you come [return to the village]. But if it's trouble from you, you say,'I don't want this boy, I'll go home,' I'll gonna put your head in the stove."

A women who is reputed to have declared on her arrival at Union Station, "So this is the country where the men work and the women are bosses!" was immediately bundled back on the train and sent home by her aghast fiancé. Believing that the New World held many temptations, dangerous freedoms and opportunities for their womenfolk, thinking men felt they had good reason to worry.[3] Moreover, to the extent that women had worked as field hands in the old country and the men emulated *comitadjis* (freedom fighters—like a warrior class), there were adjustments to be made in Canada.

The girls who were selected as brides remember making their way to the New World in a combined state of fear and happiness. They were glad to escape political turbulence, the unwanted attentions or brutalities of billeted Greek soldiers and back-breaking farm chores. They were also fearful of marrying men whom they knew about, usually from fellow villagers, but did not know personally. As a Junction bride recalled: "When I come over here [Toronto] I'm lost. I never know even my husband. I know his people, but I never know him." Many tears were shed between Cherbourg and Halifax.[4]

The women made their way to the New World over well-worn chain and travel routes. Indeed the business of bringing out brides became just that, allowing some men to make money as go-betweens. These guides were men who had the time and opportunity to travel along the Toronto-to-villages communications network. Many possessed English-language skills and Canadian citizenship papers, both of which facilitated their flow along the migration route. Stavro Gemandoff, a West-End slaughterhouse worker, took up the go-between role shortly after losing an arm in a stockyard accident. The small service fees paid by waiting husbands and fiancés to Stavro for going back and forth to Macedonia to shepherd out prospective brides provided him with income to tide him over until he was able to take up light duties at the slaughterhouse again.

Such go-betweens guided women through the train stations and port cities of Europe. Stavro Gemandoff escorted Gina Petroff—"like a little child going to buy candy"—and a friend from Bobishta in Macedonia to the Junction in Toronto. The young brides-to-be in their teens had never been outside their village area. Other go-betweens worked only the North American port cities, escorting wives and brides-to-be from Halifax, Nova Scotia, and Ellis Island, New York, to the inland settlements. Using the Hotel Balkan in New York City as his temporary base of operations, Vasil Trenton, a Toronto restaurateur and part-time go-between, successfully arranged with officials of the "Canadian Office" to escort twelve women from Ellis Island to Toronto.[5]

For the brides-to-be, marriage took place soon after arrival. Old-World weddings were characterized by elaborate week-long celebrations which included processions and receptions held by the parents of the bride and groom respectively. In Toronto lengthy ritual gave way to the demands of urban life and the work place; there evolved a spartan one-day wedding celebration. Simple foods were prepared for the reception by guests and friends of the couple. Celebrants danced to the music of a gramophone or *gaida* (native pipes) if an accomplished player was present. Married on a Sunday, a Junction barber opened his shop for business on Monday morning. An affluent East-End butcher and his wife honeymooned by taking evening drives after work.[6]

Many of the wives came to Canada reluctantly. Sorry to leave friends and relatives behind, frightened at the prospect of living in intimacy with men they had not seen for a decade, they came because the ethnoculture required them to do so, or because they feared trying to survive without a mate. Some, however, simply refused to come. Recalling the reluctance of her mother to come to the New World, an immigrant woman said: "Father [a former sojourner] wanted to bring the family to America. Mother scared. Nobody here. [sic] she never come." Such women watched their children come of age and leave for America to marry and take on family obligations. For them, the migration system and the myth of America meant only loneliness and broken families. In other cases, husbands who chose to stay in Canada did not send for their wives in the village. Some women made the decision to come in spite of their husbands. They mortgaged property or borrowed passage money from relatives and travelled to husbands in Canada who had perhaps become too fond of bachelorhood, or found other female companionship.[7]

Most women got a rude introduction to Toronto after the clean open spaces of the village: smoke, grime, identical squalid and boxlike houses greeted them as they met urban industrial life and Canadian society head on. A new bride arriving in the West End summed up her first impressions of her new home and neighbourhood by saying, "most houses look same to me, only [the] numbers are different." A woman who came to join her brothers in Toronto was appalled at having to live in a "shack on Tecumseth

Street." In her home village of Oshchima, she had lived in a six-room house with two balconies, paid for with money that her migrant father had earned in the New World.

Female Macedonian newcomers often demonstrated a critical sense and eye to match that of the city medical officer, Dr. Hastings—a student and critic of foreign quarters and slum neighbourhoods. Seasoned sojourners, men who had worked in or near European towns and cities, on the other hand, accepted matter-of-factly the less attractive aspects of the new urban way of life.[8] Like all greenhorns, the newly immigrated womenfolk had little time for reflection. Each had the private task of coming to grips with mates they sometimes barely knew and an ambience totally foreign to them. They were required to adjust quickly and take their place in the family as an efficient economic unit.

Traditionally performing a variety of material and domestic tasks, Macedonian women in the old country played a vital role in their families' search for economic stability. They concerned themselves with the demands of child-rearing and the production of their families' food and clothing. They baked an assortment of breads and pastries and produced large quantities of butter and cheese. Beginning with the preparation and spinning of sheep and goats' wool, Macedonian women went on to sew and mend a variety of garments. The preparation of a trousseau in the form of bridal linens, embroidered shirts and handkerchiefs provided the optimum challenge to the women's patience, energy and skills.

Within the household compound, women concerned themselves with stock-breeding and so raised chickens, lambs and goats. In the nearby fields, they both planted and harvested a number of crops, including wheat, hay, tomatoes, peppers and potatoes. The fields were worked primarily by hand and hoe; the men alone used the plough and scythe.[9] All of these activities saved on expenses, brought in cash and defined the family's economic status. Economic activity was not confined to their families' holdings as women frequently extended the bounds of their labour. Those particularly skilled in the art of knitting or embroidering often produced clothing for other families of the village. Poor harvests sometimes prompted the women of Tersie to obtain additional employment as harvesters on the more affluent holdings of a Turkish landowner.[10]

With the mass migration of males becoming customary, life and roles in the villages changed for Macedonian women. They played a greater part in supervising the family property and did heavier labour; they ploughed or had to manage hired help.[11] Women were also forced to conduct family business beyond the village boundaries. Long-standing concern for the honour and safety of women had resulted in the creation of tight social controls which governed their movements. Trips by women to the neighbouring villages, towns or cities had generally been discouraged in the past. The number and frequency of trips to other towns increased considerably with the men's absence. For example, groups of women from the village of Tersie now led horses bearing the supply of chopped wood for sale to the city markets. Their men had done that work before migration.[12]

Macedonian women then were ready to work when they came to Toronto. They became boardinghouse keepers. Young brides oversaw the resources of the house, cooked meals, washed clothes, scrubbed floors and tended to a host of other family and tenant needs. One East-End woman also performed banking tasks, depositing pay packets entrusted to her in the male boarders' accounts. It was through collecting board and rent money and minimizing household expenses that women helped to build their families' income.[13]

The wives of storekeepers also assisted their husbands at work. At first shy and lacking a working command of the English language, Macedonian women found it difficult to deal with strangers or to assist in the business without fully comprehending language meanings and business practice. Describing her first attempts to help her husband in the family grocery store, a woman recalled: "That time everyone worked with scales and pencil. I wasn't very fast in counting. Then my husband bought a cash register for me and then we was both happy."[14] Numerous business hurdles were overcome only through sheer persistence and great effort on the part of immigrant wives. Over time many seemed to replace their husbands as chief proprietors of small businesses, freeing them for other business or leisure activities.

The wife of a West-End shoeshine parlour operator made herself indispensable to her husband when she mastered the art of cleaning and blocking hats.[15] Another woman was so successful in managing the family's haberdashery that her husband was able to work at the A.F. Schnaufer fur and dye works in order to supplement the family income.[16] The wife of a West-End barber and grocer, as she learned English, permitted her husband to concentrate on his barbering duties while she took charge of the grocery's daily operations. Her regular work included serving customers during the factories' lunch breaks, ordering and arranging an endless stream of tobacco, refreshment and confectionery supplies and making daily trips to the nearby slaughterhouses with a wagon to purchase ice blocks for the store's cooler.[17]

Macedonian women generally did not enter domestic service, an occupation which drew a great number of other immigrant women. The absence of Macedonian women in domestic service was probably due to recruiting practices. Responding to the demand for servants, such agencies as the National Council of Women, Young Women's Christian Association and the various church organizations of both Britain and Canada recruited British and Scandinavian girls exclusively. It is highly unlikely that southeastern European girls were considered suitable. Hence, domestic service occupations long remained the preserve of British and Scandinavian immigrants.[18] The main reason, however, for the absence of Macedonian women in the job market was that few if any came to Toronto except as brides and wives, and their menfolk found ample scope for their productive energies within the family entrepreneurial unit.

The growing shift of Macedonians from factory work to keeping shops and restaurants offered many job opportunities to the younger members of the family. Parental pressure and economic necessity forced the children to obtain summer and after-school employment. Many young boys and girls in the Macedonian community worked as attendants in family-owned shoeshine parlours, or as dishwashers, sometimes doubling as translators, in family restaurants. The daughter of an East-End butcher remembered working from a very young age in her father's store every Saturday and each day after school. There she would arrange various foodstuffs on the counter, take cash and place pieces of meat in the grinder, a task which eventually was to rob her of a finger.[19]

Women also worked in factories. Those unmarried daughters who did join the work-force found employment in the city's meat-packing houses. As an employee of the William Davies Company, one woman was involved in the production of sausage casings, fancy pickles and olives. Macedonian women did join the needle trades, though on a much smaller scale than Jews and Italians. As employees of the Beaver Cloak Company, York Knitting Mills and Joseph Simpson and Sons, they worked at fashioning sweaters, coats and buttonholes.[20]

The presence of young women in the factories was often the result of economic necessity. Their role working in the stores and shops of their husbands and fathers was natural, but it should be measured alongside the countervailing opinion which held that a woman's place was in the home, preparing for marriage or performing the duties of a wife and mother. One immigrant woman recalled bitterly the stinging criticism she received from a friend for working in her husband's shoeshine parlour. She was chastised for not remaining at home and accused of wantonly seeking the attention of her male customers.[21]

Although work occupied the bulk of their time and energy, Macedonians also knew when and how to relax and play. Men relaxed in the company of other men—wives and families were excluded from the coffee-houses. Outside the informal ethnicity of the male hang-outs, most of their leisure time activities had specific ethnic content and emblematics. In church, at the athletic society, or at meetings, their gatherings were both consciously concerned with Macedonian nationalism and subconsciously an assertion of Canadian-Macedonian ethnicity. Women operated on a smaller and more familial scale. Their leisure activities were inextricably bound up with the business of minding children. Groups of Macedonian mothers socialized at Sunnyside and High Park as they watched their children play. They also met at each other's houses. In the East End women gathered to knit, crochet and have coffee together. Although such gatherings were informal or connected with specific aspects of the liturgical year, women's leisure and ethnic in-gathering were not dismissed by the men. Rather they were part of the coherence of ethnicity.

In the West End the wife of a shoeshine parlour operator could enlist her husband's help when it was her turn to entertain friends and neighbours. An accomplished performer on the *gaida*, the proprietor would close his store in order to "play for the girls" as they drank coffee and ate *zelnik*. These social gatherings easily transformed themselves into a structure of assistance in times of illness or maternity confinement. Friends came to visit as well as to perform the daily housekeeping chores such as laundry, cooking and cleaning in order to keep households running as smoothly as possible and to provide time for rest and recuperation. In that sense, neighbourhood women or those from the same village had their own informal ethnic benevolent societies.[22]

Ironically, women did not have a formal role or presence in group mutual benefit societies and brotherhoods until the societies evolved into social clubs, playing a role as centres of immigrant culture while members' working conditions and incomes became the responsibility of the government, insurance companies and labour unions in the period after 1940. The Skopia (Nevoliany) Benevolent Society thus began to offer membership of equal standing to both men and women who were eighteen years of age or over. The Banitsa Benevolent Society "Hope," in its later years, had an active and influential ladies section. The Zhelevo Brotherhood offered memberships to men of any nationality who expressed an interest in the organization and were married to women of Zhelevo family background. However, the brotherhood, unlike its counterparts, steadfastly refused to grant memberships to women. Women, of any nationality, could only acquire "honorary" membership if they "rendered invaluable service to the brotherhood."[23] In contrast, women had easier entrée into the church, SS. Cyril and Methody, and the nationalist Macedonian Political Organization (MPO).

The years in which the church—founded in 1910—struggled to create an identity as centre of the ethnic community and to define its relationship to being Macedonian and to Macedonian exile nationalism also involved a revolution in folkways and mores over the female role in religious and community life. Women, as wives and fiancées, came in numbers to the Macedonian settlement areas of Toronto at the conclusion of the Balkan and First World War. SS. Cyril and Methody Church—through its 1918 Executive Committee—for example, thought about adding female washroom facilities for the first time during the course of church basement renovations in that year.[24]

Church and religious matters had long been the preserve of the village priest and elders in the old country. Women had entered the church as worshippers, candle-makers and caretakers, dusting and washing walls on a regular basis especially after weddings and other hectic religious celebrations.[25] While they continued to make candles in the church back room on Saturday afternoons, Macedonian women in North America enjoyed a marked increase in their level of church participation and influence. As members of the parish and the Macedonian Political Organization, women became enthusiastic participants and instructors in SS. Cyril and Methody's various educational, athletic and cultural programs. Young ladies in the Bulgarian language school—Bulgarian was the language of liturgy and literature—and the Macedonian Unak (athletic society) had the opportunity, for example, to come under the spirited tutelage of more emancipated women such as Vera Matova and Mary Evanoff.[26] Women also enjoyed opportunities to perform in plays and concerts. They also sang in the church choir which had been all male.[27]

It was the women who gave the larger host community some sense, albeit at a minimal folklore level, of Macedonian culture, who showed that behind the half-acculturated and rough ways of labourers and countermen lay a sensitive and aesthetically rich culture. The women also mounted popular and prize winning embroidery displays at the Canadian National Exhibition.[28]

Beyond the social and cultural sphere, women took part in the decision-making processes of the church; they helped to determine who would be tenants of the parish hall. However, it is important to note that they had no official role to play when church committees became involved in the structure and workings of the Macedonian family. In 1923, for example, Pavel Vasileff came before the Church Committee to ask for help with his marital problems. He was "complaining that his wife, Anka, left him without any cause and [he] begs the church committee to do something and call her to advise her to come back to him."

Inspired by the Internal Macedonian Revolutionary Organization (IMRO), —an Old-World political movement which had complemented its political activities with family and social reforms— ever mindful of the reputation of the collectivity and subscribing to the notion of "let's settle it among ourselves not in the civil courts," the 1923 Church Committee established a commission to deal with this and other cases, which was composed of the priest, Rev. Velik Karajoff, and the following church members and officers: Kuzo Temelkoff, Georgi Dineff, Naum Phillips, Grigor Stoyanoff and Elia Vasileff.[29]

The Macedonian Political Organization's sensitivity to the role of women, likewise, grew quickly; women had long been participants in the Old-World nationalist struggle. A few, like Mara Buneva, gained a measure of notoriety as nationalist fighters and assassins. In the old country women acted as messengers and gun-runners who moved quietly through the night with their supplies from the villages to the *comitidjis* mountain retreats. Legends of female bravery, especially their ability to keep silent about the revolutionary effort before all manner of inquisitors, grew. In North America women played a part in Macedonian national politics through membership in the various Ladies' Sections of the MPO (one should note the archaic civility of the use of Ladies rather than Women).

The first Ladies' Section of the MPO in North America was founded in Toronto, March 13, 1927. The Toronto settlement had received many women in the immediate postwar years; it seems likely that American immigration law slowed the arrival of women there and the process of family reconstitution. Therefore, it was natural that Toronto had the first Ladies' Section. Toronto members took a great deal of pride in this fact of their organizational history and, as a result, felt obliged to take a kind of leadership role in MPO conventions. "As the founders of... Ladies' Sections we ask every Macedonian woman to join us in the struggle for [a] *Free* and *Independent* Macedonia." Membership fees were initially set at ten cents a month or one dollar and twenty cents per annum. By the 1930s annual membership fees for women had increased to three dollars. Payment of these dues was not taken lightly: "Ten cents meant an awful lot to us. You could buy an ice cream cone for five cents. [There] wasn't that much money around, and we had to save that just to pay our dues. I was very proud just to be in it."

The MPO Ladies' Section was at the forefront of the church's and community's social life. Tea parties, dances, *vecherinki* (entertainment evenings) and a host of religious and political celebrations were all organized and orchestrated in the SS. Cyril and Methody parish hall not by a parish women's association, but by the Ladies' Section of the Toronto chapter, MPO "Pravda," which was founded in 1922.[30]

As we have seen in the Old World, Macedonian women had distinct social and economic roles, obligations and restrictions. As Christian village women, they had assessed their lives in the context of the Vlach mountain women, Greek and Jewish town women and veiled Turkish wives around them. They knew well before arrival in Toronto that there were many ways of being a woman, roles to accept and reject, status to aspire to or refuse. In Toronto they responded to the real conditions of the economy and what they thought they knew to be the ways of women in Anglo-Canadian society. What emerged was neither a father-dominant nor a mother-centred household. Gender roles were distinct, but authority and duty in the family were fluid or blurred since they related to the constantly changing ethnoculture itself. Although they stayed out of the coffee-houses and nationalist debates, women played an active and often opinionated role in the running of family enterprises and households. No one of the immigrant generation questioned that the nuclear family should be a single economic, entrepreneurial unit. It was, however, more often "a joint stock company" than a venture owned and run by the male family head. As their new lives took shape in the three settlement areas of Toronto, Macedonian families cast a critical and evaluative eye upon themselves and the non-Macedonians around them.

Women took stock and compared themselves with others as mothers and housekeepers. They believed that they were more concerned and involved in the lives of their children than Anglo-Canadian mothers were. A Macedonian mother was "more warm for the kids. The mother dies for the kids. The English don't like their children that much." Macedonians also saw themselves as good and efficient housekeepers with a commitment to cleanliness that pleased both landlords—"she [landlord] look around... her new house clean. First time the house clean"—and visiting public health nurses. In *Cabbagetown* novelist Hugh Garner gives an interesting account of "European immigrant women" who aired their mattresses and "washed down their front porches and steps every day." He was writing about the Macedonian East End of Toronto.

The immigrant women prided themselves, often long after economic justification for such parsimony was gone, on how carefully they could budget and still put on a good meal for their family. Macedonian children were always clothed adequately even if their garments were often crafted out of the adults' used clothing. The memory culture recalls that some other ethnic groups were not as concerned with this. Items like bed sheets and curtains were made from flour and sugar sacks provided by family or group restaurateurs. First cut and split along their seams, sacks were then washed and bleached; these prepared pieces were joined together to make different size clothes and sheets. Macedonian women were, thus, proud of their ability to survive, if not thrive, in poverty when compared to non-Macedonians.[31]

As they moved from a village structure to a Macedonian ethnic enclave in Toronto, women experienced an intricate shifting of psychological gears. Encounters with Canadian society-at-large made womenfolk and the immigrant community modify, abandon or, alternatively, assert with even more resolve many of their folkways and mores.

Notes

1. Interview with Mrs. V. Dimitroff, 26 August 1976, Oral History Collection, Multicultural History Society (MHSO). (All interviews were conducted by the author unless otherwise stated.)
2. F.S. Tomev, *Short History of Zhelevo Village Macedonia* (Toronto: Zhelevo Brotherhood, 1971); interviews with Mrs. G. Petroff, 27 October 1976; and Mrs. T. Vassil, 2 December 1975, MHSO.
3. Interviews with Mrs. G. Petroff by R.F. Harney, 15 January 1977, MHSO; memorandum of an unrecorded conversation with Mrs. G. Petroff, 9 December 1979, MHSO.
4. Interview with Mrs. G. Petroff by R.F. Harney, 15 January 1977, MHSO. See also interviews with Mrs. F. Nicoloff, 15 August; Mrs. T. Vassil, 2 December 1975; and Mrs. R. Pappas, 23 January 1976, MHSO.
5. Interview with Mrs. G. Petroff, 27 October 1976, MHSO; interview with Mrs. G. Petroff by R.F. Harney, 15 January 1977, MHSO;

interview with Mr. Vasil Trenton, 19 January 1978, MHSO. See also the Trenton family collection of documents at MHSO; R.F. Harney, "Primary Sources," *Canadian Ethnic Studies* IX (1977), pp. 60-76.

6. Interviews with Mrs. C. Lewis, 22 September 1977; Mrs. G. Petroff, 13 December 1975; Mrs. G. Petroff, 29 June 1975, MHSO; Tomev, *Short History of Zhelevo Village Macedonia*, pp. 109-23, 134.
7. Interviews with Mr. B. Stefoff, 17 December 1975; Mrs. B. Markoff, 9 December 1957; Mrs. F. Tomev, 13 February 1976; Mrs. G. Petroff, 13 December 1975, MHSO.
8. Interviews with Mrs. Fanche T. Nicoloff, 15 August 1975, MHSO; Mrs. Donna Spero, 29 November 1975, MHSO; Mrs. R. Pappas, 23 January 1976, MHSO.
9. Lillian Petroff, "The Macedonian Community in Toronto to 1930: Women and Emigration," *Canadian Women's History Series* V (Toronto: Department of History and Philosophy of Education, Ontario Institute for Studies in Education, 1977). Also interview with Mrs. M. Kercheff, 25 November 1976, MHSO; Tomev, *Short History of Zhelevo Village Macedonia*, p. 9.
10. Ibid.; interview with Mr. and Mrs. B. Stefoff, 17 December 1975, MHSO.
11. This is the general opinion of all oral history sources consulted.
12. Ibid.; also interview with Mr. and Mrs. B. Stefoff, 17 December 1975, MHSO.
13. Interviews with Mrs. G. Petroff, 21 January 1976; Mrs. H. Petroff, 17 July 1975; Mrs. H. Paliarc, 15 July 1975, MHSO.
14. Interview with Mrs. F. Nikoloff, 15 August 1976, MHSO.
15. Interview with Mrs. D.K. Thomas, 25 February 1978, MHSO.
16. Interview with Mrs. H. Petroff, 17 July 1975, MHSO.
17. Interview with Mrs. G. Petroff, 21 January 1976, MHSO.
18. G. Leslie, "Domestic Service in Canada, 1880-1920," *Women at Work: Ontario 1850-1930*, eds. J. Acton, P. Goldsmith and B. Sheppard (Toronto: Canadian Women's Educational Press, 1974), p. 87.
19. Interviews with Mr. T. Jangel, 24 November 1975, Prof. B.P. Stoichef, 28 January 1976, and Mrs. Sophie Pandoff, 30 March 1977, MHSO.
20. Interviews with Miss H. Stamenova, 6 May 1976, Mrs. Sophie Florinoff, 23 February 1977, and Mrs. D.K. Thomas, 25 February 1978, MHSO. Macedonian women generally quit their factory jobs after marriage. Therefore, they did not have a long and sustained presence in the world of industry.
21. Interview with Mrs. D.K. Thomas, 25 February 1978, MHSO.
22. Interviews with Mrs. S. Pandoff, 30 March 1977, Mrs. T. Jassil, 2 December 1975; Mrs. D.K. Thomas, 25 February 1978; and Mrs. G. Petroff, 29 June 1975, MHSO.
23. Skopia (Nevoliany) Benevolent Association, *Constitution* (Toronto, 1956) p. 2, see Article IV, Section A. Banista Benevolent Society "Hope," *Constitution*, p. 25; Zhelevo Benevolence Brotherhood, *The Constitution and By-Laws of the Zhelevo Brotherhood*, p. 4, see Article XI.

24. SS. Cyril and Methody Macedono-Bulgarian Orthodox Cathedral, *Protocol*, no. 9, 1 September 1978.
25. Interview with Mrs. Lennie Vassil, 2 December 1975, MHSO; memorandum of an unrecorded conversation with Mrs. G. Petroff, 18 February 1980, Macedonian Collection MHSO.
26. SS. Cyril and Methody Macedono-Bulgarian Orthodox Cathedral, *50th Anniversary Almanac, 1910-1960* (Toronto: 1960), pp. 68-75; interviews with Mrs. Chris Lewis, 22 September 1977, and Mrs. Mara Kercheff, 25 November 1975, MHSO.
27. *50th Anniversary Almanac*, pp. 41, 65.
28. Interview with Mrs. Fanche T. Nicoloff, 15 August 1975, MHSO.
29. *Protocol*, no. 20, 8 June 1923; memorandum of an unrecorded conversation with F.S. Tomev, 10 December 1979, Macedonian Collection. IMRO, for example, advised village women not to waste their energies on intricate embroidery. Needlework designs were to be kept simple.
30. Macedonian Political Organization (MPO), *16th Annual Convention Almanac* (Indianapolis, 1937), p. 14. Interview with Mrs. Sophie Florinoff, 23 February 1977, MHSO; see the Ladies' Section membership cards, 1928, 1929, 1930, 1936 and 1937, in Mrs. Blazo Markoff family documents collection, MHSO.
31. Interview with Mrs. D. Spero, 29 November 1975, MHSO; Hugh Garner, *Cabbagetown* (Toronto: Simon and Schuster of Canada, Ltd., 1975), p. 274; interviews with Mrs. Nicoloff, 15 August 1975; Mrs. Lennie Vassil, 2 December 1975, MHSO.

Creating and Sustaining an Ethnocultural Heritage in Ontario: the Case of Armenian Women Refugees

Isabel Kaprielian

From the multilingual and multi-ethnic societies of the Middle East, Armenians immigrating to Canada in the early twentieth century brought with them an awareness of cultural distinctiveness, as well as traditions and techniques of ethnonational survival. For them to function as a viable minority in North America and still be a contributing component to North American society was neither incongruous nor contradictory. The fact that North America was Christian would be, they thought, an additional factor in facilitating their adjustment to Canada. The Armenians of southern Ontario, accordingly, sought to maintain their ethnoculture and at the same time to acculturate to Canadian society. This article examines the part played by Armenian women—traumatized refugees, survivors of a modern Genocide—in preserving their ethnocultural heritage from 1919-39. Many aspects of their experience in Canada were rooted in traditions that for centuries had set the Armenians apart from neighbouring peoples. These national particularities interacted with their refugee background and with their immigrant experience in Canada to produce a generation of women pioneers who helped to save the Canadian Armenian community from extinction.

Religion and language were integral parts of the Armenian heritage. In 301 A.D. Armenians accepted Christianity as a state religion; for the next 1700 years they struggled to retain their faith, and hence their identity, in the face of repeated conquests by non-Christians determined to convert them.[1] Christianity became the focus for the Armenian language and literature when the

Armenian alphabet was created under the direction of the monk, Saint Mesrob, at the beginning of the fifth century A.D.. This important event was followed by a period of rich and extensive literary activity during the fifth century, known as the Golden Age of Armenian literature.

When the Turks conquered the Armenian homeland, they excluded Christians from participation in the political and military life of the country and relegated them to the status of a religious nation or millet. In spite of 600 years of forced conversions and attempts at Turkification, Armenians clung tenaciously to their religion and language.

During the nineteenth century the Armenian vernacular tongue displaced the liturgical or *grapar* language in the written word. "A slumbering people began to awaken" as a resurgence of Armenian literary and educational activity "spread light, like a candle, among the masses." This *Zartonk* or renaissance was also influenced by the life and work of Protestant missionaries who brought modern Western ideas and expertise to Armenians and by Armenian youth who had studied in Europe and America and returned to disseminate progressive ideas and methods to their people. Underpinning these movements was the spread of Armenian national feeling and self-consciousness.

The schools stood out as powerful agents of enlightenment, and in this arena women played a critical role. One of their outstanding achievements was the formation of the Patriotic Armenian Women's Association in 1879, which in turn founded the Armenian Women's Educational Institute in Constantinople. In its initial annual report, the association emphasized its dedication to recruiting and training women as teachers, to raising the consciousness of Armenian women and to facilitating the education of Armenian girls throughout the country. Women educators like Zabel Asadour and writers like Zabel Essayan and Serpouhi Dusap regarded teaching not only as a pedagogical undertaking, not only as a career, but also as a sacred and patriotic duty: by uplifting the backward masses, the Armenian people and the empire itself would become more enlightened and progressive. Despite constraints on their behaviour because of Islamic traditions and strict Turkish government censorship, Armenian women, both those who worked in the cities and those who taught in isolated villages in the interior, carved out a strong place for themselves in popular education prior to World War One. The monumental task which these women undertook is indicated by the following contemporary account:

> [In the provinces] all children, boys and girls, aside from having no education, were ignorant even of the most elementary civil traditions... The teachers who later were sent...

> to the various provinces begged us to send along books and pens, soap, needle and thimble... They were ignorant of hygiene and of the prevention of contagious diseases. Nor did they know about vaccines; and anyone contacting measles would either die or go blind... Holding them down was poverty and ignorance...
>
> The delicate girls of Constantinople have gone into the depths of the provinces to bring enlightenment. Thanks to their dedication, their education, and their culture, they have instructed their sisters in backward areas and have brought knowledge to them.[2]

The spread of literacy among the masses and the involvement and participation of women in the field of education were developing concurrently with the first movement of Armenians to Canada at the turn of the century. For this cohort, composed mainly of migrant male workers, religion had been the major element of their separate identity within the Ottoman Empire; but the trans-atlantic crossing to a Christian land transformed them into a linguistic minority. In the non-threatening milieu of a liberal and democratic country, the Armenian pioneers tried to break out from under the intellectual vice of Turkish rule and the limitations imposed on a subject people. Their goal was to become more progressive, liberalized and Westernized. Far from Ottoman government censorship and violent suppression, the Armenian sojourners established their political parties, educational associations and reading-rooms in southern Ontario. These national institutions were aimed at perpetuating Armenian culture and strengthening Armenian national consciousness. Contrary to the myth that the crossing destroyed language and culture, these pre-1914 Armenians were able to pursue learning, to enhance their knowledge of their mother tongue, read their literature, discuss political ideologies and events, and study their national history. In this manner a small oppressed group of peasants from the Ottoman Empire bridged the distance back to their homeland and laid the foundations of a secular, liberal and nationalist tradition in Canada even before the Genocide.[3]

In 1915 the Ottoman government embarked on a systematic program to destroy its Armenian minority and to establish religious and linguistic homogeneity within the boundaries of its empire. One and a half million Armenians were murdered or died of disease, starvation, thirst or exposure; unknown numbers were taken into captivity and forced to renounce their religion and hence their ethnic identity.[4] Their homeland destroyed, the survivors were driven into exile in neighbouring countries.

Who were these "starving Armenians," these gaunt and tragic remnants of a nation? The majority were women and children.[5] The survivors came from all parts of the empire, from both rural and urban areas, and from all socio-economic and educational backgrounds. J.L. Barton, head of the Near East Relief, wrote that they:

> ... were not the by-products of irregular home life, they were the sons and daughters of... intellectual and business leaders. They were a cross section of the race, children of merchants, farmers, teachers and craftsmen. They were blighted in their schooling and starved in body and soul... wandering vagabonds searching for a morsel of food... Disease, from the insanitary crowded camps, had covered many with repulsive sores and made them untouchable. The unclean, wizened, emaciated, pathetic faces, pleading for bread, gave no hint of a forgotten happiness, an abandoned home.[6]

Some were too young at the time of the Genocide to have clear memories of life before 1915; their only knowledge of their language, customs, patterns of relationships, perceptions of roles and hierarchies had been gained not in family and community surroundings but in refugee orphanages. Their role models were not mothers and fathers, aunts and uncles, but orphanage teachers, missionaries and clergymen.

After the initial chaos, facilities for hospitals, orphanages and schools were hurriedly arranged. Those children fortunate enough to be admitted to orphanages were given medical attention: "Every orphanage was also a hospital; every child a patient and medical treatment was as much a part of orphanage routine as mealtime."[7] Children who had lost their facility to speak Armenian because they had been abducted by Turks and Kurds relearned their mother tongue. They were taught to read and write Armenian, were familiarized with Armenian literature, liturgy and music and were exposed to elements of Armenian crafts and trades such as rug weaving and needlework.[8] Indeed, it is to the credit of these orphanage workers, both men and women, Armenian and non-Armenian, that a segment of a national culture was conserved.

The orphanages played another important function. Because many of them came under the influence of Western personnel and relief organizations,[9] they became subtle avenues in spreading modern Western social concepts, such as egalitarianism, liberalism and capitalism, and of disseminating Western languages, especially English and French. Their socializing and educational role thus combined in reaffirming Armenian identity and culture and inserting Western influence in the cauldron of the Middle East.

The orphanages, however, were not agents of social reproduction. They did not transfer the structure and traditions of the birthplace to a foreign environment. The girls and women who survived the Genocide carried, at best, a disrupted and disjointed culture. Not only had the tangible elements of their culture been destroyed—the churches, schools and precious manuscripts—not only were the transmitters of the culture dead—the parents and grandparents—but the creators of the culture—the writers, artists and architects—had also been killed. The young survivors, brutally cut off from the customs and conventions of their homeland, were thus compelled to cherish the surviving fragments of their culture if they harboured any inclination to assert their ethnic identity.

Because of Canadian government restrictions against Asiatics, only about a thousand of the surviving girls and young women were admitted into Canada during the 1920s. They came in as relatives of Canadian-Armenian settlers, as domestics, or as mail-order brides for the sojourning men who had migrated to this country before 1914. Adjustment to Canada was not easy. Many suffered deep emotional and psychological wounds. As survivors and refugees they were forced to assess their life in the diaspora, to live with the recurring nightmares of Genocide and to cope with a Genocide complex in an environment that did not understand or even attempt to understand their precarious condition.

Isolated from the larger Armenian settlements in the Middle East and the United States and outside the cultural, social and political framework of the Canadian host society, these refugee women with their husbands gradually forged a new way of life in southern Ontario which inevitably acquired a quality of its own. They struck a delicate and changing balance between two ways of life and created an amalgam of two cultures, one ancient, one modern. As conditions warranted they retained and discarded from the old and borrowed and rejected from the new. In whatever they did, however, they were aware that their ethnoculture was in double jeopardy, partly because they were immigrants in a strange land, but more acutely because the Genocide and its aftermath threatened their very existence as a people.

Mindful of these issues, women participated in church work and in perpetuating customs and feasts of the Armenian Apostolic Church.[10] Others threw themselves into secular community work. Generally the women followed in their husbands' footsteps. If their husbands belonged to the Patriotic Society of Keghi, so did they; if their husbands belonged to the Social Democratic Hunchagian political party, they joined the women's group of that party. As Armenian associational and institutional life became more segregated, women's organizations evolved as one of the few legitimate channels for self-expression and service to the community. This fact was especially relevant to educated and/or bright women who could fulfill intellectual and artistic needs through such involvement.

One of the most prominent organizations that mobilized women's efforts in this period was the Armenian Relief Society—ARS. Before World War One branches of the ARS had been founded in Brantford, St. Catharines and Hamilton to give the small number of women settlers the opportunity to engage in Armenian cultural, educational and benevolent affairs. Although the ARS was not a political party, it had been organized in North America in 1910 as the women's wing of the Armenian Revolutionary Federation, an Old-World nationalist political party. With the influx of women during the 1920s and 1930s, Armenian Relief Society activities expanded and membership increased from five or six to over twenty. The mandate of this organization was threefold:

1. Charitable. To assist destitute Armenians, especially those dispersed throughout the Mediterranean world, but also in the local area, to help the needy, visit the ill and comfort the dying.
2. Artistic. To support Armenian choirs, theatrical productions, poetry readings and lectures both locally and internationally.
3. Educational. To establish and maintain Armenian language classes for the new generation.

While it is true that many members were engaged in fund-raising work—cooking meals for and serving at banquets, selling raffle tickets, preparing handmade fanciwork for sale—it is also true that there was another dimension to their endeavours. Indeed, through their enterprise the women created a forum for developing both their administrative and Armenian language skills. Through their meetings and activities the members learned parliamentary procedure and discipline; they learned how to write and respond to minutes, correspondence and reports, and they learned to speak publicly among friends on topics other than home and family. In associations like the Armenian Relief Society, members made deliberate and determined efforts to purify the language of Turkish and Kurdish borrowings. Some who were artistically inclined produced plays and directed poetry recitations. Because the organization was international in scope with branches in many different countries, members were exposed to issues affecting other Armenian communities in the diaspora. In this regard, women were encouraged to read the Armenian press, notably the political press. As they progressed from simply phrased advertisements, to serialized Armenian novels and short stories, to editorials, they improved their ability to read and comprehend their language, enhanced their knowledge of Armenian history, politics and literature, and learned more about issues and events outside the local sphere. In their pursuit of ethnocultural goals, women's organizations, both secular and religious, invariably became vital channels in the education of women and important agents in the creation and preservation of Armenian identity in southern Ontario.

For these early settlers language, even more than religion, embodied the major means of group survival and national solidarity. While the ancient mountain, Mt. Ararat, remained the holy symbol of their perseverance and persistence, the Armenian language emerged as the sanctuary of the Armenian people.[11] It was therefore deemed important to transmit the language to their children. As almost all the marriages in the community contracted in the 1920s and 1930s were endogamous, husband and wife spoke to one another in Armenian. What is noteworthy about this fact is that many of these men had come to North America before World War One. Their intention to return home and their determination to maintain their identity slowed down a major shift among them from Armenian to English. Before the war they had spoken to each other in Armenian in their boardinghouses, their coffeehouses and their work places. When they could not return to the homeland after the war, they became permanent settlers in Canada, married Armenian women and continued speaking Armenian to their wives, again both by necessity and choice. Since, moreover, the women were prohibited by custom from working outside the home, their traditional role of transferring culture was not greatly disrupted. In this respect, mothers not only spoke Armenian to their children, they also recounted fairy, folk and historical tales and taught them prayers, poems and songs. Sociologist Wsevolod Isajiw found that where parents spoke to a child only in Ukrainian, 100 per cent of the children knew Ukrainian at least in a general way.[12] Interviewees have indicated that Armenian children also exercised a basic facility in the language during the 1920s and 1930s.

The Armenian neighbourhood, moreover, was concentrated in a small geographic area, incorporating five or six streets. The community was closely knit and members were "like family." Adults looked out for each others' children, and children treated all adults like relatives, referring to elders as aunt and uncle. One informant recollected, "If you did something bad on your way home from school, someone would see you for sure, and your mother would know even before you got home."[13] In this environment, young children played in Armenian, and they spoke to all adults in Armenian.

Using the language at home and in the community, however, was only part of the language transfer. Women also organized and taught in Armenian supplementary schools. An interviewee who had attended the school in Hamilton remarked, "[The school] made my mind sharper, gave me confidence. It's a good thing we went too. We learned Armenian. We wouldn't have learned that much at home. Not that much. I learned a lot. I could write quite well."[14] The school's mandate was to make the children more than bilingual: it was to make them biliterate and bicultural. Indeed, language and literature were important factors linking and unifying the disparate Armenian communities around the world. People who read the same literature would be exposed to the same ideas and drawn into the same causes. The language was thus more than a symbol of ethnic identity or a tool of communication between the generations. It was a critical agent of ethnonational survival.

Before 1920 the arrangements for the supplementary schools were loose and informal. As the number of children increased in the 1920s, school committees became administrative necessities. These committees or local school boards were composed of both men and women. They arranged the location of the children's schools, regulated the school hours, engaged teachers, decided on honoraria and later salaries for the teachers, set fees for the children and inspected the school on a regular basis. The committees solved school related problems, sat in on examinations, assisted teachers and parents with concerts, plays and picnics, and made periodic reports to the overseeing organization.

While each school was organized by a different group, there were certain similarities among them. Both boys and girls attended school three evenings a week from seven to nine o'clock. School was held in a room in someone's house or in what was called the club, later the community centre. In the early twenties parents paid a nominal fee, usually about twenty-five or fifty cents a month per child. This fee, however, was not a prerequisite to admission; all children were admitted whether their parents could afford the fees or not. Any outstanding amount was subsidized by the organizing group.

Not only did women play an increasingly active role in administration and fund-raising, they also taught in the schools. No specific teaching qualifications were required except a good working knowledge of the language and a willingness to devote the time, patience and energy required for the job which in the 1920s was undertaken on a voluntary basis. Although teachers reflected the interests of the community they served, they had considerable freedom and flexibility in creating their own courses. For most of them, the textbook provided the core of the curriculum. Texts published after 1915 clearly indicate a strong nationalist focus, with an emphasis on Armenian history, biographical sketches of Armenian historical and literary figures, and Armenian poems and short stories.

The group lesson, which was the main method used, was held in one room. This custom, together with the assistance of the older pupils, created an environment where the children were exposed to a broad range of facts and ideas and where a camaraderie developed between the older and younger students, strengthening the bond of Armenianness among the children.[15]

In the Ottoman Empire teaching had been regarded as an act of patriotism and schooling as an instrument of nationalism and liberalism. In the Old World, young men and women had tried to raise the literacy level of the masses and to awaken their pride in being Armenians. In Canada teachers were faced with the growing influence of Canadian society and the concomitant fear that Armenian ethnoculture was doomed. Their commitment, self-sacrifice and diligence helped to create an Armenian consciousness among the young in southern Ontario and to sustain a strong bond among the group members.

Women's contribution to Armenian schools and organizations requires some further comment. Traditionally Armenian women were sequestered in the home, the ethnic community and the ethnic church. It was unacceptable for Armenian women to work outside the home. The fear and distrust of Turks and Kurds in the old country, furthermore, had been transferred to the New World with the result that, initially at least, women were forbidden even to go out of the house without a male escort. Women who were engaged in Armenian school activities and women's organizations were presumed to be safe from harm and from the corrupting influence of the mainstream society. They operated within controllable boundaries and within permitted behavioural patterns, and because at the same time they were serving the national cause, their involvement was approved both by themselves and by Armenian men.

Two other factors contributed to the community's acquiescing in this type of work. Women in the old country had established a tradition of participation in charitable and educational work.

With the spread of literacy among the masses, girls, including many from rural areas, were being educated; but opportunities for both men and women were limited in the Ottoman Empire. Teaching was one of the few avenues open to women and one of the few acceptable professions. Hundreds of women teachers and teaching assistants had solidified the place of women in education. Secondly, Protestant women, both missionaries and teachers, provided powerful role models. Women like Miss Rose Lambert had left their comfortable homes in North America to help people in a foreign and backward country. They established elementary schools, colleges and teacher training institutions; some administered orphanages, clinics and schools. Their work and their lives brought Armenians in touch with Western behavioural patterns and attitudes and paved the way for a more liberal approach towards women and their endeavours. The examples of North Americans and Europeans, moreover, after the Genocide penetrated the Armenian psyche. Women working among the refugees set up and toiled in orphanages, schools and hospitals. Their efforts were appreciated by Armenians who recognized that women's work in these fields was indispensable and indeed reputable. For all Armenians, the name of Karen Jeppe, the Danish missionary who devotes her life to helping Armenians in Aleppo, represents dedication and service.

Such developments and personalities interacted with the immigrant experience in Canada in such a way as to draw Armenian women out of their cloistered shell. As their children grew up, became less dependent and brought the host culture into the home; as their husbands grew older and less authoritarian; and as the women themselves matured and gained self-confidence, they ventured out into Canadian society. By the thirties they were doing their own grocery shopping. They took English language lessons and progressed from reading Armenian/English texts, to reading crocheting and knitting instructions in English, to reading English-language newspapers. They joined English-speaking church groups, like the mothers' meetings at All Peoples' Mission in Hamilton, and attended movies where they learned North American manners and customs. Acculturation was, nevertheless, steadfastly rooted in the Armenian community and in service to the Armenian people.

Without the support of a strong female contingent in Canada before 1914 and without the support of close relatives, most of the women refugees looked to one another for sustenance and support. They created a female collectivism which permeated their daily lives. They shared their knowledge, experience and skills encompassing all facets of life such as home-making, birth control, child rearing and adjustment to Canadian society. They rallied to each other in times of distress, doing household chores, caring for children, comforting each other during times of tragedy and sharing with each other moments of joy. So strong was their interdependence and intimacy that when conflicts outside Canada split the local group, the women continued their friendships and mutual assistance. In doing so they kept the lifelines of the community open.

Whether their behaviour was dictated by practicality, by mutual need and indebtedness or by a conscious attempt to keep the bridges of communication intact during periods of internecine struggle is unclear. What is certain is that their actions contradict many stereotypes of the Armenian women's proverbial obedience to their husbands. At a time when community survival was threatened, their communications and support networks became countervailing forces in holding the community together. Their actions also raised the issue of the efficacy of the opposing forces of political partisanship and political non-involvement in developing ethnic identity and sustaining group solidarity.[16]

While the Armenian immigrants of the early twentieth century brought with them a deep-rooted tradition of self-preservation, they did not set out to form isolated colonies of Armenians in Canada. Their allegiance to their adopted land was unquestionable; they felt an affinity to Canada and Canadians. Canadians had raised $300,000 in 1920 to aid the "starving Armenians"; they had petitioned their government to support the establishment of an independent state for Armenians;[17] and the Canadian government had been a signatory to the Treaty of Sevres (1920) establishing the state of Armenia.[18] Although Canada was not the cherished soil of their forefathers, the newly arrived Armenian refugees regarded the Dominion as a free, democratic and Christian haven. They respected Canadians as civilized and law-abiding people and anticipated a peaceful and productive life as Canadian citizens.

The post-Genocide Armenians were also united by the fear of extinction. It was to be expected that in their confusion, grief and bereavement they would search for comfort and respite in their language, religion and customs. Even more to the point, national survival became an integral part of their existence. "It is," remarked one interviewee, "the fear of dying that keeps us alive."[19] Informants have emphasized that they did not avoid the opportunities to expand their horizons and make contributions to their new country. But they nurtured that which gave them comfort and strength and they were determined to perpetuate their own ancient language and literature because it was theirs, because it was beautiful and worthy of preservation and because they feared it was destined to disappear. Having lost their homeland and all that was dear to them, the remnants of the people desperately resisted succumbing to national suicide. The burning question became how to retain their ethnic identity and to operate effectively in Canadian society.

Armenians recognized and tried to reconcile the complexities and diversities of a dual loyalty. Their attempt to practise loyalty both to a beloved and fragile ethnocultural past and to an uncertain future was complicated by attitudes which the Armenians did not expect to encounter. They had not suspected that some Anglo-Canadians would reject them and their ancient culture and would expect them to give up their identity.[20] Strident imperialists did not understand that dual loyalty was not a form of disloyalty or resistance. To them assimilation represented a break with the language, traditions, values and customs of the foreigners' homeland. Assimilation was an ethnic conversion, so to speak, a transference of cognitive, psychological and behavioural loyalty from the minority ethnic group to the majority host society.[21] As Raymond Breton stated:

> Historically, nation-building in its symbolic-cultural dimension had been oriented toward the construction of a British-type of society in Canada. This was to be reflected in the cultural character of the political, religious, educational and other public institutions, in the language of the society, in the customs, mores, and way of life, and in the symbols used to represent the society and its people... Thus 'being Canadian' was in the process of being defined as speaking English within a British-type institutional system.[22]

The ways of the homeland culture, consequently, had no prestige or status in Canadian life and a stigma was attached to being a "Bohunk," "Wop" or "Hunkie." "Foreigner" itself was a pejorative word. To Anglo-Canadians cultural and linguistic self-maintenance by the foreigner was contradictory, both in theory and practice, to Canadianization. They considered the foreigner's culture an obstacle to the objectives of the larger society, rather than a rich and worthwhile contribution to it.[23]

Although Armenians did not encounter overt suppression or institutionalized intolerance in their use of Armenian, it was quite evident that English speakers preferred them to speak English. Such an attitude of rejection weakened children's motivation to pursue Armenian beyond the elementary school level and discouraged the continued use of the language.[24] As children became more proficient in English, their speech was marked by lexical transfers from English to Armenian in their conversations with each other, with younger siblings and even with their parents, notably in areas where their Armenian vocabulary was limited: for example, in a discussion about baseball or hockey.

As the children grew older, the code switching was clearly drawn. At home and in the Armenian community, with their parents and with their parents' friends, children spoke broken Armenian. Outside, in the school yard, at play or sports, they spoke to each other in English. So serious was the deterioration in knowledge of Armenian matters that the author of a reader published in the 1940s wrote a cautionary note to teachers:

> Our young people are informed about everything. They can explain to you much about literature and science, but they are less informed about things Armenian. Because of this sad state of affairs, we have relegated a portion of the book to national themes. In this way we hope to acquaint them with the history of Armenian culture. Teachers have a responsibility to use all sources which will give our young people pleasure in Armenian literature, Armenian history, in short, Armenian culture.[25]

Armenian men and women organized their ethnoverted communities to retain at least a part of their heritage. They recognized a dichotomy between their perception of bilingualism and biculturalism and that held by the host society. On the one hand, the prevailing Canadian image of loyalty implied one language and one culture. On the other hand, the Armenian tradition of many centuries was to conserve their language and religion while speaking another language in business and commerce and formally living within a "polyglot" society. They had had centuries of experience being a minority and they were ready and able to transfer their experience to new places. For a number of reasons, some Armenians eventually relinquished their ethnic identity and for a group as small as the Armenian, each loss was serious. Nevertheless, a determined core worked tirelessly to conserve that identity. In this group were women and girls who had survived the Genocide and who steadfastly clung to the treasured remnants of an ancient culture.

Notes

1. See David Marshall Lang, *Armenia: Cradle of Civilization* (London: George Allen and Unwin, 1970).
2. Armenian text. Bibliographic pages missing. Probably published in Constantinople around 1910.
3. Isabel Kaprielian, "Sojourners from Keghi: Armenians in Ontario to 1915" (Ph.D. thesis, University of Toronto, 1984), pp. 264-97.
4. Sir John Hope Simpson, *The Refugee Problem, Report of a Survey* (London: Oxford University Press, 1939).
5. League of Nations, *Monthly Summary*, vol. II, no. 10, Oct. 1-31, 1922, p. 265, states that according to reports "the number of refugees in Asia Minor [including both Greek and Armenian] for whom relief will have to be provided amounts to not less than 750,000. It is probable that 80% of these refugees are women and children; the men are mostly old or between fourteen and seventeen years of age."
6. J.L. Barton, *The Story of the Near East Relief, 1915-1930* (New York: Macmillan, 1930), p. 20.
7. Barton, ibid., quoting Dr. Mabel Elliott.
8. The aim of each orphanage was to become self-sufficient. Trades and crafts that the children learned in the orphanage as well as farming techniques were utilized to produce items that were then sold to provide funds for the orphanages.
9. These included the Near East Relief (United States), the Lord Mayor's Fund (United Kingdom) and the Canadian Armenian Relief Association.
10. See Hygus Torosian, "The First Armenian Church in Canada: St. Gregory the Illuminator," and Isabel Kaprielian, "Armenian Folk-Belief with Special Emphasis on Veejag, " in the same issue of *Polyphony: Armenians in Ontario*, ed. Isabel Kaprielian, Fall/Winter, vol. 4, no. 2 (Multicultural History Society of Ontario, 1982).
11. The first Armenian church in Canada was not built until 1930. Language retention was of great importance within the church as well as in secular organizations.
12. Wsevolod Isajiw, "Learning and Use of Ethnic Language at Home and School: Sociological Issues and Findings," in *Osvita, Ethnic Language at Home and School*, ed. Manoly R. Lupul, (Edmonton: Canadian Institute of Ukrainian Studies, University of Alberta, 1985), p. 204.
13. Alice Torosian, St. Catharines, taped interview.
14. Norman Kaprielian, Hamilton, taped interview.
15. See Isajiw, "Learning and Use of Ethnic Language, " p. 206.
16. In conversation with R.F. Harney, Toronto, 1985.
17. See Harold Nahabedian, "A Brief Look at Relations between Canadians and Armenians: 1896-1920, " in *Polyphony: Armenians in Ontario*, pp. 28-34.

18. See Aram Aivazian, "The Armenian Revolutionary Federation in Canada: Past and Present," in *Polyphony: Armenians in Ontario*. In the early 1930s the Canadian government paid a $300,000 solatium to Armenian Canadians.
19. Bedros Tchilingarian, Toronto, taped interview.
20. "We have to abandon the idea of our infinite superiority over the foreigner; we are not their superiors but their equals, and we have to step down from our haughty standpoint and assimilate them." Rev. M.C. Kinsdale of Sydney Mines in a paper entitled, " The Non-Anglo-Saxons in Canada—Their Christianization and Nationalization," p. 134.
21. In conversation with R. Breton, Toronto, 1985.
22. Raymond Breton, "Production and Allocation of Symbolic Resources: An Analysis of the Linguistic and Ethnocultural Fields in Canada," *Canadian Review of Sociology and Anthropology*, vol. XXI (1984), pp. 123-44.
23. "The ethnic foundations of all national cultures, of most of privacy and intimacy, of much of religion, literature, and the arts, have come to be largely overlooked because dominant views of the direction of social development have no place for (or are at odds with) a vibrant, constructive, and resilient ethnicity as a component of western life. The reluctance to view language and ethnicity as consonant with modern social development has been particularly prevalent in the United States, where attention to them has been restricted to the context of immigrant dislocation and assimilation."
    Joshua Fishman, "Language Maintenance," in *Harvard Encyclopedia of American Ethnic Groups*, ed. Stephen Thernstrom (Cambridge, Mass: Harvard University Press, 1977).
24. "In those days, ethnic was not in." Frances Nahabedian, Toronto, taped interview.
25. *Ararat*, no. 3, bibliography data missing, probably published in 1940s.

Outside the Bloc Settlement: Ukrainian Women in Ontario during the Formative Years of Community Consciousness

Frances Swyripa

Although the history of the Ukrainians in Canada, like most Canadian history, has been traditionally viewed from a male perspective, for Ukrainian Canadians *baba* has surpassed *dido*[1] as a symbol of their ethnicity. This is true not only of feminist writers like Myrna Kostash, whose article, "Baba Was a Bohunk," and subsequent book, *All of Baba's Children*,[2] provoked lively debate in Ukrainian circles; and dramatists like Ted Galay, in whose play, *After Baba's Funeral*, the characters come to terms with their heritage through the recently departed grandmother;[3] but it is also true of the popular culture. Far removed from the peasant woman who arrived in Canada at the turn of the century, restaurants called Baba's Village, mass-produced T-shirts advertising Baba's Borsch Soup and middle-class cookbooks named after *baba*, featuring recipes made with packaged pudding powder, proclaim the pervasiveness of *baba* as a symbol.

Baba (and *dido*) have been described as living icons, linking Ukrainian Canadians with their roots and legitimizing their right to western Canada's pioneer heritage.[4] In many ways their symbolic role parallels general prairie nostalgia, particularly in rural farming communities, for the homesteading era when life was harder but simpler and people heroic. But why *baba* at the expense of *dido*? A recent study of ethnic identity among contemporary Ukrainian Canadians suggests a partial answer. It found that certain primary and synoptic symbols, from among those around which the peasant's world revolved, enjoyed the greatest staying power; they reflected the unique shared experience of the group and most successfully bridged past and present. Food with its close relationship to the family and, by extension, to the community constituted an especially valuable bond.[5] Food, embroidery, Easter eggs—the primary synoptic symbols isolated as defining "Ukrainianness" in Canada today—are the preserve of women. Hence, it is on *baba*'s shoulders (and those of her daughters and granddaughters) that the identity of the Ukrainian group as a distinct cultural entity largely rests, and her image has grown accordingly.

The current romanticization of *baba* idealizes the Ukrainian peasant immigrant pioneers as "women who won the west."[6] Uncritical glorification of women who managed everything—housework, field work, child-bearing and rearing—amid great isolation and poverty in a strange land predominates:

> Somebody, someone will raise a statue to those pioneering grandmothers of ours. No one, even those of us who knew them all too briefly, can fully comprehend the terror in their young hearts when the blizzard raged, coyotes howled outside the cabin door and a child in a fever tossed on a bed beneath which the hoar frost was forming. That was when they turned their eyes to the only help that was available and cried out to Him in despair. Their prayers were answered because with the passing of time everything turned out quite well and certainly beyond their fearful expectations.[7]

Progress was *baba*'s reward. There is no question about its desirability or cost, as there is in the writings of feminists who equally admire *baba* but censure her oppression and exploitation. And *baba* has received her statue. On public property in front of city hall in Edmonton two monuments erected by the Ukrainian-Canadian community testify to its mainstream, local political influence as well as to its persistent concern for the homeland. One commemorates the artificial famine in Soviet Ukraine in 1932-33; the other, a project of the Ukrainian Women's Association of Canada, commemorates the pioneer female immigrant, or *baba*.[8] This idealized and popularized view of *baba* is based on the experience of Ukrainian peasant immigrants in the bloc settlements of rural western Canada in the early twentieth century. The concurrent formulation of the role women were to play within the Ukrainian-Canadian family and community was also based on the group's experience in the prairie provinces, which absorbed the majority of Ukrainian immigrants prior to the Second World War; and it was the product of community needs as defined by the emerging political and religious élite in the West. Ukrainians in Ontario, and more particularly Ukrainian women in Ontario, lay on the periphery of Ukrainian life.

In 1911, twenty years after the first mass movement to Canada began, 4.1 per cent of Ukrainian immigrants lived in Ontario compared to 94.0 per cent in the three prairie provinces. Although by 1931 the Ontario figure had risen to 10.8 per cent, the prairies still claimed 85.7 per cent of Ukrainian Canadians.[9] And while Ukrainians eventually came to represent approximatively one-tenth of prairie residents, giving them a visibility and recognition unparalleled in the rest of the country, in Ontario they remained an insignificant proportion of the provincial population. Moreover, Ukrainians in Ontario were dispersed in urban pockets, not concentrated in large rural colonies that lent a Ukrainian character to the physical and cultural lansdcape. Only Port Arthur and Fort William could compete with Winnipeg and Edmonton in terms of their percentage of citizens of Ukrainian origin, but the Thunder Bay area lacked the bloc settlement hinterland that fed the two western cities.[10]

The general regional imbalance among Ukrainians was exaggerated in the case of women. Although by 1931 they approached the demographic distribution for both sexes, in 1911, 97.5 per cent of Ukrainian women in Canada resided on the prairies and 1.7 per cent in Ontario.[11] The preponderance of Ukrainian males over females, relatively stable (a ratio of 54:46) on the prairies through the first three decades of the twentieth century, was more marked in Ontario. In the twenty years between 1911-31 the Ontario Ukrainian population changed dramatically in its sex composition from 82.5 per cent male and 17.5 per cent female to 58.5 per cent male and 41.5 per cent female.[12] A slightly smaller percentage of Ukrainian women in Ontario was under thirty years of age than in the prairie provinces, although in both regions nearly three-quarters of Ukrainian females had not seen their thirtieth birthday.[13] Perhaps because of the comparatively greater shortage of Ukrainian women in Ontario, a higher proportion of those over fifteen were married than on the prairies and a higher proportion of girls married at an early age in Ontario than in Manitoba, Saskatchewan and Alberta.[14] Illiteracy, more prevalent among Ukrainian women than Canadian women generally or Ukrainian men for the period, was less evident among Ukrainian women in Ontario than their counterparts on the prairies, including the foreign born.[15] Reflecting unskilled male employment in primary and secondary industry, Ukrainians in Ontario were concentrated in and around Sault Ste. Marie, Timmins, Windsor, Kenora, Sudbury, Thunder Bay, Hamilton, Oshawa and Toronto. This urban pattern affected the occupational choice of women. In 1931 a smaller percentage of Ukrainian women participated in the labour force than in the prairie provinces, but whereas over two-thirds of working women in the west were engaged in agricultural labour, an equivalent fraction in Ontario located jobs in service.[16]

Although Ukrainian female immigrants to Canada shared the same peasant socio-economic and cultural background, by 1931 as these few examples suggest, they and their daughters had developed significantly different profiles in the regions where they settled. The differences were such as to have affected their ability and willingness to fulfill the functions the Ukrainian community designated for them.

In the late nineteenth century when the first and largest of three waves of Ukrainian immigration to Canada began, Ukrainian lands in Europe were divided between the Russian and Austro-Hungarian Empires. While Austria-Hungary claimed only one-fifth of Ukrainian territory, it contributed well over three-quarters of the immigrants to Canada. Most came from the province of Galicia, where the Poles had long enjoyed a political and economic monopoly; more backward Bukovyna, under the control of the local Romanian element, provided the remainder. A gradually crystallizing national consciousness among Ukrainians in both empires, although proceeding unevenly, echoed the growth of modern nationalism among other Slavic peoples and culminated in an abortive bid for independence between 1917-22.

The creation of the modern Ukrainian nation in the late nineteenth and early twentieth centuries marked the political and national awakening of a peasant mass. Over 95 per cent of Ukrainians in Galicia and Bukovyna were peasants and had been enserfed until 1848. Deteriorating conditions in the countryside after emancipation and the destabilization of peasant society under incipient capitalism found concrete expression in a growing agricultural proletariat of landless peasants, rural overpopulation, widespread alcoholism, mounting indebtedness to Polish landlords and Jewish innkeepers and, for many, seasonal or permanent migration abroad. Clerical families dominated the other 5 per cent of the population; the native nobility had long been Polonized or Romanianized; a burgher class was virtually non-existent; and a secular intelligentsia emerged only in the third quarter of the nineteenth century. The Greek Catholic clergy in Galicia led the national movement and work among the peasantry until the 1890s, when the secular intelligentsia, increasingly influenced by radical socialism, largely displaced them.[17] The enlightenment of the peasantry and improvement of conditions under which it lived became a burning issue and by 1900 Galicia was criss-crossed by a network of reading halls, *prosvita* (enlightenment) societies and agricultural cooperatives spearheaded by the local priest, intelligentsia or advanced peasants. Assisted by an expanding press whose influence percolated through the countryside, these institutions helped to weld village peasants into a large community, develop their political consciousness and encourage group action against socio-economic oppression.

A handful of individuals in the secular intelligentsia focused specific attention on the problem of women. The movement was largely identified with the national socialist and feminist, Natalia Kobrynska. She argued for educational opportunities for women (particularly higher education), universal male and female suffrage, literature to disseminate political ideas among women and the necessity of organization. On a more immediately practical level, fearing that peasant women would find life increasingly complicated as industrialization forced them to work outside the home while their domestic responsibilities were undiminished, Kobrynska advocated the establishment of village day-care centres and communal kitchens. Her socialism, however, alienated many conservatives, such as the wives and daughters of the village clergy, who were ideally placed for reaching peasant women; and many liberals accused her of undermining the family, the cornerstone of the nation, and a mother's role as "the keeper of national identity, the transmitter of patriotism."[18]

Little tangible progress was evident by the outbreak of war in 1914, and improving conditions for peasant women remained a major goal of the Ukrainian women's movement in interwar Galicia. Through the broadly based mass organization, Soiuz Ukrainok (Ukrainian Women's Union), interwar Galician female activists promoted general enlightenment and practical education (including domestic science instruction) among peasant women to raise their national awareness and the living standards of peasant families. Also present was emphasis on the role of nationally conscious educated women, as both mothers and socially responsible individuals, on behalf of a Ukrainian nation confronted with political-cultural survival in Poland and the Soviet Union. Their principles and programs were to be echoed among Ukrainians in interwar Canada.

The village intelligentsia in the Galician and Bukovynian countryside came to Canada in modest numbers in the years preceding the First World War. As a small educated stratum emerged in the new homeland, it joined the few members of the intelligentsia to emigrate in providing a nebulous immigrant group with practical and ideological leadership, moulding it into a recognizable community and laying its structural foundations. Socialist, Protestant and nationalist factions (drawing on different elements in the anticlerical, nationalist-populist philosophy of the Galician Radical party) confronted conservative opposition from the Greek Catholic church, which after 1913 mobilized its forces to re-establish its traditional hegemony in Ukrainian life.[19] Although the latter consolidated its position in the 1920s and 1930s as the most influential body in the community, its power had been permanently challenged. The nationalists, converging around the new Ukrainian Greek Orthodox Church of Canada (1918), emerged as the most dynamic voice in lay matters; they attracted defectors from the Protestant and socialist camps and came to reflect the outlook and aspirations of the rising middle class. The Protestant faction, which had become tied to Presbyterian and Methodist missionary activity and thus increasingly identified with Anglo-Canadian assimilation, lost ground rapidly with the establishment of the Greek Catholic and Ukrainian Orthodox churches and the growing sense of national solidarity fostered by wartime enemy-alien status and Ukrainian independence struggles in Europe. Lastly, the prewar socialist faction, having embraced Marxism, resurfaced from underground in the 1920s as the pro-communist, pro-Soviet Ukrainian Labour-Farmer Temple Association.

The intelligentsia that shaped the factionalization of the Ukrainian immigrant community and supervised its crystalization around three major philosophical orientations in the 1920s and 1930s formed the nucleus of the Ukrainian-Canadian élite. Representing competing religious-political ideologies, this élite was homogeneous in neither origin nor socio-economic composition. It offered differing definitions of what it meant to be Ukrainian in Canada and often conflicting prescriptions for improving the status and treatment of Ukrainian immigrants. The appeal and success of their programs varied, but each faction reached out to all Ukrainians—in western and eastern Canada, rural and urban, male and female.

Although Natalia Kobrynska had exhorted her sisters in the New World to exploit the opportunities America afforted women,[20] there were few educated women in the early Ukrainian-Canadian intelligentsia élite, and community opinion was primarily formulated and enunciated by men. The activities and attitudes of the intelligentsia élite were instrumental in the eventual transformation of the Ukrainian immigrant peasant women. Its encouragement of education, for example, opened options other than marriage. At the same time, the intelligentsia élite bore principal responsibility for subsequent emphasis on the role of Ukrainian-Canadian women within the home in preserving the group's identity. The tension between the two courses was augmented by the influences of Canadian society itself; delayed marriage, weakened parental authority, material desires and career possibilities affected the lifestyle and expectations of Ukrainian women and girls and reduced the control that the official community could exert over them. In the 1920s and 1930s the leadership within each ideological camp moved toward bringing Ukrainian-Canadian women under its umbrella—committed to and identified with its goals. By the time these national women's organizations were established, an élite among Ukrainian-Canadian women themselves had largely assumed a directorial role.[21]

Through the first two decades of the twentieth century, in the initial period of contact between Ukrainian peasant and Anglo-Canadian cultures, the intelligentsia élite was not immune to the gap separating its women from their Anglo-Canadian counterparts. It recognized the need for improvement not only to strengthen intellectual and material standards within the group for its own benefit, but also to elevate the social status and public image of Ukrainians. Embarrassment at the negative impression Ukrainian immigrants were producing was voiced as early as 1897 when the Pennsylvania-based Greek catholic priest, Nestor Dmytriw, toured the fledgling Canadian colonies. He decried the ignorance and disregard for elementary hygiene that permitted children to relieve themselves publicly and severely rebuked Ukrainian women for the filthiness of their section of the immigration hall.[22] The concern for the Ukrainians' status and image required some conciliation with prevalent Anglo-Canadian views of the womanly ideal, having some rather incongruous results. At times, the advice and stereotyping advanced by Ukrainian community leaders had little direct or immediate relevance to the Ukrainian women toiling on a homestead or bending over the laundry tub as a domestic in someone else's home. Nevertheless, the attempt was made, if only on paper, to introduce Ukrainian girls and women to ways of deportment and self-perception deemed proper in Victorian and Edwardian Canada. While a transaction involving livestock and bed linen might be an intrinsic part of betrothal for many Ukrainian girls, for example, they could still learn "correct" courtship etiquette from a 1913 guide to writing love letters[23]—a book of limited usefulness to a largely illiterate population. The Ukrainian Protestant press was also quick to translate Dr. Maria Allen's *What a Young Girl Ought to Know*, a volume in the popular American

Self and Sex Series, distributed in Canada by the publisher for the Methodist church.[24]

The intelligentsia élite equally saw the necessity of assisting its women to adjust to and function in the Anglo-Canadian world on a more practical level. A Ukrainian-English phrase-book of the mid-1920s, covering sundry topics and situations, acknowledged the needs of the Ukrainian working girl and ensured that she knew her place. Job-hunting phrases ranged from "Ai font e pozyshon for dzheneral havsvork" and "Ai kennat kuk mach" to the following exchange: "Du iu ekspekt hai veidzhes?" and the response, "Nov, ser, ai ker mor for e gud hovm."[25] The Ukrainian community press also carried columns on child care, gardening tips (including plant strains suited to the Canadian environment), home medicine, food preparation, hygiene and the like. Such articles reflected the concerns of the Ukrainian women's movement in Galicia and Bukovyna, and paralleled Anglo-Canadian attempts to promote assimilation and improve Ukrainian-Canadian lifestyles and living standards through the home.[26]

Women in the Ukrainian Protestant camp, receptive to Anglicization, denounced the condition of Ukrainian women who "merely existed physically" and argued for a liberal education so that wives and mothers could complement their husbands intellectually and raise their children as good citizens. In addition, wrote Anna Bychinska, the wife of a Ukrainian Presbyterian clergyman, "we cannot put too great a stress upon the paramount need of educating our daughters if we, the Ukrainian women of Canada, would be numbered among the cultured women of the Anglo-Saxon race."[27]

At the same time, the Ukrainian community élite outside the Protestant framework resented many of the Anglo-Canadian activities among its womenfolk. The Greek Catholic church, hostile to the proselytization of its flock by Methodist and Presbyterian missionaries, criticized Protestant methods of infiltrating Ukrainian homes and winning the people's confidence, especially through medical services and clothing hand-outs to women.[28] Anglicizing pressures in the Methodist Ruthenian Girls' Home in Edmonton were also criticized, and a letter in *Kanadyiskyi rusyn* (Canadian Ruthenian), the Greek Catholic weekly, questioned the value of such girls to "Canadian Rus'-Ukraine" if they "learn from foreigners and forget their own."[29] In a similar vein the nationalist organ, *Ukrainskyi holos* (Ukrainian Voice), greeted the first instalment of *What a Young Girl Ought to Know*—an innocuous enough biblically-inspired chapter on the origins of life—with an article stressing that what a Ukrainian girl really ought to know was her duty to her people to raise her children in its interests.[30]

The community reacted even more strongly to other foreign influences on Ukrainian women and, more particularly, on Ukrainian girls. The intelligentsia agitating for the immigrants' spiritual and socio-economic elevation was not motivated solely by genuine populism and nationalism; painfully aware of the antagonism Ukrainians were encountering in North America, it was personally sensitive to behaviour and patterns that contributed to the group's unfavourable image. Ukrainian girls and young women were considered disproportionately responsible for that image. Early letters from Canada to the American newspaper *Svoboda* (Liberty), the first forum for the embryonic community north of the border, expressed disapproval of the moral decay among young girls who gravitated to the city in search of a good time, fancy and idle living, and English husbands (who did not respect them). Too often, these male correspondents asserted, the girls became frivolous and sexually promiscuous, neglected their filial obligations and rejected parental values. They married Ukrainians only as a last resort, were dissatisfied with what their husbands could offer and, unlike "plain hard-working girls," were useless as farm wives (a particular calamity to rural settlers). A man writing from Copper Cliff, Ontario, in 1902 to lament the growing independence and disdain of custom among Ukrainian females thought he had identified the culprit—"women's rights" (*babske pravo*) in Canada.[31]

The Ukrainian intelligentsia élite and Anglo-Canadians with a stake in assimilation both condemned the evils and temptations of urban life that beset vulnerable immigrant youth—whether pool rooms and bars for young men or moving pictures and dance-halls for young women. These attractions lured them from more serious pursuits—English and Bible or domestic classes for the Anglo-Canadian reformers, or Ukrainian national and cultural pursuits for the Ukrainian leadership. Both groups also realized that youth and not adult immigrants were most vital to the success of their respective programs. To the Anglo-Canadian community, it was the young Ukrainian girl, exposed to the right influences through a rural teacherage or Protestant mission, who would introduce her parents and, subsequently, her own household to Anglo-Canadian modes of behaviour and thought. To the Ukrainian community, it was the same young Ukrainian girl who must be harnessed by the group, for its future survival, in the face of enticements from the larger society.

These interlocking themes of the fate of Ukrainian girls and their relationship to the ethnic group were developed more fully as the community ideology of the women's role evolved, reflecting a growing Ukrainian consciousness nurtured by events in both Canada and Europe. An immediate stimulus to the enunciation of a specific Ukrainian role for women within the family was the increasingly effective restriction on second-language instruction in prairie schools, especially the formal abolition of bilingual education in Manitoba in 1916, which forced the Ukrainians to rely on their own resources for the perpetuation of their language and culture in Canada. Most spectacularly, it led to a great investment of money and energy in *bursy*, or private residential institutes in prairie cities. Simultaneously facilitating the education of youth beyond the rural school and encouraging Ukrainian awareness through a Ukrainianized environment, the *bursy* produced a generation of dedicated community leaders, male and female. More modestly, it led to the expansion of *ridni shkoly*, or vernacular schools, the only public vehicle ever practicable to Ontario Ukrainians with their small dispersed population and distance from the western *bursy*;[32] and it heightened emphasis on the women's role in raising Ukrainian children.

On the eve of the abolition of bilingual schools, one woman dramatically compared the injustice being done to Ukrainian women and children in Manitoba to that inflicted on their Serbian and Belgian counterparts in the current war; "they [the abolitionists] want to take our Ukrainian heart, our Ukrainian soul, our children," she declared and urged mothers to fill the breach by teaching their language and culture at home.[33] The collapse of the nascent Ukrainian National Republic with its partition among the Soviet Union, Poland, Czechoslovakia and Romania in the early 1920s and the ensuing struggle for political and cultural survival in the homeland not only reinforced this community-imposed role for Ukrainian-Canadian women within the home, but also influenced the form their activities took outside it in the interwar years.

Not all factions in the pioneer intelligentsia élite or on its fringes, however, subscribed equally to such a role for Ukrainian women or allotted it identical weight in their respective worldviews or programs. Although the interwar communist women's press was to underline parents' (particularly the maternal) responsibility in preserving a sense of Ukrainian pride and identity among Ukrainian-Canadian youth, it stressed at least as much their responsibility in transmitting to their offspring a politicized working-class consciousness.[34] In the pages of its prewar predecessor, *Robochyi narod* (Working People), a correspondent drew attention to the paramount need of alleviating the economic exploitation of Ukrainian working girls and damned "our businessmen-patriots" who cared only whether a girl could sing patriotic songs and would willingly part with her hard-earned money for their causes.[35] Similarly, while it also emphasized a woman's responsibility to her people and nation, the Greek Catholic press stressed in equal measure her responsibility in raising her children as good Catholics.[36] It was the nationalist intelligentsia élite—aspirants to the middle class and its first representatives—which was to articulate most clearly and thoroughly the obligations of women within Ukrainian-Canadian society in the interests of both the ethnic group in Canada and the nation in Europe.

A series of articles appearing in *Ukrainskyi holos* in the 1910s on conditions among Ukrainian women outlined the budding nationalist perception of the role women were to play in the Ukrainian-Canadian community. As with earlier correspondents in *Svoboda*, focus rested on the moral deterioration and alienation of girls removed from the restraining influences of community and parental sanctions. The fate that befell "Jack" on the extra gang befell "Katie" working as a hotel maid, waitress or domestic—but more heavily and with worse consequences. Not only were women by nature morally weaker, more emotional and more easily swayed than men, they were also most responsible for the quality of the next generation. "Katie's" passion for outrageous hats, face powder and fancy clothes was only the outer symptom of a deeper malady, and the nadir of her downward journey was reached when she scorned her people and abandoned her native tongue.[37] As mothers these girls took the lead in assimilation, speaking English exclusively (and badly) to their children and often to their husbands. "And in that the mother primarily raises a child," concluded one objector, "she therefore rears it not for its own people but for foreigners."[38] Such situations existed because of indifferent parents, frequently too ignorant to teach their daughters otherwise, and because of the negligence of the community, especially the intelligentsia, in its duty both to counsel young girls and to push their parents along the path to enlightenment. "Remember," warned a correspondent to *Ukrainskyi holos*, "that their sin is the sin of those who fail to acquaint them with anything better."[39]

That the concern for the maturing generation of Ukrainian-Canadian women largely emerged from community-perceived needs, as defined by the intelligentsia, is illustrated particularly well by a 1916 article, "Why We Need Educated Women." Unsigned and drawing on a familiar scenario, it was obviously written by someone closely associated with the *bursa* movement and intended as ammunition for female dormitories at the Mohyla (Saskatoon) and Kotsko (Winnipeg) institutes. The author opened with a bleak picture. On the farm women were isolated and illiterate. Girls were kept home from school to work and married early. In town girls enjoyed greater independence but found movies more attractive than knowledge; very few joined Ukrainian organizations, where they "would learn to respect their own," and as mothers were ashamed to speak Ukrainian to their children. The result was inevitable with both mother and children lost to Ukrainian society. Mothers were the cornerstone of the family, the author continued, and an enlightened family needed a broadly educated patriotic mother: "If the mother loves her nation and is proud of being Ukrainian, then her children will not desert their people either."[40] Not mere personal development, the reader is forced to conclude, but the welfare and future of the Ukrainian nation was at stake.

For a variety of reasons the education of women was important. "National" concerns aside, uneducated women were unable to instruct their children intelligently about the workers' struggle or the Catholic faith. It was impossible for Ukrainians as a group to pull themselves up in Canadian society and Anglo-Canadian eyes if they were encumbered in the primary social unit—the family—by an ignorant womanhood content to "hide behind closed doors."[41] How could children blossom when women blindly adhered to the principle that domestic upbringing consisted of "eating, growing and nothing more"?[42] A mother's sin was particularly grave in relation to her daughters. Writing in *Ukrainskyi holos* in 1915, "Ukrainka" (Ukrainian Woman) upbraided mothers who denied their daughters education because they were going to be farm wives, who thought them adequately prepared for married life if they knew how to milk cows, tend chickens and do other farm work. This was insufficient, rejoined "Ukrainka"; a woman must also know something about world affairs, proper child-rearing, adept social intercourse—all acquired through education, the cultivation of broader interests and, even after marriage, the reading of books and newspapers.[43] The same year another commentator condemned as false the argument, popular with women, that as girls would marry they needed no training beyond basic household arts (their concerns were the "small things" as opposed to the "great issues" of life); handicapped by their ignorance, apathy and laziness, such women, the author insisted, were useless for national work.[44]

The official consensus was that an uneducated mentally stagnant woman, oblivious to pressing national questions, lacked the personal resources to ensure that her children had more than a simple passive acquisition of their language and culture. Then too, how could she contribute to that national life? Community spokespersons responsible for defining women's role did not believe they should be confined to the home; women must also participate more actively in the public sphere. This summons to direct community commitment and involvement received an impetus from events in eastern Europe, particularly Polish-Ukrainian hostilities over control of Galicia in the later stages of the Great War and ensuing months. Ukrainian women in Galicia were aiding the national struggle (*Polish* women in Galicia, one writer observed, had organized into military units and boasted of helping their men kill Ukrainian husbands and sons), but regretfully Ukrainian women in Canada sat impassively.[45] A female intelligentsia was as crucial as a male intelligentsia, a corrrespondent to *Ukrainskyi holos* had insisted already in 1910, indignant that the community concern for education focused on men; a female intelligentsia would channel the leisure time of urban girls into useful and healthy pursuits and it would preside over the creation of distinct women's organizations.[46] In 1917, admonishing Ukrainian women in Canada for their apathy toward national affairs, the wife of a labourer challenged the inaction of "our women leaders": where were they, those women of education, culture and refinement—the wives of doctors, lawyers, priests, merchants and teachers, or teachers themselves—who ought to be coming forward to undertake and coordinate national work among women? Ukrainian women in Canada, the author continued, would never be significant until organized into strong women's associations.[47] And the prerequisite for this, as she and others recognized, was education at both rank-and-file and leadership levels.

It was as organized women, through their own associations, that Ukrainian-Canadian women were seen as contributing most to national life outside the home. By the 1920s the issue of aid to the war-torn homeland dominated community projects, and women were encouraged to found and run local branches of the Ukrainian Red Cross.[48] Some women welcomed this responsibility, others did not. Tekla Lysa, the head of the Ukrainian Red Cross in Fort William in early 1920, criticized the poor behaviour and negative attitudes toward the endeavour exhibited by certain local women.[49] Red Cross work was considered ideally suited to women's character and talents, and as with their contemporary counterparts among other nationalities, Ukrainian women's organizations were to complement not duplicate the activities of male organizations, they should be concerned less with "politics" and more with the affairs of the female world, including their needs, faults, follies and special areas of competence and the development of sound social viewpoints. Not only would women's organizations define and propagate women's peculiar national responsibilities, but individuals within the movement would act as models of female consciousness and patriotism to their less enlightened sisters.[50]

While female education was largely discussed in terms of its potential to advance community goals, the matter of a woman's personal emancipation and growth was not summarily brushed aside. Some writers, most vocally women, contended that the level of consciousness and knowledge required for women to execute their national tasks satisfactorily could be achieved only if they learned to think independently and controlled their own lives.[51] At times the tone of the appeal to greater national service underlined that not everyone endorsed a public profile, or even enlightenment itself, for women, and that the appeal was made over objections, silent or otherwise, to women outside the home. The realization that women were good for something besides cooking and nursing babies was long overdue, Olha Swystun, wife of one of the most prominent male activists, told the Third National Convention of Ukrainians in Canada in 1919. Ideas to the contrary only prevented their participating more fully in Ukrainian national life.[52] Her fellow speaker was blunter: "You men, may call yourselves patriots, may have noble ideas and may speak of education, and politics, but your patriotism is of little value if you do not place the matter of the elevation of our women in the first place."[53]

Some writers, significantly from the period prior to the escalating wartime community concern over women's national role, regarded women's emancipation and enlightenment more as issues in themselves and as part of a larger problem. Only when both sexes were equally learned and liberated from traditional prejudices, when life for everyone was "regulated by reason and understanding and not a cudgel," would the Ukrainian-Canadian community experience true progress.[54] But as long as women remained men's property, bought and sold in the marriage market, they were not individuals with personal rights but objects whose thinking and decision-making were done for them by men—slaves perforce had to be kept ignorant, while knowledge did not befit the obedience demanded of a wife. "No one," emphasized the author of this particular 1910 piece, "denies that where one man decides for another, great wrongs are done to the latter, but women clearly endure a great many such wrongs." Only independent decision-making and earning power, by freeing women from compulsory marriage, would give them full personal autonomy.[55]

Thus by the early 1920s, a community ideology for women, based on the dual concerns of the group's cultural preservation in Canada and the precarious situation of the Ukrainian nation in Europe, had assumed definite shape. It would mature in the interwar years and be reflected in the outlook and activities of women's organizations. By the 1920s too, a core of Ukrainian women had emerged as spokespersons for their sex. In addition to individual voices, they were grouped around two major nuclei. The larger and more geographically dispersed nucleus encompassed the bilingual teachers and women active in the *bursa* movement.[56] The second was provided by the Ukrainian Women's Enlightenment Society, dominated by the wives of the leading male intelligentsia, that formed in Winnipeg in late 1916.[57] However, while conscious and upwardly mobile Ukrainian women were endorsing the community role being created for them, the degree to which awareness or acceptance of it had filtered downward to influence women at the grass roots level remains problematic. Meanwhile, the Ukrainian Women's Enlightenment Society became the prototype for the national women's organizations that followed: its members were active in *ridni shkoly*, participated in concerts and plays, assisted the Ukrainian Red Cross, held money-raising bazaars and did the cooking for community events.[58] Charity work within Canada was largely left to the pioneer religious order, the Ukrainian Sisters Servants of Mary Immaculate. But the charity, fund-raising and other activities conducted by interwar lay organizations focused on "national" work—museums to preserve Ukrainian handicrafts and record their historical heritage, financial assistance to *bursy* (farm women were encouraged to donate butter, cheese, garden produce) and material aid to Ukrainian war orphans, veterans and *ridni shkoly* in Europe, particularly Galicia.

Although on the periphery of organized life and the discussion about women's role, Ukrainians in Ontario felt they belonged to the larger Ukrainians community in Canada. Not only did the pioneer press link Ukrainian across the country, but the considerable movement of individuals between prairie farms and Ontario job sites also helped forge a common sense of identity and purpose.[59] Ukrainians in eastern Canada, for example, identified and sympathized with the goals of the prairie *bursy*, sharing the conviction that the fate of Ukrainian youth and the future of the Ukrainian nation were at stake.[60] Moreover, Ontario Ukrainians were expected to contribute to Ukrainian causes in other parts of Canada. In 1937, for example, the Sisters Servants visited Toronto to raise money for their orphanage in Ituna, Saskatchewan. In this particular instance the tables were turned. In response to pleas to aid the local religious-cultural community, the nuns stayed in Toronto to teach *ridni shkoly* and catechism.[61] Conscious Ukrainian women in Ontario concurred with the need for female improvement, both to facilitate raising children and to influence the quality of home life. More enlightened women, a letter from Port Arthur argued, could better persuade their husbands to join benevolent associations and abstain from alcohol.[62] Conscious Ontario Ukrainians were equally aware of women's potential role outside the home. It was wrong, the priest-author of a series of articles on Ukrainians in eastern Canada insisted in 1917, to maintain that women's value stopped with the kitchen and cradle. A people charged with a national renaissance had to mobilize everyone—not just the select few—and an enlightened Ukrainian womanhood must learn to participate in church and national life (especially those spheres suited to female talents) alongside men.[63]

Nevertheless, Ukrainian women in Ontario faced difficulties that prairie women escaped in fulfilling their public and domestic functions on behalf of the group. They were separated physically from the Ukrainian heartland and creative well-spring in western Canada, insignificant within the general Ontario population, greatly outnumbered by Ukrainian men in the province and more dispersed and isolated from other Ukrainians than was the case on the prairies. It is possible, however, that the absence of Ukrainian bloc settlements, both as areas of Ukrainian concentration and as sources of psychological support and settlers for adjacent urban centres, was a mixed blessing. Sheltered in the large rural colonies of the west, a woman could *be* Ukrainian without ever thinking about it, never forced to consider the political or broader sociocultural implications of her ethnicity or to make conscious decisions concerning her relationship to the ethnic group. The luxury of such inertia was less certain in Ontario if "Ukrainianness" was to be maintained.

Several indicators point to the problems of Ontario Ukrainians in preserving their language and culture as part of daily life, which inevitably affected a woman's ability to transmit her heritage to her offspring as well as her own ties to it. Successful assimilatory pressures are seen, for example, in the inroads of the Roman Catholic church—by 1931 over 25 per cent of Ukrainian women in Ontario adhered to it compared to less than 10 per cent on the prairies.[64] The Ukrainian Greek Orthodox church after 1918 attracted comparatively few followers in Ontario, and in many localities the Greek Catholics were able to organize parishes and secure resident priests or regular services only in the late 1920s or 1930s, while other centres remained missions. This assisted proselytization by non-Ukrainian denominations and delayed the formation of Ukrainian church-affiliated lay organizations. In Dryden, for example, a Greek Catholic women's group formed only in 1937. Before that, organizationally inclined women attended the local "English" Women's Institute, certainly no hotbed of Ukrainianism.[65] By the Second World War the Sisters Servants of Mary Immaculate had established an institutional network on the prairies (a noviciate, a private school for girls, hospitals, orphanages, a home for the aged) and taught *ridni shkoly* and catechism to approximately 4,000 children annually in nearly 100 locales, but they were still pioneers in eastern Canada. In Toronto (1937) and Windsor (1939) the sisters had made no more than a modest beginning in Ontario, conducting language and religious classes for youth, visiting the sick and organizing parish women's and girls' groups.[66] That conditions in Ontario militated against the success of the community desire to perpetuate things Ukrainian, not only through *ridni shkoly* but also the home, is apparent in the comparative decline of Ukrainian as a mother tongue. In 1931 only 86.9 per cent of Ukrainian women in Ontario reported Ukrainian as their mother tongue, compared with 94.3 per cent of Ukrainian women on the prairies; the difference was less marked in the case of men.[67]

The above factors, coupled with their urban status, higher education and lower illiteracy, suggest greater accommodation to Canadian life among Ukrainian women in Ontario than in western Canada. Perhaps too they suggest less interest in Ukrainian matters as a result, regardless of shared eastern-western convictions at élite levels concerning women's ethnic or national responsibilities. This prairie-Ontario balance among Ukrainian Canadians—with the west the demographic, ideological and organizational centre and Ontario the weaker partner—persisted through the first four decades of the twentieth century. It was to be altered after 1945 by the arrival of often intensely nationalistic Ukrainian displaced persons from Europe. Settling primarily in Ontario, they greatly augmented the province's Ukrainian population, already growing through migration from other parts of Canada and, injecting new vitality into the Ontario community, challenged the west for the leadership of the Ukrainian group in Canada.

Membership in a national minority with a strong identity nurtured by psychological commitment to the homeland dictated a special community-perceived and -imposed role for Ukrainian-Canadian women that was not only cultural and biological but also had non-Canadian political undertones. That their duties fell within traditional spheres of women's competence is not to be dismissed simply as another expression of Ukrainian male dominance, but examined within the context of the Ukrainian diaspora. While ethnicity in Canada might carry burdens and limitations, partnership in the "Ukrainian nation," as defined by the vocal élite, had both obligations and greater glory.

Notes

1. Literally, grandmother and grandfather, also used to refer to any elderly female and male persons.
2. Myrna Kostash, "Baba Was a Bohunk," *Saturday Night* (October 1976), pp. 33-38; and *All of Baba's Children* (Edmonton: Hurtig Publishers, 1977).
3. Ted Galay, *"After Baba's Funeral" and "Sweet and Sour Pickles": Two Plays by Ted Galay* (Toronto: Playwrights Canada, 1981).
4. Zenon Pohorecky, panel discussion at the conference, "Visible Symbols: Cultural Expression among Canada's Ukrainians," Winnipeg, 6-7 November 1981 (videotaped proceedings, Ukrainian Language Resource Centre, Canadian Institute of Ukrainian Studies, University of Alberta). Pohorecky does not make this point as strongly in the pubished version of his presentation, see his "Ukrainian Cultural and Political Symbols in Canada: an Anthropological Selection," in Manoly R. Lupul, ed., *Visible Symbols: Cultural Expression among Canada's Ukrainians* (Edmonton: Canadian Institute of Ukrainian Studies, 1984), p. 139. The attempt to establish historical antecedents is not peculiar to immigrant minority groups with a traditionally negative image. Parallels can be observed among the descendants of the United Empire Loyalists and Selkirk settlers, see Carl Berger, *The Sense of Power: Studies in the Ideas of Canadian Imperialism, 1867-1914* (Toronto: University of Toronto Press, 1970), pp. 84-88, and Frits Pannekoek, "The Historiography of the Red River Settlement, 1830-1868," *Prairie Forum* 6, no. 1 (1981), pp. 75-85, respectively.
5. Wsevolod Isajiw, "Symbols and Ukrainian Canadian Identity: Their Meaning and Significance," in Lupul, *Visible Symbols*, pp. 119-28.

6. This was the title of an article on Ukrainian pioneer women in the magazine, *Branching Out* 2, no. 6 (November-December 1975), pp. 16-19. That the author, Zonia Keywan, is the child of post-1945 immigrants, both of them professionals, illustrates the popularity of the *baba* myth beyond the descendants of the original peasant pioneers.
7. Mundare Historical Society, *Memories of Mundare: a History of Mundare and Districts* (Mundare: Mundare Historical Society, 1980), p. 181.
8. The statue of a young woman in an embroidered Ukrainian blouse and coiled braids, carrying a sheaf of wheat, was dedicated to all pioneer women of Alberta on the occasion of the province's seventy-fifth anniversary.
9. Based on William Darcovich and Paul Yuzyk, eds., *Statistical Compendium on the Ukrainians in Canada, 1891-1976* (Ottawa: University of Ottawa Press, 1980), Series 20.63-80, pp. 41-44.
10. In 1931, 21,459 Ukrainians formed 7.3 per cent of the population of Winnipeg Central Metropolitan Area (CMA), 5,025 formed 6.2 per cent of Edmonton CMA and 4,383 formed 9.5 per cent of the Thunder Bay CMA; although Toronto boasted a Ukrainian population of 5,138, they constituted less than 1 per cent of its residents. Based on Darcovich and Yuzyk, *Statistical Compendium*, Series 21.243-294, pp. 66-67, and Series 21.295-934, pp. 68-88.
11. Based on Darcovich and Yuzyk, *Statistical Compendium*, Series 20.63-80, pp. 41-44. The 1931 figures were 87.2 per cent (prairies) and 9.9 per cent (Ontario).
12. Based on Darcovich and Yuzyk, *Statistical Compendium*, Series 20.63-80, pp. 41-44.
13. In 1931, 73.8 per cent of Ukrainian females in the prairie provinces and 73.0 per cent of Ukrainian females in Ontario were under thirty years of age. Based on Darcovich and Yuzyk, *Statistical Compendium*, Series 22.17-56, pp. 133-62.
14. In 1931, 65.1 per cent of Ukrainian women over fifteen were married in the prairie provinces, compared to 72.3 per cent of those in Ontario. The same census year, of Ukrainian girls aged fifteen to nineteen, 12.5 per cent were married in Ontario and 9.6 per cent on the prairies; of Ukrainian girls aged twenty to twenty-four, 69.0 per cent were married in Ontario and 61.5 per cent on the prairies. The figures for all Canadian women were significantly lower in each category. Based on Darcovich and Yuzyk, *Statistical Compendium*, Series 22.17-56, pp. 133-62; Series 62.1-8, pp. 737-42; and Series 62.45-60, pp. 754-57.
15. Illiteracy among all Ukrainian females over ten years of age dropped from 37.6 per cent to 12.4 per cent in Ontario and from 38.4 per cent to 18.5 per cent on the prairies in the decade prior to 1931. In that year only 19.5 per cent of foreign-born Ukrainian women in Ontario were illiterate, compared to 36.1 per cent on the prairies; illiteracy remained higher among Canadian-born Ukrainian women on the prairies than in Ontario (2.4 per cent and 1.0 per cent, respectively). By 1931 only 1.9 per cent of all women in Ontario

and 4.5 per cent of all women in the prairie provinces could neither read nor write. Based on Darcovich and Yuzyk, *Statistical Compendium*, Series 32.1-12, pp. 277-80.

16. In 1931, 6.0 per cent of Ukrainian women in Ontario participated in the labour force, compared to 9.4 per cent on the prairies; 18.2 per cent of all Ontario women and 14.1 per cent of all prairie women worked for wages. In Ontario 68.9 per cent of Ukrainian working women were in service and on the prairies 67.6 per cent were agricultural labourers; only 46.2 per cent of all Ontario women were in service and only 58.2 per cent of all prairie women were agricultural labourers. Based on Darcovich and Yuzyk, *Statistical Compendium*, Series 40.15-30, pp. 390-91, and Series 40.119-134, pp. 402-03.
17. On the Ukrainian national movement in nineteenth-century Galicia, see Andrei S. Markovits and Frank E. Sysyn, eds., *Nationbuilding and the Politics of Nationalism: Essays on Austrian Galicia* (Cambridge, Mass.: Harvard Ukrainian Research Institute, 1982), and the following works by John-Paul Himka, *Socialism in Galicia: the Emergence of Polish Social Democracy and Ukrainian Radicalism (1860-1890)* (Cambridge, Mass.: Harvard Ukrainian Research Institute, 1983); "Priests and Peasants: the Greek Catholic Pastor and the Ukrainian National Movement in Austria, 1867-1900," *Canadian Slavonic Papers* 21, no. 1 (March 1979), pp. 1-14; "Young Radicals and Independent Statehood: the Idea of a Ukrainian Nation-State, 1890-1895," *Slavic Review* 41, no. 2 (Summer 1982), pp. 219-35; "The Background to Emigration: Ukrainians of Galicia and Bukovyna, 1848-1914," in Manoly R. Lupul, ed., *A Heritage in Transition: Essays in the History of Ukrainians in Canada* (Toronto: McClelland and Stewart, 1982), pp. 11-31; and "The Greek Catholic Church and Nation-Building in Galicia, 1772-1918," *Harvard Ukrainian Studies* (forthcoming).
18. Martha Bohachevsky-Chomiak, "Natalia Kobryns'ka: A Formulator of Feminism," in Markovits and Sysyn, *Nationbuilding and the Politics of Nationalism*, p. 215. See also Martha Bohachevsky-Chomiak, "Feminism in Ukrainian History," *Journal of Ukrainian Studies* 7, no. 1 (Spring 1982), pp. 16-30.
19. The best work on this period is Orest Martynowych, "Village Radicals and Peasant Immigrants: the Social Roots of Factionalism among Ukrainian Immigrants in Canada, 1896-1918" (M.A., University of Manitoba, 1978). See also his "The Ukrainian Socialist Movement in Canada, 1900-1918," *Journal of Ukrainian Graduate Studies* 1, no. 1 (Fall 1976), pp. 27-44, and 2, no. 1 (Spring 1977), pp. 22-31; and "Ukrainian Catholic Clericalism in Western Canada, 1900-1932," manuscript, 1974.
20. See Bohachevsky-Chomiak, "Natalia Kobryns'ka: A Formulator of Feminism," p. 217. Kobrynska also exhorted Ukrainian women in the New World to help their sisters in the homeland, encouraging the former, for example, to promote the marketing of old-country handicrafts; see *Svoboda*, 26 May 1904.

21. Three national women's organizations reflected the prewar factionalization within the Ukrainian community in Canada: the women's branch of the Ukrainian Labour-Farmer Temple Association, the Ukrainian Women's Association of Canada (representing the Orthodox laity) and the Ukrainian Catholic Women's League. A fourth group, the Ukrainian Women's Organization of Canada, was affiliated with the Ukrainian National Federation of the intensely nationalistic, republican interwar immigrants.
22. See Nestor Dmytriv [Dmytriw], *Kanadiiska Rus': Podorozhni vspomyny* [Canadian Rus': A Traveller's Memoirs] (Mount Carmel, Pa.: "Svoboda," 1897), pp. 5 and 31-32.
23. *Poradnyk dlia zaliublenykh abo iak pysaty liubovni lysty* [Guide for Lovers or How To Write Love Letters] (Winnipeg: Ukrainska Knyharnia, 1913).
24. The first instalment appeared in the Presbyterian *Ranok* [Dawn] on 27 June 1917. For a discussion of the influence of the Self and Sex Series and related literature in contemporary English Canada, see Michael Bliss, " 'Pure Books on Avoided Subjects': Pre-Freudian Sexual Ideas in Canada," *Canadian Historical Association Historical Papers* (1970), pp. 89-108.
25. *New Ukrainian-English Interpreter/Novyi ukrainsko-angliiskyi providnyk*, 3rd ed. (Winnipeg: Ukrainska Knyharnia, n.d.), pp. 94-95; the guide was first published in 1926. Each sentence or phrase appeared in Ukrainian, English and the English words in the Cyrillic alphabet; I have reproduced the last named in Latin script to illustrate how a Ukrainian girl would have learned to pronounce the words in question.
26. Those most directly concerned with Canadianization were educators and Protestant missionaries, the Presbyterian and Methodist churches establishing missions for foreigners in urban and rural centres across Canada. The Methodist Wesley Institute in Fort William included a program for foreign girls in its activities: "The one hundred and ten little girls who come to us from homes of ten different nationalities to play games, to learn to cook, sew and keep house under the guidance of the finest types of Canadian womanhood are being prepared for the motherhood of Canada to be"; see *Missionary Bulletin* (June-September 1916), p. 518.
27. *Kanadiiskyi ranok* [Canadian Dawn], 6 June 1922.
28. *Kanadyiskyi rusyn*, 8 December 1915.
29. Ibid., 4 January 1913.
30. *Ukrainskyi holos*, 11 July 1917; see *Ranok*, 25 July 1917, for the Presbyterian response.
31. *Svoboda*, 23 January 1902; for samples of contemporary opinion on the unseemly behaviour of Ukrainian immigrant girls in Canada, see *Svoboda*, 31 January 1901, 14 May 1901, 30 May 1901, 10 July 1902, 28 August 1902, 16 April 1903, 30 July 1903, 20 August 1903, 1 September 1904; only one article identified male infidelity as a cause of Ukrainian ridicule (14 August 1902).

32. *Ridni shkoly* or vernacular schools had existed in Ontario from the early days of settlement, being feasible wherever there were sufficient pupils, interested parents and suitable teachers; the latter were expected to organize concerts and plays and teach various folk arts as well as instruct youth in the Ukrainian language. For a discussion of pioneer cultural and organizational work in Ontario, see Michael H. Marunchak, *Ukrainian Canadians: a History* (Winnipeg-Ottawa: Ukrainian Free Academy of Sciences, 1970), pp. 211-19.
33. *Ukrainskyi holos*, 22 December 1915.
34. See, for example, *Robitnytsia* [Working Woman], 1 October 1924.
35. *Robochyi narod*, 18 July 1917.
36. See, for example, *Kanadyiskyi rusyn*, 26 August 1911, 28 October 1914 and 23 May 1917.
37. See, for example, *Ukrainskyi holos*, 31 May 1916, 26 July 1916 and 19 December 1917.
38. *Ukrainskyi holos*, 19 December 1917. Writing in 1897, Nestor Dmytriw disagreed with this sentiment; it was his view that Ukrainian girls, exposed to "English civilization" through domestic service, absorbed the culture of the world more quickly than did Ukrainian men (ill-prepared by their Galician upbringing for North American competition and work) and thus were better equipped to help the Ukrainians adjust to Canadian society (*Podorozhni vspomyny*, pp. 6-7).
39. *Ukrainskyi holos*, 25 November 1914. All factions in the immigrant intelligentsia (nationalist, clerical and labour) were criticized for failing in their responsibilities and betraying the example of their counterparts in Galicia; see *Ukrainskyi holos*, 4 September 1918.
40. *Ukrainskyi holos*, 28 June 1916. Similar concerns were expressed in the Liberal organ, *Kanadyiskyi farmer* [Canadian Farmer]; see, for example, 20 August 1915 and 1 February 1918.
41. *Ukrainskyi holos*, 8 September 1915.
42. Ibid., 19 December 1917.
43. Ibid., 8 September 1915.
44. Ibid., 11 August 1915.
45. See, for example, *Ukrainskyi holos*, 16 July 1919 and 19 November 1919. Ukrainian women in the United States were held up as examples for their counterparts in Canada to follow; the former had both formed their own association, concerned with national affairs, and founded their own periodical, *Rannia zoria* [Morning Star].
46. *Ukrainskyi holos*, 22 June 1910.
47. Ibid., 19 November 1919. The author's point was well taken in terms of the leadership needs of Ukrainian women in Canada, but she failed to appreciate the small number of women who qualified; priests' wives, for example, important in the Galician village, were not to be found in Canada because of the Vatican ruling that permitted only celibate Greek Catholic clergy to serve in North America.

48. The Ukrainian Red Cross Society in Canada was established in 1919 with the active participation of women; see Marunchak, *Ukrainian Canadians*, p. 333.
49. *Ukrainskyi holos*, 25 February 1920.
50. See, for example, ibid., 19 December 1917, 5 February 1919 and 19 November 1919.
51. See, for example, ibid., 16 July 1919.
52. Ibid., 5 February 1919.
53. Ibid., 5 February 1919.
54. See, for example, ibid., 18 May 1910, 14 December 1910 and 18 January 1911.
55. Ibid., 22 June 1910.
56. The Mohylianky—female students at the P. Mohyla Institute in Saskatoon—were the most vigorous group of women; in 1926 they provided the impetus for the Ukrainian Women's Association of Canada, the most active of the interwar national women's organizations. For a discussion of the early women's movement around the Mohyla Institute, see *Iuvileina knyha: 25-littia Instytutu im. Petra Mohyly v Saskatuni* [Jubilee Book: Twenty-Five Years of the Petro Mohyla Institute in Saskatoon] (Winnipeg: "Ukrainskyi holos" Publishers for the Mohyla Institute, 1945), especially pp. 172, 201-02, 297-305, 313-18, 371-75.
57. The Ukrainian Women's Enlightenment Society (Ukrainske Zhinoche Prosvitne Tovarystvo) was organized at the suggestion of Taras Ferley—Liberal MLA in Manitoba—who told an initial gathering of ladies that, "it was absolutely necessary for us to form a women's organization that would be concerned not only with child-rearing and homemaking but also the need for women to become interested in national and political affairs, in order to become the equals of other citizens of this country." See Semen Kovbel and Dmytro Doroshenko, eds., *Propamiatna knyha Ukrainskoho narodnoho domu y Vynnypegu* [Jubilee Book of the Ukrainian National Home in Winnipeg] (Winnipeg: Ukrainian National Home in Winnipeg, 1949), pp. 227-29.
58. The women's groups that emerged in Ontario also performed "traditional" female functions (organizing handicrafts exhibits, bazaars and teas, community dinners), justified on the grounds that they were both indispensable and complemented men's activities; see, for example, D.A. Nykoliak, ed., *Korotkyi istorychnyi narys Ukrainskoho narodnoho domu v Toronto z nahody 35-litnoi pratsi tovarystva* [A Short Historical Outline of the Ukrainian National Home in Toronto on the Occasion of the Thirty-Fifth Anniversary of the Work of the Association] (Toronto: Ukrainian National Home, 1953).
59. The common ties and sense of mutual responsibility being formed among Ukrainians in all parts of Canada are perhaps best illustrated by the monetary campaigns undertaken in the press on behalf of the families of workers killed or injured on the job; see, for example, the plea for help by the widow of a Hamilton worker (*Kanadyiskyi*

rusyn, 15 August 1914), or the letter of gratitude from a Keewatin woman, Maria Greskiv, for the assistance received after a train accident claimed her husband (*Ukrainskyi holos*, 19 February 1913). Three Ukrainian women writing from Port Arthur stressed the need for all Ukrainians in Canada, regardless of faith, to cooperate in helping the victims of the Hillcrest mine disaster in the Crowsnest Pass; see *Ukrainskyi holos*, 15 July 1914.

60. *Kanadyiskyi rusyn*, 2 May 1917.
61. See *Propamiatna knyha z nahody zolotoho iuvileiu poselennia ukrainskoho narodu v Kanadi* [Jubilee Book on the Occasion of the Golden Jubilee of Ukrainian Settlement in Canada] (Yorkton: Episcopal Ordinariate, 1941), p. 76.
62. *Ukrainskyi holos*, 15 July 1914.
63. *Kanadyiskyi rusyn*, 2 May 1917.
64. Based on Darcovich and Yuzyk, *Statistical Compendium*, Series 30.1-12, pp. 177-82. In 1931, 51.9 per cent of Ukrainian women in Ontario were Greek Catholic, 12.9 per cent were Ukrainian Orthodox and 25.5 per cent were Roman Catholic. On the prairies, 84.8 per cent of Ukrainian women still belonged to either the Greek Catholic or Ukrainian Orthodox churches.
65. See *Propamiatna knyha z nahody zolotoho iuvileiu poselennia ukrainskoho narodu v Kanadi*, pp. 96-126, for an outline of organizational and parish work by the Greek Catholic church in Ontario prior to the Second World War.
66. *Propamiatna knyha z nahody zolotoho iuvileiu poselennia ukrainskoho narodu v Kanadi*, pp. 73-76.
67. Based on Darcovich and Yuzyk, *Statistical Compendium*, Series 31.21-39, pp. 231-35, and Series 31.60-75, pp. 238-39.

"But Women Did Come": Working Chinese Women in the Interwar Years

Dora Nipp

There were few Chinese women in Ontario prior to World War Two. In 1911 some thirty years after the arrival of the first Chinese in Toronto, women were only 2.9 per cent of the Chinese population in the province. By 1921 the proportion of women had increased modestly to 4.6 per cent, but not until the 1960s did the sex ratio begin to reach a balance.[1] Impersonal statistics tell nothing, however, of those they represent, of who the women were and how they lived. For the Chinese community the arrival of the women symbolized the final stage of the transition from villager to settler. The arrival of a wife and the immediate responsibilities for dependents strengthened the immigrant's economic and social interests in Canada.

Chinese began to arrive in Ontario well before the Canadian Pacific Railroad (CPR) had been completed, but it was not until the western section was finished that significant numbers began leaving British Columbia for central and eastern Canada. For Canadians the CPR provided a much needed national transport system. But for the Chinese navvies who had been recruited to work on it, its completion resulted in large-scale unemployment. Unable to accumulate enough savings to return to China, the Chinese found themselves not only unemployed, but also caught in a depression. The depression further aggravated already existing anti-Chinese sentiment. As a result a series of laws and regulations designed to limit the economic, social and political participation of the Chinese was implemented. Those who left British Columbia found their way to the small communities that dotted the provinces, and many migrated to the urban centres of Ontario, which did not display the same degree of xenophobia found on the west coast. This, as well as the opportunities in the cities to establish one's own business enterprise, made Toronto a particularly attractive settlement.

Early immigrants were mostly involved in the service industries and were found in either laundry or restaurant work. Unlike either Vancouver or Victoria, in the early days Toronto had no discernible ethnic enclave. It was not until some time later that the perimeters of a "Chinatown" were set out.[2]

Immigration records noted the arrival of the first Chinese female in Canada in 1860, docking in Victoria. Mrs. Lee Chong, who had come via San Francisco, was the wife of a prominent Victoria merchant. It is not clear when the first Chinese woman arrived in Ontario. The 1901 census tract enumerated 629 Chinese in Ontario, but did not differentiate the sexes. Over the next ten-year period, seventy-nine women appear in the records as being born in China, with 2,638 men. The greatest number of women was found to be living in Toronto.[3]

Although it is not possible within this discussion to detail the factors responsible for the paucity of women, it is necessary to provide a summary of the main explanations for the imbalance during this early period. First, it has been argued that the Chinese were not true immigrants; that is, that throughout their stay in the country, they possessed a "sojourner" mentality. Their actions were supposedly proof of their intent to earn as much money as possible as quickly as possible and return to China. The sole reason for being in Canada was to support the family they had left behind.

Another explanation is that restrictive Canadian immigration policies actively discouraged Chinese immigration. The graduated head taxes that were levied—$50 in 1885, $100 in 1900 and finally $500 in 1904[4]—made it virtually impossible for most Chinese labourers to have the luxury of a wife and family. By 1923 the tax was abolished to be replaced by almost complete exclusion with the Chinese Immigration Act. Regardless of these restraints, the decision to send for a wife and children, as with the decision of the men to migrate, was ultimately a personal choice.

Much of the information found in this paper is extracted from the memoirs of Mrs. Anna Ma—the wife of Rev. Ma T.K. Wou, Toronto's first Chinese Presbyterian minister—and from the as yet incomplete autobiography of a Canadian-born woman who shall be referred to as Mrs. L. In her memoirs the latter describes with sensitivity her mother (Mrs. Y) who arrived in Canada in

1898. From taped conversations with the children of some of the early women also comes a partial glimpse of the pioneers' lives. Their roles as mothers, wives and business partners were defined by their position as women who circumvented imposed restraints and came to terms with life in Canada. For example, women widowed in Canada all chose to remain as permanent settlers and became bread-winners and decision-makers. Regardless of a woman's status prior to her arrival, her status within the immigrant community would be re-determined by her husband's social standing.

This paper focuses on the interwar years. One woman, however, Mrs. Y, arrived before this era and so discussion of her experiences in Ontario will begin before the First World War. The experiences of Mrs. Y who lived in North Bay and her youngest daughter (Mrs. L) who was born there were quite different from those of women who resided in larger urban centres. The women in this discussion had, however, shared a common experience as Chinese Christians. Unlike their sisters in British Columbia, Ontario Chinese women were actively involved with the church. The presence of China-trained Chinese missionaries and the concentrated effort of the United and Presbyterian churches among the Chinese were influencing factors. For the only Chinese family in North Bay, Christianity complemented their Chinese heritage and the mother devoted much time and effort to combine the two into a working model.

At the time of her arrival in the east, Mrs. Y was twenty years old, her husband a number of years older. He had worked on the CPR before moving east, first to Boston, then to Montreal. Mrs. Y was the first Chinese bride in Montreal, and she and her husband settled into a laundry that Mr. Y's relatives operated on Ontario Street. The family lived in Montreal for seven years during which time Mrs. Y had four children. Her second son was the first Chinese boy born in Quebec. Little is known of her life during this time until the family moved to North Bay. Here they joined Mr. Y's relatives who also ran a laundry. There were no other Chinese families in the community, nor were there any single Chinese women. In North Bay Mrs. Y had four more children, before her husband suddenly died of a heart attack at the age of fifty-one.

Mrs. Y was left to care for eight children with the youngest only eighteen months. Mrs. Y's children remember her as a deeply religious woman who struggled to support the young family. Her informal support system consisted of an uncle and other of her husband's male relatives. By her son and daughter's accounts,

Mrs. Y immediately assumed the dual role of mother and father, relinquishing the responsibility of raising her children to no one.

Mrs. Y was fortunate to have received an education as a child in China. Although this was not highly unusual, at the same time it was not a common practice. Mrs. Y was anxious that her own children would also receive a solid education and this meant returning to China. Her daughter recalls that her mother "saved frugally" and the entire family left North Bay with their "uncle."

Shortly after returning to her husband's village, Mrs. Y found that the parcel of land her children were to receive could not possibly support her family. She was not one to dwell on misfortunes over which she had little control. Mrs. Y enrolled the older children in schools close to the village, and with the two youngest she travalled in the countryside before leaving for Hong Kong and then back to Canada. "Mother returned to Canada to earn money to educate the family." With her she took the eldest and youngest sons, and the youngest daughter. Returning to North Bay, Mrs. Y continued with the small laundry. Again, "an uncle assisted mother in providing for the large family, and we were never hungry or lived on relief... we survived on our little laundry for our livelihood."[5]

Mrs. Y had no intention of returning again to China, but chose to raise her children in North Bay. It would appear that she led a somewhat insular life and that her efforts were directed entirely toward her family. Hers was the only Chinese family in the town, and she does not seem to have had any contact with Chinese women in other areas. Work seemed to consume every moment of her time. Her son says that she did not sleep much because she did not have the time, and instead stole naps in between tasks. To be able to pay for the children's studies in China and eventually to pay for their return passage, Mrs. Y gave up the laundry and opened a small restaurant. Known as the New York Restaurant, like most Chinese restaurants of that era it did not serve Chinese food. To assist their mother, the children came home during lunch hour. Mrs. L remembers that, "Sometimes we were kept so busy that at noon hour we did not have time to lunch, so we stood up to eat our sandwiches before returning to school."[6]

Mrs. Y's decision to leave the laundry and set up a restaurant was most likely due to the higher returns that the latter offered. During the early years of Ontario's Chinese community, laundries and restaurants were the preferred investments. Both allowed those involved to keep business expenses to a minimum. This ensured that they were able to make at least a small margin of profit. According to one study of Chinese in Toronto, if they could choose most Chinese would operate restaurants rather than laundries because while the initial capital investment was two to three times greater, the profit margin was also more significant.

Even before she immigrated to Canada, Mrs. Y was a devout Christian who wanted very much for her children to grow up as good Christians: "She brought up her children with a Christian upbringing, and taught us to be thoughtful of others. At the time she received much criticism [in China]. When our brothers and sisters graduated village school, she sent the girls to the Anglican mission in Fat Shan and the boys were enrolled in the school in Canton City."[7]

Mrs. Y's efforts, however, were ill rewarded, not because she did not succeed in business, but because repeated tragedies struck the family. Her son and two daughters who were studying in China succumbed to tuberculosis. Later on the youngest son, who had also returned to continue his education, contracted TB and died in 1921 in a sanatorium in North Bay. In 1921 a burglary attempt left Mrs. Y grazed by a bullet, but the second shot proved fatal to her eldest son. At his funeral service she "sobbed that each son she raised to manhood had been taken away from her. She told us of a vision she had had one night. She dreamt an angel entered through the back window and took something away."[8] No suspect in the burglary was ever caught.

Mrs. Y's youngest daughter (Mrs. L) spent little time in China, and unlike her brothers and sisters grew up in North Bay. In her reminiscence of the mother-daughter relationship of a young woman caught in the conflicting demands of growing up Chinese in a Canadian society, Mrs. L recalled that Mrs. Y tried to impress upon her children that they were Chinese, and that it was important not to forget one's heritage. In their interaction with non-Chinese children in the community, they were taught to remember that they were "different" from everyone else and had to act accordingly.[9]

Mrs. L spoke of the difficult position in which her mother's attitude placed her:

> In my strict upbringing I was not allowed to associate with many of my age, so I had very few friends. I was reminded that I was Chinese and discriminated against. Being a Canadian-born Chinese [sic] I tried to follow the ways of Canadians. Yet I found it difficult at times because of my respect and obedience to my mother.[10]

Although her companions were not many, Mrs. L did have friends with whom she felt very close. From them she learned Canadian ways. "I remember the first Christmas on our return.

Everybody at school was talking about Santa Claus and his bag of toys. So on Christmas Eve, D and I hung our stockings but found nothing the next morning. Mother did not understand the Western customs. I considered it a real treasure when my schoolmate... presented me with a beautiful used doll."[11] Mrs. L was taught proper table manners, and how to play the piano. To her these were important steps to her "Canadianization." One special friend was a major influence in her life. From her she learned to enjoy her studies at school and received much religious teaching. "When I told mother how much she meant to me as a real friend, mother used to remind me we had no friends because we had no money, but I thought otherwise."[12]

In her memoirs, Mrs. L reveals one of many obstacles facing not just Canadian teenagers, but in particular a Chinese-Canadian teenager:

> By the time I was going to high school, I was interested in my studies and in sports. I was on the basketball team. At this stage, like all others I became interested in boys, but could only [sic] admire them at a distance and was taught I was not one of them. I felt discriminated. So with a strong upbringing with Chinese customs, I was not allowed to associate with them. I recall a beautiful Chinese girl. Her mother was French. Her father was transferred to the CNR telegram office. She fell in love with a Canadian boy [meaning European Canadian] but later he gave her up because she was too ashamed to introduce him to her Chinese father. Her sister was a clever student, but lived a most unhappy life. Among the French she felt unaccepted and like-wise she was not accepted among the Chinese because of her mixed blood, but both sisters were beautiful.[13]

In her career aspirations, Mrs. L was not unlike other women of her age. In her memoirs she stated that:

> It was time to decide what I would like to be. When I mentioned nursing to mother, she was stunned. That was one of the lowest professions one could consider next to being a soldier... Financially, I knew I could not afford a college education, so I took up business administration and a commercial course. On graduation, I worked in an insurance firm.[14]

One of Mrs. L's pastimes was writing to pen-pals. Between studies and working for her mother she had little time for other activities. It was through corresponding with friends that she met her future husband. As Mrs. L was one of the few Chinese women in Ontario of marriageable age, it was only a matter of time before young men would seek her out. Mr. L was living in Brockville some miles from North Bay when they began corresponding. Mr. L had arrived in Canada at the age of twelve to help his father and uncles in their laundry business. Mrs L's family was not very pleased with her choice of husband. Her mother and brother were afraid that Mr. L, who was eleven years Mrs. L's senior, already had a wife in China.

After Mrs. L married she returned with her husband to Brockville. On the day she arrived she was wearing the sable coat Mr. L had given her as a wedding gift. "It was the hit of the town," she recalled. The environment Mrs. L found herself in contrasted with the more insular life of her mother. Mrs. L moved in with an extended family which included a father-in-law, bachelor uncles and one uncle with his wife and children. In later years, Mr. and Mrs. L established their own restaurant. The uncle and his family lived in Brockville till approximately 1918 when they moved to Iroquois, Ontario, where they too entered the restaurant business.

The largest concentration of Chinese families in Ontario was in Toronto. The city appeared to offer women already in a limited circle greater opportunities and interests in their personal lives than those who lived in the smaller communities had. The number of women in Toronto was, of course, an important factor. The internal social structure included wives, mothers and children. Another area which set those in the city and smaller communities apart was the strong Christian involvement of the Chinese in Toronto. The influence of the church helped foster a closer community.

Recent graduates from mission schools in China provided the single most significant influence on the Chinese families. The wife of the first Chinese Presbyterian minister, Rev. T.K. Ma, who had arrived with her husband in 1914 was active in church work with the women of the congregation. In July 1914 the couple had set sail for Canada aboard a Russian liner. By this time they had had a son. Rev. and Mrs. Ma settled into living quarters in Toronto that were part of a laundry owned by two church members. Later that year, the congregation was growing so quickly that the church needed larger premises. Another location was soon found at 187 Church Street. The rent at the time was $187 per month. The Ma family lived upstairs on the third floor, and the lower sections of the house were used for holding Presbyterian services, meetings, social functions and Chinese school: "We had a full program every Sunday. Our congregation consisted then of twenty to thirty males." Below is a typical Sunday program:

10:00 a.m.	Sing-song led by Mr. Dong
11:00 a.m.	Service
2:00 p.m.	Bible Class led by Rev. Ma and Mr. Mark
3:30 p.m.	Open-air meeting in Chinatown
5:00 p.m.	Evangelical meeting
6:00 p.m.	Dinner in the basement of the church
7:00 p.m.	Evening service[15]

In 1919 the congregation purchased another building to accommodate the growing number of members. Their new address was at 124 University Avenue.

Less than two years later, in 1916, three Chinese women joined the church in Toronto.[16] This group eventually became the women's auxiliary. The members included: Mrs W.L. Mark, Mrs. Lock Kwong and Mrs. Mark Park. In her memoirs, Mrs. Ma records that they met regularly at the Knox Presbyterian Church: "Because of an Old Chinese custom which did not allow women to meet in public, the women got together without the presence of men." She also states that separate meetings for women only were necessary before the women could even be encouraged to attend without going against this practice.[17]

Her church work kept Mrs. Ma very active, apparently leaving little time for the domestic chores normally expected of women. The cooking was Mr. Ma's responsibility, not because of Mrs. Ma's busy schedule but because she "simply couldn't cook." Shopping for groceries which would have required a trip to Chinatown was also left to Mr. Ma. In recalling his childhood, one of the Ma sons told how there were missionaries constantly at the house to help look after the family of six boys (one later died in childhood) and four girls.

In 1927 the family went to Hong Kong on furlough. On their return to Ontario in 1930, they moved to a three-acre farm situated behind present-day Humber Golf Course in Toronto. Mrs. Ma, at this time, was less active in church work and spent most of her time caring for the family, growing vegetables and giving Chinese lessons to missionaries at the farm.

One young woman from the Toronto Presbyterian church, Miss Dickson, asked Mrs. Ma if she would be interested in continuing her work in the city looking after meetings and teaching four women to read the Bible. For her services, Mrs. Ma received $15 a month which was later increased to $20:[18]

> It was rewarding work. Two months later, five women asked to be baptized. When Miss Dickson heard this, she was quite surprised... Miss Dickson, who was then working with the kindergarten began to join me in the afternoons visiting Chinese in Toronto; every fortnight we made a trip to New Toronto. Miss Dickson was a fine and dedicated Christian. We got along famously and worked for a year or so together until she left to return to her home in Edmonton. To increase our number, I asked the Women's Missionary Society if they could supply volunteer drivers to help bring the young mothers and their children to our meetings. They found three volunteers for three Sundays of every month. For me it was a period full of joy and happiness—to be doing God's work.[19]

But her husband died suddenly, leaving Anna Ma with a young family to raise on her own. Her son recalls: "Mother held the family together. She learned how to cook after father died. We ate fish heads for a long time... managed to get these fish heads from people at almost no cost and they were nutritious."[20]

In her memoirs, Mrs. Ma records:

> I was left with nine children all still at school. Miss Mathew was in charge of the women's work. She [sic] came to visit me, and [sic] suggested I apply for welfare to which I replied, 'I'd rather die than take charity.' When the minister of Knox came to see me, he found I only had twenty-five cents in my purse; he gave me $3:00. At a further meeting he handed me $20. Everyone was very kind. The church gave me $100; the relatives helped a bit; the Mission Department continued to pay my husband's salary and rent supplement of $140 for three months. When Rev. David Smith who was in charge of the Chinese work across Canada came on tour, he asked me to carry on the work for the next few months and he would pay me $45 a month.[21]

Mrs. Ma continued supporting her family by renting out rooms in her house. She also kept on working for the church, though perhaps less actively than before. By this time the number of Chinese families in Toronto had increased to at least thirteen.

In her study of Toronto's early Chinese community, Valerie Mah found that by 1933 thirteen families lived in the Chinatown area. She concluded that most of the marriages were arranged—that is, the couples were brought together by their families after the background and compatibility of the man and woman had been thoroughly checked. Of these women, three came to Canada to be married; three arrived with their first child; one was the minister's wife; and for six information was unavailable.[22]

Of the thirteen families, all were housewives and three had received a missionary education in China. It is difficult to classify these women simply under the category of "housewife" because, with the exception of one in the group, they all worked alongside their husbands in the family businesses. The following are samples of case studies conducted as part of Valerie Mah's research.

It was the norm for a Chinese widow in Toronto either to continue with the business her late husband began or to enter into her own. After the death of her husband, one young widow opened a small laundry at St. Clair and Lansdowne avenues, which she operated with the help of her two sons and an assistant:

> E had a bicycle for picking up socks from other laundries which needed repairs. T used to help out front. T and E turned collars and cuffs and darned socks. Mrs. X started the business with money borrowed from a Chinese credit union. Those who wanted a loan bid for an amount saying they would repay with so much interest every week. Mrs. X obtained the capital and was responsible for repayment.[23]

At the time, to start up a laundry required anywhere from $500-$600 up to $2,000.[24]

Mrs. X's laundry was open until "at least supper time" and often as late as 8:00 or 9:00 p.m. when the day's work had been completed. She did not handle large orders such as those from restaurants or hotels. Instead she dealt mainly with families and unmarried individuals who lived in nearby rented rooms.[25]

The laundry was not a large operation, and therefore Mrs. X was able to keep the overhead to a minimum. This also meant, however, that the profit margin was not large. In the mid-twenties laundries were charging twelve cents a shirt, fifteen cents a sheet, five cents a collar and three cents for hankies.[26] In her laundry Mrs. X and her helper did the washing, starching and ironing themselves. "The irons were not electric. They were the kind that leaned against the stove. They couldn't afford the electric ones."

The Chinese laundries were known for their fine hand wash. Tom Lock, the son of one of the widows, told Valerie Mah:

> To make the linen white, we used to put the soiled clothing into a big square steel tank, 4′ × 4′ × 6′ deep, on top of the coal stove. We would fill the tank using a hose and add bleach, stirring the washing with a big stick. After, ma would stand on a stool, reach into the boiling water and drag out the clothes with a stick. She would then drop them in a pail and transfer them to the washing-machine. She was less than five feet tall and her feet were once bound.[27]

If one was prepared to put in long hours, the laundry business was fairly stable. Although, compared to restaurants, the profit margins were small, laundries seemed less affected by general business fluctuations. During hard economic times, for example, it seems that laundries did not suffer as badly as restaurants and rarely lost money.

In addition to the domestic responsibilities of caring for the children, managing household affairs, cooking, cleaning and sewing, women worked: "All mothers worked in their husband's businesses, mostly in the laundries—except the wife of a merchant. She was seen as an upper-class woman because she was educated. She was one of my mother's former pupils in Hong Kong." Family outings were not common because most Chinese businesses operated six or seven days a week. On Sundays, the women and children would attend church, and later in the day, after services, the married men went to Chinatown to shop and exchange news.[28] One Chinese laundry was located at Mortimer and Pape avenues:

> My mother helped out for many long hours in the laundry. She did not go out even to shop. She worked the longest. My mother worked six days and also Sunday. We worked until eight or nine each night. There were eight children in our family and we had two to three helpers. Sometimes she had to cook for thirteen. She was too busy to belong to any group. She didn't go to Chinatown. Besides, she didn't know the way.[29]

The 1920s, 1930s and 1940s witnessed the emergence and maturation of a generation of Canadian-born Chinese from the original thirteen families. By 1931 Chinese children were enumerated in the Toronto Board of Education records.

The growing number of local-born children also inspired the establishment of Chinese language schools in Toronto, Windsor and Hamilton. The Exclusion Act of 1923 made it no longer feasible to send sons and daughters back to China for their Chinese education. The responsibility thus rested with the community itself. In his study on Chinese schools in Canada, Gordon Taylor states that there were children who were classified under three groups for whom these schools were established. The largest group was the Canadian-born of purely Chinese parentage. Although immigration legislation discouraged and then completely excluded the arrival of women, "The families here have been prolific and as a result the native-born Chinese are comparatively numerous." He further notes that, "in practically every case the father has been Chinese. Only two cases are known, both in Ontario, of white paternity and Chinese maternity, and in at least one the parents were married in China."[30]

Toward the end of the 1930s an increasing number of Chinese began to arrive in Toronto. By 1940, after the depression, some 1,500 arrived from the four western provinces looking for greater opportunities. While some were China-born, a large number were second-generation Chinese who migrated to Toronto because Ontario's attitude concerning the Chinese was less harsh and legislation was not as restrictive as in British Columbia. Unlike the Chinese in British Columbia, the Chinese in Ontario had not been disenfranchised and could enter the professions of law, pharmacy or accounting, which afforded increased social mobility. This, coupled with the active Christian Chinese groups, resulted in a community that had a greater vested interest in Canadian life than British Columbia's Chinese community. By the 1940s Toronto's Chinese Christian population accounted for approximately 40 per cent of the total number of Chinese in Canada.[31]

When British Columbia refused to admit Chinese women into the health professions, the prospective students approached schools in Ontario. The Women's College Hospital in Toronto admitted Agnes Chan, the young ward of the missionary-run Oriental Home and School in Victoria, B.C. In 1923 she graduated from nursing with honours and continued her studies in Detroit. In the same year, another Victoria woman graduated from the University of Toronto medical school. Entering on a scholarship with the help of the president of the Women's Missionary Society, Mrs. Steele, Victoria Cheung graduated with an M.B. and became the first woman to intern at Toronto General Hospital.[32]

On July 1, 1923 Canada passed the Chinese Immigration (Exclusion) Act which effectively ended Chinese immigration for the next twenty-four years. Its effect on the community was reflected in the rapid decline of the number of Chinese in Canada. Many returned to China, and the thousands who remained had to endure decades of separation from families and friends. Those who stayed probably did so for economic reasons. They existed in a peculiar ambience without the comforts of wives and families. One informant says that when she arrived in Toronto, there were seven Chinese families in the United church and about eight in the Presbyterian church. The scarcity of women resulted in relationships or marriage with non-Chinese women. The interviewee observed that many mixed couples were married at the Presbyterian church because the deaconess insisted that the children be recognized.

The impact of the act was also felt in business enterprises. In 1923 there was the greatest number of restaurants (471) in the history of Toronto, but by the 1930s restaurants numbered only 104, and the number of laundries fell from 471 to 355.[33] From the mid-1930s and into the 1940s there appeared a gradual stabilization of Chinese businesses but without the vigour witnessed in the 1920s' period of growth.

The act stunted the growth of the community, but it could not curtail the inevitable acculturation of the local-born Chinese, nor could it deprive them completely of attaining specific goals. It is unfortunate that so little has been written of the people who grew up during this era. Individuals who grew up in Canada during the 1920s and 1930s describe a small and tight group of "hybrid" Canadians who essentially "set the stage" for generations of Chinese Canadians to come. One such person, Mrs. J, like Mrs. Y, Mrs. Ma and all the other working mothers discussed here, was typical, yet remarkable in her accomplishments as wife and mother.

Mrs. J arrived in Toronto in 1935 from British Columbia. As with many who left the west coast for employment opportunities, Jean had come east looking for work. She had been born in Nanaimo, British Columbia; her mother was the first Chinese bride in that coal-mining town. Mrs. J worked from the age of twelve when her father had to take her out of school so that she could help support her family of twelve brothers and sisters. She was sixteen years old when she came to Toronto to work with her sister. When she arrived in the city, Mrs. J recalls that there were about twelve to fourteen Chinese women in Toronto. Less than three years later in 1937, she and her cousin borrowed $200 from relatives to start up their own business. Together they opened a fruit store at St. Clair and Bathurst streets, called Wong Brothers. She recalls that it took them two years to pay off their debt. Mrs. J was the first Chinese-Canadian woman in Toronto to have her own fruit business. The two did well enough to bring Mrs. J's parents and brothers and sisters to Toronto. Soon after Mrs. J and her cousin branched out to open stores in other areas of the city.

The twenty-year-old was fast gaining business experience, but in spite of her success, Mrs. J's mother still felt it necessary to find a husband for her daughter. The time came when her mother told her it was time to get married. After thoroughly examining interested parties, they thought that a certain gentleman was the most suitable. "You will meet him today and he will come over for tea," was what she was told:[34]

> My mother chose for me. I was one of the last of the six in the family to be chosen. When it came to my brother, my

> mother chose for him. He went out to meet her and said, 'No, I don't like her.' And my mother said, 'The nerve of him!' My father and mother were a little more lenient with me [sic]. They said, 'We've checked him out thoroughly...' I knew they wanted the best for me.[35]

Mrs. J had been taught from childhood that the wife was to work beside her husband. For the forty-four years of their marriage, she and her husband worked as a team in the family businesses.

Like many young Chinese-Canadian women of her age, Mrs. J was very active with the Young Christian Group and the Women's Auxiliary in raising funds for the war effort. Later on, even with a young family to care for, she still worked closely with the community. In cultural areas—she was a member of one of the Chinese dramatic associations—and political involvement, she represented Chinese-Canadian interests. During the talks with the federal government for the repeal of the Chinese Exclusion Act, Mrs. J was the only woman delegate to Ottawa. "I was speaking on behalf of Ontario, but I was really representing Chinese women across Canada. It was important to have a woman delegate because we were fighting for family unity."

Far from an in-depth analysis of the world created by Chinese-Canadian women in the prewar decades, this article explores, through perhaps the only research available, the bits and pieces of reality as remembered by eye-witnesses. Chinese-Canadian women were few, but the presence of these few women resulted in the creation of a community from what was essentially a society of bachelor migrants. It is commonplace that cultural mores and values are established in the basic family unit and that women in all societies bear the greater responsibility for their preservation. The Chinese women in Ontario were no exception. Caught between the conflicting demands of children who wished to become more Canadian and husbands who saw them as their link with traditional Chinese culture, these women were ultimately responsible for resolving those demands and establishing what it meant to be Chinese Canadian.

Notes

The author would like to thank Valerie and Daniel Mah for their co-operation in providing information for this paper. She also extends her appreciation to the Women's Issues Committee of the Chinese Canadian National Council for access to their oral history collection. Part of the interviews used will be published in the Committee's Book Project entitled, "Voices of Chinese Canadian Women."

1. *Seventh Census of Canada*, 1931, vol. 1, Table 24, "Birthplace of Population by Sex."
2. In Toronto, the early Chinese businesses and shops were found in small pockets rather than localized in a certain area. For example, in 1910, groupings were located along Queen Street West and York Street. Later on shops extended from Queen Street to Terrauley, near Denison. (See further, Valerie Mah, "The Bachelor Society: A Look at Toronto's Early Chinese Community from 1878-1924," April 1978).
3. *Sixth Census of Canada*, 1921.
4. Canada, Parliament, Sessional papers.
5. Memoirs of Mrs. L, n.d. n.p., p. 6.
6. Ibid., p. 9.
7. Ibid., p. 15.
8. Ibid., p. 24.
9. Ibid., p. 30.
10. Ibid., p. 31.
11. Ibid., p. 22.
12. Ibid., p. 27.
13. Ibid., p. 32.
14. Ibid., p. 33.
15. Memoirs of Anna Ma, n.d. n.p., p. 58.
16. S.S. Osterhout, *Orientals in Canada. The Story of the Work of the United Church of Canada with Asiatics in Canada* (Toronto: Ryerson Press, 1929), p. 185.
17. Memoirs of Anna Ma, p. 62.
18. Ibid., p. 73.
19. Ibid., p. 74.
20. Interview with D.M., September 1985.
21. Memoirs of Anna Ma, p. 79.
22. Ibid., p. 23.
23. Interview with D.M.
24. See Mah, "The Bachelor Society," p. 23.
25. Ibid., p. 24.
26. Ibid., p. 24.
27. Ibid.; interview with Tom Lock, p. 23.
28. Ibid., p. 35.
29. Ibid.; interview with Dorothy Soo, p. 25.
30. Gordon Taylor, "Chinese Schools in Canada" (M.A., McGill University, 1933), p. 70.
31. Edgar Wickberg, et al., *From China to Canada: A History of the Chinese Communities in Canada* (Toronto: McClelland and Stewart, 1982), p. 127.

32. "They Came Through. The Stories of Chinese Canadians," Toronto, Literature Department Women's Missionary Society, committee on Missionary Education, p. 7, United Church Archives.
33. Richard Thompson, "The State and the Ethnic Community. The Changing Social Organizations of Toronto's Chinatown" (Ph.D diss., University of Michigan, 1973), p. 39.
34. Interview with Mrs. J, 1985.
35. Ibid.

From *Contadina* to Worker: Southern Italian Immigrant Working Women in Toronto, 1947-62

Franca Iacovetta

On Thursday, 16 November 1956, Maria R. and her daughter arrived in Toronto from her peasant farm in Abruzzi.[1] She was met at Union Station by her husband Eneo, who had left her a year previously for work in Toronto. After eating dinner with relatives, she was ushered into her new home—a basement flat in a Calabrian's house. Next day, Maria and Eneo, who took the day off from his Royal York Hotel janitorial job, went to Honest Ed's discount department store to shop for household necessities, including an espresso coffe-maker and pots for cooking spaghetti. To Maria's delight, next morning the Santa Claus Parade passed by their Dupont Street home. At seven o'clock Monday morning, Maria went directly to work at a nearby laundry where a sister-in-law had secured her a job as a steampress operator at thirty-seven dollars a week. For twenty years Maria worked at many such low-skilled jobs—sewing, cooking, tending a grocery store and as a cashier—until 1976 when she finally withdrew from the work force to care for her dying husband.[2]

Women played an important role in the immigration of southern Italian peasant families to post-World War Two Toronto. Within the patriarchal framework of the family, Italian women performed demanding roles as immigrants, workers, wives and mothers. Their active commitment to the family helped bridge the move from Old World to New as women's labour, both paid and unpaid, continued to help ensure the survival and material well-being of their families. The transition from *contadina* (peasant) to worker did not require a fundamental break in the values of women long accustomed to contributing many hours of hard labour to the family. As workers, though, they confronted new forms of economic exploitation and new rhythms of work and life imposed by industrial capitalism. Women at home similarly performed important economic and social functions and endured the alienating and racist aspects of urban industrial life. Bolstered by networks of kinfolk and *paesani* (co-villagers) and the persistence of traditional social forms, women not only endured such hardships but displayed a remarkable capacity to incorporate their new experiences as working-class women into traditionally rooted notions of familial and motherly responsibility.

This article will consider three aspects of southern Italian women's role in postwar immigration: Old-World conditions, chain migration and early living and working conditions in Toronto. Based on documentary research and interviews, the conclusions presented here are tentative and exploratory. While the essay focuses on women's activities and perceptions, an attempt also has been made to provide the structural contexts—political, economic, social and familial—in which those experiences took place.

Following the long interruption caused by government restrictions, the Great Depression and the Second World War, Italian immigration resumed on a major scale once again in the late forties and fifties. Millions of temporary and permanent emigrants travelled to continental Europe, North and South America, and Australia. Between 1951 and 1961 overseas emigrants numbered over one million; 250,000, or 25 per cent of them, settled in Canada. A target city after 1951, Metropolitain Toronto alone attracted some 90,000, or 40 per cent, of the total Italian immigration to Canada in this period.[3]

Women and children comprised a substantial proportion of the influx. Over 81,000 women aged fifteen and over arrived in Canada from 1951-61. Between 25,000-30,000 women, many with children, settled in Toronto. Young, married women sponsored by their husbands and families predominated.[4] After 1952, for example, "dependent" women and children accounted for between 40-54 per cent of the annual wave of Italians into the country. In a typical year, 1958, dependent women alone comprised almost 35 per cent (or 6,064) of the total adult population (17, 381). And they made up over 70 per cent of the number of total adult females (8,515).[5] Most women were former peasants from the Mezzogiorno—the southern agricultural regions of Abruzzi-Molise, Basilicata, Campagnia, Puglia and Calabria. Peasants from the south accounted for nearly 60 per cent of the total Italian immigration to Canada in this period.[6]

As southern European Catholics, these women were the target of nativist hostilities. Anticipating the postwar influx of non-British immigrants, the Anglican church in 1941 depicted southern Europeans as "amenable to the fallacies of dictatorship, less versed in the tradition and art of democratic government," and better suited to the hot climate and fragile political structures of Latin America.[7] The British Dominions Emigration Society dismissed northern Italians as communists and southerners as unsatisfactory settlers.[8] Provincial officials, who worried about increasing numbers of Jews and Catholics entering Protestant Ontario, cooperated with manufacturers in recruiting skilled tradesmen exclusively from Great Britain.[9] Even federal immigration officials who did recruit from Italy focused on the inferiority of southern Italians, whom they portrayed as backward and slovenly, and they worried that these peasants significantly outnumbered their more "industrious" northern compatriots. "The Italian South peasant," one official wrote, "is not the type we are looking for in Canada. His standard of living, his way of life, even his civilization seems so different that I doubt if he could ever become an asset to our country."[10]

Immigration officials interested in recruiting Italian male labourers did not expect the married peasant woman to work and so they paid no attention to her. (By contrast, they welcomed some 16,000 females, mostly single northerners, who arrived as trained domestics, hairdressers and seamstresses.[11]) A 1950 reciprocal agreement between Canada and Italy that removed customs duties on bridal trousseaus entering either country at least recognized women's role in setting up a home in the new society. But it also reflected notions about married women's prescribed roles as wife and mother and reinforced the assumption that married southern Italian women were dependent upon their men and could make no real contribution to Canadian society.[12]

Contrary to contemporary assumptions that women were little more than part of the male newcomer's cultural baggage—a view some male scholars have also adopted—southern Italian women were active agents in family migration. A consideration of their role must begin with life in the Old World.

Southern peasants did not come from a background of isolated, closed villages, nor were they completely self-sufficient subsistence farmers isolated from a market economy and ignorant of the world beyond their village. Typically, southern Italians resided in hilltop agro-towns or villages *(paese)* situated in the region's mountainous terrain. Daily, the town's peasants (*contadini*) and agricultural labourers (*braccianti*) walked long distances to the scattered fields and landed estates below. With populations that numbered in the thousands, towns were characterized by complex social structures and class divisions evident in the presence of gentry, middle men and professional notaries as well as bureaucrats, artisans, peasants, agricultural labourers and the unemployed poor.[13] One women, Assunta C., for instance, described her home town of San Paulino in Campagnia as maintaining various commercial and retail and food services, blacksmith and tailor shops and a train station. People located in village fragments and hamlets had access to larger urban centres.[14]

Various long-term factors produced Italy's infamous "southern problem" and made life brutal for its residents. The heat and aridity of summer, followed by heavy but sporadic winter downpours, resulted in poor irrigation and soil erosion. Though more southerly areas also grew fruits, olives, nuts and poor-quality wine, peasants relied heavily upon wheat and other grain crops. Hilly and mountainous terrain precluded mechanization and encouraged traditional labour-intensive farming techniques that relied upon an ox or cow, a few simple tools and brute strength.

Another serious handicap was the highly fragmented nature of peasant holdings. Outside the latifundia, gentry-controlled estates were divided into small tenancies rented or sold to peasants who simultaneously might own, rent and even share-crop numerous small and widely scattered plots of questionable soil quality. This further discouraged mechanization or intensive cultivation and reinforced undercapitalized and labour intensive methods of farming. The region's "natural" poverty was exacerbated by decades of political neglect as successive governments failed to provide irrigation, develop industry and institute land reforms; and it contrasted sharply with the industrialized and agriculturally more prosperous North.[15]

Though tied to underproductive plots, *i contadini* were also part of a larger market economy; they engaged in regional trade networks and participated in a cash economy on a local, national and international scale. Peasants had economic and social connections to the surrounding regions and urban centres where they exchanged money for goods and services. Maria L., who came from a village in Molise too small to sustain artisan or retail activity, noted how family members frequently visited the nearby town to buy shoes and tools or call for the doctor. The women I interviewed said that their families had regularly sold surplus wheat, eggs and vegetables to co-villagers and residents in nearby villages who came to their home. A women from the Vasto-Giardi area near Campobasso in Molise, Assunta Ca., sold eggs door to door in her village. And women also purchased linens and cloths from travelling merchants.[16]

The very poverty of the South, which made total subsistence impossible for peasants, compelled families to pursue economic strategies that drew them further into a cash economy. Peasant families effectively supplemented meagre farm incomes by sending out members, usually men, on temporary sojourns as wage workers. Hiring themselves out as day labourers on the landed estates (*giornalieri*), many men found seasonal work in the local or regional economy. Other men, such as the fathers of Maria R. and Vincenza, found outside employment as seasonal woods workers.[17] Others sought jobs in agriculture, railway construction and in the building trades either on the Continent or overseas. These activities and the cash remittances families received brought them into contact with highly industrialized economies around the world—a pattern which intensified during the decade following the Second World War.[18]

Although scholars debate definitions of the nuclear and extended family, they agree that the family is the most important economic and social unit to peasants and that it provided the basis of peasant solidarity in the South. Familial allegiances were sufficiently strong to exclude membership in other institutions and (apart from some exceptional cases of peasant protests and experiments in peasant communism) communal or collectivist associations. Even the celebration of local feasts took on familial forms.[19]

As the basic mode of production and social organization, the peasant family relied upon the maximum labour power of every member of the household, and each person was expected to sacrifice individual needs and contribute to the family's survival. Women interviewed described typical work days by focusing on how every member performed a necessary task. Some, such as Julia, recalled how the relentless work of farming was made more enjoyable by the camaraderie of family and kinfolk: "we worked so very hard... we get up at the crack of dawn to go to work in the *campagnia* [fields] but we singing... happy because we're together."[20] Beyond the privileged sphere of close family, members of the extended *familiari*—cousins, aunts, uncles and in-laws—also shared this mutual trust and help when it did not interfere with the priorities of the family. (In practice, however, conflicts often occurred.) Nevertheless, such status was denied to all others except *i compari*—non-relatives who gained admittance to the *familiari* through the ritual kinship of godparenthood (*comparagio*). Extreme familialism in the South also involved a distrust of others and constant gossiping about others' misfortune, though people did share a spirit of loyalty to their native village or town and its residents (*campanelismo*).[21]

With respect to women, the literature focuses on the twin themes of sexual segregation and subordination. The patriarchal organization of the southern Italian family and society and the cultural mores of the South did impose heavy restrictions on the choices and behaviour of women. As women interviewed remarked, "honourable" women did not accompany men from outside the household in public unless chaperoned. During local dances, Sunday afternoon visits in the piazza, and at religious festivities, young adults socialized under the watchful eyes of their elders. The very concept of familial *onore* (honour) so valued by Italians rested in large part upon the sexual purity of wives, daughters and sisters and men's success in guarding the virtue of their women and in playing the predominant role of family bread-winner. Linked to prevailing notions of male self-esteem and dominance, an almost obsessive fear that women might engage in pre- and extra-marital sex and thereby bring shame to their entire family was central to women's oppression in southern Italy. Constant supervision of their activities was the inevitable result.[22]

Male privilege was exercised widely within the public sphere. Men were freer to socialize and lead the religious and social feasts celebrated within the village. Considered the family's chief decision-maker, the male head acted as the family's representative in its dealings with the outside world. This included making annual rental payments to absentee landlords, journeying out of the region in search of work, or acting as the main marriage negotiator for children—a task that carried a highly visible profile. Assunta C.'s father, for example, spent two weeks consulting people, including the local cleric and doctor, before granting final approval to his daughter's prospective husband.[23]

Nevertheless, a model of male dominance/female submission is ultimately too simplistic to account for the experiences of peasant women in the Mezzogiorno. It ignores the complexity of gender relations in Italy and serves to underestimate the importance of female labour to peasant family production. The dictates of the household economy regularly drew women outside of the home to participate in agricultural production. Though the supposed "natural" link between women and domestic labour persisted, women's work roles included domestic and farm duties. And both involved back-breaking efforts.[24]

Domestic responsibilities included cooking, cleaning and child care, as well as weaving, sewing clothes and, especially during the winter slack period, producing embroidered linens and crocheted tablecloths for bridal trousseaus. Such labours were time consuming and arduous. As Maria L. explained, doing laundry involved fetching water from the town well to boil and then soaking the items for an hour before carrying them to a nearby stream where they were rinsed and laid out on the rocks to dry. Cooking over open wood stoves was hot and dirty work, and the stoves required constant maintenance and cleaning.[25]

Women and girls also farmed—clearing the plots, sowing and planting, hoeing and sharing in the overall work of the summer grain harvest, a project that drew on help from kinfolk and neighbours. At home, women might supervise the threshing and perform the winnowing process. During the autumn ploughing, women transported manure from barns to the various field plots. Though the actual task of breaking the ground usually involved several men equipped with basic hand tools and an ox or cow, women also performed this exhausting work. All season long, they travelled back and forth between the town and the fields, carrying food and supplies in baskets on their heads. Female members helped in other ways as well. They grew vegetable gardens, fed the animals and herded them into grazing areas scattered among the family fields. Women made cheese from goat and sheep milk and often sold the surplus locally. In southern regions, women and children picked olives, nuts and fruits growing on their land, or they picked for large landowners in exchange for a portion of the produce. Girls and boys in coastal towns brought home smelts and other small fish. Women made vegetable and fruit preserves and prepared meats, and they helped collect fuel wood from communal lands. Young women might be sent to the local seamstress to learn pattern-making and sewing or train as a hairdresser. Though there were few non-agricultural job opportunities, some families sent single daughters away to work in domestic service or in garment, textile and silk factories of the region. There, they lived in chaperoned boardinghouses and regularly sent their wages home. Particularly in the latifundia regions, increasing numbers of "peasant" women after the war engaged in part-time agricultural wage labour.[26]

Distinctions between women's and men's work roles were often blurred—a vital point frequently ignored by scholars. When large numbers of men from the South were conscripted into the Italian army during World War Two, for example, women ran the family farms. Similarly, wives, sisters and daughters compensated whenever men worked in the paid labour force.[27] It was also linked to the size and character of households. When there were several women in one household, younger females were released from domestic work for field work or, as in Pina's case, a seamstress apprenticeship in town. As a single woman, Maria R. often worked in the fields with her parents, grandfather and brother since her grandmother stayed home and took charge of daily house chores. Assunta C. noted life after marriage was actually easier because she no longer divided her time between work and field duties; she now stayed at home while her husband and in-laws farmed. By contrast, Dalinda, who lived alone with her husband, performed all the domestic labours herself and shared the field work with her husband.[28]

Nor can we assume that patriarchal structures and values in effect to subordinate women meant that they were passive victims with no basis for exercising power. Scholars have stressed the importance of men's public role and have made much of women's tendency to act modestly in mixed company and to claim to outsiders that they speak and act in their husband's or father's name. This can be very misleading, for it is within the private sphere that women could wield the most influence over their families. They made effective use of their capacity to argue, nag, manipulate, disrupt normal routine and generally make life miserable for men in order to achieve certain demands.[29]

In *Women of the Shadows*, a grim look at postwar southern Italian women, Ann Cornelisen captured the public/private dynamic in her description of a married woman who had been supporting her elderly parents. When asked who made the family's decisions, the woman claimed she consulted with her parents. But when Cornelisen confronted her with the fact she did not usually confer with her parents, she responded: "The Commandments say honour thy father and thy mother, don't they? No reason to let any one know what happens inside the family." Another woman endured months of verbal and physical assault from her husband before convincing him to work in Germany in order to raise funds for their son's hospital care. In fact, she even secured the necessary work permit.[30] Mothers also acted as their children's mediators, as did Julia's mother who sent instructions to her husband in Argentina in 1955 to grant formal approval to their daughter's marriage plans because *she* favoured it.[31]

Far from Ann Bravo's model of lonely, isolated peasant women with a truncated self-identity, women's close identification with their family did not preclude bonds of friendship with other women.[32]

Joint labour projects between households permitted women to work together and, during breaks, to chat and gossip. Women performed many chores—such as laundry and shelling beans—outside the house in the company of other women. Within households, in-laws collectivized domestic and field labour and often became close friends. Not all women were natural allies; they could be suspicious of, and cruel to, each other.[33] But there were also numerous opportunities for women to establish friendships and many did so. With the exception of Maria S., whose father had discouraged friendships, all the women interviewed had confided in close women friends back home and most had chosen long-time girlfriends to be their children's godmothers.[34] As the family's social convener arranging visits, meals and gifts between kinfolk and *paesani*, women placed themselves at the centre of wide networks of family, kin and friends.[35] Men were also subjected to community sanctions should they squander the family resources or prove to be inadequate providers, and at home husbands frequently conceded to women's demands.[36] Though gender relations reflected patriarchal precepts, they were far more complex than has hitherto been acknowledged. Even victims of abuse refused to be totally submissive wives.

No longer compelled by fascist policies to remain in their home region, Italians after the war escaped worsening conditions in the South—the further pulverization of land-holdings, rising unemployment, inadequate housing, sanitation and drinking water, and extensive malnutrition and disease. Attracted to the city's boom economy and pulled by the dynamic of chain migration, many of them arrived in Toronto.[37] The poorest residents of the Mezzogiorno—landless agricultural labourers and the unemployed urban poor—did not figure prominently among the influx, however. Rather peasants, who had owned, rented or share-cropped various plots of land, sold their surplus crops and perhaps accumulated savings, predominated. They comprised 75 per cent of adult Italian immigrants to Canada during the 1950s.[38] All the women interviewed came from such families and each stressed how her family, though poor, was considerably better off than the *braccianti* and unemployed. Assunta C. recalled how poor and malnourished women in town used to beg for the water in which she had boiled beans so they could feed their babies. Assunta Ca.'s husband had even lent money to relatives and friends.[39] Far from a strategy to deal with abject poverty, emigration served to offset the dwindling opportunities of peasants, especially newly married couples, to improve property holdings. In this way, they avoided loss of status and obtained family property elsewhere.[40]

Woman were often denied a formal voice in the decision of the family to emigrate largely because migration was linked to men's work opportunities, a pattern reinforced by immigration policies in Canada and elsewhere. By making use of informal mechanisms of persuasion, they nonetheless sought to influence the timing and target of migration. Desperate to marry and leave war-torn Fossocessia, Molise, Maria S. persuaded an initially very hostile fiancé that, after their marriage in 1948, they should join her married sister in Toronto.[41] Against her parent's wishes, a spirited Iolanda, who was a hairdresser apprentice from Miamo, Abruzzi, joined two brothers in Toronto in 1956.[42] Other women could not negotiate their own future. The parents of a large southern Calabrian family in Rocella Ionica sent Pina, two sisters and a brother to Toronto in order to raise money for their butcher shop and the father's medical bills.[43]

On the other hand, many married women shared with their husbands the desire to immigrate to Toronto. They believed in the "dream of America" and were convinced that several years of hard work would secure wealth and a comfortable life for them. Assunta C. recalled how she had always been impressed by the sojourners who had returned to the home town wealthier men. Others received encouraging letters from friends and family and travelled to join them.[44]

Immigation occurred in a comparatively ragged fashion, and led by young, married men who benefited from kinfolk-arranged sponsorship and accommodation, the process frequently involved the temporary fragmentation of families. Nicolletta met her husband during his periodic visits home to Pescara while working in Belgium coal-mines from 1951-54. Soon after they married in 1954, her husband returned to Belgium and in 1956 a pregnant Nicolletta joined him. Upon receiving news a male cousin had sponsored her husband to Canada, the family returned home, and her husband left immediately for Toronto. In 1961 after her husband had sponsored his father and youngest sister, Nicolletta and daughter finally arrived in Toronto.[45]

Although after 1951 it became more common for women to accompany their men to Toronto, many women continued to stay behind while husbands explored opportunities overseas. Significantly, women were familiar with economic strategies that involved the temporary breakup of the family unit but which secured its long-term survival. Many had experienced the absence of fathers and brothers who had emigrated temporarily outside of Italy and had served in the war.[46] Even so, loneliness and hardship ensued, especially for women whose marriage and separation followed closely together. This also led to a further blurring of traditional gender-linked work roles. With only occasional help from her father and brother, Dalinda ran the farm in Vasto-Giardi, Molise, for two years while rearing two small children, including a son born just two days before her husband's departure in 1951 for a Quebec farm. Immediately after their marriage in Mountarro, Calabria, Vincenza's husband left for several years to work in agricultural and railway repair jobs in Switzerland. He made two brief visits in two years but respected his familial obligations by sending money home regularly. He returned home only to accompany a brother to Toronto; one year later, he called for his wife and child. Initially oppossed to joining her husband permanently in Toronto, Julia eventually gave in because she felt responsible for her daughter's unhappiness: "...my little girl she call 'daddy, daddy' every day... she say, 'mommy why we don't go see daddy; mommy, mommy she's a devil, she not let me see my daddy.' Oh, she make me cry every day."[47]

Travelling alone, with female kin or husbands, southern Italian women benefited from family-linked chain migration which acted as a buffer against the alienating features of immigration. A ticket was financed in a variety of ways—a father's savings, money sent home by a husband, cash raised from a woman's sale of household furniture and the Canadian government's Assisted Passage Loan Scheme. Women experienced their first direct confrontation with government bureaucracy when they visited the crowded consulate in Rome for processing and medical examinations. Six months later, they embarked upon the two-week sea voyage and the train ride from Halifax to Toronto's Union Station.

Women's reaction to leaving home and to the trip varied. Some cried; others felt optimistic about prospects in Canada. While some enjoyed the food and dancing aboard ship, others feared their children might fall overboard or disturb passengers by crying in the cabin at night. At Halifax, they feared being separated from their children. When Dalinda arrived on a cold November day in 1953, she was embarrassed by her lightly clad sons and feared she might be considered a bad mother. The train ride through eastern Canada evoked concern as the scattered wood-frame houses resembled more the poverty of home than the expected wealth of the New World. But Toronto brought familiar faces and relief, and women settled with their men in the growing southern Italian enclaves in the city's east and west ends and within College Street's Little Italy.[48]

At home and at work, southern Italian immigrant women contributed to the welfare of their working-class families now struggling to survive in Toronto. Their domestic activities and their participation in the paid labour force will be discussed separately.

In order to understand women's domestic duties, a discussion of immigrant households is necessary. They consisted primarily of two types: an extended familial arrangement in which one or more relatives owned the house and other residents paid rent, or a flat rented from non-kin or even non-Italian landlords who normally resided on the main floor. Given their intense clannishness, fewer emotional benefits could be derived by newcomers who rented separate quarters from strangers. Women resented daily infractions of their privacy, and mothers were highly protective of their children. "With the children is very hard to live in... another people's house," explained Vincenza. "You have to live in freedom... other people they get too frustrated for the children... is not fair." She detested three years spent in a tiny third-floor flat near Christie and Bloor streets: "I was think it was gonna be different. I was living worse than over there [Italy]. I live in a third floor... two kids after six months... and a kitchen in the basement... I wanna go back home. But the money was gone, the furniture was sell, nothing was left...." Julia, however, so resented her landlord's complaints regarding water and electricity bills and her child's ruining the hardwood floors that she made her husband move to better quarters within a month of her arrival in Toronto.[49]

By contrast, the *familiari* set-up held greater opportunities for social bonding between kinfolk. A central feature of Italian immigration was the remarkable extent to which family, kin and *paesani* boarded together temporarily and the high turnover rate of boarders within any particular household. Boarding served an economic and psycho-cultural function for newcomers; it provided boarders with cheap rents, homeowners with savings to put towards mortgage payments, and everyone with an opportunity to engage in "fellow-feeling-ness."[50] It held practical advantages as couples passed on household and baby things, and the group took on labour-intensive projects such as wine-making and the annual slaughter of a pig. Women preferred this arrangement and several commented on how remarkably rare serious outbursts were in a household containing up to twenty people. A Molisana woman who lived for several years in a crowded Dupont Street house, Ada, even claimed those early years were special times when *parenti* united during hard times. "We cared more for each other then than now," she added.[51]

Far from huddling indiscriminately, the dynamics of these crowded households reflected a deep-seated sense of propriety and were largely organized according to nuclear families. At supper, for instance, families sharing a kitchen ate at different or overlapping times as each woman, who alone was responsible for her family's meals, awaited her husband's arrival from work before heating her pot of water for pasta. Individual families shared private quarters and while several women might be entrusted to do the grocery shopping, each family paid for its share of the supplies.[52]

Whatever the household structure, women at home performed crucial economic roles. Like other working-class women, they stretched limited resources and found ways to cut costs and earn extra cash. To the benefit of industrial capitalism, women's labours daily replenished the male bread-winner and fed, clothed and raised children. In extended households, they served extra menfolk who were unmarried or had not yet called for their wives, as well as elderly parents and in-laws. Maria S., who stayed home to raise three children, divided her days between doing her housework, which included gardening and sewing, and helping her sick married sister who lived nearby.[53] Since some households lacked refrigerators until the late fifties or early sixties, women purchased daily perishables such as milk and bread. Without washing-machines and often with access only to hotplates located in otherwise unfinished basements, basic chores were time-consuming and arduous.[54]

Women cut living costs by growing vegetable gardens and grape vines and by preserving fruits and vegetables. With pride Assunta C. recalled how she had produced most of the family's food: "I did everything, tomatoes for sauce, pickles, olives. I did pears, peaches, apricots, everything we eat. We bought the meat from the store and I make sausages and prosciutto." Maria S. saved money by shopping at a large farmer's market at the city limits. Others earned additional cash by taking in boarders or extra washing and many baby-sat for working relatives—all of which increased domestic chores.[55]

Moreover, the wife frequently acted as the family's financial manager, allocating funds for groceries, furniture and clothing, paying bills, and depositing savings in the bank or putting them towards mortgage payments. Several women described how at the end of each week their husbands would hand over their pay cheques. In Maria S.'s words, "My husband bring the money home and give it to me and he say, 'You know what you're doing, take care of the money... I tried save money, and I did. After three years we buy a house." Women considered this task to be of the utmost importance. Though men later usurped this role when finances and investments grew more complex, it also suggests that women's influence at home, especially during the critical early years, was considerable. Certainly, when families were merely surviving men relied upon women's resourcefulness to help make ends meet.[56]

Extended households also let women collectivize housekeeping and exchange confidences. Women who were at home all day—one nursing a newborn, another sewing clothes and another unemployed—frequently shared domestic chores. For over a year Vincenza lived with a sister-in-law and their children while their husbands worked out of town on a mushroom farm. She baby-sat the children while her in-law worked as a hospital chambermaid, and each night they shared the cooking and clean-up duties. Similarly, three single working sisters daily shared cooking and cleaning tasks, and on week-ends they rotated laundry, shopping and housekeeping.[57]

Many women also made friends with non-related Italian and even non-Italian women in their neighbourhood. Maria S. and her sister befriended several Ukrainian and Jewish women in their neighbourhood. In spring and summer they spent hours outside talking, and they made a point of celebrating each other's birthday. At home with her own and her cousin's children, Assunta C. spent afternoons with a neighbour who also baby-sat children. Each would alternate working in her garden or house while the other supervised the children.[58]

Whether at home or in the factory, urban industrial life evoked anxiety and fear in women who no longer enjoyed the protection of the *paese*. Several women recalled the fear of going out alone at night, the mocking looks of native Torontonians and even the experience of being robbed in their own homes.[59] Daily they confronted prejudice. Maria S. recalled crying all the way home after being laughed out of a department store one day in 1949 when she could not make herself understood by the saleswomen. (She had wanted to purchase socks and work pants for her plasterer husband.) Interestingly, this incident spurred her on to learn English. While returning from a week-end visit with relatives in New York City, a misunderstanding at the border resulted in the jailing of Pina and her sister for ten days in Buffalo until an American aunt hired an Italian-speaking lawyer who cleared up the confusion.[60]

Mothers also feared for their children's safety at school where outbursts regularly occurred between Anglo-Saxon and Italian schoolmates, especially boys. They worried about being called poor mothers by doctors, school nurses and teachers. When school authorities sent home a girl suspected of having lice, her family became totally distraught and immediately took her to the hospital. Maria L., who gave birth to a premature son the morning after she arrived in Toronto, was afraid to leave him in the hospital for fear he would die. As she noted, the comfort traditionally provided by the village midwife had been abruptly cut off and impersonal institutions put in her place.[61]

Women's anxieties were well founded, for racism permeated postwar Toronto society. Fearing the loss of the city's British and Protestant character, native Torontonians could be very cruel to the new Jewish and Catholic immigrants of the 1940s and 1950s.[62] Women worried about police harassing their men as they congregated outside churches or clubs to chat with *paesani* as they had at home. Though some noted the kindness of certain strangers, they resented being stared at while riding the streetcars, or being treated like ignorant children.[63] Racism could run deep. In a 1954 letter to Ontario Premier Leslie Frost, a Toronto Orangeman wrote: "In regards to the Immigration to this country of so many Italians the place around here is literally crawling with these ignorant almost black people... [and] so many landing in this country with TB disease." While he saved his worst criticism for young Italian men suspected of being "armed with knives and... continually holding up people and especially ladies near parks and dark alleys," the writer expressed total distaste for foreign-speaking Catholic men and women and called for a stop to immigration from a Vatican-controlled and disease-infested Italy.[64]

Many southern Italian women contributed to their family's finances by entering the paid labour force. They were part of the dramatic postwar increase of women in general, including married women, who entered the Canadian work-force. In 1961 almost 11 per cent of over a million working women in Canada were European-born, of whom Italian-born women comprised over 17 per cent. Some 15 per cent of the over 100,000 working women in Ontario were European-born with the Italian-born making up 20 per cent of the total. In Toronto 16,990 Italian women made up 7 per cent of the 1961 female labour force. Working women, most of whom were probably postwar immigrants, accounted for 30-38 per cent of the total Italian adult female population in Canada as well as Ontario in 1961; for Toronto this was nearly 40 per cent. And these stastistics do not take into account money raised by women at home.[65]

While Canadian-born women swelled the ranks of white-collar work, immigrant women provided cheap, unskilled and semi-skilled female labour, suggesting that female migration from Europe after the war helped Canadian employers keep down labour costs. With the approval of employers who considered them hard-working and docile, Italian women in Toronto took on low-skilled, low paying jobs normally offered to immigrant women lacking English-language and other marketable skills beyond some domestic training. These included garment piece-work at home, operating steampresses, sewing and novelty-making machines, packaging, bottling and labelling, cafeteria work and domestic service.[66]

Manufacturing and domestic service were the largest employers of European-born women in Canada and Ontario in 1961. Almost 57 per cent of over 32,000 Italian women workers in Canada were in manufacturing, particularly clothing (50 per cent), food and beverage (11 per cent), textiles (12 per cent), leather goods (6.2 per cent) and unskilled factory work (6.6 per cent). In service, where 28 per cent of the total were located, nearly 76 per cent of them were domestic servants. For Ontario, over 20,000 Italian women workers were similarly concentrated in manufacturing (50 per cent) and service (31 per cent). In the former category, they included leather cutters and sewers (38 per cent), tailoresses (22 per cent), food processing workers (14 per cent) and unskilled factory workers (10 per cent). Over 61 per cent of the personal service workers were housekeepers, waitresses and cooks; 38 per cent were laundresses and dry-cleaners.[67]

Whether a woman worked outside the home depended on various factors such as a husband's attitude, child-bearing, availability of baby-sitters and work opportunities. Alone, with menfolk, or in groups of female kin, women in search of work headed for the garment and light manufacturing areas of the city, where they went door to door asking for jobs. It took Pina four months of searching with her brother, who worked nights as a bowling alley janitor, before she found work packaging men's socks in a Spadina garment factory. Following an unsuccessful two-month search, Dalinda sewed children's clothes at home for five cents a garment until a cousin landed her a factory job several months later. Many women benefited from kin-networking at the work place as earlier employed women would arrange positions for incoming relatives.[68] Scholars have stressed how these occupational enclaves eased men's concerns about women working outside the home by providing traditional checks on female behaviour,[69] but the women themselves preferred to emphasize the utility of kinship ties and the camaraderie of the work place. Several said they would have worked wherever they found suitable jobs, and some, such as Ada and Maria L., found work for a time in ethnically mixed work places.[70]

Italian women's paid labour was part of a well-articulated working-class family strategy for success, one most often measured in terms of home ownership. Female wages helped support families through periods of seasonal male unemployment, especially for the men in construction and public works or out of town on farms, in mines or on government building projects. Women's earnings paid for daily living expenses, such as groceries, clothing and household necessities, while men's pay cheques went into savings deposits and toward buying houses and other investments. Characterized by low wages and high turnover, their work experience also reflected the gender inequalities of the postwar occupational structure. Predictably, the desire of capital for cheap workers and of immigrant working-class families for additional earnings were inextricably linked.[71]

Like many unskilled male and female workers, Italian women worked long hours at either monotonous or hazardous jobs that were physically demanding. Women employed in the drapery and clothing factories endured poor ventilation and high humidity, as well as speed-ups and close supervision. Women assembling items in plastics factories put up with dust and foul-smelling fumes. Laundry work required much sorting and carrying, and steam-presses made the work place almost unbearable in summer. Italian women in factories also confronted the new time and work discipline of industrial capitalism and the impersonal relations between employers and workers. On the other and, the daily experience of the work place, where Italian women learned to speak English from co-workers and sometimes forged friendships with non-*paese* and non-Italian women, may also have had a broadening impact on women hitherto confined to the household. By contrast, domestic workers cleaning house for middle-class clients toiled in total isolation from the rest of the working women.[72]

During the fifties and early sixties, Italian women workers did not express an articulated political response to their exploitation as female workers. This was linked to their low status as cheap and unskilled labour and to the barriers of language and ethnicity erected between women in the work place. Another major factor was the isolation of domestic workers. Household duties also kept women away from organizing meetings, and many were unsure about union organizers who visited their shops. Since joining a local might endanger their jobs, they feared compromising their main goal of helping the family's finances. Moreover, southern Italians were concentrated in industries characterized by high concentrations of unskilled female workers and high labour turnover rates. As a result, relatively few joined unions.[73]

Familial priorities, especially the duties of newly married women to bear and raise children, helped shape the timing and rhythm of women's participation in the labour force. Some women, such as Virginia, a trained seamstress from Pescara, Abruzzi, who worked for three years in a Spadina Street bathing-suit factory until she had her first child, never returned to work after starting families. Others, such as Assunta C., did not work until all their children reached school-age. Ten years after her arrival in Toronto in 1959 Assunta C. found work in a crest-making factory. Having worked for several years, Vincenza withdrew from the labour force for six years between 1960-66 to rear her children before returning to domestic service.[74]

Significant numbers of Italian women, however, regularly moved in and out of the labour force. They moved from one type of factory work to another, and from factory work to service jobs such as cafeteria and chamber-maid work as well as fruit and vegetable picking. Frequently women left jobs as a protest against poor working conditions and pay. Ada quit work as a shirt packager after losing some overtime hours, but in only a few weeks she secured work as a bow-machine operator for a factory producing wrapping and party accessories. Husbands sometimes urged their wives to quit. In 1963 Maria L. quit work as a Royal York Hotel chamber-maid to appease her husband who disliked her cleaning up for strangers and working on Sundays, even though his father and sister also worked at the hotel. Several years earlier, however, Maria had spontaneously quit her job in a Woolworth's cafeteria when management shifted her into a more stressful job in inventory. That time her husband had immediately approved of her quitting, even though he had found her the job in the first place.[75]

Most often, women left work temporarily to fulfill family obligations—having children, tending to a family crisis, or resettling the family in a new home. Shortly after Angella immigrated with her parents in 1958, for example, she worked as a seamstress in a Spadina Street bathing-suit factory and continued to work there for two years following her marriage in 1959. One year later, she left to have a child and then returned in 1962 to similar work at a sportswear and leather factory on College Street. Three years later she left to have her second child and then returned to the same job two years later. Following the family's move to Willowdale, a Toronto suburb, she secured work in a local plastics factory, which she left in 1971 to have her third child only to return six months later. In 1973 she suffered a slipped disc at work, which kept her out of the labour force for ten years.[76]

When baby-sitting could not be provided by female kinfolk or *paesane*, many Italian women put off work until a sister, in-law, or cousin became available to watch the children. (These relatives might themselves be recent immigrants or new mothers.) Mothers who hired landladies or neighbours often felt uneasy about leaving their children with "Strangers" unconnected to them by links of kin or village. Maria L. recalled how each morning she hated leaving her crying and clinging son with the landlady downstairs. Suspecting that her son was being neglected by the baby-sitter, who had young children of her own, Maria stopped working for over a year (with her husband's approval) until her mother's arrival in the city in 1959 gave her the confidence to re-enter the work-force. Opting for a different solution, Julia and Vincenza worked as domestic servants while they had pre-school youngsters and brought the children to their clients' homes.[77]

Nor did outside work reduce the burden of housekeeping. Although men performed certain tasks, such as stoking the coal furnace, shovelling outside snow and perhaps watching children briefly while their wives shopped or cleaned, working women were responsible for the household chores, even during periods of male unemployment. Indeed, other women often watched the children while their mothers performed domestic tasks. This double burden hung heavily on the shoulders of Maria L., who for over a year combined full-time work as a steampress operator with caring for a son, a husband and his father and two brothers. "Oh poor me," she recalled, "full-time work... wash, clean, cook... I did all that! I was really just a girl, nineteen years old and thin, thin like a stick. I had four men, a baby. I was with no washing-machine. I would go down to the laundry tub....Then I had to cook and I had to work. And it was not only me." Julia probably voiced the frustration of many working women when she said: "Of course he should help in the house. My back I hurt it at work, it hurts to wash the floor, pick up the clothes. But what you gonna do? Can't have a fight every day about it so I do it. But no it's not right!"[78]

Notwithstanding the obstacles to unionization, assumptions regarding Italian women's alleged docility and their outright hostility to unionization may be exaggerated. At a time when female militancy in the work place was not pronounced, it is not surprising that Italian immigrant women did not become politicized during the 1950s. Nor is there any reason to assume they should have felt any sense of working-class solidarity with their Canadian-born sisters, especially white-collar workers. Some women explained that for years the topic of unionization had never come up in the work place. Employers no doubt also took advantage of ethnic and cultural divisions among new arrivals.

In contrast to Italian women radicalized by their participation in the wartime Resistance movement—women who became socialists and communists and who, by the early 1960s, spearheaded Italy's modern feminist movement with the creation of Unione Donne Italiane—most southern peasant women who came to Toronto had little if any prior experience with industrial work and the traditions of worker protest.[79] (There were communists in the South. They included former landless *braccianti* who benefited from land reforms initiated under Italy's postwar reconstruction program as well as peasants, though probably none of the latter came to Canada.) But as peasants long resentful of the exploitation they had suffered at the hands of landowners and local élites, Italian women perhaps understood instinctively the exploitative relations between employers and workers, and many were truly angered by the injustices they suffered as working immigrant women. Even Julia, an anti-unionist, dismissed what she considered ruling-class rhetoric that portrayed Canada as a land of limitless opportunity. "Why feel grateful?" she said. "We really suffered for what we got. I have four back operations. I have to leave my kids alone and work... And we don't live like kings and queens. I work hard for what I got." Moreover, increasing numbers of women grew to support unionization over the years not only because higher wages further helped their families but because they identified improved working conditions and health benefits won during the sixties and early seventies with a recognition of their labour and with self-respect. In Dalinda's words, "Sure we should get more money, we work hard for it, we leave our kids, come home tired, do the dirty jobs."[80]

The entry of southern Italian peasant women into Toronto's postwar labour force reflected a pattern of continuity, for women had been important contributors to the peasant family economy in the Mezzogiorno. Traditional values that stressed the obligation of all family members to contribute to the family's well-being eased the transition into Toronto's industrial economy. Since women's work was already justified in terms of peasant survival, no dramatic change in values was needed to allow these immigrant women to work outside the home. Women themselves argued that they were accustomed to working long and hard for the family. "I went to work to help out the family," was a common response. Given the scarcity of resources accessible to southern Italian immigrant families newly arrived in Toronto during the forties and fifties, additional wages earned by women, including those at home, amounted to an effective familialist response.[81]

To a remarkable degree southern Italian families preserved traditional cultural forms and familial arrangements and thereby resisted disintegration. Problems confronted by working women were often handled effectively within the context of family and kinship networks. Even so, women's entry into an urban, industrial work force did not occur without considerable strain and difficult adjustments, especially for married women. These strains reflected a dialectical process by which southern Italian peasants became transformed into working-class families. Their familial and collectivist behaviour was not simply the expression of traditional peasant culture; it also reflected their new economic position as working-class families coping with conditions of scarcity and restriction under industrial capitalism. This held particular significance for working Italian women, a fact ignored by scholars who view Italian immigrant women exclusively in terms of family and home. How demands of family and work conflicted with but also complemented each other also requires consideration.[82]

Motivated by a commitment to family, southern Italian women linked their self-identification as women and mothers to the paid and unpaid labour they performed for the benefit of parents, husbands and children. Whether at home or at work, they took on dirty and difficult jobs and cut costs wherever possible. In the process they developed a conception of feminine respectability that was rooted in both their peasant and immigrant working-class experiences, and that expressed the pride of women who saw themselves as indispensable to their family. Stripped of notions of reserved femininity and delicate demeanour, it also contrasted sharply with postwar middle-class models of womanhood.[83] While the nature of their labour was largely transformed when they entered Toronto's industrial economy, southern Italian women's paid and unpaid work remained critical to the daily survival of their newly arrived families in postwar Toronto.

Notes

1. I would like to thank Ruth Frager, Margaret Hobbs, Daphne Read, Janice Newton, Janet Patterson, Ian Radforth and Joan Sangster for their comments on earlier drafts of this paper. And many thanks to the women I interviewed, whose real names I used not only with their approval but at their insistence.

2. Interview with Maria Rotolo.
3. Samuel Sidlofsky, "Post-War Immigrants in the Changing Metropolis with Special Reference to Toronto's Italian Population" (Ph.D. dissertation, University of Toronto, 1969), chap. 1; Franc Sturino, "Family and Kin Cohesion among South Italian Immigrants in Toronto," in Betty Boyd Caroli, Robert F. Harney, and Lydio F. Tomasi, eds., *The Italian Immigrant Woman in North America* (Toronto, 1978); A.T. Bouscaren, *European Economic Migrations* (The Hague, 1969).
4. Sidlofsky, "Immigrants," pp. 97-110; Sturino, "Family and Kin," pp. 288-90; Freda Hawkins, *Canada and Immigration: Public Policy and Public Concern* (Montreal, 1972), pp. 47-48; Jeremy Boissevain, *The Italians of Montreal: Social Adjustment in a Plural Society* (Ottawa, 1970), p. 10.
5. Department of Citizenship and Immigration, *Annual Report*, 1950-62, tables indicating dependents and intended employment, my calculations.
6. "White Paper, Canadian Immigration Policy," 1966, cited in Hawkins, *Canada*, pp. 9-10; Sturino, "Family and Kin," p. 291; Sidlofsky, "Immigrants," pp. 97-101. See also Istituto Centrale di Statistica, *Annuario Italiano* (Rome, 1951-60).
7. Public Archives of Ontario (hereafter PAO), Ontario, Department of Planning and Development, Immigration Branch Files (hereafter IBF), "The Bulletin Council for Social Service," No. 104, Church of England of Canada, 15 October 1941, pp. 15-19. I would like to thank Donald McCloud at the PAO for making these materials available to me.
8. PAO, IBF, E.H. Gurton, Canadian Manager, British Dominions Emigration Society, Montreal, to Ontario Immigration Branch, 1 June 1951, 2b.
9. A departmental memo to the minister responsible for Immigration, William Griesinger, was critical of the federal government for not attracting more British immigrants and advised him that Ontario must secure federal help in its effort to maintain a racial and religious balance in the province, "preferably one British to four others... any preference to British is given simply because they are our greatest source of skilled help and a minimum readjustment [sic] to our way of life." PAO, IBF, F.W. Stanley to William Griesinger, 28 November 1950; see also Griesinger to Stanley, 30 October 1950; the *Telegram* (Toronto), 27 December 1950 (clipping); see also files on the 1951 plan to recruit British tradesmen for Ontario manufacturers.
10. Public Archives of Canada (hereafter PAC), Immigration Branch Records (hereafter IR), vol. 131, Laval Fortier to acting Commissioner of Immigration Overseas, 4 October 1949.
11. Department of Citizenship and Immigration, *Annual Report*, 1950-61, tables on intended occupation, my calculations.

12. PAC, IR, vol. 131, Department of External Affairs Statement, 29 March 1950; A.D.P. Heeney Memo, 30 March 1950; House of Commons, *Debates*, 28 March 1950, p. 1208.
13. Rudolf Vecoli, "Contadini in Chicago: A Critique of the Uprooted," *Journal of American History* 51 (1964); Robert Foerster, *The Italian Emigration of Our Times* (Cambridge, 1919); Rudolph Bell, *Fate and Honour, Family and Village: Demographic and Cultural Change in Rural Italy Since 1800* (Chicago, 1979).
14. Interview with Assunta Capozzi and Maria Lombardi.
15. Bell, *Fate and Honour*, pp. 123-48; J.P. Cole, *Italy: An Introductory Geography* (New York, 1964); Alan B. Mountjoy, *The Mezzogiorno* (London, 1973).
16. Interview with Maria Lombardi and Assunta Carmosino; also interviews with Maria Rotolo, Assunta Capozzi, Maria Sangenesi, Maria Carmosino and Dalinda Lombardi-Iacovetta.
17. Interviews with Maria Rotolo and Vincenza Cerulli.
18. Interviews with Salvatore and Josephine D'Agostino and Julia Toscano. See also Robert F. Harney, "Men Without Women: Italian Migrants in Canada, 1885 to 1930," in Betty Boyd Caroli, Robert F. Harney and Lydio F. Tomasi, eds., *Italian Immigrant Women*; his "Montreal's King of Italian Labour: A Case Study of Padronism," *Labour/Le Travailleur* 4 (1979); Bruno Ramirez, "Workers Without a 'Cause': Italian Immigrant Labour in Montreal, 1880-1930," paper presented to the Canadian Historical Association, Annual Meeting, 1983.
19. On South Italian peasants, general monographs include: Edward Banfield, *The Moral Order of a Backward Society* (Illinois, 1958); Jan Brogger, *Montavarese: A study of Peasant Society and Culture in Southern Italy* (Oslo, 1971); Constance Cronin, *The Sting of Change: Sicilians in Sicily and Australia* (Chicago, 1970); John Davis, *Land and Family in Pisticci* (London, 1973); Joseph Lopreato, *Peasants No More! Social Class and Social Change in an Underdeveloped Society* (San Francisco 1967).
20. Interview with Julia Toscano.
21. Vecoli, "Contadini"; Bell, *Fate and Honour*, pp. 2-3, 72-76; Leonard W. Moss and Stephen C. Cappannaro, "Patterns of Kinship, Comparaggio and Community in a South Italian Village," *Anthropological Quarterly* 33 (1960).
22. See Brogger, *Montavarese*, pp. 106-20; Cronin, *Sting*, chap. 4; Bell, *Fate and Honour*, pp. 90, 120-23; Ann Cornelisen, *Women of the Shadows: A Study of the Wives and Mothers of Southern Italy* (New York, 1970); Virginia Yans-McLaughlin, "Patterns of Work and Family Organization: Buffalo's Italians," in Theodore R. Rabb and Robert I. Rotberg, eds., *The Family in History: Interdisciplinary Essays*, and her *Family and Community: Italian Immigrants in Buffalo, 1880-1930*, pp. 180-217. Also interviews with Ada Carmosino, Maria Lombardi, Maria Carmosino, Dalinda Lombardi-Iacovetta and others.
23. Interview with Assunta Capozzi.

24. Interviews. Also, Ann Bravo, "Solidarity and Loneliness: Piedmontese Peasant Women at the Turn of the Century," *International Journal of Oral History* 3 (June 1982); Brogger, *Montavarese*, pp. 41-50, 106-09; Miriam Cohen, "Italian-American Women in New York City, 1900-1950: Work and School," paper presented to the American Studies Association, San Antonio, Texas, 1975; Cornelisen, *Women*, pp. 71-129; Columba Furio, "The Cultural Background of the Italian Immigrant Woman and Its Impact on Her Unionization in the New York City Garment Industry," in George E. Pozzetta, ed., *Pane e Lavoro: The Italian American Working Class*; Donna Gabaccia, "Sicilian Women and the 'Marriage Market': 1860-1920," paper and discussion at the Sixth Berkshire Conference on the History of Women, June 1984; Simonetta Piccone Stella, *Ragazze del sud* (Rome, 1979).
25. Interview with Maria Lombardi, Assunta Capozzi, Dalinda Lombardi-Iacovetta.
26. Interviews. Yans-McLaughlin, *Family*, pp. 26-27; Bell, *Fate and Honour*, pp. 130-33; Sydney Tarrow, *Peasant Communism in Southern Italy* (New Haven, 1967). On an earlier period, see also Louise A. Tilly and Joan Scott, *Women, Work, and Family* (New York, 1978).
27. Interviews with Julia Toscano, Maria Sangenesi, Ada Carmosino, Maria Carmosino and Josephine D'Agostino.
28. Interviews with Josephine D'Agostino, Maria Rotolo, Assunta Capozzi and Dalinda Lombardi-Iacovetta.
29. Brogger, *Montavarese*, pp. 41-109, Bell, *Fate and Honour*, pp. 120-28. On men's role in feasts, see, for example, Enrico Cumbo, "The Feast of the Madonna del Monte," *Polyphony* 5, no. 2 (Fall/Winter 1983). See also Ernestine Friedl, "The Position of Women: Appearance and Reality," *Anthropological Quarterly* 40 (1967).
30. Cornelisen, *Women*, pp. 222-24, 57-93; see also Vincenza Scarpaci, "La Contadina, The Plaything of the Middle-Class Woman Historian," Occasional Papers on Ethnic and Immigration Studies, Multicultural History Society of Ontario (Toronto, 1972); and her "Angella Bambace and the International Ladies Garment Workers Union: the Search for an Elusive Activist" in Pozetta, *Pane e Lavoro*.
31. Cronin, *Sting*, p. 78; interview with Julia Toscano.
32. Bravo, "Peasant Women."
33. See especially Cornelisen, *Women*; Bell, *Fate and Honour*; Banfield, *Backward Society*. See also Sydel Silverman, "Agricultural Organization, Social Structure, and Values in Italy: Amoral Familialism Reconsidered," *American Anthropologist* 70 (February 1968).
34. Interviews with Maria Sangenesi, Dalinda Lombardi-Iacovetta, Maria Lombardi, Ada Carmosino, Maria Rotolo, Assunta Capozzi.
35. Interviews; Gabaccia "Sicilian Women." Most studies deal with Italian women almost exclusively in terms of family and home. See for example, Vaneeta D'Andrea, "The Social Role Identity of Italian-American Women: An Analysis of Familial and Comparison of

Familial and Religious Expectations," paper presented to the American Italian Association, 1980; Harriet Perry, "The Metonymic Definition of the Female and Concept of Honour Among Italian Immigrant Families in Toronto," in Boyd, Harney and Tomasi, eds., *Italian Immigrant Women*. At the Columbus Centre in Toronto, Samuel Bailey recently described Italian women in prewar Argentina, New York and Toronto as living in insular worlds defined by the particular block on which they resided with their children and families. By contrast, men identified more easily with the larger ethnic community. The implication is that women stayed at home and played no role in the ambience of the ethnic enclave.

36. Harney, "Men Without Women."
37. Mountjoy, *Mezzogiorno*, pp .32-36; Tarrow, *Peasant Communism*. See also Carlo Levi, *Christ Stopped at Eboli* (New York, 1946). On chain migration see, J.S. MacDonald, "Italy's Rural Structure and Migration," *Occidente* 12, no. 5 (September 1956); MacDonald and L.D. MacDonald, "Chain Migration, Ethnic Neighborhood Formation and Social Networks," *Millbank Memorial Fund Quartery* 13 (1964); Harvey Choldin, "Kinship Networks in the Migration Process," *International Migration Review* 7 (Summer 1973). On Toronto, see, Sidlofsky, "Immigrants"; Sturino, "Family and Kin"; his "Contours of Postwar Italian Immigration to Toronto," *Polyphony* 6, no. 1 (Spring/Summer 1984).
38. Hawkins, *Canada*, pp. 47-48. See also "White Paper," pp. 9-10.
39. Interview with Assunta Capozzi and Assunta Carmosino.
40. On an earlier period, see: Joseph Barton, *Peasants and Strangers: Italians, Rumanians and Slovaks in an American City, 1890-1930*; John Bodnar, "Immigration and Modernization: the Case of Slavic Peasants in Industrial America," *Journal of Social History* 10 (Fall 1976); Yans-McLaughlin, *Family*, pp. 33-36; Harney and Scarpaci, eds., *Little Italies in North America* (Toronto, 1983). See also John Baxevanis, "The Decision to Migrate," in his *Economy and Population Movements in the Peloponnesos of Greece* (Athens, 1972), pp. 60-75.
41. Interview with Maria Sangenesi.
42. Iolanda Marano interviewed by Pina Stanghieri.
43. Interview with Josephine D'Agostino.
44. Interviews with Maria Carmosino, Maria Lombardi, Assunta Capozzi, Vincenza Cerulli, Dalinda Lombardi-Iacovetta.
45. Nicoletta DeThomasis interviewed by Rosemary DeThomasis.
46. Julia Toscano's father, for example, spent her entire girlhood outside the country—in Albany from 1936-38, Germany 1938-39 and Argentina for six years after the war. For a discussion of the impact of men's immigration on home life in Italy see: Harney, "Without Women"; N. Douglas, *Old Calabria* (New York, 1928).
47. Interview with Dalinda Lombardi-Iacovetta, Vincenza Cerulli and Julia Toscano.
48. Interviews. On postwar settlement, see Sidlofsky, "Immigrants"; Sturino, "Family and Kin" and his "Postwar Immigration."

49. Interview with Vincenza Cerulli and Julia Toscano. Also with Josephine D'Agostino.
50. Harney, "Boarding and Belonging," *Urban History Review* 2 (October 1978). On the importance of kin and boarding for an earlier period see also: Michael Anderson, *Family Structure in Nineteenth Century Lancashire* (Cambridge, 1971); John Modell and Tamara K. Hareven, "Urbanization and the Malleable Household: An Examination of Boarding and Lodging in American Families," in Hareven, ed., *Family and Kin in Urban Communities, 1700-1930* (New York, 1977); and her "Family Time and Industrial Time: Family and Work in a Planned Corporate Town, 1900-1924," in ibid.
51. Interviews with Ada Carmosino, Maria Rotolo, Maria Lombardi, Maria Sangenesi, Maria Carmosino, Dalinda Lombardi-Iacovetta.
52. Ibid.
53. Interview with Maria Sangenesi. See also *Canadian Ethnic Studies*, Special issue on Ethnicity and Femininity, 1981.
54. Interview with Dalinda Lombardi-Iacovetta, Maria Lombardi, Ada Carmosino, Maria Rotolo, Josephine D'Agostino. All of them obtained appliances several years after their arrival.
55. Interview with Assunta Capozzi and Maria Sangenesi; also with Assunta Carmosino. See also labour force statistics indicating Italian-born women who took in washing, boarders and children. Canada, *Census* 1951. Others, of course, went unrecorded (tables on Canada and Ontario).
56. Of course, working women might also perform this role. Interview with Maria Sangenesi, Maria Rotolo, Vincenza Cerulli, Maria Lombardi, Ada Carmosino, Julia Toscano and Josephine D'Agostino.
57. Interviews with Ada Carmosino, Maria Lombardi, Dalinda Lombardi-Iacovetta; also with Vincenza Cerulli and Josephine D'Agostino.
58. Interview with Maria Sangenesi and Assunta Capozzi.
59. Dalinda Lombardi-Iacovetta was robbed one day in 1953 while she was at home with her two children doing garment piece-work. The thief, who came to the door, armed with a knife, got away with two weeks' pay—twenty dollars.
60. Interview with Maria Sangenesi and Josephine D'Agostino.
61. Interview with Maria Lombardi. (Maria reported on the story above, in which a cousin by marriage was involved.); also with Dalinda Lombardi-Iacovetta, Maria Rotolo, Ada Carmosino. Also, in conversation with several Italian-born men who attended elementary and secondary school in Toronto during the 1950s. All stressed backyard brawls in which they engaged and the embarrassment of being put behind in school grade level because of language difficulties.
62. See, for example, *Debates*, 13 June 1950; Margot Gibb-Clarke, *Globe and Mail*, 20 October 1984, p. 18; Sturino, "Postwar Immigration to Toronto," paper given to the Colombus Centre, 1984.

63. Interviews. Also interviews with Salvatore D'Agostino, Camilo Schiuli and Salvatore Carmosino.
64. PAO, IBF, F.J. Love to Premier Leslie Frost, 1 September 1954. See also response; H.K. Warrander to J.L. Love, 2 September 1954. Following an explanation that the Ontario government carried out "a very small selective type of immigration programme... [having] to do only immigrants from the United Kingdom, it added: "Other immigrants... are dealt with by the Federal Government departments and I am therefore sorry to say that we have no control over that type of immigrant or whether or not he comes here in a healthy condition."
65. Canada, *Census* 1951. The figures for Toronto were provided by Statistics Canada researchers. On postwar women and work see: Pat and Hugh Armstrong, *The Double Ghetto* (Toronto, 1978); Julie White, *Women and Unions* (Ottawa, 1980).
66. Ibid. See also Sheila McLeod Arnopolous, *Problems of Immigrant Women in the Canadian Labour Force* (Ottawa, 1979); Laura C. Johnson with Robert C. Johnson, *The Seam Allowance: Industrial Home Sewing in Canada* (Toronto, 1982); Monica Boyd, "The Status of Immigrant Women in Canada," in Marylee Stephenson, ed., *Women in Canada* (Don Mills, 1977); Anthony Richmond, *Immigrants and Ethnic Groups in Metropolitan Toronto* (Toronto, 1967). For useful theoretical discussions of immigrant and migrant women see: "Why do women migrate? Towards understanding of the sex-selectivity in the migratory movements of labour." *Studie Emigrazione* 20 (June 1983); Annie Phizacklea, ed., *One Way Ticket.*
67. Canada, *Census* 1951, my calculations.
68 Interviews with Josephine D'Agostino, Dalinda Lombardi-Iacovetta, Maria Rotolo; also with Maria Lombardi, Maria Carmosino, Vincenza Cerulli, Julia Toscano, Ada Carmosino.
69. See, for example, Yans-McLaughlin, "Family"; Sturino, "Postwar Immigrants."
70. Interviews especially with Maria Lombardi and Ada Carmosino.
71. Interviews; Bettina Bradbury made this argument for an earlier period on working-class families in Montreal. See her "The Fragmented Family: Family Strategies in the Face of Death, Illness and Poverty, Montreal, 1860-1885," Joy Parr, ed., *Childhood and Family in Canadian History* (Toronto, 1982).
72. Interviews. Studies on working women in Canada include Ruth Frager, "No Proper Deal: Women Workers and the Canadian Labour Movement, 1870-1930," in Lynda Briskin and Linda Yanz, eds., *Union Sisters: Women in the Labour Movement* (Toronto, 1984); Joan Sangster, "The 1907 Bell Telephone Strike; Organizing Women Workers," *Labour/Le Travailleur* (1978); Wayne Roberts, *Honest Womanhood* (Toronto, 1976).
73. White, *Women and Unions.*
74. Virginia interviewed by Tina D'Accunto; interview with Assunta Capozzi and Vincenza Cerulli.

75. Interview with Ada Carmosino and Maria Lombardi.
76. Angella interviewed by Tina D'Accunto; similar patterns emerged for Dalinda Lombardi-Iacovetta, Maria Rotolo, Maria Carmosino, Maria Lombardi.
77. Interview with Maria Lombardi, Julia Toscano and Vincenza Cerulli; also with Dalinda Lombardi-Iacovetta, Maria Rotolo and Assunta Carmosino.
78. Interview with Maria Lombardi and Julia Toscano.
79. Judith Adler Hellman, "The Italian Communists, the Women's Question, and the Challenge of Feminism," *Studies in Political Economy* 13 (Spring 1985); M. Jane Slaughter, "Women's Politics and Women's Culture: The Case of Women in the Italian Resistance," paper presented to the Sixth Berkshire Conference on the History of Women, June 1984; Margherita Repetto Alaia, "The Unione Donne Italiane: Women's Liberation and the Italian Workers' Movement, 1945-1980," paper presented to the Sixth Berkshire Conference on the History of Women, June 1984. On the South see, for example, Jane Kramer, *Unsettling Europe* (New York, 1972); P.A. Allum, "The South and National Politics, 1945-50," in J.S. Woolf, *The Rebirth of Italy 1943-50* (New York, 1973).
80. Interview with Julia Toscano and Dalinda Lombardi-Iacovetta.
81. On an earlier period see Joan Scott and Louise Tilly, *Women, Work, and Family*.
82. Bodnar, "Modernization and Immigration."
83. See, for example, Betty Frieden, *The Feminine Mystique* (Harmondsworth, 1965).

The Diverse Roles of Ontario Mennonite Women

Frank H. Epp and Marlene G. Epp

The contemporary social expressions of Ontario Mennonite womanhood represent a great diversity, which includes both the traditional and the modern, the rural and the urban, the family farm and home, as well as business and professional offices. There is hardly an area of activity or "status"—a word foreign to Mennonite ideology—that does not include Ontario Mennonite women. Today, they are prominent in traditional roles but also as seminary students[1] and ministers,[2] medical doctors,[3] lawyers,[4] professors,[5] principals,[6] school board chairpersons,[7] the first graduates in MBA programs,[8] business executives,[9] social workers and administrators of social work agencies[10] and, above all, leaders in community-wide organizations.[11]

The purpose of this article is not so much to report comprehensively on this diversity of female Mennonite roles—this has been done elsewhere[12]—but rather to explain it. At least five factors need to be taken into account in this explanation, namely: 1) ideological impulses which propelled the Mennonite reality into history; 2) immigration and settlement patterns which shaped Mennonite communities; 3) isolationist cultural modes which persist to this very day; 4) institution-building and organizational activity; and 5) integrationist cultural modes, particularly in the postwar world. We will discuss each of these in turn.

Ideological Impulses

The Mennonite community had its identifiable sociological origins in the so-called religious Reformation of early sixteenth-century Europe. Like the Lutherans and the Calvinists, who were named after the religious leaders Martin Luther and John Calvin respectively, so the Mennonites were named after Menno Simons, a Dutch priest. In 1536 he became one of the leaders of a reform movement, which had already sprung up in Switzerland in 1525 under the direction of Conrad Grebel and others and which in a few short years swept through central Europe.

These forerunners of the Mennonites were called Anabaptists because of their unconventional practice of rebaptizing those who had once been baptized as infants and who now made voluntary commitments to a redefined faith and to the community based thereon. In many religious traditions, then and now, baptism has been noted for its liturgical significance in the context of observing church ordinances, but then the revolt against infant baptism represented a radical religious mind-set—the Anabaptist movement has also been referred to as the left wing of the Reformation and its leaders as radical reformers.[13] The protest against infant baptism opposed a religious culture and civic religion which inducted every person into a *corpus christianum* in which proper and loyal citizenship was equated with decent religion and in which civic rulers exercised authority over religious institutions and persons.

Indeed, according to Sherrin Marshall Wyntjes, the new doctrine of baptism was much more. It represented, "an equalizing covenant" for all, male and female, in these newly established communities. Related to the doctrine of baptism was the doctrine of the "priesthood of all believers" which "included all members of the laity, both men and women..."[14] This "priesthood," which renounced the necessity of a mediating functionary between God and the person and demanded that all believers spread the gospel, meant that all women and all men were equally entitled to hold worship services, read, interpret and teach the scriptures, distribute the sacraments, evangelize and theologize.

Elise Boulding has established that the Anabaptists "practised complete equality of women and men in every respect, including preaching."[15] Wolfgang Schaeufele has characterized the Anabaptist woman as "a fully emancipated person in religious matters and the independent bearer of Christian convictions."[16] George Williams, the famous Reformation historian, gives the following assessment:

> "Nowhere else in the Reformation Era were women so nearly the peers and companions in the faith, and mates in missionary

enterprise and readiness for martyrdom, as among those for whom believer's baptism was an equalizing convenant..."[17]

The stories of early Anabaptist women such as Ruth Kunstel of Berne, "a minister in the word of the Lord," and Ruth Hagen of Zurich, "an elder,"[18] attest to the kind of leadership roles which women fulfilled in the movement. Although there is no specific evidence that they also baptized others, neither is there proof to the contrary. In many cases, the baptizer kept his or her identity secret from the person being baptized, in order to protect both individuals from prosecution.

The leadership role of Anabaptist women is attested to by the fact that they faced martyrdom as often as did men. One-third of the 930 Anabaptist martyrs in the *Martyrs' Mirror* (a collection of stories of martyrdom from the period) are women.[19] These include such individuals as Maeyken Wens, who could "by no manner of means, not even by severe tortures, be turned from the steadfastness of her faith." She was burned at the stake in the Netherlands in 1573, and her two sons, aged fifteen and three years, searched among her ashes for the tongue screw which had been used to silence her.[20] And Elisabeth Dirks, accused of being a "preacher," "active in witnessing and teaching the Christian faith," was drowned in 1549.[21] According to Walter Klaassen, women in the Amsterdam area were often "hanged in their own doorways in the 1530s."[22] Werner Packull has documented the story of Anna Jansz, a literary leader and martyr in Rotterdam,[23] and "there are a lot more women like her whose stories deserve to be told."[24]

The new communities being formed, resembling in many ways the "base communities" springing up today in Latin America and such Asian countries as the Philippines, were alternate societies in a holistic sense—while they rejected the social order of the day (in which religion, civics, economics, etc., were integrated in one way), they established new social orders, in which the various facets of life were integrated in a new way. In these new orders everybody was related to, and responsible for, everybody else.[25]

Thus, the economics of the Anabaptists were an antidote to violent peasant revolutions, on the one hand, and the violent oppression of the self-serving overlords, on the other hand. The degree of economic communalism, of course, varied among the Anabaptists. The Mennonites never adopted the position of their Anabaptist cousins, the Hutterites, whose *Bruderhoefe* to this day eschew private property. Nonetheless, the Mennonites viewed property as stewardship to be used for the common good, both within the immediate family, defined by blood relations, and within the family of faith, defined by spiritual and social covenants.

Thus, one can find in the Mennonite tradition the institutionalized recognition of equal rights to property for both male and female. Such provisions meant that in the event of a partner's death, half the property was assigned to the surviving partner and half to the children, and within the latter grouping without sex discrimination.[26]

Egalitarianism among the Anabaptists had its limitations, however, at least measured by later standards. The fact that women did have primary roles in the early Anabaptist community may have been due in part to the turmoil of the times and the unusual circumstances created by persecution. When the dynamics of religious and societal renewal were at work and when survival was of the utmost importance, it was acceptable and imperative that everyone, men and women, work to spread the faith. However, when the period of intolerance ended, it is likely, as H.S. Bender has observed, that "the settled communities and congregations reverted more to the typical patriarchal attitude of European culture."[27]

A significant aspect of the Anabaptist movement which has characterized the shaping of women's roles throughout Mennonite history was the belief that the scriptures were the primary authority for Christian thought and practice. This biblical literalism, interpreted in given cultural contexts and reinforced by cultural practices, took at face value such biblical admonitions that women submit to their husbands, remain silent and keep their heads covered. It is the latter practice, which, among the Ontario Mennonites, historically has been perhaps the most obvious symbol of women's subservience,[28] even while the original ideological impulses lived on as sources of the ongoing struggle for equality.

Immigration and Settlement Patterns

Immigration and settlement patterns further explain and interpret the roles of Mennonite women, as they do for women of all or most immigrant groups. There were numerous migrations in Mennonite history within Europe, across the Atlantic and within North America. Driven by persecution and/or beckoned by freedoms and economic opportunities, Mennonites have often moved to the frontier to re-establish themselves.

In such movements, everybody was involved. Only infants, the elderly and the sick were bystanders. Differentiation of roles based on sex had to do not so much with power structures or status symbols as with functions and activities best suited to individual people. We all know what this meant on the frontier, socially characterized by the large families and economically characterized by agriculture. Some things men and women did equally together. Even to this day both men and women are equally engaged in milking, in making hay, in setting up stooks of grain, in filling the cellar with food for the off-seasons and, within such contexts, in the education of the young.

With respect to Ontario, two Mennonite cultures and seven migrations can be identified. The two cultures pertain to European origins. The Swiss-South German Mennonites (hereafter known as Swiss) came to North America, specifically Pennsylvania, beginning in 1683. The Dutch-North German Mennonites, hereafter known as Dutch, first arrived in the 1870s, most of them after a period of settlement in Russia. Both the Swiss and the Dutch had subcultures within the two broader groupings. Among the Swiss, there were not only the Mennonites but also the Amish Mennonites, who represented a more conservative interpretation of the sacred writings. Among the Dutch, immigration history differentiates between the more conservative Kanadier, who arrived from Russia in the 1870s, and the more liberal Russlaender, who came in the 1920s and later.

The first two immigrations to Ontario, beginning in 1786 and 1826 respectively, involved Swiss Mennonites from Pennsylvania and Amish Mennonites directly from Europe. In both cases, settlements were founded on virgin soil, and thus both groups were engaged in all aspects of community formation. In these frontier situations the ideological egalitarianism of the original movement and the practical egalitarianism of new communities were exemplified, though with some important exceptions. In the matter of official community leadership, all the deacons, ministers and bishops were men. Also, the earliest school teachers were men. However, Mennonite women were not passive or acquiescent. They were strong, outspoken and influential people, according to the realistic portrayal of Beccy Bricker and her kind, still viewed as prototypes, in Mabel Dunham's *Trail of the Conestoga.*[29]

The first Dutch migration bypassed Ontario for Manitoba, but the second one in the 1920s saw a heavy influx of Russlaender, whose urbane orientation and sophistication would generally have suited them for urban environments. While some, both men and women, succeeded, despite union opposition, in obtaining work in city factories, most followed the federal condition of their immigration and settled on farms.[30] Opportunities at that time were best in areas where orchards, market gardens, tomato and tobacco farms proved immensely profitable, depending on the availability of farm labour. Such labour was at its best when it came from large immigrant families, in which men, women and children were equally involved in planting, weeding and harvesting.

Ontario's immigration and settlement history shows that successive waves of immigrants thus performed the unique roles characteristic of large families in agricultural situations, requiring the labour-involvement of persons of both sexes and almost all ages. Thus, the Russlaender have, in their various locations, been followed by Italian and Lebanese immigrants, to name but a few, and in an amazing historical recurrence by Kanadier, who came to Ontario beginning in the 1960s from Mexico where they had migrated from the Canadian prairies in the 1920s.[31]

Also in the 1960s, additional Amish, arriving from their modernizing American environments, found new opportunities for family agriculture in Ontario where the owners of dairy and crop farms, no longer benefiting from family labour, were ready to sell to others who could still make a go of it because of the coordinated contribution of families living in communities.[32]

Family agriculture in closely knit Mennonite communities set the pace for the involvement of Mennonite women in economic activity, on some occasions extended to the sale of farm produce, as well as home crafts and quilts at public markets. In such markets, women had a leading role often because this was their only source of cash. This was especially true after 1944 for those women who followed the advice of the church and did not accept family allowances.

There were exceptions to this general agricultural situation. The immediate urban settling of some immigrants in the 1920s had its parallels in postwar migrations from Europe and South America. Of particular interest here is the phenomenon of many single mothers—whose husbands had been lost through death or untraceable dispersion in the USSR—arriving in Ontario in the late 1940s.

Isolationist Cultural Modes

From the beginning, the Mennonites represented an inherent contradiction when it came to contact with the wider society. On the one hand, they were convinced that they carried an important verbal message for the rest of the world, which could not be delivered without contact with that world. On the other hand, they were modelling an alternate society, which to some was a message even better than words, that required removal from the world. This sense of withdrawal was reinforced periodically, in Canada most forcefully in the latter part of the nineteenth century, and had implications in particular for the role of women. Before we recall that history, however, a further explanation of the isolationist mode in its original form is needed.[33]

Mennonite ideology by definition was separatist, or isolationist. Radical reform required separation not only from a stance of unconditional obedience to the state—Mennonites, though obedient, respectful of authority and in no fundamental sense anarchists, did not swear loyalty to any overlords because loyalty in the ultimate sense of an oath belonged only to God—but also from a religious society that was compromised and corrupted. The less negative separatist impulse required retreat from the present society in order to create a new society. Actually, the opposition to church and state left them no option. Local and imperial politics dictated their eradication. The urge to survive drove them into isolation, wherever it could be found—in the mountains, in the valleys, on the fringes of the empire. Gradually, the internal and external forces contributing to isolation helped to create separated communities, a distinct sociology, including a culture that nurtured, among other things, distinctive lifestyles and languages, more specifically dialects. Hence, the occasional ethnic definition of Mennonite by sociologists.

The separatist sociology in turn produced a separatist psychology, which, to explain and justify itself, turned once again to separatist theology as the cycles of the separatist mode and mentality came full circle. Thus, when so-called progressive thinking late in the nineteenth century insisted on progress in every facet of human life and when progress was defined as newness, fashion, modernity and technology, and also touched the Mennonites, they found themselves at the crossroads.

Mennonite history records three general responses to progress, namely, the responses of the so-called new Mennonites, the old Mennonites and the old order Mennonites, to use the colloquial names of the day. The new Mennonites accepted progress in a selective way. In fact, they switched from one conservative mode to another, from one defined culturally to another defined theologically.

The old Mennonites were middle-of-the-road. They wanted to preserve the best of the old order while cautiously accepting aspects of the twentieth century. No longer insisting on geographic and rural separation, they insisted on social and ethical differentiation. Their favourite word was nonconformity, as a religious doctrine, as a social relation and as a life-embracing ethic.

The old order Mennonites resisted all progress in all its forms because for them progress was not progress. City life, technology, fashion, secular mass education, the telephone, gasoline engines, electricity and later the radio, all pointed to the loss of community and spirituality. Thus, they satisfied themselves with farms, lanterns, horses, buggies and neighbourliness.

The new Mennonites, the old Mennonites and the old order Mennonites all had one thing in common: they all restricted their women to traditional roles. While they varied in their emphases on the women keeping silent and maintaining prescribed dress and head covering, they all declined to give official leadership roles to women. Men alone qualified to be chosen or elected for office.

Sometimes, the lack of women in representative decision-making bodies resulted in situations which now seem unjust, and to an extent ridiculous. For instance, an all-male birth control committee within the old Mennonite conference discussed at length such topics as women's diseases and loosening moral behaviour.[34] Or a committee, similarly all-male, advised against the family allowance benefits,[35] a program which gave women more financial independence.

There were, however, some interesting paradoxes. The new Mennonites readily commissioned women missionaries. The old Mennonites were steadfast in their support of women's organizations. And, when the old order Mennonites in the twentieth century founded their own separate school system, the majority of their teachers were women.

Institution-Building and Organizational Activity

Ontario Mennonite women have always been "doers," and their presence in the creating and building of certain institutions and organizations within the Mennonite community has been a key to the success of those programs, though their contribution is rarely given the recognition which perhaps it warrants. The Sunday school movement of the late 1800s, which brought new opportunities for educating both the young and old, could not have survived without the dedication and innovation of women. The expansion of overseas service programs saw many adventuresome women break new paths and overcome cultural barriers.

The service emphasis of the wider Mennonite community, manifested in various agencies and institutions, which focuses both on material relief and spiritual comfort to those in need, would not be what it is without the grass-roots work of women. To all these activities is brought a democratic influence, a tradition of shared decision-making and cooperative effort which is just beginning to make itself felt within other spheres of the Mennonite community.

In the latter half of the nineteenth century, a movement of renewal occurred amongst old and new Mennonites which brought into existence the Sunday school—a phenomenon which added new life and vitality to the church in many ways. It "helped to hold the young people's interest, increased Bible knowledge, elevated spiritual life, raised moral concerns, especially temperance, created lay-leadership, promoted the missionary movement, and generally enriched church activity and expression."[36]

Most significant, perhaps, was the fact that the operation of Sunday schools involved non-ordained people directly in the work of the church. For the women, particularly, this created opportunities for leadership, albeit limited, which had hitherto been lacking. Although women, at the outset, were generally found in teaching positions only, and usually only in the children's or women's classes, it was at that level that the future success or failure of Sunday school was really determined. Gradually, women took on administrative positions as Sunday school superintendents, taught in mixed adult classes and were elected to church education committees.

As missionaries in the first half of this century, Mennonite women were allowed leadership roles in distant locales which were disallowed them at home, a fact which may have prompted certain women, frustrated by the closed doors within their communities, to venture overseas to preach, teach and, in other ways, minister. On their return to home communities, women missionaries often reported behind the pulpit on Sunday mornings, alone or with their husbands if they were married, and were given a respect, bordering on sainthood, which otherwise would not have existed. Greg Lichti suggests that, "missionary experience has probably made it easier for present women leaders to achieve respect in their positions."[37] One such woman was Edna Schmiedendorf Hurst, from Preston, Ontario, who worked as a nurse and linguist in Africa for twenty-three years. Of her it was said: "she was a very gifted speaker, just as good, if not better, than most men."[38]

As a further examination of women's projects and organizations one might cite four elements, as described by Elaine Sommers Rich, which characterized women's activities: 1) working with their hands; 2) practising hospitality toward kinfolk and strangers; 3) frugality; and 4) contributing to the welfare of the community in a spirit of cooperation.[39]

All these could be seen in informal activities—the quilting, butchering and rug-making "bees," for instance— and the formal organization with its executive and sub-committees, annual meetings and budgets. The cooperative spirit pervading women's organizations is a feature rarely seen in the more hierarchical and authority-oriented structures of the church in which the men dominated, a feature the benefits of which could be witnessed in the efficiency and productivity of their institutions. Rarely was a task done in solitude, but rather in groups, where work and socializing were simultaneous activities.

The formal institutions began as "circles," a term which was an apt description of the way in which decisions were made, responsibilities shared and projects carried out. Formal women's organizations have existed in Ontario since the early 1900s, initially as charity circles or sewing circles held at the local Mennonite meeting-house or in an individual's home to produce goods for the needy in their communities and later for missionary work abroad. An Ontario-wide organization was formed in 1917 as a response to the growth in interest and activities of these organizations as the needs of war victims—from the First, and later the Second World War—were felt in North America.

Sewing circles would operate fairly independently within local congregations but would be coordinated by an elected provincial committee which would report annually to the larger Ontario Mennonite conference. In 1955 the circles were collectively known as the Women's Missionary and Service Auxiliary. The word "auxiliary" was a key to how the organization perceived itself. As a support to the central programs of the church, the circles saw their work as doing "practical deeds that God has entrusted only women to carry out."[40]

Their projects, from the very large to the very small, from the far-away to the close-to-home, were all action-oriented and geared towards alleviating suffering in some way. They sewed garments for the needy, both at home and abroad, did a variety of handwork to donate directly or sell for fund-raising purposes, canned food for war relief, provided financial support to missionaries, visited the sick within their own communities, promoted religious and missionary literature, raised money to buy equipment for local institutions, prepared large-scale meals for church functions, held annual inspirational and planning meetings and took on an endless array of other service tasks.

An early business enterprise, though not recognized as a business *per se*, was the cutting room, a venture prompted by the clothing needs of the refugees in Europe in the late 1940s, which centralized and expanded production and which designed clothing appropriate to the needs of the country.[41] This was spearheaded by the Ontario women's organization in cooperation with the Mennonite Central Committee. This venture demonstrated ingenuity, business acumen, administrative skill and dedication, far beyond what had existed in the sewing circles.

A better-known example of the output of women's organizations is in the Mennonite Central Committee relief sale held annually at New Hamburg, Ontario. Though the sale, begun in 1967, is not planned or promoted directly by women's groups, its organizers capitalize on the abilities of Mennonite women to produce vast amounts of basket goods, handicrafts and beautiful quilts. Last year, the sale, attended by over 30,000 people, auctioned off 300 quilts and raised upwards of $250,000 for relief.

The women's organization traditionally was, and in some ways still is, the primary vehicle for channelling women's creativity and leadership skills (although in early years it was always a man who performed the major "speaking" roles at meetings). Beulah Kauffman, a former executive secretary of the organization, said: "Women who would otherwise have had little opportunity to develop and exercise their leadership gifts have benefitted from the training ground provided in the women's organizations."[42]

Within the structures of their own circles and the larger collectivity, women had ample opportunity to be ministers, administrators and innovators, and thus, in a sense, were well prepared for their more recent participation in "male" church institutions. On the other hand, confining women's roles to relief and service activities within the context of a separate women's organization remains a way of channelling them away from participation in all avenues of the church.

Though still flourishing in Ontario communities, women's organizations have been called into question in recent years. Women have reacted against the "auxiliary syndrome" which suggests that their work is of a secondary or supplementary nature, hence the name change from Women's Missionary and Service Auxiliary to Women's Missionary and Service Commission in the early 1970s.

Though the work itself was seen to be a vital part of the community's heritage and the church's role, some women questioned the specialization which defined "ladies' work" apart from "men's work," and the image that women's organizations had a supportive function only, and did not share in setting priorities and decision-making with respect to entire church activities. One woman described the dichotomy which occurred when women's roles were compartmentalized:

> On the one hand, in certain areas of the church's program the women as volunteers were permitted, even encouraged, to carry the responsibility and to operate quite autonomously. On the other hand, within the context of the total ministry, this pattern was typical of the syndrome expressing a women's 'role' or 'place' in the church.[43]

In response, some women have opted not to participate in women's organizations at all. Others have attempted to widen the spectrum of activities of women's groups and develop an image which is not confined to baking and sewing. Nevertheless, it cannot be denied that the work traditionally performed by women's organizations provided the material foundation on which could be built the larger, primarily male-administered, relief agencies of the Mennonite community.

Integrationist Cultural Modes

Urbanization trends, with the concomitant migration into business, higher education and the professions, since the 1940s, and the feminist women's movement since the late 1960s has undoubtedly been a primary influence in shaping the roles and goals of Ontario Mennonite women in recent decades. The consciousness-raising prevalent in general society has also taken place in Mennonite communities, excluding the old order groups, and the issues of concern for "secular" feminists have become important to Mennonite women as well.

Compared to secular women, however, the Mennonites have been hesitant and slow to embrace the ideals of feminism. The activism and aggression, which characterized certain elements of the movement in its early stages, particularly, was too contrary to the conditioned modesty, humility and self-denial of Mennonite women for them to be comfortable with it. The traditional belief in separation of church and state and the rejection of trends that were "of the world" further reinforced their hesitancy to join the feminist bandwagon. The initial tentative public calls for equal opportunity and more just recognition were often introduced with such qualifications as, "I do not want to be identified with the 'Women's Lib' movement... however...."[44]

Nevertheless, the Mennonites, as every other group in society, could hardly remain immune to the revolution proceeding around them. After all, the changes could have religious motivation, for the Bible contained passages not only that suggested female subservience but also that celebrated female leadership. In the same way that the sacred writings could be interpreted by chauvinism in one way, they could be interpreted by feminism in another way. The feminist movement gave impetus to a close examination of the roles traditionally held by Mennonite women in their homes, churches and institutions, and these roles were increasingly seen by some, not all, Mennonite women to be secondary and often inferior to those of men and were viewed as inadequate in utilizing women's full potential.

It was recognized that women were under-represented, if at all, in Mennonite organizations, that they were in a minority in institutions of higher learning, both as teachers and students, that they were rarely seen in professional positions, and that they were confined to roles within the church community which were peripheral or service-oriented—teaching the children but not the adults, playing piano for the church choir but not conducting it, providing meals at conference sessions but not input as delegates, giving "reports" behind the pulpit but never sermons—in short, serving coffee but not communion.

As women in society as a whole struggled for and gradually gained rights of equality, Mennonite women too struggled in their own way for increased recognition and utilization of their gifts and abilities. Frequently, it was exactly those traditional attributes of Mennonite women which were viewed as potentially significant for church institutions. In the words of one outstanding woman leader, "Vision and sensitivity and the urge for practical application are among the qualities which women would bring to bear if given opportunity."[45]

Ontario Mennonite women were often at the forefront of changes which have occurred over the past fifteen years. Eleanor High Good of Kitchener was the first female delegate to the Mennonite General Conference of North America in 1969.[46] Her presence there represented a decisive statement on the need for more female representation in church organizations, and at the next meeting of that same body in 1971, six of 450 delegates were women, three of them from Ontario.[47] Also at the 1969 session, Lorna Bergey, of New Hamburg, became the first woman elected to a general conference committee.[48] Soon thereafter she was named Kitchener-Waterloo Woman of the Year in 1975, recognizing her cultural contribution as a person dedicated to preserving Mennonite history in the area.[49]

A significant event occurred in 1973 when, at the urging of a group of concerned Mennonite women, the Mennonite Central Committee Peace Section established a Task Force on Women in Church and Society. Recognizing that women's interests represented issues of social justice, human rights and peace, the task force sought to tackle the under-representation of women in church organizations, in institutions of higher learning and in the formal ministry, and to address attitudes which subordinated women in theory and practice. They did this and are continuing to do it by publishing a bimonthly newsletter dealing with women's concerns, by compiling a resource listing of Mennonite women to facilitate the use of women on boards, committees, at conferences, workshops and seminars, by lobbying Mennonite organizations to utilize women in employment to a greater extent and by supporting a variety of publication efforts aimed at educating the community. The persistent efforts of the task force together with more local, more individual efforts of women and the influence of the general societal transition meant that Mennonite women began to assume new roles which had hitherto been inaccessible.

This is not to suggest that there weren't other significant factors operating to transform women's roles. The increased assimilation of the majority of Mennonites into the mainstream of Canadian culture, the movement from isolated and close-knit rural communities to heterogeneous urban centres, the emphasis on professionalism and specialization in vocations in society generally and economic pressures which necessitated more than one income per household, all have been influences on Mennonite ethnicity as a whole and on women in particular.

On the whole, women have entered the arenas of academia and business with greater ease, though not necessarily in greater numbers, than into the structures of the church. The number of women attending universities, colleges and seminaries and also teaching at those institutions continues to increase. Currently, several Mennonite colleges, which have traditionally been male-dominated, are actively seeking female faculty members. In the professions, in business and in other employment outside the home, Mennonite women are also increasing in numbers. This has become not only more desirable for many women, but also more feasible because of smaller families, more egalitarian practices of parenting and household responsibilities and increased educational training—all, to a certain extent, byproducts of the feminist movement. In the arts as well, women artists, composers and writers have all been granted increased recognition, though overall artistic pursuits, by women or men, have had difficulty gaining respectability amongst Mennonites.

There are more women in positions of leadership within church institutions, including the formal ministry, though generally Mennonites have been slower than other mainline North American denominations in accepting women for ordination.[50] The first female minister in a Canadian Mennonite church was Martha Smith Good, commissioned to full ministerial duties in Kitchener in 1977 and later ordained. Now there are several ordained women serving in Ontario Mennonite churches, although the majority of churches—though supportive of the practice in principle—would probably not be willing to have a female minister, and a large percentage would still object to the ordination of women.

It could be that the Mennonite community is struggling to recover "the priesthood of all believers" practised by their foremothers and forefathers in the sixteenth century, and as they succeed in doing this, women will benefit in terms of increased leadership opportunities.

The above might suggest that all Mennonite women are casting off traditional roles and taking on new ones shaped by modernism and feminism. This is not so. There is also a substantial percentage of women and men for whom the "liberalism" creeping into the Mennonite community is a danger sign and who respond not only by advocating the status quo, but by calling for an increased conservatism. This group tends to insist that solid families and solid marriages are founded on the biblical admonition that women submit to their husbands, and they view dimly the changes which have occurred with respect to sex roles over the last twenty years.

In this brief study we have seen how the roles of Mennonite women have been influenced by an original ideological egalitarianism, affected adversely in time by the surrounding culture, by immigration and resulting economic activity in frontier communities, by an isolationist religious-cultural stance in the face of progress seen to be valueless, by institution building often undertaken in unofficial ways and by integrationist forces which insisted on new places for women in church and society.

We have also seen that such integrationist influences were related to egalitarian impulses centuries earlier and that in both the sixteenth and the twentieth centuries, egalitarianism had its societal and biblical origins. Further, it can be noted that different forms of egalitarianism, not commonly recognized, may have been present when men and women worked together in the economic, social and educational enterprise called the family farm; and also that the work traditionally performed by women is of far greater value in perpetuating the ideals and institutions of the community than much of the written history might suggest.

Finally, the contemporary co-existence of the isolationist and integrationist modes is of considerable interest, as is the role of institutions, largely begun and shaped by women, in bridging as well as enriching both worlds and bringing about an egalitarianism amongst Mennonite women themselves. When they come together to serve the world, as they do so often, without the divisions between rural and urban, homemaker and professional, traditional and modern, they are recapturing to an extent the "priesthood of all believers" practised by their ancestors.

Much of the Mennonite story is simply another window into society in general but not completely. After all, for Mennonites the ideological impulses toward egalitarianism came earlier, the immigration and settlement events more frequent, the isolationist mode more pronounced, the institution building more vigorous at the grass-roots of the women's world, and the integrationist mode more explosive. At least so it seems to the present writers. Their hypothesis requires further testing in comparative studies, such as those represented at this conference.

Notes

1. An example of a seminary student, only one, is Doris Gascho, attending Waterloo Lutheran Seminary, whose breaking of the sex barrier began as church council chairperson and as coordinator first of the Conrad Grebel College School of Adult Studies, then of the Pastoral Leadership Training Program.
2. Two examples: Rev. Martha Smith Good is minister at Guelph Mennonite Church. Rev. Mary Mae Schwartzendruber is one of two ministers at Stirling Avenue Mennonite Church in Kitchener. Both attended seminary and both are ordained.
3. Dr. Iva Taves is head of Pathology at Kitchener-Waterloo Hospital.
4. Margaret Janzen works in the office of the provincial crown prosecutor in Kitchener.

5. Hildi Tiessen and Ilse Friesen are professors at Wilfrid Laurier University, in English and Art History respectively. Magdalena Redekopp is an English professor at the University of Toronto.
6. Salome Bauman was for many years principal of Rockway Mennonite Collegiate.
7. Ferne Burkhardt was chairperson of the board of Rockway Mennonite Collegiate in Kitchener and was succeeded by the current chairperson, Laura Shantz. Dorothy Worden was chairperson of the board of Conrad Grebel College at University of Waterloo.
8. Ruby Weber, first business manager at Conrad Grebel College, later comptroller of Ontario March of Dimes, was the first MBA graduate of the Wilfrid Laurier University School of Business.
9. Elaine Gross manages a travel business and is secretary of the Mennonite Credit Union Board.
10. Helen L. Epp is program director at House of Friendship in Kitchener. Delphine Martin is coordinator of Shalom Counselling Service in Waterloo.
11. Alice Koch is president of the Mennonite Historical Society of Ontario. Most executive committee members of the Mennonite Bicentennial Commission are women. Dr. Betty Fretz, optometrist, heads the regional chapter of the Mennonite Economic Development Associates.
12. See Greg Lichti, "The Role of Women in the Mennonite Conference of Ontario and Quebec (1900-1984)," research paper, University of Waterloo, 19 April 1984.
13. George H. Williams, *The Radical Reformation* (Philadelphia: The Westminster Press, 1962).
14. Cited in Joyce L. Irwin, *Womanhood in Radical Protestantism, 1525-1675* (Toronto: The Edwin Mellen Press, 1979), p. xiv.
15. Elise Boulding, *The Underside of History: A View of Women Through Time* (Boulder, Colorado: Westview Press, 1976), p. 548, cited in Irwin, p. xv.
16. Wolfgang Schaeufele, quoted in Elaine Sommers Rich, *Mennonite Women: A Story of God's Faithfulness, 1683-1983* (Scottdale, Pa.: Herald Press, 1983), p. 22.
17. Geroge Williams, quoted in Rich, pp. 22-23.
18. Thieleman J. van Braght, *Martyrs Mirror* (Scottdale, Pa.: Herald Press, 1968), p. 1122.
19. Lois Barrett, "Women in the Anabaptist Movement," in *Study Guide On Women*, ed. Herta Funk (Newton, Kansas: Faith and Life Press, 1975), p. 33.
20. Van Braght, *Martyrs Mirror*, pp. 979-80.
21. Rich, *Mennonite Women*, p. 25.
22. Walter Klaassen in a Conrad Grebel Faculty Forum, 15 February 1985.
23. Werner Packull, "Anna Jansz of Rotterdam: A Historical Investigation of an Early Anabaptist Heroine," a paper presented to a Conrad Grebel College Faculty Forum, 15 February 1985.

24. Walter Klaassen, 15 February 1985.
25. Walter Klaassen, *Anabaptism: Neither Catholic Nor Protestant* (Waterloo: Conrad Press, 1981), pp. 54-57.
26. Interview with Harvey Dyck, University of Toronto, 23 April 1985.
27. H.S. Bender, quoted in Rich, *Mennonite Women*, p. 25.
28. See Frank H. Epp, *Mennonites in Canada, 1920-1940: A Struggle for Survival* (Toronto: Macmillan of Canada, 1982), pp. 70-76.
29. Mabel Dunham, *The Trail of the Conestoga* (Toronto: McClelland and Stewart, 1942).
30. Henry Paetkau, "A Struggle for Survival: The Russian Mennonite Immigrants in Ontario, 1924-1939" (M.A. thesis, University of Waterloo, 1978), pp. 32ff.
31. Hildegard Martens, "Mennonites from Mexico: Their Immigration and Settlement in Canada," research report, 1975, available at Conrad Grebel College.
32. Orland Gingerich, *The Amish of Canada* (Waterloo: Conrad Press, 1972), pp. 159ff.
33. For elaboration on the isolationist theme, see Epp, *Mennonites in Canada, 1786-1920*, chapters 1, 6, 10, 11; *Mennonites in Canada, 1920-1940*, chapters 2, 9, 10, 11.
34. Merle Shantz et al., "Birth Control Committee," *Calendar of Appointments—Mennonite Church of Ontario* (1945-46), pp. 38-40.
35. See J.B. Martin et al., "Family Allowance Study Committee," *Calendar of Appointments—Mennonite Church of Ontario* (1945-46), p. 41.
36. Frank H. Epp, *Mennonites in Canada, 1786-1920: The History of a Separate People* (Toronto: Macmillan of Canada, 1974), p. 244.
37. Lichti, "Role of Women," p. 18.
38. Ibid., p. 7.
39. Rich, *Mennonite Women*, p. 35.
40. Mrs. E.C. Cressman, "Women's Missionary and Service Auxiliary Report," *Annual Report—The Mennonite Conference of Ontario* (1968), p. 123.
41. Alice Koch, ed., *W.M.S.A.: 1895-1967* (Waterloo: WMSA, 1967), p. 10.
42. Beulah Kauffman, "Adjunct Not Auxiliary," *MCC Committee on Women's Concerns Report*, no. 18 (Feb. 1978), p. 3.
43. Erna J. Fast, "Observations on Concepts of the Ministry," in *Which Way Women?*, ed. Dorothy Yoder Nyce (Akron, Pa.: Mennonite Central Committee Peace Section, 1980), p. 109.
44. Beulah Kauffman, "The Role of Women: Time for a Fresh Look," *Gospel Herald* 67 (8 Jan. 1974), pp. 26-28.
45. Eleanor H. High, "Woman: The 70's, and a Time to Speak," *Ontario Mennonite Evangel* 15, no. 4 (April 1970), p. 5.
46. Ruth Ann Soden, "Traditions yielding as more women vote at Mennonite meet," *Kitchener-Waterloo Record*, 18 August 1971, p. 57; also Lichti, "Role of Women," p. 26.

47. Ibid. According to another source, there was only one woman delegate in addition to the three from Ontario. See Lichti, "Role of Women," p. 26.
48. Ibid., pp. 26-27.
49. "Outstanding women include 84-year-old and teen-ager," *Kitchener-Waterloo Record*, 15 October 1975, p. 59.
50. Gayle Gerber Koontz, "Focus on Women in Ministry," *MCC Peace Section Task Force on Women in Church and Society*, no. 19 (April-May 1978), p. 1.

Bibliography

"Annual Report of the Sewing Circles of Ontario." *Calendar of Appointments*. Issued by Mennonite Church of Ontario yearly, 1930-58.

Barrett, Lois. "Women in the Anabaptist Movement." In *Study Guide on Women*. Ed. Herta Funk. Newton, Ka.: Faith and Life Press, 1975, pp. 33-38.

Boulding, Elise. *The Underside of History: A View of Women Through Time*. Boulder, Colorado: Westview Press, 1976.

Dunham, Mabel. *The Trail of the Conestoga*. Toronto: McClelland and Stewart, 1942.

Epp, Frank H. *Mennonites in Canada, 1786-1920: History of A Separate People*. Toronto: Macmillan of Canada, 1974.

Epp, Frank H. *Mennonites in Canada, 1920-1940: A People's Struggle for Survival*. Toronto: Macmillan of Canada, 1982.

Gingerich, Orland. *The Amish of Canada*. Waterloo: Conrad Press, 1972.

Irwin, Joyce L. *Womanhood in Radical Protestantism, 1525-1675*. Toronto: The Edwin Mellen Press, 1979.

Kauffman, Beulah. "The Role of Women: Time for a Fresh Look." *Gospel Herald* 67 (8 Jan. 1974), pp. 26-28.

Klaassen, Walter. *Anabaptism: Neither Catholic Nor Protestant*. Waterloo: Conrad Press, 1981.

Koch, Alice et al., eds. *W.M.S.A.: 1895-1967*. Waterloo: WMSA, 1967.

Lichti, Greg. "The Role of Women in the Mennonite Conference of Ontario and Quebec (1900-1984)." Research Paper, University of Waterloo, 19 April 1984.

Martens, Hildegard. "Mennonites from Mexico: their Immigration and Settlement in Canada." A Research Report, 1975. Available at Conrad Grebel College.

MCC Committee on Women's Concerns Report. No. 18, February 1978.

MCC Committee on Women's Concerns Report. No. 43, May-June 1982.

MCC Committee on Women's Concerns Report. No. 50, July-August 1983.

Nyce, Dorothy Yoder, ed. *Which Way Women?*. Akron, Pa.: Mennonite Central Committee Peace Section, 1980.

Ontario Mennonite Evangel. Vol. XV, no. 4 (April 1970).

Packull, Werner O. "Anna Jansz of Rotterdam: A Historical Investigation of an Early Anabaptist Heroine." Paper presented to a Conrad Grebel College Faculty Forum, 15 February 1985.

Paetkau, Henry. "A Struggle for Survival: The Russian Mennonite Immigrants in Ontario, 1924-1939." M.A. thesis, University of Waterloo, 1978.

Rich, Elaine Sommers. *Mennonite Women: A Story of God's Faithfulness, 1683-1983*. Scottdale, Pa.: Herald Press, 1983.

Schlegel, Florence et al., eds. *W.M.S.C.: 1968-1983*. WMSC, 1983.

Van Braght, Thieleman J. *Martyrs Mirror*. Scottdale, Pa.: Herald Press, 1968.

Williams, George H. *The Radical Reformation*. Philadelphia: The Westminster Press, 1962.

"W.M.S.C. Report," *Ontario Mennonite Conference Reports*. 1958-78.

Contributors

Marilyn Barber is Professor of History at Carleton University in Ottawa. She has published articles on education and on women's history in Canada, most recently in the *New Canadian Encyclopedia*.

Jean Burnet is retired Professor of Sociology at Glendon College, York University, and Chairman of the Multicultural History Society of Ontario. Aside from her extensive academic career, she is a member of several editorial boards as well as author of *Next-Year Country* and *Ethnic Groups in Upper Canada*.

Paula Draper received her Ph.D. from the University of Toronto in 1983. She has presented several scholarly papers on Jewish refugees interned in Canada during the Second World War. She has also acted as historical consultant for the Holocaust Memorial at the Toronto Jewish Congress.

Marlene Epp has a B.A. degree from the University of Manitoba and is a research associate at Conrad Grebel College, University of Waterloo. She is currently working on volume III of the history of *The Mennonites in Canada*.

Frank Epp, the late Professor of History at Conrad Grebel College, University of Waterloo, was actively involved in Mennonite community affairs and was on the board of directors for the Canadian Ethnic Studies Association. He published various studies on minorities and was the author of *Mennonites in Canada, 1920-1940: a People's Struggle for Survival.*

Robert F. Harney is Professor of History at the University of Toronto. He is Academic Director of the Multicultural History Society of Ontario and has written numerous works on ethnicity, primarily on Italian emigration and settlement in North America. He is co-author of *Immigrants: a Portrait of the Urban Experience, 1890-1930.*

Elizabeth Hopkins is Professor of English at Glendon College, York University, and one of the editors of *Susannah Moodie: Letters of a Lifetime.* She is currently working on "The Letters of Catharine Parr Trail."

Franca Iacovetta is a doctoral candidate in History at York University and is completing a dissertation on the post-World War Two southern Italian immigrant experience in Toronto. She has also written on Canadian women in politics and currently sits on the board of directors of the Canadian Ethnic Studies Association.

Isabel Kaprielian received her Ph.D. from the University of Toronto. She is a post-doctoral fellow at the Ontario Institute for Studies in Education. She is the author of several articles on immigration and ethnic studies and the guest editor of *Polyphony: Armenians in Ontario.*

Janice Karlinsky received her M.A. in History from the Ontario Institute for Studies in Education. She currently teaches history at the Toronto French School.

Apolonja Kojder is a doctoral student at the University of Toronto. She has written widely on the role of women in education.

Varpu Lindström-Best is a Ph.D. candidate as well as Sessional Assistant Professor at Atkinson College, York University. She has produced numerous documentary films for television as well as a radio series. Her various writings on Finnish immigration include most recently, *The Finns in Canada.*

Dora Nipp received her Masters degree from the University of Toronto. In 1984 she began doctoral studies on overseas Chinese as a Commonwealth Scholar in Hong Kong. She has written several articles on the Chinese-Canadian community. Currently she is coordinating the Ethnic Press Project for the Multicultural History Society of Ontario.

Lillian Petroff received her Ph.D. in education from the University of Toronto in 1983. She has given several lectures and seminars, and published articles on the immigrant experience in Toronto. At present she is a post-doctoral research fellow at the Multicultural History Society of Ontario, curriculum advisor to the Multiculturalism Project, Secretary of State, and sits on the board of directors of the Canadian Ethnic Studies Association.

Eleoussa Polyzoi is Managing Editor of *Specialnet* at the University of Texas at Austin. Her conference presentations and publications include articles and reviews on Greek immigration with a special focus on education.

Franc Sturino is Assistant Professor of History at Atkinson College, York University. He has written several articles on chain migration and kinship patterns in the Italian immigrant experience.

Frances Swyripa is currently a Ph.D. candidate in History at the University of Alberta, completing her dissertation on Ukrainian women in western Canada through the Second World War. She has been a research associate with the Canadian Institute of Ukrainian Studies and has written numerous articles, reviews and research reports on Ukrainians in Canada. One of her most recent publications is *Loyalties in Conflict: Ukrainians in Canada During the Great War*, co-edited with John Herd Thompson.

Other Publications from the Multicultural History Society on Related Subjects

The Italian Immigrant Woman in North America. Edited by Betty Boyd Caroli, Robert F. Harney and Lydio F. Tomasi. 1978 ISBN: 0-9690916-0-5, $7.00 paper.

Pane e Lavoro: the Italian American Working Class. Edited by George E. Pozzetta. 1980 ISBN: 0-919045-00-6, $8.00 paper.

The Finnish Diaspora. Edited by Michael Karni. Vol. I: Canada, Australia, Africa, South America and Sweden; Vol. II: United States. 1981 ISBN: 0-919045-08-1 (set) 0-919045-09-X (vol. I) 0-919045-10-3 (vol. II), $14.00 (set) $8.00 (single) paper.

Dutch Immigration to North America. Edited by Herman Ganzevoort and Mark Boekelman. 1983 ISBN: 0-919045-15-4, $9.00 paper.

The Finnish Baker's Daughters. By Aili Grönlund Schneider. 1986 ISBN: 0-919045-25-1, $8.00 paper.